the HEART at WAR

ALSO BY CATHERINE BANNER

The Eyes of a King
Voices in the Dark

The Heart at War

❦ The Last Descendants Trilogy ❦
Book III

Catherine Banner

Fic
T
Banne

Doubleday Canada

Doubleday Canada and colophon are registered trademarks of
Random House of Canada Limited

Library and Archives Canada Cataloguing in Publication

Banner, Catherine, 1989-, author
The heart at war / Catherine Banner.

(Last descendants trilogy)
Issued in print and electronic formats.
ISBN 978-0-385-66309-0 (pbk.).--ISBN 978-0-307-37610-7 (epub)

I. Title. II. Series: Banner, Catherine, 1989- . Last descendants trilogy ; 3.

PZ7.B217He 2015   j823'.92   C2011-900160-8
                                                   C2011-900161-6

Issued in print and electronic formats.

This book is a work of fiction. Names, characters, places and incidents are products
of the author's imagination or are used fictitiously. Any resemblance to actual events
or locales or persons, living or dead, is entirely coincidental.

Cover image: (boy) © Tracy Whiteside/Dreamstime.com;
(illustration) © 2015 Jessica Cheng
Cover design: Jennifer Lum
Printed and bound in the USA

Published in Canada by Doubleday Canada,
a division of Random House of Canada Limited,
a Penguin Random House Company
www.penguinrandomhouse.ca

10 9 8 7 6 5 4 3 2 1

Penguin
Random House
DOUBLEDAY CANADA

I

❧ BIRTH ❧

$\mathcal{M}$y name is Harlan North, and I was born in Capital, in the year zero, on the night of the invasion. But from my earliest childhood, I have been able to remember a time before I was born. I looked down on the world from a great height then, the way I look down now in dreams. I remember darkness and a white light piercing it. I remember a city of walls and red stonework. I remember my mother crying—a sound which came to me sometimes like a voice on the wind, and sometimes like the rushing of a mighty river. I remember the night my great-great-uncle was killed, the dull snap of the rifle and his dizzying fall. I remember their weeping.

Even as a small child, I could see pictures and hear sounds that were not my own, that never could have been. Sometimes the voices in me fought so fiercely that they became a kind of static in my head. What is it like, not seeing the world the way you're supposed to see it? Like a traveller from another country, you are at odds with your surroundings, disoriented. Everything is too fast and too bright and too real.

Ever since then, I have struggled to try and figure out how I came to have these impossible memories. I think I know now. It was because of what went wrong at my birth.

My mother had a hard struggle to bring me into the world. She was washing plates when it began. No one else was at home that night. My father had escaped the city weeks before, fleeing the men who had killed my great-great-uncle. My grandmother and my brother, attempting to keep things as ordinary as possible in the face of the impending invasion, had gone to watch my sister's school play. They should have been home earlier, but on this particular night they were held up in the city. So my mother was utterly alone when pain out of nowhere made her straighten. The plates went smashing to the ground. The neighbours came upstairs to complain about the noise, but ended up sending for a doctor instead. That was the twenty-fourth of December, a frost-bitten night and very still. She was brought to the hospital through dead and silent streets. The whole city seemed to be waiting, not for Christmas but for war.

The doctors struggled from the start. I was turned the wrong way inside my mother and could not be shifted. The cord was wrapped around my neck, and any false movement could have strangled me. The priest was summoned and my family brought running from the chaos of the city and told to prepare themselves. The doctors thought for a while that I would die, but that my mother could be saved. Then they thought that perhaps they could rescue me instead. My mother, on the bed, flopped weakly. In the corridor, my brother and sister and grandmother sat, imprisoned in a painful silence, Jasmine still in her costume of homemade cape and sackcloth robe.

While the doctors were struggling to keep me alive, rioting started in the streets. Foreign armies had crossed the border. Now they marched on Capital. Some rejoiced, some prepared to flee, and in the alleys and squares of the city these factions came to blows. My sister heard the shivery noise of glass shattering, hoarse voices crying "Long live the king!" and "Long live the New Imperial Order!" The same people who had taken my great-great-uncle's life wanted the rest of ours too. Very quickly, the city became fevered. Beyond the hospital window, a single flare rose against the dark, and on the horizon was the dirty orange glow of fire.

But in the tiled corridor of the hospital, all was silence. Other families were bundling up their belongings and fleeing the city, but for my own family nothing could be resolved until I made up my mind to live or to die.

Then a strange thing happened. I gave a great shuddering heave and turned myself around, just like that, and came out into the grey hospital room. The nurse freed me from the cord, clawed at my face to break the caul of slime, and, dangling me from my feet, hit me on the back—once, twice, three times. The doctor laid me on a metal tray. She spoke to me and slapped me and pressed my tiny heart over and over with two fingers. The doctor had been on duty for seventeen straight hours and her hands were shaking. "Come on," she said. "Come on, baby—damn it." My mother wept silently into her pillow.

This is where things become complicated. During that time, when I showed no signs of life, I was not really on that metal tray at all. During that time, I was elsewhere.

I remember this quite distinctly: I travelled, as though flying low over the earth, towards a land of green sunlight and dark water. Kind hands took hold of me and pulled me towards them, into the sun. They spoke to me, using the name I had not yet been given: *Harlan, Harlan.* They crowded around me in a circle, faces old and young, the living and the dead, and sang songs to celebrate my birth.

And in that green world, I was happy.

But before I became properly aware of my happiness, I felt a sharp tug behind my eyes. It brought me back. The hands in the green world loosened their grip. I opened my eyes and saw the cold hospital light above me, felt the sharp edges of the metal tray, heard the doctor's voice, harsh and raspy in my ears, saying: "Breathe, breathe, breathe." I closed my eyes again, but it was already too late. The green world was vanishing.

In a rush, the breath entered my lungs. With it came something else. That other place I had lived in for just ten minutes had left its trace on me, and into my body rushed its power. Suddenly, I could see and remember. I was not really a tiny baby at all. I was someone who had lived a long time.

My heart gave its first beat. I gathered up the air in my lungs and let out a cry of grief. Out in the corridor, my brother and sister and grandmother heard that cry and knew that I would live.

Meanwhile, in my head, pictures fought for space—that green world and my mother's face and the city before my birth. Other pictures too: my sister running up the narrow staircase of our shop with flowers in her hair; my brother, amidst the whirling snow, pacing the streets of the city in search of his history. Somehow, my new mind was full of old memories. Not just my own memories but theirs. I know this makes little sense— I know that memories cannot be inherited—and yet forever afterwards I would share the happiest and saddest recollections of my family, watching them flash across the screen of my mind at odd moments like visions, as though they belonged to me alone.

For now, though, I didn't know what to do with these memories which were not my own. It would be years before I had the understanding to unravel them. For now, my world was confusion.

The doctor listened to my heartbeat. She shook her head. "This child is a miracle," she said. "See how healthy he is. Time will tell if there is some problem with his heart, some effect we can't see. Take good care of him."

There was something wrong with my heart, but not in the way the doctor had meant it. Because of those ten minutes in the green world, my soul now didn't want to live in the place where it had been born. My heart was now at war with the world I had been dragged back to. And though I didn't know it yet, I was destined to spend my whole life trying to get home.

I was hurriedly baptised with my father's name, Leo. It didn't suit me, but no one could think of another. Then I lay quiet, exhausted after the ordeal of my birth. Eventually I slept, and while I slept war crossed the borders and darkened the cities and Malonia, my native country, ceased to exist. The New Imperial Order, our future masters, renamed it the year zero, for a fresh start.

$\mathcal{W}$e left the hospital to find our apartment building burnt to the ground.

My grandmother wept when she saw it. She knelt in the ash and dug for her things, unearthing only a little bone comb, blackened, and half a silver candlestick. Once, she had been a wealthy woman. In all the years since, she had carried the relics of her rich house around with her—now they were gone.

And yet in some ways, to lose our apartment was simpler. It left us with less to carry.

For in those first panic-stricken days of the new regime, everyone seemed to be leaving the city. In carts, in hired carriages, in long processions, walking away from the looting and burning with whatever they could carry in their pockets. Already, the place was empty, as though it had suffered a plague. My father had gone west to Holy Island. We had nothing to do but set out. So I was bundled up in an old overcoat and we left. The old religions were outlawed now, punishable by death, but it was a priest named Father Dunstan who helped us to escape. After we left the city, we never saw him again.

We left at night, when the fighting in the streets was at its quietest. My mother led the way, carrying me and holding my sister by the hand, and my brother and grandmother followed. The streets were mostly unlit, but around us we became gradually aware of other families in the darkness, all heading to the west, towards the coach station. We heard them rustle and murmur around us, the trudge of their footsteps through the dirty snow, the cries of children quickly silenced. It was bitterly cold, but something in the air that night must have told me to keep quiet, not to cry or make a sound, until we were safely away.

At the coach station, the first disaster happened. There was space for only women and children in the coach going west. My mother and sister wept bitterly. They said they would rather not leave at all than leave my brother behind. But Anselm made us. He forced my sister's small hands off his wrists, and pushed us all onto the coach. Through the window, he grasped my mother's hands. "I'll be there as soon as I can," he said. "I promise. Find Papa—go to Holy Island. You'll be safe there."

It was dark and terrible, leaving him behind in the middle of the fighting. I can picture the way he looked as we drove away. He was standing very still and straight on the top of a ridge of snow. Lamplight shone on his reddish-brown hair and the firm set of his features. My brother was seventeen, barely old enough to be abandoned in the city. Jasmine hung out of the window further and further, straining to keep him in sight until the last possible moment. Then the coach turned a corner and he was gone.

Jasmine changed her mind about leaving him, and tried to get the coach door open. She would have done, only Grandmother caught hold of her wrist and would not let go. "Just you dare," she whispered. "Just you dare, Jasmine." She held her grip until we were almost out of the city, on streets that no one recognised. Only when all chance of return was hopeless did she finally let go.

Broken-hearted, Jasmine flung herself down on the floor of the coach and cried. "Hush now, Jas," soothed my mother, suppressing her own tears. "I need your help. Help me with the baby."

They passed me between them. They were alike as sisters, my mother and Jasmine, or would have been if twenty-five years had not separated them—now I looked up into identical eyes with luxuriant black lashes, was soothed by the swaying of their identical dark hair. My grandmother's beauty must have once been of the same variety, rather faded and scraped back now. She attempted to knit, ignoring us all, but that was just her way of trying to keep things ordinary in the face of all this fighting.

So, in the arms of the three women of my family, I was taken away from the war-torn city. Everyone cried except Grandmother. Even I cried. That, my sister told me, is when she first began to love me, because it was as though I missed Anselm too. She kissed my scrunched purple face. I swear I can remember her hot tears on my forehead. We didn't know it, but that was the last time we would see Anselm until both of us were quite grown up and the city was just a blurred memory in our past, never to be returned to.

3

*I*t took us three days to reach the west coast. We were put down at a port called West Ravina. There was very little here. The town itself was submerged in a chaos of shipyards and warehouses around the quay. Gusts of fierce wind swept over us, battering indignant seagulls and carrying a scent of fish and tar. Towards this smell we hurried, following the crowd. We passed under the shadow of great corrugated warehouses, and beneath the skeleton of a half-built ship. At the docks, the four of us were swallowed up in a horde of grey and disconsolate people—people like us, trying to make their way further west, across the ocean. This crowd shoved and shouted and argued. They had run out of land to cross, and still they were desperate to go west, away from the fighting, across the black and churning sea. So was my mother.

The journey had diminished all three of them. Jasmine was wearing a charity coat and her usually luxuriant hair, limp from days on the road, had been scraped into a single braid by Grandmother's tough hands. She looked smaller and more waif-like than her city self. I know as surely as I know anything that this was how my sister looked. She had never seen the sea before, except in pictures. No one had told her about the great waves rolling darkly in to crash against the quays: "Like a monster breathing," she said, and cried.

Grandmother still grasped her knitting, grimed around the edges from the three days' journey. "There's nothing to be afraid of," she said.

The whole great crowd of us were united in one desperate wish: to flee, to get across the ocean, to reach Holy Island. At the ticket office, everything was chaos and disorder. The captains of rusted fishing vessels and cargo barges, sensing a profit, had brought their ships into dock and now hung about the quay bartering over prices, accepting gold jewellery and household treasures in place of money.

To get tickets, my mother and grandmother went into an office full of smoke and swearing to pawn the few possessions we still had. They left me outside in my sister's arms. Jasmine sat on a bench with her head turned firmly away from the sea so she didn't have to look at it. Snowflakes fell like stars and adorned the black coat in which I lay. Jasmine worried that I would catch my death, and she kept trying to brush them off. I can remember the damp touch of her hands on my face. "Hush, baby," she said. "Not long now until we're with Papa."

That was why we were going to Holy Island. Because our father was supposed to be there. But beyond that—where he was, or how to find him—we knew nothing at all.

A thousand accents surrounded us, and Jasmine heard, without fully understanding, "borders will be closing" and "next ship west" and "leave while we can." A great homesickness came over her, as awful as the black waves of that ocean, and at the same time another gust of gritty snow attacked her. Jasmine hunched her back to shelter me and keep that homesickness away. When she looked up, someone was standing over us: a man about the age of our own father, in a greasy-looking coat. He had a stubbly beard, and under it he was smiling. "That's a charming baby," he said. "Is he your brother?"

Jasmine said nothing.

"How old is he?" said the man. "How many days?"

"I can't remember," Jasmine said, which was a lie. The man sat down beside her. He leaned over and breathed his hot breath into my face. Jasmine tightened her arms around me. She felt the warm and heavy shape of my body inside the overcoat and held me fast around the middle.

"Why doesn't he cry?" said the man. "It's cold for such a small baby out here by the docks."

"He doesn't," Jasmine said. "Not much."

"Ah. He's a good child, is he? And see how well you look after him. Like a good sister." After a pause, the man edged closer. "You come from the city? I can tell by your accent. Don't be scared—I don't mean any harm."

Jasmine gave one reluctant nod. "Malonia City."

"Tssk." The man let out a soft hiss, like he was scolding. "You must call it by its new name now. Capital. You mustn't forget. That's very important." He looked at me with a kind of scientific curiosity. "You know what they're doing in the city?" He didn't wait for her reply. "Something very strange indeed. They're arresting all the babies about this size. Nine- and ten-day-old babies, newborns. They're trying to find a child born on the first night of the revolution. You won't understand all this; you're only small."

"I'm not small," said Jasmine, shocked into speech by this insult. "I'm seven years old!" Her cheeks flushed; her grip around my middle became suffocating. "Why are they doing that? Why are they arresting babies?"

"They want to find one with special powers. One that got away from the city. A baby everyone is talking about right now. A relative of Aldebaran's. You might have heard of Aldebaran. He worked for the king, and he was assassinated."

A cold dread came over Jasmine, and she shivered. Aldebaran was our great-great-uncle. "That's silly," she said, gripping my tiny foot through the overcoat.

"Well, grown-ups are silly sometimes," said the man confidingly.

Jasmine inched down the cold steel bench. "My brother's tired," she said. "He wants to sleep now and not talk anymore, if you don't mind."

The man bent over until his face was almost in mine. Through his mess of stubble, beady eyes blinked at me. He looked into my face, then made a sudden grab. With both hands he caught hold of me and pulled. Jasmine screamed. The man had hold of me by one wrist and one ankle and was dragging me from the overcoat. "*No!*" she shrieked. "*No!* Thief! Murderer!"

Her ferocity must have startled the man, because he lost his hold for a second, and that was enough. Jasmine got a grip of me by the other ankle, and she clung to it as though my life depended on it. I was pulled in two directions and screamed, hysterical with fright. My head rolled back; my tiny fists clenched. I let out a roar of rage and pain.

Then all at once the man let go. Another person had given him a hard shove from behind. A red-haired stranger with a worn-out face was standing over him, glaring through a battered pair of gold spectacles. "You let that child go," he said.

The man did not need to be told again, and besides, people were staring. He threw one final look at me, then plunged into the crowd.

My sister pressed me against her chest and glared up at our saviour. "Are you going to take my brother too?" she demanded, furious. "Because if you are I'll have to kill you."

"No," said the red-haired man. "Don't be scared. Is your brother safe? Is he hurt?"

Our grandmother appeared then in the doorway of the ticket office, drawn by the commotion. "Jasmine!" she scolded. "What have you done to your poor brother? If I hear any more crying from him, you'll get a hard smack, do you hear me?"

11

My mother came running, with the tickets in her hand. Jasmine shoved me, still shrieking, into her arms. "Take him, Mama, take him. He isn't safe."

"Hush, hush," said my mother. "What's the matter, love?"

Jasmine was incoherent in her terror: "That man—the baby—something about Aldebaran—take him, Mama! He isn't safe!"

A horn sent a low pulse through the quay beneath us, and made the crowds surge in panic. "That's our ship, Jasmine," said my mother. "It leaves in three minutes. We need to get there in time or we might not have another chance. Come on. Can you run?"

And in the panic to get down to the quays, Jasmine somehow lost sight of the red-haired man.

4

$\mathcal{W}$e were bundled onto a small, rusty ship with the name *Prince of Khazan* painted on it. I had stopped my terrified shrieking, though my breath was still hoarse and snuffly. My mother brushed the tears from my face and bent to kiss me. "You see, baby? We're safe. We're on our way to Holy Island."

More and more people crowded onto the ship around us. When it was quite packed, some crewmen began blowing whistles. We were shoved to the back of the deck to make more space. Another two or three people were loaded on board. The ship's engine growled. Jasmine stretched onto her toes to hold my foot, the only part of me she could reach. She did that because she thought I might be frightened. The ship cast off. We were leaving the land behind now and setting out across the grey water with a low, throbbing note that made the deck tremble.

People were still desperate to get onto our ship, though they had no tickets. They clawed and clutched at the railing from the edge of the dock, preventing the ship from leaving by their joint desperation. In the end, the men had to push them away from the side with sticks so that we could leave the quayside and move out onto the open sea. The people, as they were struck, began to clamour. One old man hung on. He clung to the top rail until the crew beat his fingers and he dropped into the grey water.

So that was how our journey began: on a freight ship, in the cold, fleeing a war. Jasmine stood at the rail and watched the only homeland she had ever known disappearing into the night, and Anselm with it. He had not caught up to us. My mother, valiantly, talked about what a great adventure it all was. My grandmother put one arm around Jasmine's shoulders, and held her fast. I slept.

As we crossed the sea, the wind began to drive violently against the ship's nose. Lightning cut the sky in two and lit up the churned surface of the water. The ship pitched and rolled, and Jasmine clung around my grandmother's waist, their usual enmity abandoned. But my mother was not frightened by the storm. She put her hand on Jasmine's shoulder and began telling us, in quiet and steady tones, about the life we would have on the other side of the ocean, when the night was past.

"We should never have taken this ship, Maria," my grandmother interrupted. "There's hardly space to breathe, and these people keep knocking me about. Didn't I tell you we should have gone later?"

"For all we know there wouldn't have been any ship later," said my mother.

"But then what about Anselm?" said Jasmine, starting to cry. "If there are no more ships, how will he get across?"

Just then, a great wave rolled up and sent the ship dizzily high, then plunged us into a grey trough where icy spray soaked us. Someone screamed. A sailor started clanging a loud bell, yelling orders. "What is it, Mama?" said Jasmine.

"They want us to go below deck," said my mother. "Just for a while, until the storm passes. They say it will be safer that way."

Jasmine did not want to descend into the darkness of the ship; she had seen the sailors go in and out of the black hatches and she had a great terror of going down there too. But our mother was not frightened. She led the way down the metal stairway into the dark. Other people were bundled in after us, and the hatch banged shut over our heads. In the dark there was some panic, some crying and fumbling with rosary beads. In the middle of it all, my mother, serene and fearless, gathered her small family.

"Come on," she said. "Let's find somewhere quiet for the baby." By now, the fear had permeated me too, and I was grizzling inside my wrapping.

In the metal rooms and corridors below deck, every noise seemed strange and startling. The ship creaked, and behind one door there was a thundering, like barrels rolling over and over. One of the metal doors was unlocked. In this room, my mother found a corner with an old tarpaulin and huddled us on top of it. She wrapped me tighter in my overcoat blanket. All the while she talked to Jasmine about the life we were going to have at the end of this night, when we reached the other side of the ocean.

My grandmother could not sit still. She fussed over the luggage and scolded Jasmine because she was complaining too loudly. "Why you brought another child into the world, Maria . . ." she lamented.

"Stop it," said my mother. "Take care of the baby for a minute, can you, Mother?"

I was tipped into my grandmother's arms. For all the bitterness in her face, she held me with nothing but care. She linked her gnarled finger in my own small, new one and grudgingly hummed me a lullaby.

Seasick and miserable, Jasmine clung to our mother and breathed the familiar smell of Mama's scarf.

"We used to have a fire in every room, and a chandelier on the stairs," said my grandmother to no one in particular, or perhaps to me. "We used to have a cook, and an under-cook, and a butler, and an under-butler, and three chambermaids. When I was a young married woman." My grandmother spoke these words without expecting a reply. Maybe it was the only way she knew to assert her value against the impersonal and raging force of the storm. Maybe she merely thought that I should be aware of these things.

"Shh, Mother," said my own mother.

My grandmother studied me, taking in every detail: my miniature face, still wrinkled in the aftermath of birth; my squashy head, inadequately covered by a wispy tuft of hair; my fragile ears and hands. In the warmth of the old coat, I breathed with a soft sucking sound and slept.

Jasmine asked our mother if we were going to die.

"Haven't we lived through enough troubles already, eh?" said my mother, smoothing back Jasmine's lank hair. "Haven't we always prevailed?" My mother got to her feet and gestured for Jasmine to do the same. Very carefully, across the swaying floor, she led her to a round window, and beyond it the grey surge of the sea. "Do you see the light over there?" said my mother.

"No."

"Look harder."

The sea receded from the glass for a second, and Jasmine said, "Yes. I see it."

A faint light, man-made, on the horizon.

"That light can only be one thing," said my mother. "Holy Island. Look how close it is."

"It doesn't look so far after all," said Jasmine reluctantly.

"We're almost there. See? Papa is there, where that light is. Our new life is there. We just have to get across that patch of sea. It might be a lighthouse, that light. It might be what's guiding us safely to the island."

"What's a lighthouse?"

"A tall tower with a lamp on top, to show ships the way to go when the weather is bad." My mother had never seen the sea either. She knew lighthouses only from books. "If you lie down and sleep, we'll be almost there. I think the storm is getting better too, love."

In fact, the storm was getting worse. Jasmine lay down, more out of misery than anything else, and eventually she fell asleep. In her fevered dreams, the lighthouse became a tall man with grey eyes holding out his arms.

The light was not a lighthouse but a fishing boat.

When I was much older, I would read accounts of what happened to the *Prince of Khazan* that night. According to these accounts, the ship's engine cut out in the early hours. One of the holds began leaking. The crew did what they could to save the ship, but it was clear that it was going down. So they made the decision to abandon it.

One of the many inadequacies of the *Prince of Khazan* was that it had only one lifeboat. When the six crew had launched it, they saw quite clearly that there wasn't space for any passengers. Faced with saving themselves or giving their places to six of the old, young and weak from below deck, they decided to cast away into the dark. I had no idea, as I slept, that anything had altered. But the other passengers began to understand that something was wrong. First of all, with a watery gurgling, the engine cut out. It came alive again—once, twice—then died altogether, replaced by the uneasy silence of the storm, with its creaking and sucking. Passengers began to emerge from the rooms in which they had shut themselves away. In the corridor, they paced back and forth, asked each other hushed questions. "Hey?" someone called. "Hey!"

No answer. "Hey!" called voices, louder. A few of them hammered on the ceiling. Crowding together, they braced themselves against the hatches and pushed.

But now the hatches could not be opened. Even when five or six people shoved at each one, they would no longer give. Something heavy had been dragged over the trapdoors.

The passengers set up a clamouring. Still no answer. Through the rain-washed porthole, they made out the green light of the lifeboat drifting away from us in the dark.

By this time, the panicked clamour outside the door of our small room had woken my mother and grandmother. They opened the door and cold seawater sloshed in, dousing Jasmine awake. Somewhere, the *Prince of Khazan* had sprung a leak.

The ship was drifting without direction now, spun by the waves, and the passengers gave way entirely to panic.

Then, something unexpected happened. A large fishing boat drew up alongside the *Prince of Khazan*. We heard its spluttering quite clearly, and the panic ebbed a little. It was their light my mother had seen from the porthole. "Hail them!" someone cried.

"Flash a light!"

"If only we could get these hatches open—help me—shove harder!"

It was common in time of war for refugees from the mainland to try to get across the channel to Holy Island without proper knowledge of the currents. This, I discovered much later, was the reason for the fishing boat's approach. But seeing no one on deck, the fishermen concluded that the ship had been abandoned.

People who had given way to despair now roused themselves. They hammered on the hatches with renewed vigour. But with the wind shrieking across the ship's deck, the fishermen couldn't hear that dull thumping. They too prepared to leave the ship to its fate.

Then something strange happened. I woke and twisted my body as though I was hurt, or possessed. My eyes opened wide. I let out a shudder, then a scream. The scream went on. It seemed to take hold of me. I shrieked without pause, stiff and red-faced, until the corridors below deck were ringing with it.

My mother, really frightened for the first time that terrible night, tried to hold me, but my body had gone rigid in her arms. "What is it?" she cried. "What's wrong, angel?"

But something about my screaming must have cut through the storm the way no adult voice had done. It rose up the stairs and through the ship's deck, into the wind-racked air. The captain of the fishing boat, about to pull away from the *Prince of Khazan*, heard it and paused. From the account I was told afterwards, there was some debate among the fishermen. "We can't get on board in this storm," said the first mate, "even if there is someone trapped in there. The ship's going down—it's too late."

But there it was again, the sound of a baby crying. The captain, resolving himself, ordered his crew to fix ladders and go on board.

The fishermen worked with quiet haste, racing the storm and the influx of water through the *Prince of Khazan*'s left flank. They scaled the ladder, and between them shifted the half-ton crates which had been dragged over the hatches. The captain descended the steel steps with a thumping of boots. The crew followed. They appeared among us, men with strange accents and grimy clothes but faces kinder than those of the crew of the *Prince of Khazan*. "Come out," they said, in our own language. "You've been abandoned here on a sinking ship. Come out, quickly."

With slow, frightened steps, we followed them up into the light. There were fifty-eight of us. I didn't stop screaming until the last person, an elderly man clutching his hat to his chest, was led up onto the deck.

We were brought to Holy Island on the great rusty fishing boat that had saved us. The waves still rolled under the hull, and spray like ice scoured the deck. But overhead the clouds had thinned and a few rays of light cut through. I was treated like a miniature hero by the superstitious fishermen. My mother held me very firmly and would not let anyone take me from her.

The island was a grey-green slope with grey houses stacked at the bottom and a pale grey beach. Grey concrete docks overshadowed by great metal cranes lined the port, where fishing boats lay high up on the shingle with their rusting undersides exposed. My grandmother began gathering up our luggage and stuffing Jasmine into her coat and scarf. My sister retreated behind our mother, away from her scolding. I woke and cried to be fed.

The tone of the engines changed as we approached the town. The crew threw out ropes. There were more than a hundred people waiting for us.

"Are we stopping here?" Jasmine asked our mother, tugging her sleeve. "Is this Holy Island?"

"Yes, love."

"What's the name of the town?"

My mother did not know. She had hoped for Valacia, the capital, but this was just a fishing place with fifty or sixty square grey houses.

"Who are those people?" asked Jasmine.

"They're waiting for the ship. Maybe their relatives were meant to be coming across the sea today, and they're waiting to meet them."

"Yes," said the nearest fisherman, a balding man my father's age. "They get wind of a refugee ship coming in and they rush down the coast to meet it. It's been going on since the first refugees got here. People hoping for the rest of their families to catch up."

"Are there many refugees here already?" said my mother.

The man, with a sad half-smile, said, "Are there many? Thousands, I'd say."

"Maybe Papa is there!" said Jasmine, squirming with excitement. "Maybe he's waiting for us!"

But Papa was not there. On the damp, grey side of the dock, there was no familiar face to greet us.

"Why isn't he here?" said Jasmine, sniffing back tears.

"We'll find him," said my mother. "We'll be with him soon."

"Well," said my grandmother. "We'll see about that. Oh, for pity's sake, look at that stain on your sleeve, Jasmine! Stand still—let me clean it."

Grandmother knelt on the concrete and began to scrub at the coat. Jasmine, still tearful, scowled. My mother had no idea how we were going to find my father.

So my family took their first steps onto the shore of our new homeland.

5

When I was fifteen days old, my sister told me a great secret about myself. We were in our dingy room, lying on the mattress on the floor while my mother and grandmother were in the next room cleaning. They were always cleaning, those first days, on account of the filth that was everywhere in our temporary home.

In the half-light of the evening, my sister leaned close to me. "Harlan, listen," she whispered. "You probably don't understand this, but I'm going to tell you anyway. You're special. You're going to grow up with powers. I think there are bad people trying to get you because of it. I think that man at the ship place was one of them. But look at the miracles you've done already." She counted them on her fingers. "One, you were born blue and you breathed and lived. Two, you almost got taken from me by that horrible man, but you didn't. And three, you saved us from the storm. Everyone here thinks you're a hero. Maybe they know that there's something special about you too."

In answer, I flailed my tiny, clenched hands and looked up at her.

"You're supposed to save our country in a time of trouble," Jasmine continued. "That's what Uncle told me about you.

You're our family's last descendant. You're going to grow up to do great things. Don't forget it."

Jasmine began to love me so passionately in those days. She would not leave me alone even for a minute, but was forever hauling me about like a doll, singing old city songs in my ear, bathing me in a tin bucket with water warmed over the gas stove. And, in those first days on Holy Island, she told me the story of our family. "Look," she said one rainswept afternoon, drawing for me a map on a scrap of newspaper. "Here's our family tree." She pointed to a small stickman and wrote *Aldebaran*. From him she had drawn lines descending, whole branches. My father, my mother, my brother, Jasmine and me. Also others, a separate grandmother and grandfather, and an uncle, Stirling. "But something's gone wrong," said Jasmine sadly, studying the map. "Half the people on here are lost. There keep being all these wars. That's the problem. Last time the war happened, Papa lost his mother and father. They were exiled. It means they had to go away. He never saw them again. His brother died—Stirling—when he was still a little boy. And now we've lost Anselm, and Papa too." She sniffed and rubbed her nose on her sleeve. "What we need is someone with powers to find out where they all are and get them back. To find Papa's lost mother and father, and find Papa, and bring Anselm across the sea to us. I thought I could do it, but a terrible thing is happening, baby." Jasmine's eyes in the half-light were immense oceans of sadness. "I'm losing my powers," she whispered. "Soon, you'll be the only one left who knows anything about magic. You're in charge, baby. You have to do it. You've done three miracles already. You have to do three more."

A fourth miracle did happen, shortly after our arrival, though it wasn't entirely my doing. The story of our rescue from the sea spread north, far enough to reach a small town on the outskirts of the city. That town was called New Maron, and in that town was a market, and in that market was a tall man with grey eyes and a shock of hair more grey than gold—my father and namesake, Leo. Over bread and cheese and bitter tea, a stallholder whose brother was a fisherman told the others about a sea rescue he had read about in the newspaper. He told how all the refugees on an abandoned boat had come safely ashore at Port St. Martin, thanks to a baby's crying. The Holy Islanders were a superstitious people, and some were tentatively calling it a miracle. My father said nothing. He just heard the story and wondered. Then, later that night, he packed up his things and set out.

So it was that twenty-one days after I was born, my father stood outside the little house, in his hand a crumpled paper with the directions he had been given, and looked up at the grimy windows. As he looked, a baby's cry drifted down to him in the street below and made his skin prickle. Could it be his child? My father had been walking for three days, and now he didn't know if he was ready to knock on the door, to risk losing the hope that his family was behind it.

For twenty-one days, since the first news of the invasion, he had been haunted by dreams of the rest of us burned by fire, shot through with bullets, separated and lost. He had tried to buy a ticket back to the mainland, but no ships travelled in that direction anymore. In desperation, he had walked to the capital, Valacia, and waited for the refugee ships from Malonia to come in. But among the faces, his family's never appeared. He had not greeted the newest ship, the ship at Port St. Martin. It had been too far to walk. But as soon as he heard the story of the miraculous baby, he began to wonder.

By now, his child would have been born. There was something about the story of the baby that reminded him of Jasmine as a child, the way she would wake suddenly and turn to you, cry a kind of warning if there was any danger in the night. Might this baby be his own? That hope, rather than food or water or sleep, had sustained him on his solitary journey down the coast, through the sleet that was the closest Holy Island came to snow. The fishermen at the dock had directed him to this house. And now, like a fool, he didn't dare to knock on the door.

The house was tall and narrow and black, on a back street of the town. Further up the street, someone was sloshing soapy water out of their front door, and it ran down the gutter and under Leo's boots. In front of the house stood jars with the brown skeletons of flowers in them. There was also a porcelain figure of a saint, quite new. For the miracle baby, he supposed. The island was a superstitious place.

An old woman came tap-tapping up the street towards him, heaving her body painfully uphill. She paused and leaned on her walking stick with both hands and looked up at Leo. "You'll be looking for the baby," she said.

"Yes."

"You're in the right place. Go on. Foreign family, they are. Refugees."

"Who—who's with the baby?" said my father, as clearly as he could manage with the painful constriction that had come over his heart.

The old woman opened her mouth and twisted it this way and that, thinking. "A young woman, his mother. Just a girl really, her."

It could be Maria, who was thirty-two. Leo knew well that habit of the old to see everyone under fifty as a child. "Who else?" he said.

"An older lady and a little boy or girl—I don't remember so precisely."

"What about an older boy?"

"No older boy," said the old woman definitely. "Not that I've ever seen."

Leo's stomach gave a painful twist. It wasn't them; it wasn't right. His son should be with them too.

"Go on," said the woman. "Knock at the door."

She leaned on her stick and watched him. She didn't seem about to leave, so Leo knocked. The sound echoed behind the door and made the baby cry harder in the upstairs room. When his hand came away from the door, Leo found that it was slick with sweat. *Please, God, let it be them*, he thought.

"What's that?" said the old woman. "Don't mumble—speak up."

He must have spoken out loud. "Nothing," said Leo.

On the other side of the door, someone said, "Who is it?"

In his confusion, Leo did not recognise his wife's voice; it sounded hard and suspicious. "I'm just looking for my family," he called. "I mean no harm. Maybe I've come to the wrong place."

Very quietly but with certainty, the voice on the other side of the door said, "Leo."

There was a fumbling of chains; the woman could not get the door open.

"Leo," said her voice again.

Inside, there was a thundering on the stairs, and a shriek. "Papa!" Jasmine was screaming on the other side of the door. "Papa!"

The bolts were drawn back. The door opened. Leo raised his hands to his eyes, to assure himself that the two of them were real. "Maria?" he said. "Jasmine?"

Jasmine pushed past my mother and looked up. There stood a grey-faced and grey-haired man, drenched through with sleet and shuddering with fear and joy. Perhaps he had faded to match the island. His face was all stubbly and his hair had grown long. Jasmine smelled the familiar tobacco that had been part of the air of home, and like a demon unleashed, she threw herself at our father.

What I remember—I mean to say, the memory that is truly my own out of all this—is quite different. I had been left upstairs, looking up at the ceiling of the shabby apartment. I turned my face to the door and as he came up the stairs I saw him, my father: a thin and worn man with his arm around my mother. I remember the quick intake of his breath when he first saw me, the sure grip of his hands as he lifted me from the old mattress for the first time, beheld me, adored me. His face was lined and faded well beyond his years. My father's grey eyes met my own, and I swear I recognised him. "Not Leo," my father said. "That name's not right. Let's call him Harlan." From that day, I was never called anything else.

6

*T*he first thing my father said, once all the crying and hugging was done, was this: "I'll never leave you again, Maria. I swear to God I never will."

My grandmother, who was of the opinion that my father should never have left us all in the first place, said so. "Running off like that, leaving us to flee the city without you. It's a wonder you found us again, Leonard!"

"Leo had no choice," Mama retorted. "He was a wanted man. Those criminals from the new government were after him. What could he do but leave?"

"No," said my father, shuddering as he held my mother to him. "She's right. I'll never leave you again."

At the back of the house was a yard where thorny acacia bushes wrestled in the wind. My father and Jasmine escaped there to get away from my grandmother's scolding.

Jasmine would not let go of our papa's sleeve. She pressed herself up against his side to inhale the warm tobacco smell of his old coat. "Papa," she said. "I have to tell you something."

Our father crouched down and looked at her very seriously. "Yes, Jasmine?"

"A man tried to take Harlan from us. At the place with all the boats. I never told Mama, but it happened."

My father knelt in the earth in front of her. He gripped her arms. "Tell me."

"He came up to me and tried to snatch the baby. He was a horrible-looking man, with his face all covered in beard." She wiped away tears. More fell. "He said they were trying to arrest babies in the city, and then he tried to take ours. But I held on and screamed and screamed. I was supposed to be looking after Harlan. I almost—I almost let him get taken," she finished in a wail.

"My God, Jasmine. What stopped him?"

Jasmine swiped at her nose with the back of her hand. "It was another man. A red-haired, army-looking man. With gold spectacles. He came along and pushed the other man away."

Leo frowned. He watched the flapping bushes, but he seemed to see something quite different. "A red-haired, army-looking man," he said. "Did he look like an important man, a great one?"

The great ones were the ancestral possessors of powers. Jasmine wrinkled her nose. "No," she said. "Nothing like that. He looked quite ordinary."

"Why would someone snatch Harlan?"

"He said—Papa, he said they were kidnapping babies. Something to do with Aldebaran—looking for his last descendant. Because of what he wrote."

"Kidnapping babies? Jasmine, did you tell this man anything— anything at all about Aldebaran, about our life in the city—"

Jasmine, in terror, shook her head.

"What are we going to do?" said Jasmine, timidly taking hold of his wrist. "Are they going to come and get Harlan? Is it all my fault?"

Leo pressed her into the comforting warmth of his old coat and stroked her hair. "No, Jas. You're my brave girl. You've done well. You've looked after him well. Now it's my turn to take care of him, mine and Mama's. But no one's going to take Harlan from us. I promise you that."

Jasmine sniffed and gradually recovered herself.

"Everyone on this part of the coast is talking about the miracle baby," said Leo, frowning. "That's how I found you, thank God, but I'm worried the rumours are going to spread and spread. If people come looking, this miracle baby story will lead them straight to this house. It's a simple process to connect the miracle baby with the last descendant of Aldebaran."

Jasmine began to cry in earnest. She clung to our father's side and watched the bushes twist wildly in the wind.

"We need to disappear," Leo murmured. "Change our names, go into hiding. We'll go back to New Maron, where there are more refugees and we can stay anonymous. We'll burn your papers and apply again for them here, as refugees, under false names. It's what I've done." My father straightened with a kind of resolve.

"Papa?" said Jasmine. "We won't get split up again, will we? Because I don't know if I can be as brave again as last time."

"I'll cross hell itself before I leave you again. We'll move at once, tonight, before anything can get in the way. We'll find somewhere to live safely, in hiding, and that way we can always stay together."

Jasmine asked if we could leave Grandmother behind, to save space. Leo just laughed and said, "Grandmama's family."

"She doesn't act like it sometimes," said Jasmine.

"Poor Jas. I know things have been tough for you. They'll get better now. I'll make sure that they do. I want you to have a better life, now we're here on Holy Island." Leo stood and dusted the dirt from the knees of his trousers. "Tonight, if we can, we'll leave and go north."

———

Bumping along in the cart, in the greyness before dawn, we travelled along the edge of the water, with the angry ocean seething below us and high hills soaring to our left. My mother and my father hardly saw the dreary land we travelled through. They held me close, and each gripped the other as though afraid even a gust of wind might separate them. Both understood the incredible luck that had brought us all back together.

My grandmother knitted crossly. She didn't see why we were leaving the first home, she didn't believe in powers, and she was sure that Jasmine had been mistaken about the strange man trying to take me away.

But that very same night, the house where we had been staying had its windows smashed and its door kicked in. A gang of men from the mainland ransacked the rooms. They ripped open the mattresses and pulled out the damp, sour stuffing; they kicked about the old pots in the kitchen and sent the tin bath in which Jasmine had bathed me flying out into the yard. They pounded on the neighbours' doors, demanding where the miracle baby had gone.

No one in Port St. Martin knew anything about it. Back to the mainland, someone claimed. The men left, and made for the port again, back the way they had come.

By that time we were ten miles away, rattling in the hired cart towards our future. As the cart attained a ridge, creakingly, Leo pointed out to Jasmine the hills where our great-great-uncle, Aldebaran, had grown up. That made Jasmine feel better about this strange new place, to remember that her beloved Uncle had come from Holy Island when he was just a child like she was. "Sometime, Harlan, I'll tell you the story about Uncle," she said. Then she remembered the assassination, and frowned. "It ends sadly, though. Poor Uncle."

Jasmine retreated under the seat of the cart to cry a little. Shortly after the hills had vanished behind us in the dark and rain, she re-emerged with a troubled look and tugged our father's hand. "Will Anselm still be able to find us," she whispered, "if we've all changed our names?"

"I hope to God he will," said Leo.

Jasmine wished our father had just said yes.

We settled in the fishing town, New Maron, where my father had been living. From the day we arrived there, my father forbade us to use our real names. He had already burned his own papers; the inhabitants of New Maron knew him as Joseph Karol, a refugee from the mainland. He rented a small apartment up a back street of the town. We spent our days inside at first, Jasmine and my grandmother caged and irritable, my mother displaying the patience of a nun as she navigated their cross silences. A side effect of this was that she talked to me, and I listened. "You'll have a better life here," she told me, just as my father had told Jasmine. "You'll go to school and get a good education and grow up strong and safe, and I promise, love, that I won't let anything happen to you. Maybe it's for the best that we're here. We're not refugees, not properly, if we have a home and work to do. We're luckier than most."

But the way my mother talked to me about the city, I could tell she missed the old life that had been swept away.

Before I was born, my father had kept a second-hand shop which dealt mainly in books. My mother had been a governess and tutor to the children of the rich. They lived on the safe upper edge of poverty. That life, which I never lived, remains in my head mostly in pictures: Jasmine, in her wool coat and fur mittens, running through the streets to school with Anselm, while the snow whirled around them; the way the sun blazed on the riverside houses in which my mother worked; long walks beside the city wall and the river that flowed around it, and the kind shadow of the castle.

That old country was vanishing even as we inhabited it. No one realised it yet.

Other pictures come to me: Our mother by the fire, marking her pupils' work in green ink with her beautiful, steady hands. Our father bending over a cabinet in the back room of his shop, his old leather jacket shrugged up over his shoulders. My grandmother, her mouth set firmly as she unwrapped the box of Christmas ornaments salvaged from her rich house and allowed Jasmine to hang them from the frames of all the doors.

In the fire, each Christmas ornament had exploded in a burst of light.

As my grandmother was fond of reminding us all, our family had once been rich and important. As it was, the only person of any importance left during the winter before I was born had been Aldebaran. Jasmine, soon enough, told me his story. My family had loved him dearly. He was a thin and stern man who had spent his best years with the secret service—and yet he had a great kindness within him. He would sit by the fire and toast bread for my mother on Sunday afternoons and hold Jasmine on his knee. On her birthday, in the dead of winter, he somehow always found for her a fresh red rose, which he produced with a flourish, holding it delightedly between his big hands for her to accept. He taught Jasmine to do tricks with cards. He taught her to make grains of rice jump on the kitchen table. In those days my sister believed that people could possess strange powers, and in her childish mind Uncle was full of magic.

That winter before I was born, Uncle was the king's chief advisor. For this he was made to pay. He was found with a bullet through his head in his room at the castle. Someone had shot him at long range through the window. The assassin was never found.

Aldebaran had the largest state funeral in a hundred years, with drums and cannons and a procession through the streets.

Jasmine, sobbing, walked with her hand on Uncle's coffin. From then on, our family's luck came to an end. Royalists were out of favour, and by the logic of the New Imperial Order, we were all royalists by association. This was why my father had left the city in a hurry, pursued for his family name and his great-uncle's political allegiance. This was why we were all now refugees.

Every day after work, my father begged a lift into Valacia, the city that passed for a capital here on the island, to try and find out what had happened to Anselm. My brother should have been on the island by now. But there was no record anywhere that he had passed through the ports yet, and my father's enquiries in the lists of the Missing Persons Bureau went unanswered. No Anselm Andros had ever arrived. "You brought Papa back," whispered Jasmine in the darkness, lying restless on her mattress beside me. "Now do another miracle. Bring Anselm too."

7

*T*ime passed, and the miracle we all hoped for did not come. Jasmine, however, was full of fierce impatience. She talked constantly about Aldebaran, and Anselm, and the lost grandfather and grandmother she had never met. "Maybe now that everyone's moving around, Papa's mother and father will come back," she said. "Maybe they'll end up on Holy Island too."

"Oh, Jasmine," said my father. "I haven't seen either of them in twenty years. I don't think they're going to come back to us."

"Of course they are," said Jasmine.

That first spring on the island, when I was two months old, I began to cut a tooth. I became fractious and scowled and would not sleep. The summer heat began early, and it was stuffy and oppressive in New Maron. When my grizzling got too much for my grandmother's nerves, my father took me out of the apartment and walked with me down to the sea front. From there, you could see along the bay to the big port in Valacia, where the refugee ships came in. I know my father was looking for Anselm. He carried me in his arms up and down the dock as dusk fell. A couple of people nodded to us and said good evening. The people of New Maron accepted that we were the Karol family: Joseph, Sylvia, Stella and Isak.

On this particular night, my father decided to tell me a story. Everyone talked to me in those days, and none of them talked to each other. "Listen, Harlan," my father said. "You're named for my father, a man called Harold North. I lost him when I was a child. He was a political exile during the last war. A writer. I last saw him when I was eight years old." My father rocked me in his arms. "I remember that night he went away. He put me to bed and read me a story. A perfectly ordinary night. I lay in the dark and listened to his footsteps go along the corridor, and next thing it was morning and my mother and my father were gone. I never saw them again. That's what frightens me about war. The way it takes your real life away from you, without any warning, in the middle of the night. I lost them all. My mother and father disappeared. My little brother died."

I listened. I stopped crying and listened.

My father rocked me and said, "At least it stops your tears, Harlan, even if you don't understand."

I couldn't understand; that was why he was telling me these things. But I could remember. I remember every word of his.

My father had carried me all the way along the sea wall. This was a fish-smelling, grimy place, where fishermen and market traders shouted, but at nights it was swept clean and unusually quiet. The masts of the ships made a forest beyond the harbour wall, which sang faintly in the wind. A woman was out on her step, washing grey sheets with a sluicing noise. She looked at us through narrowed eyes.

"Never have I woken so easily as I did that morning before I knew that my parents were gone," my father told me, still just as if I were a grown-up person and not a two-month-old baby. "And that's the truth of it, Harlan. That's why I've promised never again to leave you. Because what I did to you—to Maria, to Jasmine—was the same. I left you all in the night, with no real promise to return, and that was a terrible thing. Poor Jasmine is still struggling to get over it. I can see that now. I was lucky to find you again. I'll admit it. I should never have left."

In answer, I made some babbling sounds. I remember doing it—at least, I think I do.

"But here's the strange thing," said my father. "Since my father died, someone has written books in his voice, as though they were carrying on his life's work. I found one last year. *The Darkness Has a Thousand Voices*, by a man named Harlan Smith. Just exactly his written style. It's my father's voice in those pages. I know it is. A dead man can't publish a book, even a man as formidable as my father was. So either it's an old manuscript someone dug up, or . . . or he's alive. Out there, somewhere, looking for me perhaps, living. He's been living all this time. He's sending me signs."

My father sighed. "That's why I gave you the name. In honour of him. If you really have powers, Harlan, show me some sign of where he is, whether he's still living." He laughed abruptly then, painfully, folding me against his chest to shield me from the cold. "I'm crazy—I don't know what I'm asking. And yet— I don't know—I wonder about you, Harlan. This rescue from the sea, and your birth, when by rights you should have died. There's something in you that wants to fight, to live, to prevail. Something I'd almost call powers. I had them too, a little, but they disappeared when I was a boy. If you have these powers, then you may turn out to be somebody quite remarkable."

These words lodged in my mind. They altered me, defined me.

Years later, when no one believed in powers anymore—not even Jasmine—my father would deny that he had ever spoken them.

At that precise moment, another miracle really was occurring: somewhere in that black night, ill and coughing but alive, with a crumpled picture of my father folded up in his suitcase and a wish to see his family still burning in his heart, Harold North thought of my father. And into my newborn dreams crept his face.

How does a baby dream? Not in words, supposedly, for babies possess no language. But somehow, I can still remember the wrinkled face of my grandfather speaking to me, quite clearly. He told stories. He told them as if he were speaking them directly to me. "Well," he said. "Here I am on Holy Island. I've come a long way to look for you."

Once or twice, the old man took out a picture. This picture was not a photograph but a painting, and it looked as if it had been torn from its frame. It was faded almost beyond recognition. But when the old man shone a light on this picture, I laughed and clapped my hands, because three of the people in it had my father's familiar grey eyes.

Three times in my life someone came back from the dead. I'll tell you about the others in good time. But the first to come back was my grandfather.

8

I was three months old, and my family was eating potato stew and talking about me. Out of the window, a foul, spitting kind of weather. Inside, draughts, because our money for fuel was never quite enough. In the street, someone kept coughing. We were living in a new apartment now—above a disused shop that my father was slowly trying to restore. Every day, new refugees kept coming, making the demand for jobs more desperate and trying the patience of the existing islanders. My father felt a shop would be secure. "Harlan is showing no signs of powers," my mother said.

"No," said my father, who had harboured seeds of doubt since our conversation. "I think you're right. I did wonder at the start, but now I think he's quite ordinary."

"Thank the good Lord," said my grandmother.

"But he *is* showing signs of powers," said Jasmine, indignant. "What about saving us from that storm?"

"I don't know," said my father. "I don't know about that. Any baby could cry."

"What about being born?" said Jasmine. "When he turned all blue? What about him being Aldebaran's last descendant? What about all that?"

"That's nonsense," said my grandmother. "No one believes that anymore."

"They do!" said Jasmine, stamping and shouting. "They do believe it, because it's true! 'Magic is dying, and a time will come when no one remembers the old ways'!" recited Jasmine, who had memorised the whole strange prophecy my great-great-uncle wrote before his death. "'I name my last descendant as your hope in times of trouble, a very certain help in the darkness of the road.'"

"Stop that!" shrieked my grandmother. "Stop that blasphemy!"

"It's what Aldebaran wrote!" yelled Jasmine. "He wrote down that prophecy. It was in all the newspapers and everyone in the city believed it. It's about Harlan! It's not blasphemy—it's a prediction." She picked me up and clutched me to her chest. "Why are you saying he doesn't have powers when he does? He's going to be special. I just know it."

Still that coughing in the street. My father got up and went to the window. "There's someone out there," he said sharply. "Stay back from the glass."

"Who is it?" said my mother.

"I can't tell. He's in the shadows." My father strained towards the window in the half-light.

My mother stood up and put her hand on his shoulder, making him start. "I can't see anything."

"There he is. He's just ducked out of sight, but he's there, I swear."

My mother frowned into the drizzle.

"All this foolish talk," said my grandmother. "I hope to goodness the child *doesn't* develop any abnormality. Lord knows the trouble we've had with Jasmine, though thankfully that seems to be over now."

Jasmine, in tears, carried me to the next room and sat stroking my face, saying, "Don't listen to them. I hate them all." Which was not fair, since strictly speaking the only one she had hated at any time was our grandmother.

Defiantly, she whispered the last words of the prophecy into my ear: "'But there are those who will not return, those who will go forward into another place. Have courage.'"

Whatever it meant, it made me cry.

My mother came into the room. She sat down and stroked Jasmine's hair. "Angel," she said quietly. "Have you done anything impossible since coming to Holy Island? You know, like you used to? Made things move, or . . ."

Jasmine twisted the quilt between her hands. I lay on my back and looked up at my mother's face and listened. "No," my sister said eventually. "I don't have powers anymore. They're gone. They must have gone away when we crossed the sea." She started to cry. "It's what Uncle said. Powers must be dying."

"It doesn't matter. It's better that way. Your papa has heard bad things from the other refugees at the market, stories about the way children with any trace of powers are being treated under the new government. It's better to be ordinary."

"How can you say that? What about Harlan? He's special."

"Can you be very brave for me and try to understand what I'm going to say to you?"

"I'm listening."

"Your papa thinks that bad people may try to find us. Because we're related to Uncle, to Aldebaran. Because your brother is his youngest descendant, the one who everyone believes might have special powers. Because of those words Uncle wrote. They may already be looking for us."

Jasmine said nothing, but by the glittering of her brown eyes our mother could tell she was paying attention.

"Your papa and I think it's best that we don't say anything about powers again. You can't do anything impossible anymore, and neither can Leo. We've got no reason to believe that Harlan has any strange abilities."

"But he can—"

"No, Jasmine. I want you to promise me you won't say anything to Harlan about powers. I mean to say, when he's old enough to understand, I want you to promise me you won't say anything."

"He's old enough to understand now," said Jasmine.

The two of them glanced at me. I stared back. Neither of them had any idea that the next miracle was already taking place. But at that moment, someone knocked on the door.

My mother picked me up and carried me into the living room, Jasmine at her heels. There was some hesitation, because my father didn't want to open the door to a stranger. Eventually my grandmother marched down into the empty shop below, and the rest of us followed. The drizzle had washed away the dust on the front window, and we could see clearly a white-haired man in an old-fashioned suit and hat. I knew at once that this was my father's father. I laughed and smiled in delight—my first real smile, according to my mother. I strained against her grip and reached for the old man with both arms as the door opened.

"Yes?" said my grandmother sharply. "Who might you be?"

The old man took his hat in his hands. "I'm sorry to trouble you," he said. "I'm looking for the refugee family called Karol."

"That's us," said my grandmother, still keeping the door open no more than a half foot. "Well, them. I'm Andros. Sylvia Karol is my daughter. What do you want?"

She rolled her eyes slightly as she said this. My grandmother did not believe in the business of the false names.

"I've been trying to find you," said the old man. "May I come in and speak with you a little?"

I carried on reaching for the old man, straining and wriggling, and when my mother did not hand me over at once, I began to cry. This drew the old man's attention to me for the first time.

"I see I am troubling the baby," he said. "I'm sorry. I didn't mean to frighten you all."

Jasmine said, very clear and loud, "He wants you to pick him up."

When the old man did not reach out for me, I began to struggle in earnest.

"Oh dear," said the old man. "I'm sorry. I don't know what I'm doing to upset him. Perhaps he's frightened to see a stranger."

"He knows you," said Jasmine. "Can't you see he recognises you?"

"None of us have ever seen this gentleman in our lives," said my grandmother, "let alone Harlan."

"Harlan?" said the old man. "Is that what you call him?"

Something must have unnerved my father, because he shivered and rubbed at his arms as though he was suddenly very cold. My grandmother had used my real name.

"You'd better come in, if you have business with our family," he said, levering my grandmother away from the door and opening it wider.

The old man, hesitant and coughing, came in.

As soon as he was inside our shop, I renewed my struggles

for the old man's attention. My father took me from my mother and held me to his chest. "What's wrong, eh?" he said. "Why so sad, Harlan?"

"He wants the old gentleman to take him," said Jasmine.

"Why did you name the baby Harlan?" said the old man. "If you'll forgive my asking."

"It was after a writer," said my father, "from Malonia City."

"You come from the city too, don't you?" said my mother. "I can tell by your accent. Won't you please sit down?"

My mother pulled out an old folding chair. The old man sat with a sigh and rubbed at his rheumy eyes.

"Thank you," he said. "You're very kind. I come from the city, yes. I've been away from there a long time. Twenty-two years."

"Hush, Harlan," said my father, still wrestling with me.

I was screaming so shrilly now that the glass in the window-panes rattled.

Over the noise, Jasmine shouted: "Why won't you listen? I keep telling you all! He wants the old gentleman to hold him!"

My father, startled, did what he might not have done if he had thought it through properly: he put me into the man's arms. Instantly, my crying stopped. I looked up into the stranger's face and smiled in recognition.

With trembling hands, he held me. "There," he said. "There, son. That's what the fuss was about, was it? How strange."

"What did you want to say to us?" asked my father.

The man felt in the pocket of his jacket. He took out a crumpled picture and unfolded it. In it, a woman with curled hair posed self-consciously in an armchair with a fat and merry baby not unlike me. Behind her stood a small boy, very serious, grey-eyed and gold-haired. In fact, all three of them had the same grey eyes. The only one who didn't was the man, who was dark-eyed, handsome in an old-century way, in a new blue suit of clothes.

"Do you recognise this picture?" said the old man to my father.

My father held it between his two hands. "Where did you get it?" he said.

"I carried it with me from the city," said the stranger.

My father stared into the old crinkled eyes. "Who are you? What is it you want?"

"I'm looking for my son. By chance, a few weeks ago I met a boy named Anselm and he told me to look here on Holy Island."

"You met Anselm?" My mother broke in here, in a breathless rush. "Is he safe? Is he well?"

"Perfectly safe. He's in Arkavitz." In a steady voice, the old man told her how he and Anselm had been thrown together on the journey west from the city, how the two of them had pieced together their stories, and the pieces had fit. "How strange it was," he said. "I'd been circling you for years, homing in, but it took the chaos of war to bring us back together—that meeting with Anselm in the coach going west, our long conversations. I became convinced that I'd found the son of my son. I proved to be correct. He sent me here, and I made enquiries at the missing persons office in Valacia. They had no news. So I've been working my way south systematically. And yet I've felt—I don't know—guided in all this. As though some guardian spirit drove me."

Jasmine reached up and squeezed my foot in suppressed joy.

The old man handed my mother a letter. When my mother read it, she began to cry. "It's Anselm's writing," she said. "He's all right."

Meanwhile, my father was still held captive by the matter of the picture. "This was made in the city, twenty-four years ago," he said at last. "I'm the boy with the grey eyes. My father ripped this picture out of its frame as he was leaving the city. I've never seen him since. Where did you get this? Do you mean us some kind of harm?"

The old man reached up with one hand, took my father's

wrist very firmly, and said, "Look at me." His voice held steady. "Look at me," he said again. "Do you not recognise me? Have war and twenty-two years done so much?"

And finally, my father understood.

That was two miracles in one: on the same day we learned that my brother was safe, my grandfather came back to us from the dead.

But still Jasmine hissed at me at nights over the matter of Anselm. "You've done five miracles," she pleaded. "Now do one more. Bring back our brother from the north. Please, Harlan."

9

*M*y father did not sleep for a week after his father returned to him. At nights, I could hear him pacing in the empty shop below our apartment, alone in the dust and the silence, lighting cigarette after cigarette, writing a long letter to Anselm.

The best thing about the letter the old man had delivered, besides the fact that it told us that Anselm had escaped the city safely, was that pencilled on the back was a return address, the address to which my brother was heading. *Anselm Andros, c/o Damonti Steel Factory, Arkavitz.* Arkavitz was in the free north, and we could write to him there.

While my long-lost grandfather made preparations to move to New Maron to live out his life near us all, my father resurrected the old shop. He ripped out rotten boards and coated the walls in whitewash. He built counters and cabinets. He sanded the floor on his hands and knees, and polished it until it was smooth as a tabletop. The shop, when it was finished, became Karol Family Second-Hand Dealers, and it shone.

Sometime during the weeks when the shop was first open, my father carried me to the harbour. In his other hand he carried all his remaining tobacco and cigarette papers, bundled up in an old paper bag. When we got to the sea wall he climbed up on top of it, balancing me precariously in the crook of his arm, and flung the cigarettes into the sea.

"I'm done with dying now," my father told me.

For the first time in his life—the first time since his mother and father left and his little brother died—he wanted with his whole heart to live.

This newfound belief in life must have rubbed off on my grandfather. The doctor in New Maron, an old-fashioned, ponderous man who had been around since the oldest fishermen were children, listened to my grandfather's rattling chest and shook his head. He predicted that my grandfather might live two or three years, if he ate well and rested. Harold North took the decision to defy him. "That's all nonsense," he said. "I didn't come all this way to find my son only to lie down and die at the end of the journey. Two years? Why, I'm only sixty-three."

While my grandfather lived, my father got younger. After he gave up the cigarettes his face lost its grey look. Soon, the monster that had been sitting on his lungs lifted its weight. His fingers, which had been tarry, grew smooth and clean again, and the cigarette burns in his skin faded to white. Even his hair regained some of its former gold. He began to walk straighter and speak more clearly, and he lost the frowning look he had always possessed when he was thinking. His forehead smoothed, and now that he shaved properly and cut his hair with some regularity he lost his rough, dishevelled air and became almost youthful.

By the time I was a year old, he looked like a man in his early thirties again.

10

*T*wo months after my father sent his letter, Anselm wrote back to us. My mother wept for joy when she received the letter.

It was all my father could do to prise it out of her hands and read it out to us.

19th March, Year '89, Anselm wrote. *Dear Mama, Papa, Grandfather, Jasmine, Grandmother and Harlan, I can't tell you what a joy it was to get your letter, and to know that you're together on Holy Island. At least I can console myself that one good thing has come out of this war.*

I'm in Arkavitz, working in the steel factory here while I decide how to proceed. I know I should explain myself. I promised to come and meet you. I set out from the city fully intending to follow you to Holy Island. But the truth is, I can't leave the mainland without knowing what's happened to Michael. He was my greatest friend until he left the city. I must be honest: far more than a friend to me. I'm sure you are aware of this, though I haven't spoken directly about it.

"Yes, yes, everyone knows Anselm was in love with Michael," said Jasmine. "Get on with the letter, Papa. Did he find Michael or did he not?"

But the adults were startled—for no one had known that Anselm was in love with his friend Michael except, apparently, my seven-year-old sister. "Did he talk to you about this?" asked my father. "Why didn't he tell us sooner? Did he think we'd be angry? Was he afraid?"

"Oh, no," said Jasmine. "He didn't tell me. I just knew."

"The New Imperial Order won't allow it," my mother said, weeping. "Homosexual offences—he'll be imprisoned—he'll be beaten—"

"Hush, Maria," said my father, grasping the letter. "He says more about that—listen."

You mustn't worry about my safety, wrote Anselm. *Here in the free north, I can search for Michael without fear of imprisonment or persecution. The resistance here have been helping homosexuals and followers of the religions who have had to go into hiding, getting them across the border. They think Michael may be with a resistance* cell further north. I'm considering going north too, to look for him, but I'll have to wait for the warmer weather to get across the mountain passes. I should be able to go within a month or two.

"See," said my father, putting a consoling hand on my mother's wrist, "he's safe. He's all right. The place where he is isn't occupied any more than Holy Island is. He isn't subject to their laws."

"But what if they cross the border—what if they catch him?"

"Wait. Let me read on."

The situation in the occupied part of the mainland is bad, from what I understand, wrote Anselm. *All homosexuals and followers of the old religions are being interned. Also those descended from any family lines in which powers have been recorded. It's like the stories you used to tell me about the first occupation, before I was born. There's no news of the king. As far as I can tell from the news we have here, he set out in a coach to flee west on the same night you left the city, but never arrived in West Ravina. Therefore it's likely he was intercepted on the way. People have been spreading all kinds of superstitious miracle stories—that he was seen in Angel City in the south, on Holy Island, in Ositha. It's very hard to separate the truth from the rumours.*

But the Alcyrian army haven't advanced any further—which is good news for us here north of the border. There's still a good deal of fighting from the resistance in Capital, which has held them up. I saw smuggled photographs of our old street. The whole place is burned. But the general feeling here is that it's almost impossible for the Alcyrians to take the north, the south or Holy Island, because of the mountains here and the sea currents between you and the mainland. And the resistance is gathering force day by day, hoping to make a counter-attack. I give thanks that all of you are in a free sector, and so am I, and so, God willing, is Michael. I'll write more when I can. Love, Anselm.

"He's safe," said my mother, kissing the letter.

Jasmine cried too, because she knew now that until Anselm found Michael there was no chance of him coming to Holy Island anymore.

Grandfather Harold lived in a little apartment above a tobacconist's shop, two streets away from our own. That was how I always knew him, as Grandfather Harold. Truth be told, he was the one I loved the best of all my family. It was because of his stories.

War and exile and loneliness hadn't destroyed him, only turned him inwards a little. He loved his new grandchildren with a fierce passion. He taught Jasmine to make a kite and draw a treasure map, and he told us stories about our family's past—stories that had been lost for years. Now Jasmine had an ally in her campaign to educate me in my role as the last inheritor of Aldebaran's powers.

In the companionable lamplight of his apartment above the tobacconist's shop, I learned that our family had a whole past life as different from this one as air is from water. My grandfather told me of the great ones, the way they could cut stone like water, make houses tremble, conjure light out of dark. He told me about their lines of apprenticeship. Aldebaran had learned from Sheratan, and his own disciple had been Rigel. They were named after the stars. "What happened to Rigel?" asked Jasmine.

"He vanished years ago—no one knows."

Everyone seemed to have vanished in those days. No one had any news of the king either. The Holy Island newspapers which my father brought home told daily of the search, but even they could not fashion this utter lack of news into good news.

But as my grandfather told me his stories, I saw the king hiding in a black house on a moor, where lonely gulls circled and the ice on the well had to be cracked every morning. Then, later, far away in a land of bright lights and roaring traffic, a land quite different from our own. England, my grandfather called it, a legendary place that no one now believed in, into which great men and women with powers had once journeyed as naturally as stepping through a door. I saw these great ones—my dead great-great-uncle and his allies—making the crossing by ship, through the ruins of great castles, by hidden paths and tunnels. I saw these things and knew that they were real.

We had to wait another four months for a letter from Anselm. By the time it arrived, it was the height of my first summer.

10th June, Year '89, he wrote. *Dear Mama, Papa, Grandfather, Jasmine, Grandmother and Harlan, I have found Michael. I had a difficult journey north to reach him. He was in Bernitz, with a resistance cell. We've broken with them, but the truth is the two of us feel we can't leave the mainland just yet. Both of us feel bound in some way to see this battle through to its end. The resistance here are communicating with cells in the free south and west sectors, planning a counter-attack which may drive the Imperialists out of Capital before Christmas.*

"He'll be killed!" cried Jasmine.

"No, no," said my father. "It's all right. He isn't fighting."

You mustn't worry about us, wrote Anselm. *I don't intend to fight, and I've persuaded Michael to stay here too, where it's relatively safe. We're manning a telegraph post. It's in the most isolated part of the mountains, further north even than Bernitz. Which is why it may take this letter some months to get to you. But you see, I'm the furthest possible that I can be from the fighting at the border.*

The resistance here talk a good deal about Aldebaran, Anselm's letter continued. *There's a general feeling that his last descendant will come forward and rescue us all, that the prophecy still holds some weight. This is strange, for hardly anyone believes in powers, but I suppose it's a kind of superstition. Then there are those in the resistance who disagree, who think that there's no sense waiting for some sign from a long-dead great one, and that we should push over the border and force them out of our land by violent means. I don't know what I think, myself. Michael and I transmit messages between the various northern cells. Without the telegraph, they would be cut off from each other, and from the rest of the movement in the south and the west. But these messages are grim. The resistance along the border have sustained very heavy losses. The prison camps in the occupied mainland are full, and people don't come out of there once they enter. I don't want to write too much about this, but it's clear dark things are happening under Imperialist rule.*

It's very beautiful here, though. The silence of the mountains at night is like crystal, the purest silence I've ever heard. Since finding Michael, I have a good deal to be thankful for.

I'm told Holy Island is safe, though I doubt the place can accommodate many more refugees. Like the villages here, it must be full to breaking point. Be careful and stay out of danger. Love, Anselm.

What Anselm wrote was true. Holy Island could not accommodate any more refugees. In New Maron, we were refused food in half the shops. The government in Valacia had imposed a system of rationing. Grandfather, on the little terrace of his apartment, planted potatoes and beans in pots, afraid we would have nothing to eat. In Valacia itself, there had been riots. "Couldn't we go and join Anselm?" Jasmine cried, coming home from school one night with thistles in her hair, thrown at her by the local children as she left school with her bundle of second-hand books. "In that mountain place? Not here, where they don't like us or care about us?"

"Oh, Jasmine." My mother teased out Jasmine's beautiful hair, strand by strand, with Grandmother's bone comb. "It's not safe to cross the sea. We'd have to go too close to the fighting."

"Then how will Anselm come to us?"

"I don't know. He'll try his very best, Jas, but for now we must be patient and write him lots of letters to tell him we're safe."

Jasmine wrote and wrote to our brother. She walked about the house clutching his letters. Writing to Anselm became a part of my childhood as important as those lamplit winter

afternoons in Grandfather Harold's apartment. And my grandfather's stories must have worked their magic, because I saw a
little of Anselm's life when those letters were read to me: the
cold crystal silence of the north, and the frost on the branches,
and the tapping of the telegraph machine. And these things
were real too.

12

On each of Jasmine's birthdays, Anselm wrote to her person-
ally. On my fifth birthday, he also wrote to me.

1st December, Year '93, he wrote. *Dear Harlan, A very happy
birthday for the 24th—you will be five years old, and I haven't seen
you since you were eight days. Soon, I suppose, you will be starting
school. I can't imagine how big you must have grown!*

*Do you celebrate Christmas there on Holy Island? Here, we cel-
ebrate a little. We put candles in the windows, though the telegraph
post is so isolated that there's no one around to see. There's a big battle
going on at the border, so everyone there lights candles in their windows and it helps the resistance soldiers know that people are with
them. Do you have candles, or Christmas ornaments?*

*I hope that by the time you celebrate your sixth birthday, I will
be there to light the candles on your cake and make a wish for you.*

Love, your brother, Anselm.

And how could I write back to him that we had no money for
Christmas ornaments, no candles, no birthday cake? Still, the
thrill of receiving a private letter from my brother was better
than any cake or candles. I slept with it closed in my hand.

At the end of that winter, I suffered from silent fever.
It nearly destroyed my father, who wept and paced the house
and almost drove the doctor to violence with summoning and
resummoning him to my bedside. Silent fever was what had

taken my father's brother from him. Because Jasmine had never been exposed to the disease, and my grandfather had, Grandfather wrapped me in coats and hired a carriage to take me to his apartment.

This was the first time I stayed with him; there had never been any need before. The silent fever lingered. I was racked with coughing and my head felt like it was weighted down with stuffing. I spent half the days asleep. When I did wake, it was always to my grandfather, watching over me with kind eyes or sponging my forehead with cool water, or ordering me, very gently, to drink.

After a week, I was well enough to sit up. My grandfather brought out an old chessboard and taught me how to play. I loved the game—not for the rules, which were dry and strict and slipped out of my fevered head too easily, but for the stories it brought out of my grandfather while he considered his next move. He told about his exile in Alcyria, how he worked picking potatoes and the way the light is gold and thick in that country. He told about his time as a young writer in the city, and about his wife—my other grandmother—a singer and a dancer named Amelie. When he described the flowers that rained upon her as she stood in the spotlight, surrounded by velvet darkness, I could almost feel the brush of rose petals against my cheeks. My grandfather himself was showered with roses once, when he spoke to the Malonian Literary Academy. To be showered with roses is not a gentle thing, he told me. It feels like an assault. The stalks scratch you; the thorns stick in your hair. "Why, I was picking those thorns out of my hair for a week!" he said. "They could have chosen daisies or violets— but no, they had to bombard me with great sticks cut off thorn bushes, for my sins."

We both laughed at that, but I decided that day to become a writer.

When I was almost better, my grandfather moved me into the living room, carrying me with surprising strength. He laid me on the battered sofa which had come with his apartment and covered me with a blanket. "Your father brought something over," he said. "Look."

Standing beside the fireplace was a great wooden box, stout as a dog, with a grille on its front. It was patched and scuffed and a wire protruded from one side. "What is it?" I asked.

"A wireless radio."

"Where did Papa get it from?"

"He made it."

I knew my father made things out of old parts, for there were no electrical goods on Holy Island like those they had on the mainland. But he had never made a wireless radio before. This was his first. "Does it work?" I asked my grandfather, breathless with fever and excitement in equal measure.

"Let's see."

My grandfather approached it warily. He turned the dial. At first a noise like the sea, then a ghostly voice, which strengthened, as though it were coming towards us from a long distance. A woman, who spoke even more beautifully than my mother: ". . . resistance casualties currently stand at just over 75,000," she said. "The resistance leaders now state that it is doubtful they will have a victory before Christmas, as previously hoped. Meanwhile, in the Alcyrian-operated death camps—"

With a snap, my grandfather killed the wireless radio. "Hey!" I cried. "I was listening to that."

"We'll listen to it later," he said.

But after that, my grandfather turned on the radio every night.

As well as the free station, which was broadcast out of Arkavitz, we got other stations occasionally, stations from the mainland on which Alcyrian voices rattled out foreign announcements, or marching bands played. There was a voice that yelled from the wireless again and again—a voice that shouted, that threatened, that barked. That voice's name was General Marlan, and it was in charge of our old country.

One night, just after we heard the news that Angel City had fallen to the Alcyrian army, my grandfather turned the dial and came upon one of their stations. But instead of the rattling voices, something so surprising struck us that we listened in awe for several seconds without speaking. An Alcyrian voice, singing. It crackled and fizzed a little, but in spite of that it rose and soared until our room was inhabited by it. It overtook the falling night with its exact clarity, its beauty, and went on, and became still more beautiful.

We both listened in utter silence, enraptured, as darkness fell.

I remembered that night forever. I remembered the exact sound of that voice but more than that the way my grandfather listened to it. My grandfather told me afterwards that the woman was singing, in Alcyrian, "I Would Follow the One I Love," a song that had once been ours, a song my grandmother had adored. "She sounds a little like my Amelie," my grandfather murmured.

Another voice spoke at last. "'We have just presented to you, in association with the Culture Board of the Alcyrian Empire,'" my grandfather translated, for he knew their language well, "'a recording from the concert of Anastasia Fortuna in Anshelle'— Angel City, they mean, that's just their name for it—'the first time a singing voice has ever been transmitted by radio waves. The glorious government . . .'"

"Why have you stopped translating?" I asked.

"You don't need to hear all this nonsense about the glorious government." Feverishly, my grandfather wrote down the name: Anastasia Fortuna. "The first time a singing voice has been transmitted," he marvelled.

———

I got better from my silent fever, but every Sunday after that my grandfather and I listened to Anastasia Fortuna on the wireless radio. Sometimes, my grandfather turned off the lights and opened the windows, so that her voice mingled with the rushing of the sea. And I saw Anastasia Fortuna, in a black dress, singing, with roses in her hair. And around her was a theatre out in the open, a sort of circle of black stone, beside a bluer sea. And this was real, and joined the other memories in my mind.

Thanks to my grandfather, I grew up surrounded by stories of other places, other worlds.

13

15th February, Year '94, wrote Anselm, shortly afterwards. *Dear Mama, Papa, Grandfather, Jasmine, Grandmother and Harlan, I find it very difficult to write this letter. The Imperialists have taken Angel City. What this means is that the south of our old country is no longer free. Now only Holy Island and the north sector remain liberated from Imperialist rule.*

I know I used to write to you about my hope for a quick resistance victory—a battle over by next year. Now I think it likely that we are in for a longer occupation. Michael and I are swamped with telegraph messages. We take three-hour breaks in each twelve and get what sleep we can, alternating our shifts on the telegraph machine so as not to miss any. The lines are full of appeals from families looking for missing fathers, mothers, sons, daughters. If I stopped to think about it, I'd grow melancholy. We hear just enough about the prison camps to deduce where they have all gone. Meanwhile, the resistance numbers are too depleted for any quick victory anymore.

Things will get a good deal tougher in the next couple of years, he wrote. *But I still believe you are safer where you are, in the free part of the country, than returning to Capital as I hear some are now doing. Stay there and be very careful. Love, Anselm.*

My brother was right. During my fourth year, the rationing on Holy Island had got so grim that whole shipfuls of refugees returned to the mainland to live under Imperialist rule. But the following year, another wave arrived. The harvest was better. The crisis passed.

But now the wireless reports from the free radio station no longer talked about revolution. Instead, they spoke of a resistance preparing itself, "mustering its forces." "The leaders of the Arkavitz Partisan Cell have issued an announcement," the wireless told us, the winter I was six years old. "Due to divisions in the Partisan movement and heavy casualties, all preparations for a march on Capital have been indefinitely suspended. The resistance must undergo a period of recruitment and preparation before it is strong enough to be certain of winning back Capital."

It was that same year that I discovered I was the only person living in the world who could remember things that had never strictly happened to them.

It was a grey and drizzly day, and my mother was at the sink washing potatoes. "Mama," I said. "Do you remember, before I was born, when you used to cry? You used to cry all the time, and sometimes we could hear the sound of a gun too. Lots of guns, outside. Do you remember that?"

My mother abruptly stopped washing her potatoes. One of them, half peeled, went bouncing to the floor. She turned to me with a frozen kind of look. For several seconds, she looked at me like that, without picking up the potato. So I did it for her.

Then she said, "Oh, Harlan, you can't possibly remember."

"Why not?" I said.

"Because no one in the world remembers anything from before they were two or three years old. Your mind can't make memories when you're that young. It's just the way it's designed.

Things happen to you, but you don't remember them. They just—slip away, I suppose."

"To where?"

"I don't know."

"But I do remember," I insisted. "You wore a red dress with roses on the collar. You wore little earrings with birds. Out of the window of your room was a grey brick wall. We lived with Grandmother."

My mother blotted her hands, grainy with the mud from the potato bowl, on her skirt without really noticing she was doing it. Eventually she said, "No, Harly, love. I never had a dress like that."

The strange thing was, I could tell Mama was lying. I could tell by the way she looked sideways. And I could also tell because, for a brief moment, her own thoughts flashed onto the screen of my mind: the collar of a red dress like the one I had described, and that window with its flat brick wall beyond.

My mother knelt down in front of me and took my hands. Hers were cool as glass. "Harly," she said, "I want you to promise you won't tell things like that to anyone else. It isn't safe to tell people that you can see things when you can't."

I squirmed away from my mother and started to protest, but something in her disbelief crushed me, so I said, in a very small voice, "All right, I promise."

My mother kissed my forehead and gave me a stick of toffee, then she let me turn the pages of the big atlas that was really Jasmine's and look at the names of the towns. As I looked at the out-of-date borders, all the towns like stars on each page of the atlas, I could hear in my head what my mother had said. "No one in the world remembers anything from before they were two or three years old." Each of these dots was a city with a thousand, a million people—and yet none of them was like me. Which made me the loneliest person in the world.

That was the first time I realised that there was something not quite right about me.

I told my grandfather. In the continuing darkness one Sunday night, I told him. I could feel his frown rather than see it, because of the dark. "And you say you see these things as if they're memories?" he said. "As if they really happened?"

"Yes, Grandfather."

"And they aren't just your imagination? Because you have plenty of that, Harly, let me tell you."

"No," I said. "These pictures are different. They sort of . . . come to me. Without me telling them to. I dream about the city before I was born, and I dreamed about you before we met you. That was why I recognised you, that day you came to the shop. Because I'd seen you before."

"That's something I can't argue with. You certainly seemed to know me. But are you sure you aren't misremembering somehow, Harlan?"

"I'm sure," I said. My voice sounded weak in the darkness, and I felt the need to say it again, louder. "I'm *sure*. Grandfather, I'm not mad, or lying. I'm just different from everyone else." I spread my hands hopelessly.

My grandfather rested his head on his hand and considered. "All right," he said. "I believe you."

"Is it true?" I said. "Am I the only one who can see things that never really happened to them?"

"I don't know," he said. "No one wants to talk about powers anymore. A strange thing happened, around the time you were born. It was said that people who had once possessed powers were losing their special abilities. They just dried up and went away."

"Like Papa's," I breathed. "Like Jasmine's."

"Maybe."

"Do you believe in powers, Grandfather?"

My grandfather thought for a long time, then said, "I don't know."

"What about me? Do you believe I have something strange about me? Something special?"

My grandfather put his hand on my forehead as though to test for a fever. "You seem perfectly fine to me," he said with a laugh. "But either way, you're special."

"So what shall I do?" I asked him sadly. "Mama says I'm not to tell these stories anymore."

My grandfather thought for a while, then went to his little study. He came back carrying a stack of notebooks and a pen. "Write, Harlan," he said. "No one can tell you not to write stories. Write these dreams down. Maybe they will turn out to be something quite remarkable in the end."

And so I wrote.

And here are the stories I told.

II

❧ LOSS ❧

14

I dreamed of a rickety town besieged by snow, in the shadow of great grim mountains, and my brother in the light of a single lamp writing his letters to us.

My brother's story began in Arkavitz. It wasn't much of a town—just a few streets huddled around a clapboard church; an inn; a steel cutlery factory. Bleak forest and windswept mountains overshadowed it on all sides. Inaccessible by road, harsh of winter and short of summer, Arkavitz proved impossible for the New Imperial Army to invade during midwinter with modern artillery and tanks. So, when most of the country that had once been Malonia had ceased to exist, the very north was left free.

It was here, among the men and women of the newly formed resistance, that Anselm began looking for Michael. The resistance fighters travelling into the hills were occasionally willing to carry messages. Anselm wrote letter after letter. Sometimes, lying sleepless at nights, he imagined the messages he had sent out blowing like great snowflakes in the wind.

This is why Anselm left us. Because, in the end, he couldn't bring himself to abandon the place where Michael might be.

One frostbitten day, when the wind rolled off the mountains and scoured the alleys and the streets, a message arrived for Anselm. It was delivered by a shabby man who waited in the shadows outside the tenement building where Anselm lived. The street was not lit, so Anselm could only make out the person in outline. "Anselm Andros?" said the man.

"I'm Anselm Andros."

"I've an urgent telegram for you. From Bernitz. From a person called Michael Barone."

Anselm seized the telegram and tore it open. *Anselm*, it read.

Received your messages. I'm in Bernitz, but not for much longer. Get here as soon as you can. Michael.

Anselm ran with the telegram to the top of the house, where he had his attic room. Standing in the cold and dark behind his door, he pressed it to his chest and gave thanks to a God he did not really believe in that Michael was safe and well.

In the middle of the night, Anselm packed his belongings and set out. He had no idea where Bernitz was, except that it was further north. He had no map and no proper boots. As he ran past the clapboard church, elderly widows in their black, sheet-like dresses were arriving for the first Mass of the day.

Three miles north of the town, the forest began. Anselm passed a small shack where the snow had banked up. All at once, the forest trembled at the harsh rap of a gunshot. Anselm stumbled in a snowdrift and tripped, sending his belongings flying out of the leather backpack he carried.

When he sat up, an elderly man was watching him from the trees nearby, a dead rabbit dangling in one hand and a shotgun across his shoulder. "Where are you going?" the old man asked, his voice echoing across the silent clearing.

"I'm walking to Bernitz."

"Walking," said the old man. "To Bernitz." He let out a wheezing laugh.

Anselm began gathering his belongings from the snow: his shirts and underwear, his notebooks and pens, and a stack of banknotes, all covered in a fine dusting of snow.

"You'd better come inside and get those things dry," said the old man. "You can't walk to Bernitz wet with snow."

Beside the fire, the old man showed Anselm a map. He traced the route which led to Bernitz from Arkavitz.

"It goes over the top of the mountains," said Anselm, in dismay. "I didn't realise that."

"Exactly so, son," said the old man. "You'd do better to wait until spring."

"It's already March," said Anselm.

"Call that spring? Why, spring here doesn't begin for two and a half months yet, and when it does, it happens all at once. You'll know spring when it comes."

"I need to get to Bernitz," said Anselm. "I can't wait for spring to arrive. If I have to go over the mountains, then that's what I'll do."

"There is a way *through* the mountains," said the old man. "But I don't know if it would be responsible for me to show it to you. I used to be a logger, and we worked those passes even with snow on the ground." He narrowed his eyes and leaned over to stoke the fire, sending steam hissing from Anselm's thawing clothes. "Why are you so intent on getting yourself to Bernitz, anyway? Eighty-three years I've lived in these mountains, and here I am telling you to wait. Maybe you should listen."

"My friend Michael is in Bernitz," said Anselm. "I've been looking for him for weeks. He told me to get there quickly to meet him."

"I see," said the old man. He heaved himself up onto his feet and held out a hand so gnarled it struggled to grip Anselm's. "I'm Peter," he said. "You'd better let me show you the way. You might come to harm otherwise, a city boy like you."

Anselm and old Peter started up a rocky path black with ice, and under trees heavy with snow. Old Peter was so ancient that it was hard to tell his features from his wrinkles. His eyes were wet and his hand only awkwardly grasped his walking stick, the fingers pointing in all directions the way a tree grips a rock.

At some point as they climbed, the sun rose, and cut down through the mountain pass onto Arkavitz below, making an ice-like sheen on the metal roofing of the factory.

Peter puffed and coughed in the sharp air, stumping ahead. Soon the path widened, and intersected with others. Men on horses became visible on the high mountain roads on either side of the valley. They rode with guns across the saddles, their bodies wrapped in worn leather coats and bedraggled furs. Where they were coming from, it must still have been deep winter.

"Who are they?" Anselm asked. "Resistance men?"

"I should think so. Anyone you meet in this part of the world is resistance, son. No one else has any business travelling around the mountains before the spring has properly come. People stay put. Even this so-called new government. We haven't seen the worst of them yet, up here. Not nearly the worst."

"Do you think they'll invade Arkavitz? The people in the town aren't so sure."

"Aye, they'll take Arkavitz when it suits them. They'll do whatever they like. When you get to eighty-three years old, lad, you'll be able to tell these things just by looking back at the same things that have happened before. Always full of war, this world is, and I don't see any end to it."

They were climbing in earnest now. Peter gulped in air like a drowning fish.

"Are you all right?" Anselm said. "Do you want to stop and rest?"

"No, lad—I'm perfectly well. Stop your fussing."

"It's good of you to show me the way."

"You're not the first I've helped to find his way between resistance posts this winter. I'm sure it will lead to trouble when those damned Imperialists come for us all, but that doesn't frighten me." Peter let out a wheezy laugh.

"Are we almost at the start of the mountain pass?"

"Aye, lad. That's where I'll leave you to go on by yourself. Just remember, Bernitz is a long journey in the snow."

"I know it."

"Don't get caught on the mountain after dark. Get into the town before night falls."

"I understand," said Anselm.

Now the trees thinned, and ahead was bare mountainside. The two figures, the eighty-three-year-old and the seventeen-year-old, were still walking in dusk because the sun hadn't reached this side of the mountain. Peter took Anselm as far as the edge of the forest plantation, where the track was scraped bare of snow by the strength of the wind. The sun crossed the horizon and illuminated the world at last.

"See that track?" Peter said. "See where it continues through the snow, further up where it's more sheltered?"

Anselm looked. "I see it."

"That's the way you need to go."

"Up that path between the two rocks?"

"Aye. It's an old logging track. The way should be passable. It's about fourteen miles from here to Bernitz. But remember, you've got a long climb ahead of you. Two thousand feet. It'll be cold and tough up on top of the pass, and you're not dressed properly. Get down into shelter as quickly as you can, that's my advice. Don't stop to rest until you're on the other side. Is the route clear?"

"It seems clear enough."

"From here," said Peter, "you have to make your own way."

The old man waved Anselm's thanks aside with his twisted hands. After he had gone, the mountain was very quiet. Anselm watched the bent figure descend the narrow pass and vanish among the trees. He touched the corner of Michael's telegram in his pocket. Then he turned his face to the wind and began to climb.

15

*F*rost had gathered in the hollow of the path; it was as brittle as glass, and treacherous. The sun made a dim patch of light behind foggy cloud. Sometimes Anselm walked through whole stands of black and lifeless trees. Other times, he had to cross snowdrifts as deep as he was tall, treading gently so as not to fall through the surface.

Once, when Anselm lost his footing, sending the snow thundering down the mountainside, a startled mountain cat sprang away from him. Its fur rippled in the wind like it was running underwater. That cat was the first living thing Anselm had seen since old Peter turned back. He stood waist-deep in the snow, watching it vanish. The icy wind scalded his hands and face, but a small piece of his heart felt bigger somehow for seeing these things. Anselm had only ever lived among buildings. His city boots and old leather jacket were inadequate for this terrain, and he had never heard a silence as profound as the gap between gusts of wind. But he was glad to be in this place. And somewhere in his heart was a fierce hope that he would arrive in Bernitz and Michael would be waiting for him there.

Anselm climbed quite confidently all that afternoon, and then it started to get dark and he was still climbing and he began to be afraid.

Anselm stopped, put his hands inside his overcoat to warm them, and assessed the situation. Up ahead, it looked as though the path would level out. He quickened his pace and reached what he expected to be the crest of the mountain, but the mountain was deceptive and another peak rose in front of him, and at the top of that one a third reared up. By the time he reached the real summit, it had become entirely dark.

Up there, the wind tore straight through his jacket as if it were nothing at all. He could see lights far away down in the valley, and he began to feel a cold that was not real cold, but fear, in his heart. Snow was beginning somewhere to the left; he could feel its grains on his face. If it continued, those lights in the valley would vanish.

Anselm managed another mile or so at a jog, then came to a section of path obscured by snowdrifts and had to go slowly, one step at a time, for fear of sinking. He became entangled in something that was not just dead branches under the snow. Barbed wire. It pricked his hands and caught and ripped his jacket. Piece by piece, Anselm freed himself from the wire.

Bruised and bleeding, he sat down in the snow. This proved to be an error, because after resting for a while he didn't feel like going any further. Instead, he ate the last of his food, some ordinary bread and cheese from the stores in Arkavitz, still in the brown paper wrapper. That world seemed a thousand miles away, as did the city where Anselm had been born, where even now the streets were full of fire and fighting. Dimly, that thought reminded him of Michael and he got to his feet and staggered on.

His bones were getting as cold as stone. When he had gone about another mile, he reached a kind of half shack and rested again. He crouched down between its two walls to get out of the wind, pulled his coat over his head, and began lighting his matches. He cupped his hands around the flame to warm them and waited for the snow to stop. It didn't.

"Michael?" he said, into the darkness. "Are you there somewhere? Give me a sign."

In answer, Anselm heard only the growling of the wind as it raced through the remains of the shack.

The way my brother survived, in the end, was by tripping over a telegraph line. It was half buried in the snow, and it caught his boot and sent him headlong into a snowdrift.

Somehow, that woke him from his trance. This telegraph line, he decided, must lead somewhere. He pulled it up with one hand and began to follow it. It led him across a frozen stream, past another ruined shed, and through a thicket of barbed wire. After a long time, it led him directly to the feet of a horse.

"Who's there?" someone called sharply, in the northern accent.

Anselm looked up. He made out a man in thick furs with ice in his beard. "I'm very cold," he said.

"I can see that. Who are you? What are you doing with our telegraph line?"

"Following it. I didn't realise it was yours." Anselm tried to drop the line, but his fingers were immobile with cold.

Two more men appeared out of the snowstorm. "What's this?" said a quieter voice.

"Sabotaging our telegraph line. He's pulled it all up, just here. Says he's following it. He might have come across from the Occupied Territory. If you ask me, he's a spy."

The men looked sternly into Anselm's face.

"Not very old," said one of them. "Who sent you across the border and into our camp? Eh? Declare yourself."

"I'm looking for my friend," said Anselm. "He's in Bernitz. He sent me a telegram. I haven't crossed the border; I've been in Arkavitz."

"No one sends telegrams round here but the resistance," said the bearded man sternly. "Let's take him into the post for questioning."

Anselm, in a daze, allowed himself to be marched down a dark slope towards the lights of the town. He felt a rifle tapping against his shoulder blades. The main street, its lights suspended on rough wires, dazzled him with its glare. Bernitz was merely a line of clapboard houses, bracketed between two noisy bars. A white chapel, a warehouse in which two trucks stood half-submerged in snow, a scattering of farms across the steppe. This town was clearly the heart of resistance country. As Anselm was marched along the street and into the narrow house beside the chapel, a group of men in ragged furs turned to stare all the same. Along an unlit corridor his captors marched him, and into a firelit room where men sat around a table laughing, arguing, roaring. Then they flung at him a series of questions, which

Anselm, dropping with exhaustion and cold, could not answer. And at last, sleep, and a disordered confusion of dreams, clutching Michael's telegram to his chest.

16

*A*fter a long time—just how long he could not tell—light cut down through the window and Anselm woke. The whole of him ached, as though he had just come out the worse from a fistfight. He was lying on a prickly straw mattress, still in his clothes. He became aware that the telegram from Michael was gone. He scrambled for it, flung the blankets from the bed, searched the floorboards.

The bearded man was standing in the light of the window, holding the telegram in his hands.

Anselm straightened. "What are you doing with my telegram?"

"This hasn't been sent from our machine," said the man. "It's come from the resistance post at High Farm. It's got their code stamped on it. We have nothing to do with them."

"Where's High Farm?"

"A few miles out of town. As I say, we have nothing to do with that resistance cell. What's your business with them?"

"Nothing. I told you, I'm looking for my friend."

The bearded man surveyed Anselm through narrowed eyes for several seconds, then put the telegram back into his hands.

"Are you going to let me go?"

"If you've got something to do with the men at High Farm, we won't do anything to stand in their way. But be careful. The resistance fighters at High Farm are not God-fearing men." He gave directions, reluctantly, then stood and watched Anselm until he was out of sight.

Anselm headed through Bernitz and out along the north road, following the signs for High Farm until, after a short while, they gave out altogether. His head was still clouded with exhaustion. The backs of his hands were prickling with the beginnings of frostbite from the night before. Icicles hung in lethal rows from the trees, and occasionally one dropped like a spear into the powdery snow. Even so, Anselm could hardly keep elation from overcoming him.

Michael was his only thought. His voice, how Michael was passionate about anything that angered him, the smallest injustice. His abrupt laugh, almost a shout. Michael had dark grey eyes, Anselm remembered, and wore an ancient hat with a moth-eaten red feather, and under it his black hair was always untidy and restless. Anselm loved him, and now he would see him again and take him across the sea to Holy Island, away from the resistance and all this fighting.

As Anselm crossed the snowy plain, a grey house rose into view. It was surrounded by a barbed-wire fence, at which frenzied guard dogs barked. A broken cart loaded with sandbags stood in front of the door, and a mess of rifles was stacked up on the porch.

"Hello?" he called. "Is this High Farm?"

A dull thunking sound. Someone cutting wood. Anselm made out a figure in the darkness of the trees.

"Hello?" he called again.

The figure straightened. He set down his axe and shielded his eyes against the light, then on second thought picked up the axe again and approached. A boy, skinny and yellow-haired.

"Hello," said Anselm. "I'm looking for Michael Barone. He sent me a telegram to meet him here."

The boy said nothing, just chewed on something with one side of his mouth. Finally he called back the dogs and opened the gate.

Anselm followed the boy up the track to the farmhouse. Other people appeared: another skinny boy and an old, fat man in a ripped shirt. They followed Anselm's progress into their camp with watchful eyes. In his head, Anselm thought, *These are not the kind of people who trust, or can be trusted*. Even so, he followed. The boy led Anselm along a rough path that had been scraped out of the snow behind the house, and up a slope where dead pine needles prickled underfoot. Now that he might only be minutes from seeing Michael's face again, Anselm's heart began to thump in his chest and made it difficult to breathe or reason clearly. *Please love me*, he thought. *Please love me, like you did before*. He clutched the telegram like a precious relic.

"Give that here," said the boy, abruptly. "Whatever you're holding."

"It's only a telegram. I told you—"

"Give it here."

Anselm handed it to him. The boy read the telegram with difficulty, word by word. "That's ours," he pronounced eventually. "It has the code of our machine. Michael didn't have permission to send it. He shouldn't have led you to our camp."

"I mean no harm," said Anselm. "I promise you, I'm not here to cause trouble."

"Are you with the resistance?"

"No."

"No? And yet you come here—"

"I support you. I'm sympathetic to your aims. I just haven't joined yet, is all."

"Sympathetic to our aims?" mimicked the boy. "I don't deal with talk like that. Either you're with us or you're against us."

"Then I'm with you," said Anselm. "Of course I am. Now can I see Michael, please?"

Still, the boy looked at him with hard, suspicious eyes.

"I mean no harm," Anselm said again. "I'm just here to see my friend."

From the building ahead, a barn, Anselm heard a low sawing.

"Michael!" shouted the boy. "Someone here for you!"

The sawing stopped. A pause, then the door swung open. In

the doorway, bundled up against the cold, stood a figure. Older and rougher and with a new scar on his cheek stood someone who might be Michael. Then the person said, very quietly, "Anselm?"

In spite of the men watching, Michael closed the distance between them and gripped his friend in a tight embrace. It was a long time before either of them had the strength to let the other go.

Later, Michael and Anselm sat hunched in the hayloft of the barn, talking in quick whispers. The problem was how to get away from High Farm, now that they were here. Michael did not let his friend's arm go.

"I've made a mistake," said Michael. "I was so desperate to join the fight that I've joined the wrong cell. These men are hard-line, even by resistance standards. I'm going to cut free from them; I have to escape. Come with me."

"You can't escape," said Anselm. "There's nowhere to go. I almost died in the snow just getting over the mountain pass."

"Anselm, we have to leave. We don't have much time either. They're planning to move base as soon as the weather gets better, and we're supposed to be making an assault on villages along the way."

"An assault?"

"There are collaborators. We're supposed to make an example of them."

"What does that mean?"

Michael shrugged. "Some of the men in this cell have already killed for the cause."

"I didn't expect the resistance to be so . . ." Anselm searched for the word.

"The resistance isn't just one group," said Michael. "Any more than the Imperialist government is."

Anselm shuddered. "They don't like it—the fact that you sent me that telegram."

Michael put his arms around his friend's shoulders and held on. "When I got your letter, they were already making preparations to leave. There was no time to send a letter back. I broke into the telegraph room and used the machine."

"I never thought I'd hear from you. I never thought I'd find you. Not really."

"I'm so very glad you're here, Anselm."

The barn below was restless. The sheep, imprisoned for the winter, steamed in the chilled air. In the dusk of the hayloft, Michael's grey eyes looked almost black and his new scar took on a sculpted quality, as if someone had chipped it out of stone.

"I can't leave the resistance altogether," said Michael. "I've sworn my allegiance. But I might stand a chance if I move to a different cell and ask for their protection." He shivered. "Will you help me? You'll have to join too, of course, but we'll find a better cell to be part of, and they'll station us together. I can't do this without your help."

"I thought we'd go to Holy Island, Michael. Wouldn't that be better? My family are there. We can live in hiding with them and wait for all this to die down."

"But what if it doesn't? Will we just hide out there while everyone else takes responsibility for the fight?"

"Maybe." Anselm took Michael's hand. "This will die down, Michael—it has to. They've taken a whole continent. They can't keep hold of it forever."

"This isn't going to die down," said Michael sternly. "Not unless people like us do something about it."

And Anselm knew with an awful certainty that he was not going to see his family again for a very long time.

In the black night, on a stolen horse, Anselm and Michael left High Farm behind and started up the final mountain pass. Stars littered the sky like grains of sand. Anselm clung to his friend's waist and looked back at the sleeping town. By the time lights showed in the farmhouse, the two of them were gone.

In Maritz, in return for an oath of allegiance from Anselm and a renewal of Michael's vows, the local resistance cell offered them protection. They were stationed in a telegraph post so remote no one else had agreed to man it, where they would remain until the revolution. That was the agreement.

From the telegraph post, if you looked in any direction, you saw only black mountains, white snow-light, the distant glow of a scattering of farms. More important resistance men—and occasionally women—passed through from time to time. Otherwise, they were utterly alone. On those nights—their mattresses dragged up against the fire grate for warmth, listening to the silence outside—happiness came over Anselm almost too intensely to bear. "Soon things will be better and we can go to Holy Island," Michael promised. "The revolution will come soon. You'll see."

Meanwhile, Anselm learned to use a telegraph machine, and for the first time he understood what was happening to his country.

In the occupied territory that had once been Malonia, people were locked away for clinging to the old religions, for attending political meetings, for suffering illnesses of the mind—for living as he and Michael did now. The reports Anselm transcribed for the local resistance chiefs, made in secret from within the old country, brought news of imprisonment and death. Anselm knew that after reading these things, neither he nor Michael would turn their backs on the resistance. The unfinished business of their former homeland bound them here.

Anselm received a letter from his family; it found its way to him, forwarded via his old attic room in the shadow of the factory, three months late. They were living in New Maron, settled under new names. He wrote care of Harlan Smith, his grandfather, telling them he would join them but knowing in his heart he never would, not until the resistance had taken back the land that had been theirs.

When I was eight years old, photography—an Imperialist invention—came to the island; my mother saved her earnings for three months and paid for us to have a studio portrait taken. She sent it to Anselm. By a tortuous route, four months late, it reached him. And I dreamed of the way it looked on his windowsill as he set it there, sadly, knowing that when he saw me and Jasmine again we would be unrecognisable, quite grown. Anselm wrote to us almost weekly, but we all knew by that time that he was not coming back any time soon, not during our childhood. And yet, all through my childhood, he inhabited my dreams.

17

*A*round that time, I stopped dreaming of my brother altogether and started to dream instead of a black house inhabited by a stranger. It's not clear what caused this dream, except that people were still talking a good deal about the king and I began to develop a kind of obsession with him. He seemed to belong to an old-fashioned, kinder world. People talked almost daily of his return.

The problem was that, since the invasion, no one had seen this king.

Members of the Imperialist government, who according to my grandfather were living in our houses and walking in our streets, insisted that the king was dead. But no refugee on Holy Island believed that—it would have been sacrilege. No, he was just hiding, waiting for the time when he would march to victory at the head of the resistance army.

My grandfather told me stories of the time when the king still ruled. He told me these things to amuse me more than anything—to convince me that our family had once been at the heart of some romantic old-world drama—but the result was that I became obsessed with finding the king and his family. I would study the atlas for hours, pointing out towns to my grandfather. "Would he hide here? Anshelle? Would this be a good place to go? What about this place? Ositha? It's in the middle of the hills. That would be a good place to hide."

"If he is alive," my grandfather told me, "he's probably living a different life somewhere, right under our noses. That's what I like to think."

My grandfather showed me a picture of the king when he was a young man, and explained that this was how he had looked when he first became the ruler of our country. He warned me that in the occupied territory even looking at a picture like this was punishable by death or imprisonment, because you were not allowed to be what was called a royalist.

I asked my grandfather if he was a royalist. He said that he had been all his life but wasn't anymore—but he still wanted the right to look at a picture of the king.

I glued the picture to the wall beside my bed. And that night, I dreamed of a man with a face like the king's, drawing water at a cold tap in a yard in rainy weather, living in hiding just as my grandfather had said.

Raindrops fell on the tin bucket and the former king's grey head. He straightened himself and walked with uncertain steps in his mud-caked boots up the yard to the unpainted farmhouse door. On the horizon, the sun was driving great thick clouds across the sky. The wind attacked the farmhouse, running through the walls with a low, fretting moan. Crows clung precariously to the trees. In one of them, a silver birch, a love-heart was carved with the letters *G.M.* and *M.B.*, relics of the farmhouse's former inhabitants.

No one was left now. The former king was utterly alone.

Inside, he put down the bucket, stretched his aching arms and turned over the pages of a week-old newspaper scavenged from the edge of a nearby town. *I just disappeared*, thought the king. *And now all the talk is progress and war and expansion. If there is a revolution, they'll do it without me. So why does my heart feel so cold?*

The former king made a ritual of ordinary tasks. He lit the stove and cut the black spots out of old potatoes. He felt the cold of the storm entering his bones.

When he had left the capital city, bundled into a carriage by his advisors in the dead of night, they had told him they would meet him here, in this house. It was not safe for the king to travel with anybody else. Carriages were supposed to be following his, but in the firefighting they were separated from the king's, and so he ended up quite alone. The king, unrecognised, made the sea crossing in solitude just before the outbreak of war.

A long time he had been waiting now for news of his advisors, his government, anyone who might have survived the invasion. He had heard nothing. A strange weightlessness overcame him when he thought of that old life.

This house was where his closest advisor and greatest friend, Aldebaran, had once hidden from his own enemies. It had stood empty for decades, and no one thought to look here now. *He's another one who's gone*, thought the former king. *Shot, and that was when all the trouble started. Lord, how I miss him.*

When the former king went to sleep, on a rug pulled up close to the stove for warmth, with his overcoat wrapped around him, he dreamt of a place full of green light and laughter where he was once happy, and in love.

I woke with a start from this dream, stunned. It was the green world where I had gone as a baby—the two were the same.

I transcribed this story into the notebook my grandfather gave to me, word for word. My grandfather was very thoughtful when I read it to him. "What's that place?" I asked. "Do you know it?"

My grandfather frowned and shook his head. "It sounds to me like England," he said.

"England?"

"It's the place we used to believe the great ones could go."

But my grandfather was more interested in the house where I claimed the former king was hiding. "Think, Harlan," he said. "Was it on top of a hill? Were there trees? What did the building look like? Is there anything you can tell me that might help us work out where he is?"

But I shook my head. The details of the place had not been revealed to me. It was hardly more than a blur.

For several years I dreamed about the king in this house. Then, one stormy night, there was a knocking at the door.

A branch crashing in the storm drew the king out of his sleep. When he woke, the crashing solidified and became someone knocking on the door of the farmhouse. Slowly, the king rose. He drew his overcoat around him and picked up the gun he didn't know how to use from the table in the corner.

The knocking on the door came again. The former king unbolted the door, then stood aside and raised the gun.

A filthy man stood in the doorway. Mud covered him from head to foot, and his clothes hung limp. His eyes shone white in his otherwise grime-covered face. "Hell," he said. "I've had trouble finding you."

"Who are you?"

"My name was Rigel."

"Aldebaran's old apprentice?" The king, blankly, levelled the gun. "No one's seen Rigel for twenty years. He escaped to England; he abandoned his duties."

"I've taken them up again."

"After twenty years?"

"Aldebaran made me promise to find you if the revolution happened. Now I'm here."

"And I'm supposed to believe you've been in England?"

The filthy man rummaged in his pockets, ignoring the gun. Carefully, he brought forth first a plastic-topped car key, then a handful of coins with an unfamiliar queen's face. A scrap of London newspaper. "I can bring you to England too," said the man, "if you stop pointing that gun at me and trust me for a second."

The former king put the gun down and let the man into his house.

"This place is filthy," said Rigel. "How long have you been hiding out here?"

"Since just before the invasion."

"No news from anyone else? Your advisors? Your government?"

The former king shook his head. "I read the newspapers. I listen to the wireless radio."

Rigel crouched down in front of the stove and rubbed his hands together.

"What are you doing here?" said the former king. "What made you come back, after all this time?"

"Aldebaran gave me orders. I'm here to follow them. I was to rescue all the great ones and bring them to England. You. My own daughter. Aldebaran's last descendant. This whole continent is a bloody mess. I've had a hell of a job finding you, like I said. Only I remembered Aldebaran showing me this place once. A dangerous idea, hiding in his old house. I'm surprised you risked it."

"The place is abandoned."

"Anyway, you're to leave. You're to go into hiding."

"I am in hiding."

"Real hiding," said the filthy stranger. "A long way away."

"Until when?"

The stranger spread his hands helplessly. "I can't answer that."

"What about the country?" said the king. "What about the people?"

"You can't help them. There's nothing to do but leave, and wait for a time when things are better."

"Are you sure this is what Aldebaran wanted?" said the former king. "Are you sure this is what he told you?"

"I'm certain. Now prepare to come with me, please."

The former king and Rigel struggled across the moor without speaking, while the wind and rain assaulted them from all sides. When they reached a stand of trees, Rigel stopped in the shelter of their branches and attempted to light a cigarette.

"I do remember you," said the former king suddenly. "I met you once, when I was young."

"Probably so." When he was done struggling with his cigarette, Rigel straightened and said, "Did Aldebaran tell you anything about his last descendant?"

"Something," said the king. "There was something like a prophecy. Why do you ask?"

"People are after him already, you know. We can't leave the little boy here to grow up. He'll have to come with us. That's where I'm taking you now. We'll get the boy, and we'll bring him with us to England."

"Aldebaran was very close to his family," said the king thoughtfully. "The baby must be his great-great-nephew. He told me all about them. A poor family, from the city. The father kept a shop."

"Yes. I know where they are. I'm under orders from Aldebaran to watch over them. I've been following them. But we're going to have to take the child with us. It's a crime to leave him at risk from these Imperialists who want his blood. It's getting too dangerous for him here."

"What about the family?"

"The family don't need to come. That's too much of a risk. Just the child."

"No," said the former king. "No, that's not what Aldebaran would have wanted—to take a little boy away from his family. No one even believes that prophecy anymore."

"The resistance believe it," said Rigel. "That prophecy is a political tool. It makes the boy special. The Imperialists are after him. The resistance will be after him for their cause too pretty soon."

"Even so, we can't take a little child away from his family. We can't do it, Rigel. You have a daughter yourself. You know that to take a little boy away from his mother and father in the middle of this war could never be right."

Rigel thought for a moment, then flicked his soggy cigarette away. "Maybe not," he said, "but we'll bring him with us anyway."

The former king stopped still in the middle of the rain-swept moor. "If you take that boy from his family," he said, "then you'll have to leave me here. I won't come with you."

In desperation, the filthy man bent his head before the former king, imploring. "If the boy stays here, then I also have to remain. I'm under orders to watch over him. I'll never get back to England. My daughter—my home—"

"I won't let you take the child, Rigel."

In a flash of lightning, I saw the man's face properly for the first time.

I woke crying in terror from that dream, because the man in the flash of lightning was not a stranger but the red-haired man who had saved me when I was eight days old. How could that be possible? I could not make sense of it.

After that night, maybe out of fear or maybe because he really had gone away to that green place, to England, I had no more dreams of the king.

18

*W*hen I was seven years old, my mother had to take me to Valacia to register me for school. The schools on Holy Island were full to breaking point. Jasmine had got a place, but by the time I was old enough to start my education the New Maron schoolroom was so crowded it would admit no more children, not even a single skinny refugee boy with a head already full of books. There was no more space. So I must be put on a national waiting list, and I would start school, God willing, next year.

My mother didn't want to make the journey to Valacia, for fear of being seen in the city, but neither did she want me to lose my chance for an education, however makeshift that education might be. To my mother, learning was a holy thing, a salvation. That was what it had been for her, and she was very firm that I would get an education too.

We stood in a queue in a shabby office. The woman behind the desk pinched my cheek and told my mother I was a darling, which made me squirm with embarrassment. My false papers were checked and the seven-year-old refugee Isak Karol was given a certificate allowing him to enrol in a first-year class at New Maron Charity School in the Year '97, the following September.

That year, fear of invasion hung over the island the same way the fish smell hung over the harbour. We were all troubled by the wireless reports out of Angel City. While she finished copying and stamping my papers, the woman behind the desk said, "If there still is a school next year. If we haven't all ended up under the thumb of the Imperialists."

My mother sent me and Jasmine outside while she finished the interminable stack of paperwork.

I had never been to Valacia before. The school office was in a dusty square, and on the other side of it was an old fountain. Jasmine, fourteen and restless, dragged me over to the fountain on the pretence of seeing whether there were any fish, but really because three teenage boys on bicycles were standing in the road next to it. Jasmine kept giving them little glances and smoothing down her hair.

Once we had looked into the empty fountain and the teenage boys had ridden away, my sister said, "Let's see what's down this next street."

"Mama said to wait."

"She'll be hours in there. You saw that pile of paper."

"Jasmine, I wish I could have gone to school this year."

"You can have my place," said Jasmine, who hated school—but of course, that was not how it worked.

"Jasmine, do you think there'll really be a war?"

"Of course not," she said. "That's why people like Anselm are fighting with the resistance, to make sure there isn't one."

My sister could be bossy and overbearing sometimes, but she also knew when she was right and I found that comforting. I put my hand in hers and we walked along the narrow street towards a market or a square that was blaring a good deal of noise. But somehow the street turned and took us away from the commotion, and soon it was quiet and full of shadows.

Then I realised someone was following us.

My sister could not have realised it yet. He moved too silently, and he was out of our field of vision. I only understood it first by the shiver on the back of my neck, and when I turned, I saw him a long way off, standing in the shadow of a building.

"Jasmine," I said quietly, pulling at her hand. "He's following us. That man."

My sister turned. "He's just a stranger standing over there."

"He's following us," I hissed. "He is."

We walked a little farther, and my sister quickened her pace. I glanced back. The man had come into the light now.

"Look at him properly," I whispered again. "Take a proper look. We know him. He's that red-haired man who saved me when I was a baby. Look at the scar on his face."

Jasmine looked for a long time. Then all of a sudden she jerked my arm and ran, dragging me behind her. "Come on!" she said. "Come on, will you?"

"It's him, isn't it? He's here to take me! I know it!" I began to wail.

"Come on, can't you?" my sister raged. "Hurry up!"

At the end of the alleyway we joined a proper road, and when I looked back the man was coming on at a jog that almost matched our run.

My sister was wild with panic. "Run, can't you, Harlan?" she yelled at me. "Come on!"

I ran like a child possessed, through alleys and up steps and past a great cathedral and under a bridge. We came out, abruptly, by the sea, and ran along the docks, where we were lost in a mass of people who shouted and shoved us from all sides. I could not see the man now, but my sister continued to drag me along behind her. We didn't know where we were. I was crying a little and had dropped my overcoat. Eventually Jasmine pulled me into the shadow of a shop doorway and crouched down in front of me. I was gasping in air like my life depended on it.

"Harlan," she said. "Look at me. Take my hand. Are you all right?"

I nodded. "That—man—" I managed to say. "He's the man from before. You saw it too. He saved me. When I was a baby. Didn't you recognise his face, and his red hair?"

My sister shook me. "You're lying," she said. "It isn't the same man."

"Then why were you running too?"

"Because I didn't like the look of him. That's all."

"It was the same man."

"You're lying."

"I have powers."

Jasmine shook me so hard my teeth clashed together. "You don't!" she said. "You don't have powers! I don't believe in them!"

Haltingly, I began to cry. Jasmine had always been my ally. Off she hauled me again, at a run. My sister would not let go my wrist. "You're hurting me," I whined, but she said, "Shh—I'm trying to think." She was trying to find the square where we had left our mother. It took us half an hour, but she found the way at last. Past the fountain, right up to the front of the office. Here, we ran headlong into Mama.

"Jasmine! Harlan!" she said. "Where have you been? I came out and I couldn't find you. My God, don't frighten me like that." She kissed us both on the face several times, seized us by the shoulders, clutched us to her.

I peered into the shadows over her shoulder to see if that man was anywhere to be seen.

"Come on," said my mother. "I've got Harlan's papers for school. Let's go home."

We hitched a lift on a cart back to New Maron. All the way, I looked for that man's face in the dark.

I dreamed of the red-haired man that night. I dreamed of him longing for the green and bright world I had also longed for since my birth, where other people waited for him. They spoke the man's name and reached out: *Rigel. Rigel.* I woke, and did not know whether I was crying out of fear that the red-haired man would take me from my family, or sorrow that he could not live in that green world the two of us both dreamed of.

I had thought he meant to harm me, but now I wasn't so sure.

That was the day I stopped writing down my dreams. The whole encounter had shaken me, and I wasn't sure I wanted to see what I couldn't explain.

But there is one more dream to tell.

19

*T*he first night I heard Anastasia Fortuna on the wireless radio, I began to dream about her. I saw her in a white marble room. Musicians were scraping away at violins and cellos, and there she was.

Notes fell. A song rose. The harmony would not come right, and Anastasia Fortuna was frustrated. In a black dress and pink shawl, perspiring slightly in the heat, she paused the music with a gentle flick of her hand. She frowned and crossed the room and began the song again.

Out of the window the music drifted. The afternoon sun scorched a narrow courtyard and turned its surface to red dust. It heated the green depths of an ornamental pool and made the fish sluggish. On the edge of the pool, hunched up in a shawl like her mother's, a little girl sat and glared. The girl had clear brown eyes that became dark when angry and at other times seemed almost amber. She had very black hair, which her mother insisted on having cut and styled at a proper salon in the town. Little Antonia had almost no features from her father, which made it harder for the mother to identify who that father was. Either way, Antonia did not know.

Anastasia and her daughter had lived in poverty until the child was three years old. They slept in a damp room in a dark back alley of the city, and Anastasia sang in smoky clubs and bars for a few crowns a week. This was because Anastasia Fortuna was Alcyrian, and Angel City was still ruled by the Malonian resistance then. Having skin too fine and hair too black to be Malonian, the singer was treated with suspicion.

One day when her daughter was four years old, the Alcyrian army marched into the city. The air was thick with shrieks and gunshots. Anastasia Fortuna closed the blinds of their tiny room and plunged it into darkness. She held her daughter on the mattress on the floor and sang to her under her breath. For many hours they sat this way, awaiting their fate. Once, a bullet splintered off the shutter and made them both cower in the darkness. Then the fighting died away.

At last, Anastasia and her daughter emerged into the light. The child was thirsty and listless. Anastasia filled their one metal cup from the tap outside the door and gave it to the child to drink. The silence that lay over Angel City was so profound that it made her tremble, but she and her daughter ventured out into the street.

The new rulers of the city belonged to the Imperialist government. A beefy, red-faced man in uniform, not entirely unhandsome, was making a speech in the town square; Anastasia held her daughter by the hand and edged closer as his words filled that summer night.

"You are all citizens of a new world order," he said. "You are now part of the Alcyrian Empire, and those who are unacceptable to our society in any way—the homosexuals, the followers of the old religions, the sick, the depraved—will have their privileges stripped from them. This is the chance for the loyal and obedient, the enterprising among you, to seize for themselves a better life."

Anastasia Fortuna did not care about a new world order, but she did care about seizing for herself a better life. The Malonians had never treated her well, and now she saw for the first time that her life held promise, if she were brave and enterprising enough to take it. That night, brushing out her daughter's hair, Anastasia spoke to her child. "Your life will be better now," she promised, in her own language. "From now on, neither of us will talk Malonian again. This, my Antonia, is our chance for a better future."

Little Antonia slept blissfully that night in her mother's arms, unaware that her life was about to change. All she knew was that some strange man had shouted in the square, and that for once her mother was happy.

Anastasia's prediction came true. Through various small confessions of loyalty to the new government, her fortunes changed. Now she would be the first singer whose voice was transmitted by wireless radio, a great honour. Early that summer an important army man had driven into town in his motorcar and spoken with the manager at the theatre where Anastasia sang. The Alcyrian government loved culture, this army man said. They also needed a singer with the right pitch, the right clarity, to transmit over the radio waves. They wanted music broadcast for the world to hear, and Anastasia was the singer chosen. But the concert must be perfect, because any mistakes would be transmitted into the living rooms of twelve million people, undermining the cause. Anything that undermined the cause was punishable by death. Anastasia Fortuna must understand this. She understood, and signed.

It was for this concert, in the restless afternoon heat, that Anastasia Fortuna and her musicians were now practising. Because of this concert, little Antonia was glaring down into the dark water, cross at being ignored when her mother had once worshipped every lock of her black hair. Sometimes, Antonia wished her mother had never got famous. Now Anastasia Fortuna seemed to belong to everyone, when in poverty she had been only Antonia's.

The song stopped again. Antonia kicked off her shoes and stood on the hot stones of the fountain. She spread her arms wide and sang like her mother, startling the doves from the roof. "Bored, bored, bored, bored," she sang. "Bored of listening to this song."

Someone gave a short laugh. Anastasia Fortuna's shoes clicked on the marble. She appeared in the black shade of the doorway. "Antonia, *princessa*," she called, in Alcyrian. "Stop that. We can't hear ourselves in here."

Antonia flung herself down and turned her back on her mother.

On the night of the concert, the singer was brought to the theatre in a motorcar, her daughter beside her. The little girl was kept behind the scenes, but she was allowed to stand beside a hot spotlight in a scratchy party dress and watch as her mother took the stage. The open-air Theatre Libertas was built in great stone rows, and behind her mother, lit by eight spotlights, were tall black date palms and the glossy waves of the sea. The band members tuned their instruments, and the audience shuffled restlessly. The first five rows were taken up with fat, important men in army uniform, and around the entrances stood armed guards.

Antonia did not like the army men. One of them had once beaten a stray dog to death on the doorstep of her mother's house while Antonia, frightened, looked on from the upstairs window. He only did it because she was watching, as a kind of warning, though she didn't understand exactly why. Others brought her sweets and showed her kindness, disappearing behind closed doors with her mother in the great house with the fountain.

Now, from the wings, Antonia watched her mother. Anastasia Fortuna wore a red ball gown. Her hair lay coiled over one shoulder, as black as the sea itself. Her arms were bare, no bracelets that could jangle and interfere with the purity of the transmission.

In the shadows stood men with large coils of cables and micro-phones on metal stands, waiting to catch Anastasia's voice and send it, with a kind of strange magic, around the world.

The band began. Anastasia Fortuna took a breath and sang. And twelve million people listened.

20

*T*here was a fortune to be made by singing Imperialist songs on the wireless radio, and Anastasia Fortuna made it. By the time Antonia was ten, her mother was the third-richest woman in Angel City. Around this time, Anastasia Fortuna received a letter from a former lover, a minor official in the Censor's Office, asking for a favour. *Dear Anastasia*, the man, a Mr. Bercy, wrote, from a grim little town on the edge of the empire called West Ravina. *I wonder if I might trouble you for a transfer to the Censor's Office in Angel City, where I hear the opportunities for promotion are greater. Yours, Victor.*

Anastasia received a hundred such letters a week, but this one made her pause. She had reason to suspect that Victor Bercy was her daughter's father. The man knew nothing about the child's existence, and Anastasia had long since moved on to other lovers. After some consideration, she returned the letter to its envelope, unanswered. Better to leave such things in their proper place.

One night shortly afterwards, Antonia came weeping home from school, her hair straggling, her uniform disordered.

"What is it, *princessa*?" Anastasia said, taking her daughter's face in her hands.

The girl was secretive and would not be drawn out; she just wept.

"I have to go to the theatre," said Anastasia. "Drive with me."

The car was still a novelty—one of only five in the town, belonging to the Chief Censor of the theatre and sent for

Anastasia Fortuna before every performance—and usually the girl loved to sit beside her mother, glorying in the speed and the snarls of the engine. Not tonight. Instead, she watched the dark streets passing and remained silent.

"What is it?" said her mother again.

"Mama, is it true that the government kill people who don't agree with them?"

Anastasia cast a glance at the Chief Censor's chauffeur, then closed the glass hatch between them with a snap.

"Who's been telling you so?" she asked.

"And that there are rules about the beliefs you can have and the things you can say?"

"Every country has laws."

"And that there are prison camps where people are sent?" Antonia persisted.

"Who's been telling you all this?"

From her pocket, Anastasia produced a crumpled pamphlet. It bore, clearly, the mark of the Malonian resistance, two crossed knives and a single star. "What's this?" cried Anastasia, her rage filling the car. "Where did you get it?"

"People were scattering them all over the street."

"It's nonsense. You're not to believe it. They'll catch those people—they'll hang them, or put them in prison."

Antonia only wept harder at this.

Anastasia Fortuna stroked her daughter's hair and murmured, "Hush, hush."

"The Imperialists paid for our house." Antonia's voice was rising. "They pay for my clothes and my school and the food we eat. This car." She gestured at her mother's ball gown. "That dress."

Anastasia bent close to her daughter, pretending to straighten a loose strand of hair at her ear. The engine roared, and obscured her words. "Listen, my love," she whispered. "I did this for you. I'm not a political woman, but I wanted you to have this life. So I work for the Imperialists, and see how much better our life is than the life we lived under that Malonian resistance. Eh, *princessa?*"

Anastasia reached for her daughter's hand, but the girl pulled hers away. They bounced along the dark road to the theatre in silence. When the car drew up, Antonia followed her mother at a short distance. With cold eyes, she watched her mother apply rouge and lipstick.

"Sit here in the wings," Anastasia coaxed. "Like you used to when you were a little girl. Eh, *princessa?*" She kissed the side of her unresponsive daughter's hair.

When her mother had gone on stage, Antonia crept forward into the wings. She watched the spotlights find her mother, move with her, track her across the stage. Today, five government officials occupied the front row. They sweated in their uniforms and fanned themselves with their programmes. Sometimes, when Anastasia Fortuna sang, tears coursed down their well-fed cheeks. Now, as she reached the microphone, these men of the new world order stood and roared their ovation.

Their roaring frightened Antonia. She wrapped herself in the velvet stage curtain and listened in the dark.

21

Somehow, Anastasia Fortuna got sick. She didn't know exactly what caused it, but her face grew drawn and her eyes were shadowed. She found it more and more difficult to sleep and was racked with a terrible cough. The agents at the theatre ordered in sorbets and exotic fruits, which were kept in a great casket of ice in a spare room, and doctors plied her with tonics in glass bottles.

One night, Anastasia went onstage and no music came out at all, only a wheezy gasping. The singer was led from the stage and a doctor was brought to her dressing room. Anastasia Fortuna sat slumped across a chair, weeping. "I am finished," she gasped. "I am finished."

That night, she sent a letter in secret to the man she believed was her daughter's father. *Dear Victor*, it read. *I apologise for overlooking your previous letter. You will have heard that I have had good fortune since we parted. I can't say much, for fear this letter is being read. I have a little girl, now eleven. I am certain she belongs to you. I am not well, Victor. Please, if anything happens to make me unable to care for her, will you send someone for the child? She can live with you in the north. There's no one I trust here to take care of my precious girl.*

One night, Anastasia and her daughter returned home to find men in leather jackets with cigarettes in their mouths carrying their belongings out of the house.

"What's this?" shouted Anastasia, running into the hall. "What are you doing with my things?"

"These aren't your things anymore. They're being seized by the government. Stand aside."

A man jostled past, carrying a potted fern which trembled with every step.

On the front step of the house, Anastasia crumpled. The man stepped over her and loaded the fern into his truck anyway. All at once, a great anger came over Antonia. "I won't have you take my mama's things!" she said, standing in front of him. "I won't!"

The man sighed. He put his hands on his hips and looked down at Antonia. "Look, we're just the bailiffs. Talk to the men at the government office if you have an issue with this ruling."

"I'm not letting you take my mama's things."

Anastasia, hauling herself to her feet, led Antonia inside and up the stairs. Their footsteps echoed, because the rugs were gone. Almost everything had vanished. Their rooms were strangely empty and almost unrecognisable. Only their least valuable belongings were left: Antonia's box of childhood treasures from her bedside cabinet, Anastasia's photographs and music books. She gathered them up in a pile and cradled them to her chest. Antonia went to the window. Outside, the bailiffs were still piling the truck with their things, moving back and forth in the glare of the headlights.

"I won't have this!" said Antonia. "These things are ours!"

Her mother seized her wrist. "You want them to take us away too, and put us in some prison camp? Is that what you want?"

A man appeared in the doorway. "I'm here for the music books," he said.

Weeping, Anastasia handed them over. But Antonia, full of rage, reached out and took hold of them. "No!" she said. "No!"

Gently, the bailiff prised Antonia away. "Who has ordered this?" said Anastasia at last, weakly.

"The Chief Censor's Office. Apparently, your singing is no longer up to the standard required. You are undermining the cause."

"I'm sick!" cried Anastasia. "I've been nothing but loyal!"

The truck roared to life. The man vanished. Antonia ran down the stairs. She caught hold of her mother's bedside table, the first thing her hands lit upon. She began tugging it from the truck, hair flying. "Help me, Mama!" she called.

Anastasia, shakily, descended the stairs. From the doorway, she watched her daughter, sobbing in humiliation.

The bailiff stopped the truck again and got out, regarding Antonia with a flick of the ash from his cigarette. "Stand aside. We're under orders to take these things."

"Stand aside, Antonia," said her mother.

Sobbing with suppressed rage, Antonia let go. The man got back into the truck and closed the doors. He sat still for a moment and let the engine run, and then he drove away. There were two other trucks. Laden with the belongings of Anastasia Fortuna and her daughter, they followed him into the night.

———

In the silence left behind, Anastasia and her daughter sat on the edge of the fountain in their courtyard. The fish darted in the water as though nothing had changed. "Mama," said Antonia. "Are you really sick? Badly sick, I mean?"

"Yes," said Anastasia. "I think so."

Antonia felt like she was falling from a great height, and her breath came in little gasps. She said, "What's going to happen to us now?"

Anastasia went inside, slowly, like an old woman, then she came out carrying a letter. "This is from your father. If anything happens to me, he'll look after you."

Antonia reeled a little, for this was the first time she had heard any mention of a father.

Dear Anastasia, the letter read, in Alcyrian. *I must say I was surprised to hear from you, though not altogether displeased. Yes, I will take the child if necessary, but please understand that I have my career to think of. If the government has decided that you are disloyal, I run a considerable risk in sheltering her. Send her here to me in West Ravina, and I will see what can be done. I enclose the address. Yours, as ever, Victor Bercy.*

Antonia wept. She said, "How can you send me to this man, this person I don't know, who doesn't care anything about me at all?"

"He'll take care of you. He's an officer who works for the government, in a branch of the Censor's Office, an Imperialist. He's still in their favour. You'll be better off with him."

"How can I be better off with someone I've never met, Mama, than with you?"

Anastasia bowed her head. "I'm certain he will look after you," she told her daughter. "I believe that he is, at heart, a good man."

That night, Anastasia and her daughter slept side by side on the floor in Anastasia's big room, surrounded by emptiness. The next day, her current concert series was cancelled, and men arrived at eight in the morning to tell them that they had a day to leave their home. They packed their remaining things. Antonia felt sick and distant, almost feverish, as though none of this was really happening to her. Her mother alternated between anxious pacing and tears.

She was never told the charge against her, but it did not matter. It wouldn't have made a difference anyway.

Antonia could not bear to leave the goldfish in the fountain; she had always thought of them as her pets, though they came with the house. They needed feeding with breadcrumbs every day, and their water needed constant refreshing with new plants. Leaning up to her elbows in the icy water, she spent an hour shepherding them into a chipped glass bowl from the kitchen. Then she carried them down to the municipal gardens and released them into the pond there. As she watched them swim away, a light wind began and it started to snow. Antonia had never seen snow before; it rarely fell this far south on the continent. She lifted her face and watched it unfurl from the sky towards her. The snow made the city seem part of the dream world she had begun to inhabit.

That last year with her mother, Antonia was reminded of her earliest childhood. The two of them were rarely apart. Anastasia had hidden savings in gold, bought on her behalf by a former lover, and from this money they rented a two-room apartment in the grimy part of Angel City where Antonia had been born. Anastasia was very sick now. She was not yet fifty, but she suspected that she was dying. She did not tell her daughter this, but lavished care and attention on her instead. Either way, telling Antonia would be pointless. The girl already knew.

Antonia, at twelve, had grown very beautiful. All that winter, she stayed home from school because her mother could not afford the fees. Antonia had a voice that was at times as good as Anastasia's, though with a special quality that was different. Anastasia could not tell how good a singer her daughter was because she had never been trained; she had refused to have singing lessons when she was a child, and Anastasia never pushed her. Instead, the girl played an old guitar that had been a gift from the same former lover of her mother's, Pietro, in happier times. She played this guitar so beautifully that her mother demanded its music almost constantly as her illness wore on. It seemed to give Anastasia a kind of peace to hear the guitar on hot nights when her bones ached and nothing else would soothe her.

Antonia played and played, because there was nothing else to do. She played the songs her mother used to sing in that great theatre by the sea.

On the first of November, Anastasia Fortuna died.

22

*A*ntonia, weeping, with a small suitcase, her guitar and her mother's old pink shawl around her shoulders, found herself alone on a train north. *My life is over*, she told herself. *I can never love anyone so much again.*

She passed the wire fences of the prison camps. She passed cities with new apartment buildings that hid the light. She passed large factories that puffed smoke over the horizon. As she went north, it rained. The train rattled along the edge of the grey sea. It passed through a checkpoint where men with guns shouted orders. Some of the Malonian people on the train must have disobeyed these orders, because they were dragged from the train into a nearby stand of trees and the train left without them. Antonia heard gunshots and covered her ears. She shut her eyes too, and imagined that she was back by that other ocean, in the old stone theatre where her mother had been the centre of the world.

Her mother had told her that her father worked in the Censor's Office, giving out permits to performers and reading plays to decide whether they were suitable to be performed, whether they agreed with Imperialist values. He also had the job of tracking down all the books that had been banned and burning them. Her father had a good future with the Imperialist government, and this would protect her. Antonia imagined a great fierce man tearing up books and throwing them on a fire and yelling like General Marlan on the wireless radio.

In West Ravina, there was only one person waiting for the train, so Antonia knew he must be her father. A tall man, slightly balding, in the suit of a bank manager.

"Antonia Fortuna?" he said, as she struggled with her case across the wind-racked platform.

Antonia nodded. It was awkward, because she had to have her papers checked by an official before she could pass through the barrier. There they stood, on either side of a metal fence, while the man fumbled with the papers. Antonia noticed that her father was rubbing his palms nervously on the sides of his shiny black trousers.

At last Antonia was allowed through. Her father reached out and gripped her hands, then let them go. His were very cold, probably from the wind.

"Well, this is a strange business," he said, in an Alcyrian accent different from her mother's. "I never expected to meet you."

"No," said Antonia, in a small voice.

"You're very like your mother, in looks," he said. "Anastasia didn't see fit to tell me that you were mine—not until recently. I might have made some effort to contact you sooner, child."

Her father waited for a response.

"You are a bit like Mama described too," she managed at last.

"Am I?" Her father nodded approvingly and took her suitcase. "Come on. You'll meet your aunt—my sister—at the house.

We've got everything in boxes at the moment. When we establish a presence on Holy Island, I'm told I'll be stationed there, so I'm just waiting for the command."

"Holy Island?"

"Yes. It won't be long now. You'll come with me over there, I suppose."

The two of them walked through the half-dark of the town without speaking. They passed a lighted bar, a port, a fountain in a square. To Antonia, this northern place seemed infected by a great damp that made her head ache. At last, they came to a low house whose lights were lit. Antonia's father pushed her ahead of him up the path.

The sister opened the door. She was a thin woman, with lank beige hair. She said, "Glad to meet you," without smiling. From the beginning, sitting in her new bedroom—which was really just a storage room half full of old mouldering coats and suitcases and cardboard boxes—Antonia understood that this new aunt would be trouble.

She unpacked her mother's photographs and tried not to cry. She had managed to salvage from the house two music books. Quietly, on her guitar, she plucked a few lines of the song that her mother had sung on the wireless radio all those years ago, "*Seguirar mein Amor*," which in Malonian they called "I Would Follow the One I Love." Antonia thought of the poor people across the sea on Holy Island, who didn't know Imperialists like her father were preparing to enter their country.

"Love brings down many captives," sang Antonia very quietly, in Malonian, the private language she and her mother had spoken together when she was a tiny girl.

Her aunt rapped on the door. "I don't allow music in the house," she said. "Just so you know for the future, Antonia."

The girl, hugging her guitar to her chest, thought of that future and wished for it to disappear.

In the first family argument, the guitar was broken clean in two.

Around the time I dreamed that dream, my grandfather told me that Anastasia Fortuna's death had been announced on the radio. We had not heard her songs for a while—not since that concert where instead of singing there was only coughing and silence, and the singer was led from the stage, disgraced. It was a short announcement, my grandfather said, no more than ten seconds' worth, read very briefly and dispassionately: Anastasia Fortuna had died of a consumptive fever in Angel City, leaving behind only a daughter.

"You can never be their friend, Harlan," my grandfather mused that evening over the washing up. "You can never win with those Imperialists. They do what they want with you. That's what Anastasia Fortuna learned, to her cost. Ah, well. God rest her soul. There will never be another singer like her. She reminded me a little of my Amelie."

I missed that voice on the radio. And though I did not tell my grandfather, I missed the story of her daughter that had occupied my dreams. After the two of them were separated, I dreamed of Antonia Fortuna no more.

But now, in my mind, two obsessions haunted me. The first was to get to that green world I had seen only twice—at my birth and through the eyes of Rigel. And the second was to find that girl, Antonia Fortuna, and see for myself if she could sing in the voice of her mother, that voice my grandfather loved.

III

❧ DEATH ❧

23

*T*ime passed.

We waited for the resistance to make their push into Capital and take back our old country.

It didn't happen.

At school, sitting on the floorboards because there were not enough benches, holding between my knees an old-century slate because we had no paper, I learned the history of our country. I learned about the king and the great ones and the wars for possession of the city. I also learned that no one now believed in powers anymore.

10th March, Year '02, wrote Anselm. *I know I kept promising you that the revolution would happen and that I'd be with you all on Holy Island. Now I fear that promise was unfounded. The resistance here has hit a kind of stalemate. There are those of us, like me and Michael, like most of the original members who remember the free country, who believe that our numbers are now too few to take back Capital by armed struggle. There are rumours circulating about Aldebaran's descendant, about a disciple, a last great one who will lead us to revolution. Now most of the old members think we should wait until this last descendant shows himself. You can imagine how I feel about this. Keep Harlan very safe, and be careful.*

Meanwhile, the newer members, people coming of age under this government, incline to a different view. They think that we should muster troops by force, and use violent means to undermine the Imperialist rule. Now almost every meeting is a pointless argument, getting us nowhere, wasting our energies.

Without greater numbers, we can't ever take back the city. This I know. But, God willing, Holy Island and the north will remain free, and you will remain safe. Love, Anselm.

On my grandfather's wireless radio, we heard that the conditions in the other free sectors of the continent were no better than our own. "The Imperialist government is offering deals to the free sectors," said the news announcer now. "Those governments who enter into agreement with the Imperialist government are guaranteed safe passage of food supplies in and out of their territories, and protection from civil war. In return, the free states must agree to collaborate with the Imperialists, and allow an Imperialist presence within their territories. All have refused."

But that autumn, the last free sectors of Alcyria and Titanica entered into agreement with the Imperialists. Now only the north remained free, and Holy Island.

They could not invade us openly, but they were cutting off the ships. My fourteenth winter, we existed mainly on potatoes and bread. Meanwhile, refugees had begun leaving, going back to the mainland, into their ports. "It's a sad day," said my grandfather, "when people think it's better to give up their freedom than to remain here."

Maybe so, but we were all hungry, and the Imperialists had great industrial farms, and hot and cold running water, and motor trucks, and electric light.

The following spring, the resistance broadcast a message on the wireless radio. "We need greater numbers," a man's voice growled. "We urge you, free Malonians, men and women, to join our cause. And we urge Aldebaran's disciple, the fabled last descendant, if he exists, to come forward so that we can deal with him directly."

Take care of Harlan, wrote Anselm. *Keep him safe.*

Jasmine and my parents came to blows. I woke one night to hear her yelling in the front room of the shop: "I'm twenty years old—I'll do as I like—"

"No," cried my mother. "You're not leaving, and that's final."

"They want us to join—they want us to fight. Anselm fights. Michael fights. And here we are, stuck on this island in the middle of nowhere, hiding, scraping a living—"

"I won't let you go."

Jasmine stormed up the stairs. My door opened; light cut in. "Harlan," she said. "I'm leaving. There's a ship to Arkavitz. I'm going north to join Anselm and the resistance."

Sleepily, I began to cry. Jasmine hugged me so tightly that it took the breath from my lungs. "I'm coming with you," I said. "Let me get my clothes."

"No!" Jasmine's fury halted my tears. "Don't you dare! Harlan, you're to stay here!"

She prised me off her and was gone, down the stairs, embracing briefly my mother and father. "I'll see you soon," she said. "But they need more people. I'd never be able to stand the sight of myself in the mirror if I didn't go."

She left on the next ship north. But without my sister, the shop felt empty, a place with a great cavern at its heart.

I went to school every day, and every afternoon I sat in the back room of the shop, next to the gas fire, and studied the books my mother told me to—history and geography and science—to make up for the things we didn't learn very much of at school. Once, she had been a tutor in the city, educating the children of wealthy Malonians, and now she devoted herself to my education. Then, in the evenings, I went to see my grandfather, who told me stories and loaded me with more books to carry home with me. "These," he told me eagerly, "will make you a writer." My days were full of learning. All the members of my family, it seemed, wanted me to grow up an intellectual.

Truth be told, I did not mind this learning. All those books opened the world and showed me another life, at a time when my own real life on the island seemed to be narrowing and narrowing. So did Anselm's letters. So did my grandfather's stories. So did my dreams.

Time passed. Jasmine wrote us a letter from Maritz. *I reached Anselm*, she wrote, *and he's taking care of me, so you don't need to worry. We'll all join in the resistance push and be back before Christmas.*

No one now believed in the resistance push any longer.

My grandmother went about shaking her head at Jasmine's "wildness" and "headstrong nature" and "caprice." "Cutting her hair so short," my grandmother muttered. "Running about with those wild resistance boys." By this, I knew how much my grandmother missed her. That winter, without seeing Jasmine again, my grandmother died.

At sixteen, I finished school. There was a university college in Valacia, and my mother thought for a while that I would attend it, but she had a great fear of letting me go to the city and in the end it was resolved that my formal education, for what it had been worth, would end here. I found work as an apprentice clerk in the shipping office by the harbour. My mother was proud that I had found clerical work. Clerical work, according to her, was a way to make your life better, just like education.

I realise that this is no way to tell the story of a life. I am jumping five years all at once, from that day at twelve when I last dreamed about Antonia Fortuna to a moment five years later when the life I knew ceased to exist. The reason for this is simple. Those five years were spent waiting. I was waiting for the resistance to be ready to take back the country, as we all were, and I was waiting to find Antonia Fortuna.

At the end of the waiting is where my real story continues. That's the part I want to tell.

24

*T*he day before death came for my grandfather was dull and ordinary. Dressed in a suit too tight around the collar, sweating a little from the heat, I made the climb through the town to my grandfather's apartment. It was a little after six o'clock, a

Thursday early in July, and the sky was hazy. When I looked back over the town, I could just make out the dark line of the mainland on the horizon. That line had grown more threatening in the past few weeks, and the distance between us now seemed hardly any distance at all. "The government of Holy Island," the wireless radio had announced the week before, "is considering entering into an agreement of truce with the government of the New Imperial Order so as to put an end to the ban on shipping in the channel and the resulting food shortages."

I paused in front of the tobacconist's window and bent to straighten out my hair and necktie. My grandfather always looked at me so carefully, with such admiration, that I felt the need to be dressed with a kind of old-world formality in his presence. The suit had been a gift from him on my seventeenth birthday. It was navy blue and made me look paler than I really was. "Intellectual and interesting," my grandfather said, half joking and half serious, "much like myself as a young man." There I stood: blue, too-tight suit, brownish hair, grey eyes, halfway between my mother and my father in colouring, halfway between child and adult in age, impatient with my life on the island and this revolution that never came.

I was old enough now to understand that, in part, they were waiting for me.

I wish I had been thinking of other things the day before death came for my grandfather, but I was seventeen years old and I was preoccupied with my appearance and the stuffiness of my small-town home and my great-great-uncle's assertion that one day I would be a great man.

I slid the knot of my tie up to my neck and climbed the dark stairs behind the tobacconist's shop. Outside my grandfather's apartment, on the cool-tiled terrace which led to his front door, was a miniature jungle of potted plants. They were wilting this evening, which meant they had not been watered as usual. And the curtain was drawn in Grandfather's front window, also strange. I tapped on the door. While I waited, a grey, flea-bitten cat twisted in and out of the potted plants, glaring at me.

"Grandfather?" I called.

Within, something crashed. I could not tell what.

"Grandfather!" I called again, with more anxiety this time.

I tried the door. To my surprise, it was open.

"Grandfather Harold?" I said, as I entered the apartment.

An awful noise greeted me, a kind of groaning. Fear twisted my heart and I ran. In his usual chair, my grandfather was struggling to get up.

"Harlan," he tried to say, but it came out lopsided. One whole side of him had slumped, like he was melting. He struggled to open his eyes.

"Grandfather?" I said. "Grandfather! Open your eyes! Tell me what's wrong!"

His eyelids flickered. He said something incomprehensible. On the second try, I understood. "I'm all right," he was trying to say. "I'm all right."

He wasn't, and we both knew it.

I don't remember running the mile to the doctor's house. The next thing I knew, I was back there, beside my grandfather, tears running down my face while the doctor examined him, gripping his unresponsive hand and shining a light into his sagging eyes.

"Help me get him to the bed," said the doctor.

We heaved him there between us.

"How old is your grandfather?"

"Eighty," I said.

"Hmm," said the doctor. "That's a hell of an age. Eighty?"

"What's wrong with him?"

"I can't tell exactly," said the doctor. "A seizure of some sort. An attack of the brain. We'll make arrangements to take him into the hospital overnight."

105

In New Maron, the hospital usually meant that you were dying.

"No," I said. "It can't be that bad. He was fine yesterday—there was nothing wrong."

"Isak K.," said the doctor—people in New Maron always addressed you that way if you were younger than them—"your grandfather needs to go into the hospital where he can be properly observed. I'll make arrangements for the ambulance."

The ambulance—really just a dusty old cart—was soon there, clattering outside the door. I held my grandfather's hand. The two orderlies, just two off-duty fishermen who I knew by sight, manhandled him down the narrow staircase and loaded him into the back. The tobacconist's children stared as we rattled away along the street.

"Aa-aa-aargh," said my grandfather, without opening his eyes.

"It's all right," I said. "I'm with you. Can you hear what I'm saying?"

If he could hear me, he didn't answer.

The hospital was on the edge of town, in an old convent building. My grandfather was unloaded and carried into a narrow stone room with an arched window. On the bare, stripped bed, he writhed and groaned.

"Someone needs to get my family," I said, feverishly trying to think. "My mother and my father. Someone needs to get them."

"I'll send word," said the doctor, and disappeared. When he returned, he wound a strip of cloth around my grandfather's arm, made a cut in the papery skin of his shoulder and spread a vial of solution on the wound. I could tell it pained my grandfather by the wincing of his eyelids.

"What are you doing?" I said. "What's that for?"

"Injection," grunted the doctor, unfastening the band from my grandfather's feeble upper arm. "They've run out of damn hypodermic needles, so there's no other way to do it. With this shipping embargo, none of the proper supplies get through."

I sat beside my grandfather's bed and held his hand. The doctor reached out as he left, and gripped my shoulder in a manly sort of way. "The nurses will be in and out to make him comfortable," he said. "They are to call me if there are any sudden changes."

In the profound and awful quiet, I came to understand that my grandfather was dying. On the other side of the hospital lawn, beyond the road, I could hear the sea. Gulls called in the gathering darkness. Away across the water, I could see lights approaching and hear a bell clang. Enclosed in my own private misery, I did not realise this was the first warning of the invasion.

A short while later, heeled shoes came running up the hospital path. They approached along the corridor. Through the door, her hair flying, came my mother. She fell to her knees beside Grandfather Harold's bed and stroked his face and his poor thin arms.

"Oh, Harold," she said. "Dear Harold."

My father appeared at the doorway. He stood uneasily at the end of the bed, running a hand over the back of his hair.

"Sit beside him," I said. "Take his hand. Here. Sit here."

I got up, and my father sat down beside Grandfather. He gripped my grandfather's hand very lightly. "Pa," he said, and his voice held firm. "Can you hear me?"

He had always called my grandfather "Father," but that day he called him "Pa." I still don't know why. Maybe it was what he used to call him when he was a little boy.

"It's going to be all right," said my father. "Pa, it's going to be all right. I want you to know that. We've had seventeen years with you here. We found each other again, and we had seventeen years. We all love you very dearly, but if you want to go now, Pa, you can."

Those words made it better somehow. We waited.

25

*T*he doctor came back at midnight. The nurses had lit a lamp for us, and by its light we sat and watched my grandfather. Strange sounds came from outside the window: the clanging of bells, and people shouting hoarsely.

"They say this really is some kind of invasion," said the doctor, taking my grandfather's pulse. "You've a shop, haven't you, Joseph K.?"

My father nodded and licked his lips nervously.

"I'd advise you to stay there tonight," said the doctor. "You'll be looted otherwise, you mark my words. There won't be any change in old Mr. Karol's state for a while, I'm sorry to say."

After the doctor left, we held a whispered conference at the end of Grandfather's bed. Neither my mother nor my father wanted to leave, but the shop was standing empty. Eventually it was agreed that they would go home overnight and return around dawn. I would not consider leaving. I listened to their footsteps go away from me along the corridor. Then I sat beside my grandfather and watched his face. I could not tell if he was awake or asleep. His skin looked sunken by the lamplight.

"Grandfather," I said. "Can you hear me?"

He didn't grip my hand. I wished he'd give me some sign he was still living.

Six hours is a long time to wait alone in a hospital room praying for your grandfather to wake up. The silence was so profound it made my head ache. I went to the window and let in air, and after I had closed it again I paced the room, just for something to do. Time passed no more quickly. Around three o'clock, a nurse's footsteps went by in the corridor, but she didn't come in.

Then I must have fallen asleep, because I dreamed.

My grandfather opened his eyes and sat up, like a much younger man. He swung his legs down off the bed.

"Grandfather!" I said, half glad and half terrified. "Are you alive?"

He rubbed his hands over the wrinkles of his face and yawned. "Of course I am," he said. "Listen, Harlan, I don't have much time. This is important—" He was trying to get to his feet.

"Grandfather, you aren't well. You've had some kind of seizure. You're in hospital, you see? You need to rest, not get up."

But my grandfather, quite well, shook off my hands and got to his feet. "I'm glad to see you in that suit," he said. "Though it's getting a little short around the ankles. Get the tailor to let it out."

"All right," I said. "I will. But, Grandfather—"

He raised one hand imperiously. "Listen carefully. I've remembered what I had to tell you."

He was so like his ordinary self that at the time I did not realise it was a dream.

"Your mother and father have lied to you," he said. "It's a kind of lying that comes from love, but it's still lying. They haven't told you the truth about your past. You know that, of course."

I waited. My grandfather did not seem to want to approach me. He stood instead in the moonlight from the window.

I made to get to my feet, but he said, "No, no—I'll forget what I'm saying if you distract me. Don't move."

"All right, I won't. Tell me what you've got to say."

"Papers."

"Papers?" I said. "What papers?"

"Your great-great-uncle, Aldebaran, left you papers in his will. They were supposed to pass to you when you were a child, but they never did. They were in my possession when I came to the island. Your mother and father wanted them destroyed, but I didn't do it."

"What kind of papers?"

"I don't know. I've never read them. They weren't addressed to me. It'll be something to do with this last descendant business. We've all pretended, all these years, that it isn't you they're looking for."

My grandfather was moving again, his steps quite agile. He made for the door. I got up from the rickety chair and followed him along the corridor and out of the main door of the hospital. Dawn was just breaking. The pathway was cool through the soles of my shoes. A light wind troubled the grass. My grandfather was still in the suit he had been about to die in, a light linen suit which rippled in the breeze.

"And another thing," he said abruptly, turning to face me. "I wanted to tell you about writing. I'll tell you all I know. Now, before I go a long way off from you, too far to tell you anything at all. I won't give you platitudes. There aren't any worth giving, and the reality is quite simple."

My grandfather coughed to clear his throat. "You want to write," he said. "The only secret I ever found to writing was to tell how things are. Not the great truths, the great wisdoms—let those take care of themselves—but all the little details that might never have been told otherwise. The way an old man's hands look when he doesn't have the strength to clench them. The way the rain sounds when your roof has a leak. The dry and bitter taste of jealousy."

"How can jealousy taste dry? How can it do that?"

I was seventeen and too slow for his genius. I see that now. I can still hear the petulant way I asked it.

My grandfather turned to me with a kind of fire in his eyes. "Make them feel it, Harlan," he said. "Make them believe it.

That's what the book worth writing does. The book worth writing is a bulletin sent back from the front lines of real life. So that when the war is over, the truth remains, and people can look at your words and say, *Yes, yes, this is how it was.*

"Right," I said, trying to fix all this in my memory. "A bulletin sent back. Don't go so fast, Grandfather, or I won't remember."

He crossed the damp road in his bare feet. There were no trucks passing at this hour; the edge of the town was deserted. He walked down the beach towards the sea. Just recently, in fear of invasion, a tangled line of barbed wire had been laid out in the shallow water, a few yards from the shore. My grandfather walked right down into the waves so that the water came up over his feet, then soaked the trousers of his suit.

"Wait, Grandfather," I said. "You're not well."

"I assure you," he said, "I'm perfectly well. I've never felt as well as I do tonight."

Out in the sea, we could hear the low growl of ships. Lights rose across the water, bright fireworks that flared and died away with a faint popping sound. Then we heard a staccato rattle that I learned later was machine-gun fire.

My grandfather straightened his necktie. The nurses at the hospital had loosened it, but now he rearranged it. His face in the grey light was sweaty and zealous, but maybe that was just his illness. Another flare, or else a shell, rose briefly over the sea and died in the dark. Out there, something was starting.

"Be careful," he said, nodding towards the distant fires. "The first thing they do when they take over a country is burn the books. It's always the way. A great writer needs books. Read all you can now, while you have the chance. Learn from those greater than you. Be humble, and then—you'll see—one day you'll eclipse them."

That was how he had always been: both humble and arrogant, so certain of his genius but conscious that his work was a lifelong apprenticeship to a craft whose victories were minor. I realised that this was my grandfather dying, and I began to weep.

He said, "Harlan, lift up your head."

I lifted up my head. The dawn was rising. My grandfather walked a little farther out into the bone-aching cold of the waves. I followed as far as the barbed wire, but I could get no farther. My grandfather had found a way through, but I couldn't, and in a panic I ran this way and that, cutting my hands and arms up to the elbows on the new wire, while he walked out into the sea, his old-fashioned suit billowing around him, his face raised to the cold dawn.

My mother called my name. I heard her and came back. Dawn was rising, and my eyes stung in the light. I was standing on the edge of the sea, up to my knees in the rough breakers, and my grandfather was nowhere to be found. I shielded my eyes against the sun and searched the horizon. "Where is he?" I said.

My mother pulled me up the beach and into her arms. "He's gone," she said, shaking with tears. "He's gone. Oh, Harlan, we couldn't find you to tell you. It happened just ten minutes ago. What are you doing out here? Come and say goodbye."

She led me to the room and showed me my grandfather where he lay on the bed. His tie was loose, just the way the nurses had left it. The lamp still burned. When I touched it, the papery skin on the back of his hand was quite cool.

But forever afterwards, I believed in the reality of that dream: that my grandfather had died not lying passively in a bed, but raising his face to the sun and walking out into the waves, bequeathing me his last secrets.

26

We wrote to Anselm and Jasmine. My grandfather was buried on a high patch of ground overlooking the sea. There was fighting just off the coast now, and the funeral had to take place hurriedly or not at all. We did it in a rush, with just a few acquaintances and neighbours. After the undertakers and well-wishers had left, I sat beside the grave a long time with my father, keeping a private vigil. We sat there until it got quite dark. At ten o'clock, my mother brought us blankets and sandwiches. "Don't sit up too long," she told us.

At eleven, my father sighed and got to his feet. He seemed to have got much older in the past days, as if he had inherited some of my grandfather's great age. He shivered and pulled his blanket around him. "Will you stay here a while longer, or will you come back with me? I'm scared there's going to be trouble in Valacia tonight, and it could easily spread south. Wouldn't you be better coming back to the shop with me?"

"I want to stay," I said. "I'll see any trouble if it happens, anyway." I gestured at the sweeping expanse of the sea below us.

My father knew not to argue. He went very slowly down the hill and through the overgrown alley that led back to the town.

The night was full of stars. I sat a little closer to my grand-father's grave. I was waiting for some sign to tell me what to do without him. I sat there so long that the night passed entirely, and the sun began to rise behind pale clouds. My legs were aching, and so was my throat, as if I myself had suffered a long illness. There was no one near, so I knelt on the grave and sort of prayed, the way I had when my grandfather was ill three years earlier. "God, if there is a God," I whispered, "something's gone wrong. This wasn't meant to happen."

The wind rolled a can around, somewhere on another grave. I found it and righted it, and put the wilted flowers back in. It was what my grandfather—always so polite in an old-world sort of way—would have done himself.

"Listen, God, if there is a God," I said, "take me back to my real life. Or make my real life different. My grandfather wasn't supposed to die. He always said great writers endure forever, but I would sooner have him back with me as he was, living and real."

I clenched my eyes shut until my eyeballs ached, but the world continued and my grandfather remained where he was.

In the morning light, the graveyard had a shabby look. The birds made a racket in the trees, squalling and chirping. The sun illuminated the crest of the hill, and touched each wave of the grey sea with light. I stood up, brushed the mud off my knees as best I could and turned away from the grave to look out over the sea. I could make out black ships, and smoke. Still a bell somewhere was clanging. I left the graveyard behind and went home.

That same day, Holy Island fell.

My father had brought Grandfather Harold's belongings home to our apartment: his wireless radio and his books and papers and the odd ornaments he had gathered around him. There they stood, stacked neatly in the corner of our living room. My grandfather had mostly avoided possessions of value, but the wireless was truly his. Now it stood forlorn in the middle of our floor, bereft of its owner. I wound the crank. The dial was still tuned to the news station. But no sound emerged today, only a faint buzzing.

"That's odd," said my mother. "Maybe it doesn't work in our apartment. I can't think of it except in his living room, next to his chair. Oh, poor Harold." She dabbed at her eyes.

My father knelt in front of the wireless and turned the dial. All at once, a voice blared from the speaker, filling our whole apartment. General Marlan.

The voice ended, and a kind of strutting, marching music came on. Imperialist anthems.

My father tried to shut the music off, but this time when we turned the dial, it would receive no other station. Eventually, in frustration, my father turned the radio off altogether.

Out in the street, people were banging their doors and calling to each other. It was not yet seven o'clock. My father put his head out of the window and called to our neighbour, Mrs. Winter: "Mrs. W., do you know what's going on?"

"I'm sorry for your loss, Joseph K.," called Mrs. Winter.

"Thank you—that's kind."

"I don't know any more than you what's going on. Looks to me like the agreement with the Imperialists is really happening at last. Maybe we'll have something to eat this winter."

Mr. Cortez, a refugee from the western islands who was my father's oldest friend in the street, appeared in front of his printing shop and looked up at us. "All I get is the bloody mainland station," he said. "It's crazy, this music and shouting. General Marlan yelling all morning into my living room—I can't stand it. I was forced to take the battery out of the wireless to make it stop."

"It's the same with us," said my father.

My parents and I sat around the wireless, listening to the shouting turned down low. Around midday, we heard a series of gunshots. My father tensed and shivered. He ran his hand over the back of his head, as though he was checking to see that he was still solid.

The neighbours began congregating in the street. From the window, I listened. The rumours were wild. Someone said that there were soldiers down at the harbour. Others said that the governor of the island, Mr. Valentin, had been shot and a new Imperialist governor was already in place. An hour or so later, we heard the sound of many boots marching, somewhere down in the town.

Out of nowhere, the wireless crackled into life. A voice came from it, tinny and faint. My mother turned up the dial. The free news announcer came on, his voice more flustered and hasty than usual. "The free republic of Holy Island," he said, "has come to an agreement with the New Imperial Order. Shipping will be restored, and an Imperialist cooperative presence established in Valacia. From now on, we will work together much more closely. Hail to General Marlan."

My father banged his hand down onto the table. He made it into a fist and kept it there. My mother shook her head. The news announcer carried on with what was clearly a prepared speech. We were not to be anxious. We were to cooperate fully. We were to go to our town square and await instructions. This marked the start of a new chapter in the island's noble history.

There was nothing to do but obey. My mother, my father and I walked hand in hand. Many of the neighbours were doing the same. At the end of our street, soldiers were waiting. They shifted restlessly in the heat and pointed guns at us. "March," they said. "Go to the town square."

One of them, the youngest, was barely older than me. His hat stood up ridiculously on his head and no one had told him. That is what I remember most about that day, a boy my own age and just as nervous ordering my mother and father and neighbours about in the July heat of our town.

There was some confusion when we reached the square, because there was no one there to address us. We waited in front of the town hall. Finally a senior-looking soldier came out onto the balcony and addressed us in broken Malonian, the language the majority of us spoke, standing beside New Maron's flustered mayor. "You must not be afraid," he kept repeating. "This is a good thing for your country." This soldier did not seem frightened by the situation. He stood very tall on the balcony and breathed in our sea air. "Now go to your places of work as normal."

My mother and father did not want to let me go to the shipping office, but they had no choice. We were being shepherded in different directions. My mother gripped my hand and said, "It's all right. We'll see you soon."

In the shipping office, two young soldiers were waiting. They made the four of us clerks hand over our documentation and strip what they called the "patriotic" posters from the walls. Then they demanded our books. Since there were none in the office, they eventually settled for our shipping charts and records of cargo, and left with them in an old sack. "Now carry on as normal," they told us. "Your island is still free."

As soon as we were dismissed from the shipping office, I ran home. My father was waiting behind the shop counter, my mother beside him.

"Some of the other shops in the street have been searched," he said urgently. "Is there anything you have that could cause trouble? Tell me quick, and we'll burn it now."

On the shelf that ran all the way around my narrow bedroom were the books my grandfather had given me over my seventeen years of life. Could some of them be dangerous? I knew, very firmly, that I didn't want to declare them either way, to see them bundled into sacks and hauled away like rubbish.

"No," I said. "Nothing that could cause trouble."

I went upstairs. Very quietly, I examined my books. The old Harold North novels and political writings in their faded leather covers. Stories by the great Malonian writers of the last century. A book by Diamonn, our old country's national poet, *On the Art of Poetry*. Diamonn's *Complete Works*, a book that my grandfather told me Aldebaran had loved. I think I already understood, then, that I was bidding them farewell.

Towards evening, a lone soldier came up to the shop door and knocked. I heard him speak to my father in the street. "I am under orders to search this place of business," he said, almost apologetically, in his faltering version of our language. My father must have submitted, because the soldier came in. I went down the stairs and watched him from the darkness of the back room. He turned over

117

the things in the shop window, half-heartedly, and went through the drawer of the counter. He paused at a photograph of our family and held it to the light—Jasmine, aged about fourteen, awkward and halfway to beautiful; me, still a seven-year-old child; my parents on either side, smiling, protecting; and Grandfather seated in the middle. "I am a father too," the soldier said. "Yes, yes. I have two little boys back on the mainland. I'll wait to bring them out here. Once things have settled."

My father nodded and licked his dry lips. "How old?" he said.

"Seven and two. My young princes, they are."

"Very nice ages," said my father. "My own are grown up now."

"Look," said the soldier, handing the photograph back, "we mean you no harm. We come here to help you bring yourselves into the new century, understand? A new world order. It . . ." He paused, then brought out, tentatively, a phrase from our own country: "It is all for the best."

"Yes," said my father. "I understand that."

"I have to take your books, I'm afraid," said the soldier. "Part of the agreement."

"Very well." My father nodded to the stack of second-hand books behind the counter. The soldier began carrying them from the shelves into the street. Other soldiers with handcarts wheeled them away.

My own books remained. My father said nothing about them, and neither did my mother. We locked up the shop for the night, went upstairs and listened in silence to the wireless radio, which told us nothing new.

Eventually, because no one knew what was going to happen next, we went to sleep. I woke once or twice to the sound of my parents' anxious voices through the wall. I felt at the edge of something, light and weightless, as if tomorrow might bring anything at all.

———

I was woken suddenly at about two o'clock. I had been in the very deepest sleep, and when I woke it was like coming up out of the sea, or else like drowning. I stood up all at once and stumbled to the door, and leaned my head against it to stop myself from falling over. "Harlan!" my mother was calling. "Harlan!"

They were in the living room, their faces as white and blank with confusion as mine must have been. Someone was hammering on the door. My father flicked the switch for the light. Nothing. The gas was out. Very quietly and tremblingly, he drew us together and encircled us with his arms, as though I were still a little boy.

"Joseph!" the voice was calling. "Joseph K.! Sylvia!" Their false names.

"Who the hell is it?" said my father. "What do they want?"

"Isn't that Cortez's voice?" said my mother.

My father listened more closely.

"Joseph!" came the voice again.

"It is," I said. I recognised it too.

My father sagged with relief. He went to the window in three strides, pushed it up and called, "Cortez?"

Mr. Cortez's voice came hurriedly up through the night. "Yes," he said. "Yes, it's me. You heard the gunshots from the harbour?"

"You scared us half to death, Cortez."

"Karol, listen, you must come and join us. Bring your boy. We've got a group to go down and join the men already at the harbour."

"To do what?" said my father.

There was a pause. "To join the resistance, Karol. It's time we armed ourselves, we island people. Too long we've been cowering on the edge of the empire, scared to do anything. We heard it on the wireless radio. The resistance mean to make their big push now, at last."

My father withdrew from the window. He looked at us both with grey eyes full of darkness. Then he put his head back out of the window. "No," he said finally. "No, I don't think I will."

"But, Joseph—"

"I don't think I will," he repeated more firmly.

"Everyone is going!" called Mr. Cortez. "There are not so many of them on the island. Not as we first thought. But a new wave is coming, and if we have luck we'll repel them. Come on, Karol. Don't be a coward! You, with your brave son a revolutionary across the sea!"

"Be quiet!" said my father, in the sharpest tone I'd ever heard him use in my life. "I don't want to hear you saying anything about that. I've had enough of fighting. Long ago, I had enough of that."

So it was that this particular part of the invasion passed us by. We sat safe in the house, while at the harbour farmers with their pitchforks and fishermen with their harpoons and men from the hills with their old rusted hunting rifles waited to confront the next wave of soldiers. In the end, it was no kind of confrontation. The soldiers with their submachine guns and tanks ordered the islanders to submit, and they did. Then a whole crowd of them were taken off for questioning. We didn't see Mr. Cortez again.

27

Starting the next day, foreigners brought across in ships seemed to be everywhere. The police force had a new chief, and Mr. Walcott, my boss, was replaced with an Imperial man named John Vincent, immensely fat, and well-meaning by their standards, but unable to speak a word of our language. We got by in signs and awkward grunts as well as the scattered Alcyrian I had learned from my grandfather, and the productivity of the shipping office dwindled almost to nothing.

Meanwhile, New Maron was given a new leader, the soldier who had addressed us that first day they took over. Captain Vilnius, he was called. New Maron had never had a leader before, and most residents felt that it didn't need one now.

About a week after the new government entered into agreement with ours, Captain Vilnius paid our street a visit. I had just got home from work and was sitting with my father in the back room of the shop. We first saw his entourage, a procession of men with guns that gleamed black in the sunlight, whose shadows crossed our front window. Then the captain, sweating in his full ceremonial uniform. He came up to our door and rapped on the glass.

We glanced at each other, then my father stood to open it. There was nothing else to do, with him looking at us through the shop window. The captain came in, trailed by his entourage. "We are looking for information," he said to my father. "Do you know any of these names?" He thrust forward a document. "Delmar. Donahue. Rigel. Jameson. North."

My throat went dry, though I didn't show it. I just gripped the handle of the counter drawer, a cold little glass ball.

"I don't know those names," my father said quite calmly. The way he stood there straight and tall astounded me. I hadn't thought he had that strength in him.

"Pictures," said Captain Vilnius, snapping his fingers. "Bring out the pictures. We're looking for the people in these pictures. You understand, yes?"

"I understand," said my father.

One of the soldiers brought out a stack of pictures, and they were put before my father. One man, with greying hair and dark eyes, I recognised immediately.

"He used to be the king," said my father, very evenly. "Yes. I know this man's face."

"Yes?" said Captain Vilnius. "You know anything about this man, Cassius Donahue, or where he's gone?"

"No more than I've said. Everyone on this island will recognise him if you show them. He vanished in the year '89—I mean to say, what you call the year zero."

"Hmm," Captain Vilnius grunted. "We suspect he's somewhere on the island."

He went on flipping over the pictures. Men and women in resistance furs. A few young faces who might have been anyone. And then an ancient man with a face like a skull. An old-century newspaper photograph.

"You know this man?" the captain said, shoving the picture in my father's face. "Aldebaran, he used to call himself? Assassinated in the year zero? I saw your face—you recognised him?"

"No," said my father. "I've never seen him before in my life."

"That's odd," said Captain Vilnius. "Because you come from the city, yes? You lived there once?"

"Yes," said my father. "But I never saw Aldebaran address the citizens, if that's what you're thinking. I know his name, but not his face. That isn't odd. He kept to himself. Not like the king. Maybe I saw him in the newspaper once, but I certainly don't remember."

Captain Vilnius regarded my father for a long time, blinking slowly. Then he thrust the picture at me. "You know this man's face? Take a look."

I looked, and like my father I shook my head.

Captain Vilnius held my eyes for a long time, then turned away. He put the pictures down on the shop counter. "I shall leave you with these," he said. "In case you remember. There's a lot of silly rumours about a last descendant on this island, which need to be properly dealt with."

After the men had gone, my father put the pictures in the bottom of the drawer of the counter. "Papa, do you think they know something about our past?" I said.

"I don't know, Harly. I honestly don't. I hope they're just questioning everyone."

"Why would they send the most important soldier here, to our shop?" For the first time in my life, I felt the fear my parents must have known when I was still a tiny child.

My father watched the soldiers turn the corner of the street. Then he said, quietly, "I know you hid your books."

I sat down beside him. His hands, I could see, were shaking.

"Those are the books Grandfather gave me. I won't watch strangers take them away."

"I know, son," said my father. "It's difficult. All of this. I wish I could protect you from it—I wish to God I could." He stood abruptly and shoved the counter drawer shut. "Bring them down to the yard."

I shook my head.

"Harlan, please," he said gently, and took me by the wrist.

"No!" My heart was thudding. I had never confronted my gentle father like this before. "You're going to set them all on fire, just like the Imperialists."

"Harlan!" He clamped his hand over my mouth. "Watch what you're saying!"

"Grandfather wouldn't have done it." I found myself on my feet and shouting. "He wouldn't have acted so shamefully, and neither should you."

My father looked at me for a moment through narrowed eyes. Then he turned and went up the stairs. He came clattering down a moment later with his arms full of my books. I tried to wrestle them from him.

"Don't make this any more difficult," he pleaded. "Just do as I say."

And I saw that the books he had brought down—the first ones he was going to burn—were his own father's, irreplaceable because they were out of print. The books he least wanted to see destroyed, surely, out of all of them.

"I don't want to do this any more than you do, but we'd better get it over with. In the circumstances, wouldn't Grandfather rather we were alive, without the books, than dead for the sake of them?"

I hadn't thought about it coming to that. "We can burn every other book, but let's just keep these. Just the Harold North books. Just for a while longer. Please."

My father caved in. He set the Harold North books aside. The rest of the books we piled in the centre of the yard. He put his arm around me and together we watched them burn.

28

*W*hen my mother got back from the market, she cried tears of anger at what my father had done. "How could you, Leo?" she said, picking up the charred remains of the books. "We'll never get these back. Never."

I had seen my mother cry more in the last month than I had in the whole seventeen years of my life. The two of them seemed to be falling to pieces since Grandfather's death.

We went upstairs and tried to eat dinner as normal, but it was a dismal meal. Afterwards, I told my mother and father that I was going to sleep at my grandfather's old apartment. It was not that I was angry with my father, though my mother certainly was; I just wanted to think, and I had always thought best at Grandfather's.

No one went out after dark anymore in New Maron. Shortly after I reached my grandfather's apartment, dusk fell and the streets emptied. A few trucks roared by on the main road to Valacia. The Imperialists brought more and more of them to the island every day, unloading them from ships with great rusty cranes. Now they were everywhere, coughing out smoke and rumbling on the steep uphills and downhills of our island.

The first thing I did at my grandfather's apartment was go

to the sink and fill a cup with water. My grandfather's plants were all but dead—it made my throat ache when I saw them—and I wanted to try to bring them back to life. It would probably do no good, but I did it anyway.

When I went back to the sink, the tap let out only a brief dribble. Of course, that was the last of the water. My father must have shut it off when he closed up the apartment. It would have to be put up for sale, if the commotion of the invasion ever died down. But it still felt to me almost more like home than my real home. There was the sagging sofa where my grandfather had coaxed me back to health after my bout of silent fever. There was the worn table where he had set up the chessboard, and the writing desk under the window where he used to sit and read. There was the bed where he had slept every night, lying as straight as he later did in death, with the covers drawn up to his chin.

The bed was stripped bare, but I lay down on it in my clothes and tried unsuccessfully to sleep. There was shouting down in the town, not the ordinary drunken shouting of the bar at the harbour but shouting that meant trouble. And my chest ached with thinking of my grandfather. Maybe I shouldn't have come here at all.

I went to the writing desk. I sat at it as he used to sit, drew up the chair and closed my eyes. I opened and closed the lid to let out the desk's dry, woody smell, which I remembered from when my grandfather used to rummage around inside to find me a pen or sheet of paper for my drawings.

That was when I saw the letter.

It was wedged under the desk's brown lining paper, so that only a corner showed, but deliberately, a whole neat triangle, as though it was meant to be found. I slid my hand under the lining paper and took it out. *Harlan*, the writing on the front said.

I opened the envelope. Inside were just a few words. *Dear Harlan*, it read. *Your great-great-uncle left a bundle of papers for you after his death in the year '89. From Anselm's possession, they passed to me. They are being held for you in my name at J. Harcourt and Sons, Lawyers, Avenue Delacroix, Valacia. I can't say more here. Love, Grandfather.*

The back of my head prickled. My great-great-uncle's papers. I had no great-great-uncle but Aldebaran.

I searched the whole apartment by the light of the candles my grandfather had kept carefully wrapped in paper for when the gas cut out. There was nothing else but this letter.

When dawn came, I locked up the apartment and went home via the cemetery. It was a raw, wind-blown morning, and my hands burned as I bent to clear old leaves and papers off my grandfather's grave, where they were already accumulating. "Grandfather," I muttered as I worked. "Why would you tell me this now, in the middle of an invasion, when you've had seventeen years to tell me?" How could I go to Valacia now, the centre of the fighting?

I got back to the shop and found my father in the back room, heating water for tea. He put a cup in my hand and patted my shoulder. "You were all right, were you? At Grandfather's? I heard trouble at the harbour."

"Yes, Papa. I was fine." I sat down with him behind the counter. I still had an hour left before work. "I've been thinking, what if Grandfather had a will?"

"A will?"

I shrugged. "Maybe he left one somewhere—with lawyers, say."

"They would have sent us a letter telling us so. There's only one lawyer in New Maron, Mr. Jones."

"But what if he left a will with some other lawyer? In Valacia, say, or further away?"

My father looked at me sharply over his chipped teacup. "Did you find something in Grandfather's apartment?"

126

"No," I said.

My father gulped his tea. "If there was some document with a lawyer, we'd have difficulty getting it now. There'd be some Imperialist in charge, sorting through all the papers." He shrugged. "But it doesn't matter. He didn't have anything to leave. He told me himself he'd bequeathed nothing; all of it was to come to us here—the wireless, the handful of books."

He got to his feet and began arranging the display of oil lamps in the window, brushing a speck of dust from one with his sleeve. He moved even more shufflingly today. The books my grandfather had left were already burned.

"What have you been doing?" I asked. "Didn't you sleep?"

My father shook his head. "I've been reading those last books. My father's."

"Where are they now?"

"Out in the yard. Waiting." He sighed deeply. "We'd better do it, Harlan. Mrs. Winter said they've put up posters outside the town hall with all kinds of restrictions—new laws, and penalties for not following them. Time to burn those last books."

I followed him out to the yard. There, stacked neatly against the wall, were the Harold North books. My father touched each one gently before setting it alight. *The Sins of Judas*, *The Golden Reign*, *The Darkness Has a Thousand Voices*, *Political Essays*, *The Shattered Wheel*. One by one he fed them to the flames.

"He told me once what his next book was going to be called," I said. "*The Heart at War*."

"What was it going to be about?"

I didn't know. My grandfather had never written it. I had always hoped, secretly, that the title referred to the heart that didn't belong, the heart that was always searching for another world—the heart like my own. But of course, he could have meant war quite literally. His life had been interrupted by enough of that.

My father nodded but said nothing. He kept his eyes on those books until the fire had taken them from him entirely. I braced myself against feeling anything too deeply. As my father said, there was probably nothing else to do.

On the way to work, I stopped to look at those new notices. The whole front wall of the town hall was papered with them: "Homosexuality Prohibited," "Discussion of Supernatural Powers or Happenings Prohibited," "Following of the Old Religions Prohibited," "Speaking of Malonian in Public Buildings Prohibited," "Opening of New Prison Camps for Juvenile Offenders Decreed," "All Relations Between Alcyrian Occupiers and Non-Alcyrian Citizens Strictly Prohibited." And a last one that made my stomach a little cold: "All Mention of Aldebaran and Last Descendant Punishable by Death." On the beach where the fishermen put in during stormy weather, a few men in overalls were rolling something out along the sand. As they uncoiled it, I saw that it was barbed wire. They were spreading it across the bay, halfway into the water, where our own feeble strand of defence had been. Two soldiers in the mainland uniform watched very seriously, directing them how to arrange it.

That day we were released early from work. The explanation given was that a government inspection had to take place at the shipping office. A great decisiveness came over me. I would go to Valacia, to J. Harcourt and Sons, Lawyers, and find those papers my grandfather had left there. This last descendant business haunted me, possessed me. If Aldebaran had anything at all to say to me about it, I needed to read his words. I wouldn't tell my mother or father, or take anything with me—I would just go, and try to get these papers before the Imperialist presence on our island made it even more difficult.

I had to walk, because it was no longer safe to hitch a lift in a truck now that most of them were driven by Imperialist soldiers. There were rumours of them slitting travellers' throats and dumping them at the side of the road. I didn't believe those rumours, but I didn't want to test them either. I took off my jacket and tie and walked along the side of the road, keeping my head down when Imperialist trucks passed. No one stopped me. Though the day was warm and the schools had finished, the little bays along the coast road were empty except for the new barbed-wire defences. Someone's greasy papers, relics of some fried food eaten on the roadside, now drifted eerily across the grey sand. That was all.

As I passed the hospital, I stood and looked out to sea where I had seen my grandfather go from me. The sea looked quite ordinary in the afternoon light. My heart hurt with thinking about him.

29

*I*t took me three hours to get to Valacia. It was the first time I had been to the capital since I was seven years old and my mother took me to register for school. The first thing I noticed was that there were more soldiers here. They seemed to be everywhere— idling in trucks at the docks, sitting on the steps of the city hall playing cards, clinging to every patch of shade with their rifles on their shoulders. I wasn't sure that I should have come after all. I had the address of Harcourt and Sons on a scrap of paper in my pocket, but I needed to ask someone the way to Avenue Delacroix, and there was no one in the streets who wasn't one of the Imperialists.

As I walked, I kept thinking about my grandfather. Why leave the papers at a lawyer's office in Valacia, where I had to go and fetch them? Why not just give them to me?

A gunshot cut across my thoughts. I dropped and cowered on the pavement. The roar of trucks was close now. I felt my heart thump against the dust. Two trucks swung round the corner and screeched along the tarmac, sending up an acrid smell. I got myself into the shadow of a parked cart.

"Please!"

A quick cry made me half raise my head. In the shadows of the houses on the other side of the road, someone was pleading, his hands raised. A man about my father's age. "No," he was saying. "No. Listen. Please listen."

Soldiers encircled the man with shouts and orders. "Answer in Alcyrian. Get down on the ground. Now!" I understood that much.

The man opened his mouth to say something else. There was another gunshot, then a storm. And I had my hands over my ears and my face in the dust and was saying, out loud, "No, no, no!" because I didn't want to see what they had done to the man.

In the end, I didn't see anything at all. The man no longer shouted. The soldiers dragged him into the back of one of the vehicles and drove him away.

A fluttering made me start. A cloud of crows had descended from the tall palm trees at the end of the street and were pecking at the blood in the road. The trail it had left was almost black.

I got up, very carefully, without looking at the blood. I recall I even had the presence of mind to dust off my suit. I dusted it, and walked without hurrying in the other direction. Not knowing how to make sense of what I had seen, I refused even to admit to myself that I had seen it. *This place is not safe*, I told myself. *You have to get into town, get the papers, get out. Otherwise that could be you dragged away in a truck. Come on. Go quickly.*

I asked a lone woman at a street market the way to Avenue Delacroix. She gave me careful directions and called after me, in Malonian, "Be careful!"

Avenue Delacroix was a wide street, and at the end of it was a building I recognised from pictures. It was the old Kalitz mansion, the house of the former rulers of this island. Fronted by lofty cypresses and glowing in the light of the bay, the building was beautiful. Lines of Imperialist trucks stood outside. On the corner of the square, a workman was nailing up a new Alcyrian street sign beneath our own. It read *Plaz Capitansk Lucien.* The lawyer's office also had a new sign on the railings outside. *J. Harcourt and Sons*, it read, *Lawyers and Notaries.* And underneath, *Victor Bercy, Censor of the Imperialist Government.*

Something about that name made me pause. Where had I heard it before, Victor Bercy?

I climbed a dusty staircase and tapped on the door at the top. I could not speak very much Alcyrian, but I would have to hope that this wouldn't get me into trouble. If I hadn't been so determined to get the papers, I would have turned back long before this point.

A frail man answered the door. I cleared my throat and said, "*Monsegneur Bercy?*"

"No, no," said the frail man, in my own language. "He's out. Come in. I'm Mr. Harcourt."

"Oh." Relief overcame me. "You must be the lawyer. You have some papers of mine. I'm just here to collect them."

"I can show you in. You'll have to wait for Mr. Bercy. This isn't my office anymore. It's been requisitioned."

The office was a mess of papers and documents that seemed to have been pulled out of the cabinets at random. A shiny new typewriting machine stood on the desk, and an Imperialist flag hung over the mantelpiece. Mr. Harcourt looked at it and flattened his lips. While he listened, I told him about the papers.

"Yes, yes, I remember your grandfather," he said. "A very particular man. I first met him when he was trying to find his family on the island. Later, he came back and said that he had found them, and that he wanted to deposit a bundle of papers in your name. Because the rest of your family might not be receptive to the idea of keeping these papers. Something from before the war. Sensitive documents. You must be his grandson. Isak Karol."

"That's right," I said. "I don't need to take up much of your time; I just need the papers." For reasons I could not explain to myself, I had a great dread of meeting this Mr. Bercy.

Mr. Harcourt shook his head. "Mr. Bercy, you know, is from the Censor's Office and he's overseeing the running of the business now." The man spread his hands helplessly. "You'll have to speak to Mr. Bercy. It's the only way. He's out at the moment, but he'll be back soon. You'll hear the roar of his motorcar, I daresay. Sit here, please."

I sat on one of the chairs that stood in a straight-backed, austere row by the window. The breeze gusted in with the scent of warm sea air, and the flapping of the birds in the cypresses could be heard quite distinctly. The world had not realised that anything was wrong with our island. Mr. Harcourt politely offered me tea but seemed relieved when I declined; he appeared preoccupied with his own troubles. Then, while I waited, he knelt down and began scrubbing the floor with an impossibly tiny rag. I wished I could offer to help, but he was enclosed in his own private sadness and I didn't want to interrupt it.

As the last sun left the square outside, a motorcar drew up with a sharp cough and a slamming of doors. From the dusty window, I looked down on a tall man with a bald circle in the middle of his dusty-coloured hair. I saw him march smartly round to the front of the building, then heard his boots clicking on the stairs. He pushed open the door and regarded me. He was about fifty-five or sixty, and wore an Imperialist band on his sleeve.

"Harcourt," he barked. "Why isn't that finished? I asked you to do it at ten o'clock this morning."

"Yes, sir."

"So why isn't it finished?"

Old Mr. Harcourt cringed. "Perhaps if I had a bigger cloth . . ." he ventured.

"Anya!" yelled the man from the Censor's Office, removing his leather driving gloves and throwing them with a slap onto the desk.

A shadowy figure appeared behind a glass door. "Yes?" came a girl's voice.

"Make me coffee. Black, three sugars. Then bring it here."

At last, Mr. Bercy was ready to give me his attention. "What can I do for you?" he asked without offering me his hand. He spoke decent Malonian, but he spoke it grudgingly, and I could tell he didn't like me sitting here in his newly requisitioned office, felt that I shouldn't have been shown in in the first place.

"Mr. Harcourt has been holding some papers which my grandfather left here for me. I'd like to collect them."

"Name?" said Mr. Bercy.

"Isak Karol."

Mr. Bercy became thoughtful. "Yes," he said. "I know the papers you mean."

"May I have them?"

Mr. Bercy, all at once, was obliging. "Yes," he said. "Certainly. There's nothing wrong with those papers. Only they're in storage. I must just go and fetch them."

"Another room?" I said.

"Elsewhere."

Mr. Bercy whipped round at a soft sound from behind him. In the shadow of the doorway stood a girl about my own age, with the cup of coffee for her employer held carefully in both hands. Without saying anything, the man took it and began gulping it down. The girl reached up to push her black hair away from her face, then shrank back from the door and disappeared.

"You'll need to wait here," Mr. Bercy told me. "Harcourt, make the boy tea." He retrieved his leather gloves from the desk and pulled them on with a snap. "I'll be back soon." He marched down the stairs, and in a moment I heard his motorcar cough into life and drive away.

Mr. Harcourt raised his ancient head. "Be very careful," he said, hoarsely. "Be very careful indeed."

A strange feeling broke over me. "Careful of what?" I said. "What do you mean?"

"The other week, there was someone else here to collect papers. Mr. Bercy told him to wait, and went for the secret police. Is there anything about those papers which could be incriminating in the eyes of the Alcyrian government? Because if there is, I'd leave now, Mr. Karol."

"Incriminating?" I got to my feet all in a rush. "I don't know. I've never seen them. They were written for me by my great-great-uncle before I was born. My grandfather was keeping them for me. I haven't got any idea what's in them."

Mr. Harcourt shook his head. "I'll get into trouble for telling you so, but it's best you leave."

Quite suddenly, as always happens on Holy Island, the good weather was over and clouds had descended. Rain began to assault the windows of the lawyer's office.

"I'll show you out," said Mr. Harcourt.

He ushered me down the stairs, still carrying his dripping rag in one hand. At the bottom, he tried the door, but it would not open.

"Damn," he said. "Mr. Bercy has locked it. He does mean to bring someone back for you—I knew it." He wrung the cloth onto his shoes. "Oh dear, oh dear—I should never have let you in."

Panic was getting the better of me. I wished I'd never come. All at once, what I had seen that morning overwhelmed me: that man shot at, and the blood on the road, and the truck roaring away with him inside.

"It's no good," said Mr. Harcourt. "He's done this before. Even if I could open the front door, there'll be surveillance. Soldiers hanging about. Come with me. You'll have to try and go out the other way."

I followed the old man back up the stairs. Everything in the office seemed very bright suddenly, like I had come up out of a dark tunnel. In the doorway, the girl called Anya was hovering again. I had a strange feeling that I knew her, as I had known the name Victor Bercy. But when I looked at her, she turned away, offering no assistance.

"Anya," said Mr. Harcourt. "This young man needs to leave quickly, by the fire escape. We must let him go, now, in case Mr. Bercy has gone for the secret police."

The girl looked at the ground in front of her. She had very straight, almost-black hair, and her face was delicate, as though sculpted out of some fine stone. Definitely Alcyrian. But when she spoke in our language, she spoke quite fluently. "I can't," she said. "I don't dare. I'm the only one with a spare key. He'll know it was me."

"Anya, please," said Mr. Harcourt. "Have some decency. This young man has done nothing wrong." He lowered his voice coaxingly. "You aren't like the rest of them; you aren't a true Imperialist. You're a good young woman at heart."

"What do you know about me?" Her anger erupted unexpectedly. "Five days I've been on this island. You don't even understand what's happening. You think you can resist? You don't know what Mr. Bercy is like. If he tells you to do something, you do it. Otherwise he'll make sure your life isn't worth living."

"Please, Anya," pleaded Mr. Harcourt. "I'll take the blame. I just can't stand to see this poor young man sitting here waiting for the secret police to arrive. You remember what happened last time."

"Listen, I don't want anyone to take the blame," I protested. But my protest was half-hearted, because mostly I just wanted to get away. Fear like I had never felt had gripped me when Mr. Harcourt mentioned the secret police. Anselm's distant world of terror and disappearance had overtaken the island—it was here.

Meanwhile, the rain went on, beating down like a drumroll, shaking the branches of the cypress trees. Thunder split the sky. I could not think. Mr. Harcourt looked at the girl, and she looked at the floor.

"Very well," she said eventually, in no more than a whisper. "I'll do it."

As she turned, I gripped her arm. "Thank you," I said.

The girl narrowed her amber eyes. I could tell from the way she did it that she half recognised me too. But there was no time to ask. Already she was ushering me down a corridor to the door of an office. Her hands shook on the key.

"Listen," I said. "I don't want you to get into bad trouble. If it's too risky—"

"No," the girl said, very steadily. "I've said I'll help you."

The office was full of the big Imperialist man's presence—a great military overcoat on the back of the chair, a handgun on the desk, an Imperialist poster covering the wall. On the desk itself were stacks of papers, and I saw my own name—*Isak Karol*—on the front of an envelope at the top of the pile. In fact, there were several carbon copies of the same envelope, all stamped with red ink.

Without thinking, I did something very stupid—I grabbed one of the envelopes and shoved it under my jacket. I'd come here for my papers, and I'd take them all the same. The girl was too preoccupied with getting the window open; she had not seen. "Quickly, quickly," she kept saying. Everything was heightened in my fear. As the girl struggled with the glass, I saw that on her neck, where her hair was pulled back into a gold-coloured clip, was a mark like a thumbprint, a thumb-shaped bruise.

"Here," I said. "Let me."

I got the window open and one leg through it before we heard a sound that neither of us could mistake: the sweep of tires on the gritty road at the front of the building. The girl pushed me over the windowsill and out onto the rusted fire escape, which creaked in the high wind. The rain hit me full in the face. "Thank you," I called. But she vanished behind the window and closed it with a bang. The fire escape was not a proper staircase; I doubted anyone had used it for years. It swung violently in the storm. The steps were eaten away and the railing had broken off altogether. I didn't dare to climb down it. All I could do was cling to the outside of the building and hope that Mr. Bercy didn't know this was a way out. I hunched down under the level of the windowsill and made myself as small as I could, praying for the infernal storm to stop.

He was inside the main office now. From behind the door, a voice called, quite clearly, "Anya!"

"Yes, Father?"

His daughter? I pressed myself against the wall and waited. The incriminating papers weighed heavily against my stomach. I heard, quite clearly, the clicking of the girl's heeled shoes. Then came her father's voice, startlingly clear.

"Anya, where's that boy? The one I told to wait here."

"I don't know."

"I let him out the front door." It was Mr. Harcourt, his voice quavery but strong. "I took Miss Anya's keys from the door of her office. He said he had to leave very urgently, so I let him go."

Inwardly, I cursed the old man for his bravery. *If there is a God*, I thought, *don't let anything happen to them because of me.*

Mr. Bercy's anger erupted in all directions and both languages. "I left that door locked! Harcourt, you had no right to let him out! And Anya"—this in Alcyrian—"didn't I tell you not to leave those bloody keys in the door, time and again? They're all the same, these damn islanders—they can't be trusted!"

"I didn't realise that you wanted him kept here," lied Mr. Harcourt mildly, in our own language. "I thought you had merely locked the door by mistake."

"You did, did you? You mindless old bastard! Get back to the floor."

"Father," said the girl. "Leave him."

Mr. Bercy's anger descended on his daughter. The words came so fast that I could only make out fragments: "Important breakthrough in the last descendant case—chance for promotion—look what you'll cost me—ungrateful cow—stupid bitch—"

"Please, sir—you're being unreasonable." The old man again, very gently. "You're frightening this poor daughter of yours."

All at once, Mr. Bercy's voice was cool and dangerous. "Harcourt, go and wash the floor of the front office as I have been asking you to do all day, or I'll make you clean it with your tongue. Do you hear?"

Now only the voices of the girl and her father remained. I could hear her sobbing quietly, just feet from where I cowered.

"Anya," said Mr. Bercy. "If you aren't absolutely loyal, then I will"—then a phrase I could not work out, yelled—"*rendert da sein vitas ein enfier vivend!*"

Slowly, I pieced it together, word by word: *make of your life a living hell.*

Something about this man made me shudder, worse than the chill rain sluicing down my neck and the three-floor drop beneath me.

"Is that completely clear? Or do I have to make it clearer?"

I willed the girl to say yes, because I didn't like the tone his voice had taken.

"Yes," she said. "It's clear."

"Good. Now I'll have to sort out this damned mess—"

"It's clear, Father," Anya interrupted, "but I don't think what you're doing is right."

"What was that?"

Louder: "I don't think what you're doing is right."

Her father waited. Then I heard a sudden scream, which made me almost lose my hold on the windowsill.

"Please, Father, don't. No!"

Something incomprehensible, and a thud. The girl was weeping. The thuds came quicker and quicker, followed by muffled sobs, as if the girl didn't dare cry out loud. It was the saddest noise in the world. I could have pushed the window up—could have tried to stop him—but horror and fear kept me locked to the precarious step where I crouched, listening to every thud.

"I don't have anything else to say to you, Antonia," called Mr. Bercy as his boots thundered back along the corridor and down the stairs. "Get up and wash your face. Then make me some coffee. I'll be back in ten minutes."

Very quietly, I raised my head. As I did it, the window opened slowly, and the girl appeared. She was in a bad way. A line of blood ran down the side of her face, and she clutched her right arm stiffly to her.

"I thought you'd gone," she said, very faintly.

"I'm sorry. I couldn't get down the fire escape in this storm. What I just heard . . ."

The girl shook her head. Blood dripped from her hair and onto my wrist.

"Are you badly hurt?" I said. "I'm sorry. I wish to God I'd never come here."

"Help me," she said, very stiffly because of her injured face. "You aren't the only one who needs to get away from here. Help me get down the stairs, now, before he comes back."

"It isn't safe. We can't climb down in this storm."

"I don't care. Help me."

"Take my arm."

She gripped my wrist and climbed awkwardly out the window. The fire escape was still swaying. We got down, in the end, by crawling backwards down the steps on our hands and knees. At the bottom, she straightened her shawl and turned away.

"Thank you," she said. "Now make sure you get away from here, while he's still distracted. Goodbye."

"And what about you? Where are you going? He'll be after you in a minute."

She stumbled away from me, ignoring my questions.

"Let me help you," I said. "You can hardly walk. At least let me help you, after what you've done to help me."

She limped into one of the alleyways that must lead to the docks. I followed. "Where are you going?"

"I need to get away from him. Right away this time. I need to leave. I've tried before, but I always went back. Not this time. Leave me—I can manage."

The girl was shuddering in the rain.

"Here," I said, taking off my overcoat and draping it over her shoulders. "I'll help you. I'll take you wherever you want to go."

"You don't have to do anything for me." She held herself as straight and tall as she could. With her good hand, she plucked off the overcoat and returned it.

"Is it true you've been on the island for only five days?"

She nodded, then winced and clutched her shoulder.

"You'll need help. You don't even have a coat. You're Alcyrian. Where are you going to go, with resistance starting everywhere along the coast? You think people will help you? You're completely on your own on this island."

The girl went on shuddering, whether from cold or pain I could not tell.

"Please let me help you," I said.

"You're Malonian. We're not even supposed to associate with each other."

"For God's sake, you can barely walk." That father of hers had badly frightened me and I wanted to be far away too, but

I could not abandon her here. "Stop arguing with me. We don't have time. He'll come after you once he knows you're gone. He's already after me."

I put one hand under her elbow, and she let me. Wincing, she began limping down the next alleyway towards the town. I went beside her, taking half her weight.

"I'm sorry," I tried again. "I had no idea—"

"He's the one who should be sorry, in this life or the next, and I hope he will be." She said it very simply. I admired her courage, this girl, even if she was an Imperialist's daughter.

"He's your father? You live with him?"

"I live with him and my aunt. They're both like that. I stay with them only because I have no choice. I'm no Imperialist."

"Where will you go now you're on your own?"

"Back to the mainland, where I come from."

"In this storm?" I knew enough about the sea to understand that the weather was too violent even for the Imperialists' great steamships. "No ship will cross—not even the big ships from Valacia. Look—you see? They've all come into the docks early."

The fishing boats were lying high up against the quays, with their storm moorings fixed.

"Then I'll find somewhere to stay until they do," said the girl. "I have money." She turned out her pockets awkwardly, holding her injured right arm high. A few cents fell out into the mud. At last, she succumbed to tears, wiping them angrily away. "Damn it," she said. "Damn it all—this island and my father. I hope they both go to hell."

"I can help you," I said. "I owe you that much. I'll take you somewhere your father can't find you, and I'll try to help you get to the mainland. The ships won't be crossing now—I've lived all my life in a fishing town, and I know that much—but maybe in a few days you can leave from a smaller place. New Maron, where I come from."

"All right. I don't see what else I can do." It was almost a whisper.

With the precious papers inside my jacket and my arm about the girl's shoulders, I led her down towards the town. In the storm, the alleys and streets were very dark. The girl's breath came in light gasps that were not quite sobs, because after those few proud tears she had got control of herself again. There was something tough as knives about her, this Alcyrian girl. We went—half limping, half walking—along the coast road. The rain had washed the worst of the blood from her face. I tried to smooth it from her hair, where it had congealed in damp tangles at the edges, but this was more difficult, and the girl wrestled away from me. I found a bruise on her forehead to match the one on the back of her neck. The girl looked up at me strangely. "What?" I said.

"Why are you being so kind?"

I didn't know, so I just shrugged and stopped smoothing her hair. There was no point; I couldn't get the blood off anyway.

The rain still came in torrents, and the wind made havoc of the trees and sent the waves flying up against the houses. It made our old coast road impassable for trucks, which meant that we left Valacia unobserved. The girl leaned heavily on me now, but when I asked if she wanted to rest, she shook her head.

As we entered the outskirts of New Maron, she stumbled and I had to take almost all her weight to stop her from falling altogether. "We're almost there," I said. "This is it."

"I haven't even heard of New Maron," she said hopelessly. "What kind of a place is it?"

"It's an old fishing town. There isn't much here, but we'll find somewhere for you to stay until you can get to the mainland." I didn't see where, in this gossipy little place where I had grown up. Then I thought of my grandfather's apartment, standing empty.

"What?" said the girl. "What is it?"

I didn't know if I wanted to take her there. Every stone of its walls, every patch of flooring, was sacred to me because it was his. This girl was a stranger. But I felt, somehow, that she was my responsibility now. "I know a place you can stay," I said at last. "Just for tonight. It's my grandfather's apartment. You'll be safer there than if I take you to someone in the town."

The girl seemed uncertain.

"It's all right," I said. "My grandfather isn't there. He died a few weeks ago, so the place is just empty."

She didn't look reassured by that, but I couldn't see what else to do. Could I risk sheltering this Alcyrian girl under my parents' roof? Probably not. Mrs. Winter was one of the worst gossips in our town, and she surveyed everyone's comings and goings on our street like a prison guard. No one in this town would have any sympathy for an Alcyrian. I wasn't even certain why I had.

The streetlamps had been lit early in the storm. By their light, I saw that the girl's face was very grey. "It's just up this side street," I said. "Come on."

In the pouring rain, we reached the tobacconist's shop, climbed the stairs and got through my grandfather's door. In the sudden quiet, I looked at her and she at me. Again, that sudden flash of recognition, as sharp as the lightning outside. I didn't know what was happening, but I could tell that it was something very strange.

I know you, I thought. *I've met you before. But how?*

IV

❦ LOVE ❧

30

*T*he girl stood in the doorway, shivering, waiting for me to invite her into the apartment properly. I guessed that she could tell from the way I crossed the floorboards that to me it was a sacred place.

"Come inside," I said. "You'll be safe here. The apartment hasn't been put up for sale yet. No one comes in and out. This is where I grew up, partly. My grandfather's old place."

Outside, the storm crashed. While she looked the other way, I shoved the soggy envelope I had stolen from her father's office into the writing desk. I would have to deal with that later.

I puffed up the sofa cushions as best I could. "Sit here. I'll try and get the water connected again, and bring a cloth for you to wash with."

The girl, painfully, sat. I found the main water tap under the kitchen sink and turned it back on. I filled a bowl with water and gathered the cleanest of the rags my grandfather kept under the sink. Anya was sitting very still on the edge of the sofa when I came back.

"Do you want me to help you?" I said. "I don't mind."

"I'll do it myself."

I got the little chipped mirror from the bathroom. She positioned herself in front of it and wiped the blood carefully out of the edge of her hair with firm strokes, then bandaged her arm with one of the rags. She did all this without wincing. Because she would not let me help, I checked the gas fire instead and with a couple of kicks got it working.

"You'll be all right here," I said. "Don't go anywhere in this storm. Stay overnight. Since the invasion—I mean, since the agreement with the Imperialists—nobody leaves their houses after dark."

"When will the ships be going tomorrow?" She huddled close to the fire in her wet clothes. "I need to leave as soon as I can."

"You can't do anything about the sea. That's the way it is on this island. If it's too rough to make the crossing, you have to wait. It might be a week."

"A *week*?" She looked crestfallen, as if she had expected the storm to clear in a few hours.

"Look," I said. "If you stay here, in this apartment, I promise you'll be all right. No one has seen us come in, and the neighbours think it's standing empty."

She hesitated, then said, "All right. Thank you."

I sat down a little way off from her on the sofa. She let me, but she still held herself very tall and proud. "How do you speak our language so well?" I asked her.

The girl relaxed her shoulders just a little. "I grew up in Anshelle—Angel City," she said. "I lived there with my mother before she died. Until it was invaded, I spoke your language every day."

"Angel City?" I said, excitement getting the better of me. "Then you'll know of the singer Anastasia Fortuna. I used to listen to her music here in this apartment, with my grandfather, on summer nights. I loved that music."

All at once, this unbreakable girl started to cry. Great tears welled out of her eyes and made black streaks down her face.

"I'm sorry!" I said, horrified. I jumped from the sofa and hovered over her, trying to think of some way to halt her crying. "I don't know what I've said. I really am sorry. Of course, you must miss your home. Is it that?"

The girl turned her face away. "I'm being stupid," she replied. "I'm being so damn stupid."

I tried to reach for her arm, but she gave a little gasp and jerked it away. So instead I knelt unhappily on the floorboards while she cried and would not look at me.

Eventually, when she had regained possession of herself, she said, "Don't you need to go home to your family?"

It was already half past six, and I knew my parents would be anxious. "I'll come back later this evening," I said. "I'll bring a blanket for the bed. It gets chilly in this apartment in weather like this. The damp gets into you; that's what my grandfather used to say. I'll bring you food. Whatever you need."

The girl hunched closer to the fire. There seemed nothing to do to make her any happier, so I left.

When I got back, my mother was out in the street in the pouring rain. As I approached, she came splashing down the road to meet me.

"Harlan!" she said. "Where on earth have you been?"

"Just at Grandfather's."

"I checked there."

"I've only been there half an hour. I'm sorry, Mama—I didn't know you'd worry."

"How could I not worry? Oh, Harlan!" She hugged me to her. "I get so worried about you now, in the middle of this fighting, that's all. Come in out of the rain. We'll tell your father—he's been searching too."

All through dinner, I kept thinking of that Alcyrian girl alone in my grandfather's apartment with the storm growling around the windows. As soon as I could, I pushed back my plate and said, "I think I'll go to Grandfather's again tonight."

My mother took my hand. "Not again. I'd rather have you here with us. If there's any trouble in the town, I want you close by. What if we can't reach you?"

"I'm only two streets away."

My mother, with her glance, said no.

"I'll be careful. I promise. I'll go straight there and stay inside the apartment."

She looked at my father for support. He nodded. "Let him,"

he said. "If he wants to sleep there, I see no harm, as long as he goes now, while it's still light."

I glanced a silent thanks at my father, put on my overcoat and left. I had wanted to take food from the kitchen for Anya, but there was no chance with my mother hovering around me. Instead, I raided the back room of the shop for supplies—luckily my father kept bread and butter and tea for busy days when he did not have time to go up to the apartment and cook lunch—then I left by the side door and ran the two streets to my grandfather's apartment.

I let myself in quietly. Anya had fallen asleep in front of the gas fire. Her hair had dried thick and wavy, and she was lying peacefully, one arm around the sofa cushion and her hair spread out behind her in a trail as black as the soft darkness that was falling outside the window. She had little gold rings in her ears, which glinted in the orange light from the fire. The cut on her forehead had stopped bleeding. I knelt beside her quietly and wondered if she was badly enough injured to need a doctor. Then I decided against it. I had the uncomfortable feeling that it would not be very difficult for her father to find her if she showed her face. They all seemed to be in league with each other, the Imperialists. Better for her to lie low until she could get away.

Anya's clothes looked mostly dry, but she was still shivering a little in her sleep. I hadn't been able to get a blanket for her, but I remembered there was a threadbare one in the bedroom wardrobe and went to fetch it. When I laid it over her, she clutched at one edge with her good hand and murmured. Slowly, she was coming to the surface.

"It's all right," I said, so that she wouldn't be frightened. "It's only me—Isak Karol. Remember? The—the Malonian boy," I finished awkwardly.

Anya rubbed at her face and sat up. She looked at me for a long time, then said, very evenly, "You took some papers from my father's desk. I saw you. Why didn't you say anything about it?"

I didn't know what to say about it now. I sat back on my knees and looked at her.

"What did you want with them? Those were copies of papers that my father seized as part of what they call Operation Last Descendant. I know you took them, so there's no point lying."

"Operation what?" I said.

"Operation Last Descendant. It's a big manhunt that's been going on for years. A hunt for a Malonian family—the North family—who are supposed to be descended from an important royalist politician. They used to call him Aldebaran. That's what the red stamp on the envelope means." She studied me carefully. "Why did you take them? What have you got to do with that operation?"

I got up and went to the writing desk. The envelope was there, in just the same place. How could I tell her I had everything to do with it?

"I haven't touched it," she said. "But I saw you put it there."

I took out the envelope and examined the red stamp. *For the attention of Sgt. Daniros, Operation Last Descendant*, it read.

"Who's that?" I asked. "Sergeant Daniros?"

"He's chief of the operation. Believe me, you should be very careful, taking things like that. It's their most important operation of all."

I got a sick feeling in my stomach that nothing could quite dispel. What had my grandfather let me in for, bequeathing me those papers? "What do you mean, be very careful?"

She ignored my question. "Do you recognise these papers? Because if so, you're a relative of the family they're looking for. The North family. That's their name."

High in my chest my heart had begun a light, insistent drumming. I slit the soggy envelope open and pulled out what was inside. Another envelope. The words *To the baby* were written in narrow, sloping writing, yellowed with age. My skin prickled, the way it always did when I thought of Aldebaran. This was from him, for certain, the letter he had supposedly written to me before his death, before I was born. This was what I had been looking for.

I opened the second envelope. Out fell a stack of stapled papers. Copied pages from a book: *Poetical Works*, by Diamonn, our old national poet. "He must have left me the real book," I said. "But look—I've ended up with a copy." I flipped through the pages. *To my dear great-great-nephew* was inscribed on the first page.

There was another stapled stack of papers, larger pages this time, like writing paper. The date on top was *10 6 88*—six months before my birth—the very end of the old century. But the hope in me sank as soon as it had risen. I could not read the handwriting.

"This isn't Alcyrian, is it?" I said, putting it in front of her face.

"Of course not." She frowned. "That isn't even a language."

"What is it, then?"

"It's numbers. Look."

It was true. Though the handwriting looped and joined, what I had thought were words were really just sequences of numbers. *11143, 12735, 1826, 437 . . .*

The girl's interest was piqued, in spite of herself. She drew herself up onto the sofa and took the papers in both hands. "It's some kind of code, maybe."

"Be careful with them," I said; I couldn't help it.

"Don't worry." She studied the pages. "My father sometimes receives coded documents, and they look a lot like this. Like words, but made of figures. I can't believe I'm telling you all this. It would be enough to get me imprisoned. But I told you, I'm no Imperialist."

"I know," I said, and believed her.

I took the pages back from her and scanned through them. The next page was the same, and the next. But there was something more promising at the bottom of the pile. A map, drawn in spidery black lines, with little stars marked on it at intervals. No explanation of what the stars might mean, but the map was of our country. This too was stamped with the same words.

"Operation Last Descendant," I said. For seventeen and a half years, I'd been Aldebaran's youngest descendant, the last to be born before the old world ceased to exist. I thought of the strange man trying to snatch me as a baby, when we were fleeing the city. I thought of the way the house we had once lived in had had all its windows smashed and its rooms ransacked. I thought of Anselm's letters: *Keep Harlan safe*. And those old resistance men across the border, waiting for me, for a sign. I was afraid that in taking these papers, I had unleashed something from the past that I simply did not understand.

"What has all this got to do with you?" said Anya, putting her hand on my wrist.

It made me start. She had woken up from her sleep less distant, more human.

"I don't know if I can tell you," I said. With cool eyes, she regarded me. I still don't know what made me do it—the gaslight, maybe, and her cool touch on my wrist, and the altered world I now inhabited—but I decided to. "I'm a relative of that family," I said. "My real name's Harlan North. These papers are from my great-great-uncle, and he was that political man you talked about. Aldebaran, his name was."

Anya said nothing. She just kept hold of my wrist, and looked at me with wide and frightened eyes. I was half terrified myself.

"Is this true?" I asked. "That they're looking for me and my family? That they've got a whole secret operation about it? That they're tracking us down?"

"The trail went cold years ago. At least, that's what I gather from the way my father talks about it. Of course, they don't tell people like him, small-town censors, the truth. Listen, I don't want you to underestimate them. You seem like a good person. I'm no Imperialist, but I know what they can do. Don't tell anyone your real name, ever. Trust me. You shouldn't have told me just now."

"You're the only person."

For a moment longer she looked at me. Then she got to her feet carefully. I put all the papers back into their envelopes and hid them in my grandfather's writing desk.

It was too much to think about for now: that code, and the map, and the secret police hunting my family. "Listen," I said. "Don't worry about all this. It will be all right." I was telling myself, not her.

"What's in that bag?" Anya asked.

"Oh, this." I opened it up. "I've brought you some bread and butter and tea. It was all I could get, I'm afraid. I don't want anyone knowing you're here."

"That's fine. That's good." She smiled at me a little awkwardly. "Let's make some tea, and agree to keep each other's secrets." She put out her hand. I took it.

I rooted around in my grandfather's abandoned kitchen for the things we needed. While we were waiting for the water to boil, the girl said, "Anya isn't my real name either."

"No?" I said.

She shook her head. "It's just the name my father insists on calling me, because it sounds more Alcyrian. I've always hated it. My real name's Antonia."

My real name's Antonia, she said carelessly—and the streetlights dimmed and the room turned sideways like a ship in a storm and my small world fell apart and put itself back together again.

And I said, "Antonia?"

"What is it about the name Antonia?" she said, amused. "You say it like it's a curse word."

153

I knew I had to set myself to rights, because how could I explain what that name meant to me? *When I was growing up I dreamed about a girl called Antonia, and I've been searching for her half my life.* I shut my mouth and breathed in once. I said, "Oh, it's nothing in particular. I met someone with that name once."

She narrowed her amber eyes and appraised me. "Did you?" she said at last. "Well, I've lived in Angel City my whole life, so I can assure you it wasn't me."

"With who?" I said. "Until when?"

The girl laughed. "What is this—some kind of interrogation?"

"Sorry." I laughed too, to keep her company, because I could tell I was frightening her a little.

"No, no. I'll tell you. You talked about Anastasia Fortuna earlier. The truth is, she was my mother."

I had to bite down on my lip to stop myself from saying, *I know, I know. I know everything about you. I know your face, your voice, your laugh. I can sing a thousand Alcyrian tunes you played on your old guitar as your mother lay dying. I've seen you grow up; I've watched the twelve-year-old you cross the continent, weeping, your guitar case in hand. And the man who took you in, Victor Bercy, the small-town censor. Antonia, it's you.*

"That's interesting," I said instead. "Having Anastasia Fortuna as a mother."

"Interesting?" said Antonia. "Painful, mostly. All those lovers, all that waiting for her backstage at the theatre, those crowds of admirers. She died when I was twelve." She shivered, with a trace of the sorrow that had overwhelmed her earlier. "That's why I became so upset before. The way you mentioned her out of nowhere." She occupied herself with the tea, avoiding my eyes. "She wasn't always someone I agreed with, but she was so loving, and my God, how I loved her in return. Nothing like my father."

"We used to listen to Anastasia Fortuna on the radio," I offered. "My grandfather and I."

I must have been looking at her strangely, because she frowned and said, "What is it? Something more."

"Nothing. Nothing." Stupid! Why was I repeating it? I gulped my tea.

The storm raged on outside the window. Shamefully, I prayed it would continue raging and keep her here, rather than letting her go to the mainland, where I would never see her again. Wonder overcame me. I had found her. I had actually found her. Eight million people in the empire, and here was Antonia in my grandfather's apartment. It was a miracle—it meant something. But now that she was here, I didn't have the first idea what to do about it. I had always imagined that when I found her, she would recognise me too.

I could tell she felt awkward about staying under the same roof by the way she kept glancing at the narrow bed, so I left her and went back home. I told my mother and father I had decided against sleeping in Grandfather's apartment. They seemed to believe me—a strange mood had come over all of us since my grandfather's death. Turning over and over in my chilled sheets, I didn't sleep at all. I listened to the storm and tried to make sense of what had happened to me. How was she here? What did all this mean?

Around dawn, I fell into an uneasy sleep and all my dreams were of her.

31

*A*ntonia herself was asleep again when I arrived the next evening after work. Those first days, she seemed to be sleeping off the sickness of her father's house, barely surfacing at all. Through the half-open bedroom door I made out the curved shape of her under the blanket on the bed. I stood in the doorway, in a beam of rainy grey light. It seemed an intrusion to wake her, to go up to her where she lay and touch her or say her name. So I retreated from the door and left her. I arranged the groceries I had brought in the kitchen, and waited for her to wake up. And while I waited, I took out Aldebaran's papers.

The map was the only thing worth anything to me at the moment. What did the code and the book mean? I had read the works of Diamonn a hundred times. The map, at least, was clearer. It had been drawn by hand in ink. It showed our country, a rough hexagon. In the centre was the city where I had been born, marked not *Capital* but *Malonia City*, its old-century name. On the left, in the middle of the sea, was a long sliver labelled *Holy Island*. I could see other cities—Arkavitz in the far north and Angel City in the far south; Ositha and Bernitz in the east; Maron, the place for which our tiny fishing town was named; and West Ravina, that great grey port where a stranger had tried to steal me as a baby, and where Antonia had lived with her father in the dark house at the edge of the town.

The little stars, however, did not lie exactly on top of these cities. There was a star near to Arkavitz, and another in the immense expanse of countryside between Capital and Angel City. One of them was on Holy Island, but somewhere in the centre where I knew for a fact that there were only moors and marshes—land that people had once tried to farm and given up on. Perhaps that marked the place where my great-great-uncle had grown up. I did not know.

Another star was drawn on Capital. Next to this one, Aldebaran had made an enlargement in a rough circle and sketched out a network of spidery streets. The star became three. One of them fell on a place called New Square. In the centre was marked *fountain* and to the left, *church dome*. Some kind of directions, perhaps, but to what? Someone's house? Some place full of miracles? The second star fell on what looked like the castle, and the third on a place called Royal Gardens.

My stomach gave a great leap. Maybe these stars marked other people with powers, others who had the strangeness about them that I had. People who might lead the resistance to victory. But then, why were the stars marked so precisely? Wouldn't these people have moved in the eighteen war-torn years since my great-great-uncle had drawn the map? And anyway, wasn't I the only one left?

I turned the map over and examined the back of it. There was nothing to explain what the stars—or indeed the map itself—might mean. That must be in the coded document, I realised with a jolt of disappointment. I had to work on that before any of these papers would be of use to me.

I began reading the numbers again. A code for sure, but I had no way of working it out. I turned the groceries out of their paper bag, found an old pencil and began experimenting, exchanging each number for a letter. But it gave no words. I could tell from the unpredictability of the pattern that there was something more complex here. I wished my mother had taught me mathematics along with the history and geography and poetry she had plied me with since infancy.

Antonia appeared in the doorway, her eyes still heavy with sleep. She pushed her unruly hair out of her face. "What are you doing?"

"Looking at this code."

She peered over my shoulder. She was still wary of coming too near to me, I noticed.

"I brought you groceries," I said. "They're in the kitchen."

She felt in her pockets, and I realised she was trying to find the money to pay me.

"No," I said. "Don't do that."

"Why are you being so kind to me?" she said.

I could have told her then. Instead, I said, "It's only a few old potatoes and beans."

She smiled, but her smile faded behind her bruises. "I feel so *helpless!*" she said, all at once. "Especially given what my people are doing to yours. I don't want to prey on your kindness like this, believe me. I'm ashamed to be here in your country at all."

"It's not your fault," I said.

"It isn't yours either."

I tried to make things better. "You're like an exile. Someone who has to go into hiding for a while. It's no different. My grandfather—Harold North—was a writer. He was exiled to Alcyria during the last war. When he was there he lived in a peasant village somewhere in the mountains. I don't know exactly where. The villagers kept my grandparents safe. They gave them food and homemade wine and hid them in a barn when patrols came over the border. All through the war, those villagers helped my grandfather. All without having read even one of his books. Every person in that village was illiterate, my grandfather said. When his wife, my grandmother, fell sick and died, they contributed money to pay for her burial. They sat up with him to keep vigil over the grave. But I'm not trying to say it was heroic, not exactly. Your people did for my grandfather what was right and proper. You deserve the same from me."

She said nothing. She just reached out and gripped my hand. It was like static, the touch of her, and she must have felt it too because she drew back and stirred herself and said, "I didn't mean to sleep so long. Did you find out about ships to the mainland?"

"They're not running until further notice. Not until the storms die down."

I hoped she couldn't hear the badly disguised gladness in my voice. She flung herself down in my grandfather's old armchair, and brooded at the rain-filled dark.

Within me, a kind of madness had taken hold. How do you fall into loving someone? Is it because of the persistent flick of her hair, her voice, the clear depths of her eyes? Is it through knowing her better? Both take a part. But also, it happens by degrees, without consciousness, so that you marvel at the distance you've travelled when you stop to look back.

Well, that's how this was.

32

I was not the only person hiding someone in those first chaotic days of the agreement with the Imperialists. I heard some gossip about it from Mrs. Winter across the road. But the people in hiding were mostly our own. Imperialists wanted to seize and interrogate everyone who they suspected of being homosexual or of following the old religions. Our own government let them. My mother, who believed devoutly in a higher power, might well have been guilty of the second crime, but they didn't care about people's homemade faiths. No, it was the former priests and nuns they were rounding up—people who had committed the crime of dedicating their lives to these religions. New Maron's former priest, Father Patrick, had moved into the baker's little back office and was lying low there, pretending he had left the town. The two women who ran the postal office had put their business up for sale and moved away in the middle of the night, without even saying goodbye. With that blind familiarity that comes from growing up in a place, I hadn't even known they were in love with each other.

I thought of my brother when I heard the news about the two women, Ruth and Susanna. I hated to think of soldiers arresting Anselm and Michael, dragging them out into the street, beating them with sticks. The idea had given both Jasmine and me nightmares when we were children, and my mother and father had to forbid us from listening to the news reports when the war on the mainland was particularly bad.

We still received letters from Anselm, but sporadically now, and sometimes they had clearly been ripped open. *Everyone is safe here*, he wrote. *Michael and I continue as before. The north is still free. I can't write much now that your situation is altered there. Be careful, that's all.* He had stopped addressing us by our real names.

I wished I could write to Anselm and ask him what to do about the Alcyrian girl I was hiding in Grandfather's old apartment, this girl whom I was now more than half in love with. What to do about these rumours of the last descendant, about the papers from Aldebaran, about the occupation of our island. Anselm would understand more than my mother or father, more than even Jasmine would have done. My grandfather would have understood too, of course. I even tried going to his grave and talking to him, but I got no sudden wisdom, and with the way our town was going I was afraid to talk too loudly.

After a week, the storms stopped. That fact troubled me as I climbed the stairs to my grandfather's apartment and softly called Antonia's name. I had started going there on the way to work too, on different pretences. That morning, she opened the door and smiled. "Harlan," she said. "I'm glad you're here earlier today. I have something to give you. I've got the money for a ticket to the mainland, and I'd like you to buy it for me if you don't mind—if it isn't too much trouble?" Into my hand, tremblingly, she pressed a stack of crown notes.

"Where did you get those?" I asked her. "You didn't go outside?"

"I went to the market." Before I could protest, she carried on. "It's all right. I went early, before many people were up. I sold my earrings."

Sure enough, the gold rings were no longer in her ears. "You did *what*?" I knew that I was angrier than I had a right to be, but I couldn't help it. "It's not all right at all! Antonia, anyone might

160

have seen you! Don't you realise the danger? Don't you realise you look like a foreigner?"

She shrugged. "It doesn't matter if anyone sees me. I'll be gone soon. Tomorrow you can buy me a ticket, and I'll be gone the next day. And look—" She counted out a few notes and handed them to me. "That's for all the groceries you've bought, and the water and the gas I've used, and—"

I flung the notes back in her face. "No!" I said. "I won't accept money! That's not why I'm helping you! Don't you understand anything? How could you go out into the town and risk your safety without telling me first?"

I stopped my ranting only because of the look on her face, the real fear in it. I remembered then the violence of her father, and all at once my anger left me.

"I don't have to answer to you," she said.

"I'm sorry," I said. "I didn't mean—"

She turned and went into the kitchen, slamming the notes down on the sideboard very firmly. "If you won't accept them, I'll leave them here anyway," she said. "My country and yours aren't friends. You've taken a risk to help me, and I appreciate it, but you don't owe me that help. I left you with very little choice, the state I was in."

"That's not why I'm helping you," I said again, as steadily as I could. "Not because I have to, or because it's the right thing to do."

"Then why?" she said, with the same quiet indignation I had heard in her father's office when she told him she didn't think he was right. The same indignation that had made her drag her mother's belongings from the bailiffs' trucks as a girl of eleven years old. "Maybe you'll finally tell me the truth," she said. "There's been something strange going on from the first day I met you. I'm not too stupid to see it."

Cornered, full of cold grief and rage at the thought of her leaving, I lied. "There's nothing strange going on," I told her. "I'm just worried about you."

161

"Look, I spoke more coldly than I meant to." She shook her head, as though to throw off the weight of our argument. "Don't take the money if you don't want to. You've been a good friend to me. I'll send you my address when I have one. Maybe we'll write to each other and meet again when all this madness of war is over. There."

"*Write* to each other? Is that all? Letters don't even get through anymore. I hardly hear from my brother. What if I never see you again?"

"What else do you want from me, Harlan?"

I didn't know. Or at least, I didn't know how to explain.

Antonia was full of her journey to the mainland; the hope of it buoyed her, made her steps light. I could do nothing but submit. I found and dusted off my grandfather's old carpetbag, and packed it with a few supplies for the journey.

With my stomach twisted and painful, I went to work.

At lunchtime, another of the clerks, Martin, called me to the window. "Look out there," he said. "That man has been hanging around all morning."

I looked through the grimy glass and saw a man in an overcoat with a cigarette, showing something to the sailors at the docks. Whatever he was showing was quite small—money or papers or more likely a picture. Some new person they wanted for questioning. I hoped it wasn't one of those poor women from the postal office, or the old priest, Father Patrick.

"Who is that man?" I asked. "Do you have any idea?"

"Alcyrian border police," said Martin. "They wear those overcoats. See the yellow stripes on the shoulders? Different from an ordinary soldier."

I saw, and was frightened.

The man went on hanging about the docks. At about half past four, he knocked on the door of the shipping office. Our new employer, Mr. Vincent, went to greet him, all smiles and wobbling eagerness. He found our visitor a chair and sent Martin running for a cup of coffee. Then he and the police officer held a whispered conference in their own language.

"Listen, boys," announced Mr. Vincent importantly when the man had gone. "I have here a list of people who are not to be allowed to leave the docks. This is our responsibility in the shipping office now. The borders of Holy Island are closing for a while so as to allow the new arrangement to settle down."

Since none of the others understood Alcyrian, I made a rough translation. A storm of questions broke out. Who were these people? How were we supposed to stop them? And what did it mean for us that the borders were closing? What about the promised ships full of grain and potatoes, which still had not come?

While the others were questioning poor blundering Mr. Vincent—who could not answer—I edged closer to the list and looked at it. *Denied passage at the ports: Wanted for questioning*, read the headline. The people in the pictures were, for the most part, clearly Malonians like me, with goldish skin. Only one was a pale-skinned, dark-haired Alcyrian, and with an awful certainty I knew it was Antonia, even before I made out her name beside it. *Antonia Fortuna Bercy*, it said, with a description: *Missing from her father's home, suspected abduction by Malonian militants. Her father and aunt are very anxious about her whereabouts.*

The note at the bottom of the page said that the list had been distributed to all the ports. As I left the office, I saw more police hanging around.

"Antonia!" I called as I ran up the stairs of my grandfather's apartment. Her carpetbag was by the door. "You can't leave yet," I said, catching hold of her arms. "You can't go."

"What is it?" She half smiled. "Catch your breath. What do you want to tell me?"

"The police came to our office; they brought round a list of people wanted by the government. Your picture is on it, and your name. It says that your father and aunt are looking for you. You're denied access at all the ports. You can't leave New Maron on a ship, not anymore."

As I spoke these words, the hope leached out of her, until she seemed very small in front of me. Then she flung herself on the sofa and wept bitterly into the dusty cushions.

I edged closer and sat beside her. Now I felt like the situation was my doing, somehow, because I had wished for it, and guilt knotted my stomach.

"Please, it's not so bad," I said. "At least we found out before you tried to board a ship." I tried to take her arm. "Look, all this will die down. Stay here a few more weeks, wait until your father loses interest—"

"He will never lose interest," cried Antonia. "He will never let me be. You don't know what he's like."

"You're safe here. Remember that."

"I should never have gone out of the house," she said, weeping. "You were right. Now I've exposed where I am, and I can't leave. You were right."

"Even if someone recognises you on the poster, no one knows which house you're staying in," I reasoned, "or even if you're staying at all. You might have just been passing through."

Antonia sat up. She rubbed the tears from her face. Despair never took hold of her for long; always, she mastered it.

"Stay here a while longer," I said. "Don't go near the windows. Stay inside. You're safe enough—there aren't any direct neighbours. No one knows you're living here. I'll protect you—I won't tell anyone. You'll have another chance to leave."

"But I'm putting you at risk, Harlan. I can't stand the thought of something happening to you, after all you've done. The longer I stay here, the worse it gets."

"We're not breaking any laws. This is about you and your father, not politics or nationality."

"Try explaining that to the secret police."

"I understand the risk," I said. "I'm willing to take it." I had never felt so brave or certain about anything.

That evening, at dinner, I tried to fight the elation growing in my heart, but my father must have noticed it. "Harlan," he said. "You're the happiest I've seen you since your grandfather died. Anyone would think it was because of a girl."

"What?" I made a feeble attempt to scoff. "No. Nothing like that."

My mother met his eyes and they gave each other a quick smile.

"There's no girl," I protested.

"Well," said my mother, flicking on the wireless, "I don't see what else there is to be happy about these days. But it's not our business to ask you."

The news on the radio was certainly bad. More arrests, more new laws and more armed fighting in the north of the island. But nothing so frightening as the first days of the cooperation with the Alcyrians. The island, it seemed, subdued and angry, was biding its time.

That night I slept badly again, Antonia in my head like the sweetest of nightmares, depriving me of rest.

33

*A*ntonia felt imprisoned in the apartment. I knew it, though she never said so. She spent her days sitting in front of the gas fire, unable even to look out because someone might catch a glimpse of her in the window. I brought her everything she needed, and several things she didn't. I smuggled second-hand clothes out of my father's shop, and spent my pay on groceries from the market. It

165

was true what they said—at last, new ships had come in and we ate better than we had eaten in a year. Each gift that was more than a necessity—a fresh peach or a scarf that matched her eyes—Antonia accepted with a response halfway between unease and pleasure.

As for me, I couldn't have stopped myself from buying them.

She had taken to watering the plants and feeding the grey cat, and although going out onto the terrace was risky in itself, I didn't have the heart to stop her. I knew that she invited the cat into the apartment during the day. He was her only company apart from me, and from me she still kept a wary distance.

One day, just as I was leaving for work, a man came into my father's shop carrying a battered and stringless guitar. My heart gave a strange kind of leap. People were selling things with desperation now that the Alcyrians showed no sign of leaving, funding their journeys south and east again, back the way we had all come.

"Can I sell this to you?" said the man. "I'll take any price for it. I'm going with my family back to the mainland, and I haven't got the last few cents for the fare. I need to leave today, right away."

"We don't take instruments," my father said, in the gentle voice he reserved for desperate customers like this. "I'm truly sorry to disappoint you."

The guitar had a bluish finish and great scrolls on its back, and I could tell it must once have been beautiful.

"I'll take it," I said. Without looking at my father, I counted out the three crowns the guitar was worth.

The man couldn't believe his good fortune. He grasped both our hands, then took off with his three crowns. My father was watching me thoughtfully.

"It's for someone else," I said. "For Martin, at work. He's always wanted to play the guitar."

"Really? That junior clerk? Mr. Wilson's boy?"

I understood my father's doubts. Martin's main interests were bare-knuckle fighting and drinking, and he wouldn't have known a guitar if someone had smacked him in the face with one.

"Mr. Wilson's boy," I said, wading deeper. "It's for Martin. He's always secretly wanted to play. He asked me to keep an eye out for a guitar."

"I didn't know the two of you were such good friends," said my father. "We'll fix it up after you get home from work."

That evening, instead of going straight to my grandfather's apartment, I ran home to the shop. I knew Antonia would be waiting, but I wanted to see about the guitar. It was lying in the back room on my father's woodworking table.

"It needs new strings," he said. "We can't do that here."

There was an instrument-maker on the next street, Mr. Romero. He had closed up his shop after the Alcyrians arrived and was still refusing to open it, but after I had knocked on his door for a long time, he answered. I explained about the guitar.

"All right," he said. "Come in quickly. I'll string it for you."

I waited while he examined it.

"These are sad times," he said, and the new strings hummed mournfully in reply. "It's not a bad instrument. It will have been beautiful, once."

To fix the rough woodwork would have cost me two crowns, and my money was running short, so I took the guitar back to the shop and did it myself with furniture varnish, laying the instrument across my father's workbench to dry. When I ran my fingers over the strings, it gave a soft thrumming.

My father regarded it critically. "Is that my best furniture varnish?"

"Yes. Do you mind?"

"I don't mind about the varnish, but I don't know whether the guitar does. Will it still sound right after that treatment? Isn't there something special for instruments?"

I shrugged. "We'll see." The truth was, the three crowns had cleaned me out. It was furniture varnish or nothing, and I wanted the guitar to look its best.

I couldn't wait the two days it would take for the varnish to dry properly. That same evening, while the instrument was still sticky, I lifted it carefully and took it to Antonia. I felt like some awkward suitor in a book, grasping the guitar by the neck with clammy hands and proffering it the way an old-fashioned gentleman would a bouquet of flowers. I attracted a couple of curious glances, but I didn't care. Eagerness had made me incautious.

When I opened the door to the apartment, Antonia was standing to the side of the window, behind the curtain, watching the ships come in and out of the docks. A light rain was falling, giving the town a misty glow as dusk fell. She turned as I came in.

"Where have you been?" she said. "I expected you at six, like normal. I was worried that something was wrong."

Then she saw the guitar. She came towards me, softly, dreamingly.

"Harlan?" she said. "What's this?"

"A present." My voice came out cracked and feeble, like a boy's. I cleared my throat and tried again: "It's a present for you, Antonia."

"A guitar." She reached out her hands in wonder. "I haven't had a guitar since my aunt snapped my old one in two."

"Careful! The varnish is still wet."

Antonia took the guitar and held it gingerly in her hands. "My aunt destroyed my old guitar," she said, still in that same dreaming voice, "and it was burnt with the firewood, and after that no one cared enough about me to buy me another."

"My books were all burned," I said. "They were my most precious possessions. If someone gave me another book, I think

I'd find it the most precious gift in the world. For you, a guitar must be the same. That's what I thought, anyway."

Antonia tentatively touched the strings.

"Let's put it close to the fire," I suggested. "It'll dry like that. Just not too close, so the wood doesn't warp."

I laid the guitar across the fender. When I straightened, Antonia was watching me with a look which made me unable to meet her eyes properly. But then the guitar let out a few twanging notes as she brushed the strings, and I realised the fool I had been. "How can you play a guitar," I said, "when you're supposed to be in hiding? How can you risk making the noise?"

"Bring me rags—we'll muffle it."

Still, I was doubtful. Antonia, carefully, tore up the rags from under the sink and stuffed them into the guitar until its tone was deadened, an underwater noise. "Go outside the door and listen," she said. I listened breathlessly. I heard a light twanging. But as I descended the stairs, the noise vanished, swallowed in the noise of the town. No sound. It was safe after all.

When I came back into the apartment, without warning, Antonia threw her arms around me. She clung to me, and in a confusion of arms and legs, we were on the sofa, kissing each other and holding each other so tightly, so fiercely, that I never wanted to let her go.

Antonia broke away all at once and said, "What am I doing? No, Harlan. No."

"What's wrong?"

"This is. Stop it."

"I'm sorry," I said. "I'm sorry."

"I think it's better if you go home."

I tried to approach her, but she wouldn't let me.

I didn't know what to do, so I left and shut the door. But I stood a long time on the terrace, my thoughts disordered. Inside the apartment, after a very long time, I heard Antonia's footsteps,

169

then the soft shivering thrum of the guitar strings. Very quietly, she plucked each string in turn, adjusting its pitch. Then a few twanging notes came to me faintly, so quiet that they were almost imagined, and not quite in tune with each other. Again, she adjusted the strings.

The real tune began, distant and silvery, a waterfall of notes. The music that escaped from my grandfather's old apartment, in this back street in the middle of nowhere, made the place the centre of the universe. As I listened, the song spoke to me of a land far away, of the place our country had once been. It was "I Would Follow the One I Love," but it was also a song that I had never heard before. Hearing her play it made everything new.

It was a long time before I could drag myself away. Insistently, a small voice was telling me, over and over, *She'll have to love you now.*

"Did Martin like his guitar?" asked my father, as I let myself back into the shop.

"What?" I said. "Martin?"

"Martin." My father grinned, very pleased with himself about something. "His guitar."

"Oh, yes. He said he's going to take it home and practise this evening."

My father looked at me, still half amused. "Sometimes I think you're in another world entirely these days, Harlan."

34

*W*hen I got to the apartment the next day, I could sense something was wrong. Antonia was sitting on the edge of the sofa, her arms folded. Because of her bad arm, she did it stiffly. The guitar lay before the fire, still drying, untouched.

"I never told you I could play the guitar," she said very quietly.

"What?"

"I never told you anything about the guitar. So how did you know to bring me one?"

My stomach went cold. She was right. I knew about the guitar only from my dream.

"I never said anything to you about my aunt breaking my guitar, not until yesterday. You bought me one without knowing that I used to play it."

The only way out of this difficulty was to lie. "You did, Antonia. You told me you played when you lived with your mother. You must have forgotten."

"No," she said quietly. "I didn't. I'm quite sure."

"How else would I have known?"

Her silence asked the same question.

After that day, there was a distance between us. That clumsy kiss and the mistrust that now possessed her were the cause. I still visited every evening, but she avoided my glances and kept a foot or two away from me, so that I felt we were playing some awkward game whose rules I didn't understand. She played the guitar I had brought her, sometimes, but only when she thought I was out of earshot.

Just once, late in September, I heard her singing as I climbed the stairs. Not singing, exactly, but a gentle hum over the notes of the instrument. The sound made my spine tremble. That humming was so beautiful that it made the rest of the world— New Maron and the incessant rain and the sea and the ships and the hills—look like a grey photograph from a newspaper, bleak and uninspired. It was also dangerous. The notes of the guitar were too fragile to be heard at the bottom of the stairs, but the singing carried.

I found myself sitting on the other side of the closed apart-ment door. I sat there so long the mangy grey cat crept over, curled up by my feet and went to sleep. In my head I could see her clearly: her hair with its rich black and brown notes falling over the guitar strings, her eyes half closed to concentrate better. When the song ended, I remained where I was. Then I heard the guitar set down with a soft thrum. Antonia's footsteps approached. I dragged myself up off the step, too late. She didn't seem startled to see me when she opened the door. Her eyes travelled over my face quite calmly.

"How long have you been sitting there?" she said at last.

"Not long."

"Just sitting there, listening to me play?"

"No, not exactly."

"Come in."

"You shouldn't sing. It carries." I came in, as awkward as a visitor in the home that had once been mine. I felt too large for its rooms.

"I don't sing."

"What does that mean?"

"It means just what it means. I don't. I haven't. Not ever in my life. And I don't intend to."

"I heard you sing just now."

Antonia brushed a pretend speck of dust off the guitar's varnish. I tried to think of something to say to cut short the silence. Why were things getting more and more difficult, the more attached I became?

Eventually I said, "Well, then," and went to the kitchen to put away the groceries I had brought.

As I opened the cupboards, I felt the tremor in my hands. I seemed to be permanently on edge these days, as we had been on the day the Alcyrians crossed our border. At night I barely slept, and by day my head felt strange and insubstantial.

Antonia was leaning in the doorway. "Harlan," she said. "Stop that a minute."

"Stop what?"

"Put those down. Leave them. Look at me."

I did as she said.

"The fact is, you've been very kind to me. I like you a good deal. You're one of the best people I know. Maybe even the best. And I'm staying here in your apartment, and it's only natural that, spending so much time together, we might start to—I don't know—believe we were falling in love. We might get confused."

I looked down at the floor.

"It's better that I'm direct with you," she said, "without any pretence. Yes?"

I felt the blood surging behind my eardrums. "Yes."

"You act as if you're falling in love with me. That's how you act. Don't deny it. Bringing me the guitar. All these presents."

I ran my hand over the back of my hair, just as my father always did when he had no words and wanted time to think. I wondered what my grandfather would have told me to do, and settled at last for the truth.

"It's not just that," I said. "There's more to it."

"I knew there was something. Tell me."

"Since I was a little boy," I said, "I've had strange dreams and memories. I used to tell my family, but they reacted . . . badly, so I've kept it a secret since then. You know how it is. No one believes in powers anymore."

"Go on." It was a mark of Antonia's wisdom that she didn't panic there and then, just listened.

"I'm not sure how you'll take it."

"I'll just listen, first of all," she said. "And then I'll make up my mind."

"I can remember the time before I was born," I went on. "I mean to say, I actually *remember* it. I know it's crazy, but I can remember what it sounded like to be inside my mother's womb—a kind of surging noise, like a howling wind. I can't believe I'm telling you this. It's true, but it's crazy at the same time. I've never told anyone."

Antonia sat down. "Tell me," she said.

"You've never met my sister, Jasmine, but we used to be close. Very close. And I've always been able to . . . I don't know . . . share her memories."

"What do you mean by that?"

I forged on blindly. "It's hard to explain, but any time she was angry or upset, any particularly dark or bright memory, I remember too. Like the time my father went away and left them in the city. I can see it through Jasmine's eyes, in my own mind. I can see her grabbing hold of the suitcase, crying, pleading with him not to go. Only it's like her hands are my hands—like I'm seeing it from her eyes. That was two full months before I was born, but I remember the hollow way Jasmine felt. I remember my mother, looking down on her. She was saying things: 'Jas, don't cry. Jas, come back.'"

Antonia said nothing, but from the way her eyes were fixed on me I could tell she understood what I was saying. She understood it had something to do with Aldebaran and Operation Last Descendant. She understood a lot of things, Antonia.

"Then, when I was older, I started to have strange dreams," I said. "First, I dreamed about my grandfather. He didn't always live with us. He was in exile for years. Remember I told you? Well, when he found us again, I recognised him even though I'd never met him before. I was just a tiny baby, but I recognised him. And I dreamed about my brother. I dreamed about people I didn't know too. The former king. Rigel, Aldebaran's apprentice. And, after I heard her on the radio, I dreamed about Anastasia Fortuna too."

"My mother?" Antonia put a hand to the side of her face as if she were in pain. "How could you dream about her? You didn't even know her."

"These dreams aren't like ordinary dreams. I don't understand why myself, but I don't even have to have met the people I dream about. And these dreams feel like real life, in proper colour, not in mixed-up colour and darkness like normal dreams are. They happen as though I'm living them. As though the things happening are really happening to me. As though I can travel across the world and inhabit other lives at will, without leaving Holy Island."

Antonia shook her head. She went on shaking it. I knew, now that I had come this far, that there was nothing to do but go on.

"You were the main point of these dreams, Antonia," I confessed. "I mean, you were at the centre of them, not your mother. Like someone was trying to fix you in my memory. Maybe it was Aldebaran—some magic. Maybe someone wanted me to have some kind of map, to know when I met you at last that I had to rescue you from your father. I know all kinds of things about you. I know that you grew up poor, but then your mother made a fortune. I know she sang for government officials in a theatre in the open air beside the sea. I know that you were cross when she had to rehearse for the radio performance. She was wearing a pink shawl. You used to sit beside a fountain filled with big orange fish with black lines along their backs."

"My God," said Antonia. "My God. How do you know these things?"

"I don't know how." I shook my head, marvelling at it myself now that it was in the open between us. "I'm the only person I've ever heard of who can dream like this. Look, it's better that I tell you, even if you don't want anything more to do with me. It's better that I tell you the truth." I took hold of my courage and said what I had been working up to all along. "You see, Antonia, it's not that I'm falling in love with you. It's that I was in love with you when I first met you. It's like I'm *condemned* to love you. Like I always have. Like I was supposed to."

She looked at me as if I was some kind of stranger. Eventually she said, "Leave me alone for a while. I'm not angry, but I need to think."

I didn't have to be told more than once. I went.

35

I waited three days for her to think. On the fourth day, I could stand it no longer and went back to my grandfather's apartment. The door opened at my knock. Antonia gestured me inside.

"Harlan," she said, all in a rush, "I've been thinking a good deal. Let me say what I have to, with no interruptions, so that I say it right."

I nodded and waited in the doorway, hope and despair fighting within me.

"I'll admit that I was frightened," said Antonia. "A bit, anyway. I've never met anyone with powers before. I didn't even believe that they existed. But that was wrong of me. I think what you have is a kind of . . . I don't know, a gift. And you should be developing it, not hiding it away. If you knew these things about me without ever having met me, then who knows what else you might be able to do? You might be able to see visions. Important things, which might do some good. All this last descendant business—Harlan, it might all be true after all."

"You think it's a gift?" I said, overcome with wonder. No one, not even my grandfather, had talked about my powers like that before.

"You're the only person I know of—the only person left, maybe—with powers. Maybe the Malonian resistance are right. You might be the answer to"—she shrugged—"all sorts of things."

"But it isn't real powers. I don't see how my dreams can achieve anything."

"Harlan, is there anything else you can do? Can you move

objects, like the great ones used to? Can you turn the pages of a book or extinguish a gas flame?"

"No," I said. "I've never been able to do anything like that. My father and my sister could do those things, but their powers went away."

"Everyone's powers died out. That's what they say, anyway. But somehow not yours." She was staring at me more intently than she ever had. "You're special, Harlan. You're unique. When everyone else's powers went, yours remained."

I didn't exactly like the way she was looking at me. "Antonia," I said, "I'm not some circus curiosity. I'm still just my ordinary self."

"I know you are. I didn't mean it like that." Her eyes turned soft then. "But someone has to tell you to take this gift seriously. Not to just let it die away."

I shrugged. "My family always thought that would be better."

"But don't you see? Your powers may be the only supernatural thing we have left in this modern world of radio communications and electric light and tanks and motorcars. They may be something very precious—and not just to this little island. Do you understand what I'm saying?"

I thought of the words my great-great-uncle had written, just before I was born—words my sister had repeated to me before she too forgot them: *Magic is dying, and a time will come when no one remembers the old ways. I name my last descendant as your hope in times of trouble, a very certain help in the darkness of the road.*

I repeated these words to Antonia.

"What if these are the times of trouble?" she said, a strange light in her eyes. "What if you're the very certain help? You and your strange dreams. Now that you've told me, I'll help you, Harlan. The two of us can figure this out between us."

"Why would you do that? It's a punishable offence to even talk about supernatural powers in your country."

She looked at the floorboards. After a while, she said, "Because I'm falling in love with you too. I wish it wasn't true, but there it is."

A tear ran down her face.

"Hey, Antonia. Please don't cry. How is that a sad thing?"

"It is," she said. "Of course it is. Because nothing can ever come of it."

I reached for her hand, but she twisted hers and caught my wrist so that we were touching only through my shirt, with no warmth.

"We can't be in love," she said firmly, "unless you want to be sent to some prison camp. That's final."

It was true. The agreement between our two countries was that we would have nothing to do with each other. My heart felt a real pain. "But maybe—"

"You could end up sentenced to death—it's happened on the mainland. Just after I arrived in West Ravina, I saw an Alcyrian woman who was the lover of a Malonian resistance fighter. They shaved her head and paraded her through the streets and hanged the man she was in love with."

I moved closer to her. "I'd never let that happen to you."

"How would you stop it exactly? What would you do, supposing we became lovers, and the secret police caught us?"

I had no answer to that.

She stayed where she was for a moment, and I felt her breath hot on my ear. Then she moved away.

"You know more about me than any living person," she said, "and I'm the only one who really knows everything about you. We can't be together, and that's final. But their laws can't stop us from being closer than family, in some ways, in the end."

What she said was unbearably sad. Even so, walking home that night, I felt that I was walking through a dream. She loved me. I had found Antonia, and she loved me back.

———

I had never thought myself in love before. Still, there had been other girls. The first girlfriend I had was a strong-willed former classmate called Rosanna, who worked in the bar down by the harbour where a crowd of us went after work on Friday evenings.

Rosanna had made eyes at me across the bar. I was flattered and vaguely surprised by her interest at first, then impressed by her persistence. Eventually I went up and spoke to her, and she promptly claimed me for her property. Every night from that point forward, she would take me to the back room behind the counter and kiss me urgently until a customer called from the main room and she had to return to work. Martin and the other clerks always smirked and sniggered when I returned to the table.

One night, the rain was heavy, and Rosanna invited me up to her family's apartment over the bar to wait for the storm to stop. Her mother and father were away visiting a relative. Once there, Rosanna lost no time. She led me firmly to her bedroom—a musty pink room which smelled of roses and wax candles—pushed me onto the bed, and proceeded to take off my clothes with all the romance of a nurse stripping an elderly patient. I had nothing to do but acquiesce.

Rosanna was never tender or demonstrative. On those rare nights I spent with her, she would ignore me while she applied night cream and brushed the tangles out of her hair, pay me her brief attentions, then throw me out shortly before twelve. Those minutes while she brushed her hair were when I felt the greatest tenderness for her, knowing that I was about to be dismissed. In the light of the gas lamp, she did look very pretty. Her pale gold hair fell halfway down her back, and under it her body curved beautifully.

"Rosanna," I ventured once, feeling I ought to say something to mark this moment, "I love you."

She turned. The hairbrush lodged in her hair and dangled absurdly. "No, you don't, you stupid boy," she said, and that was the end of it.

On my walks home through the town, dodging the glances of the elderly gossips outside the bar, avoiding the questioning of Mrs. Winter, I nurtured great hopes for what this romance with Rosanna might become. I imagined the conversations we would have, the way we would tell each other every particular detail of our lives. I tried to talk to her one night about my family's history, but I could tell she didn't really understand. She was faintly scandalised to learn that we were refugees, and that my brother was in trouble with the mainland government for homosexuality. I told her no more. She always knew me as Isak K., never Harlan.

One day that spring, she took my hand across the bar counter and said, "I don't think we should see each other anymore." I tried, for the sake of decency, not to look too relieved.

After Rosanna, there was one other girl, Dolores, a niece of one of our neighbours who had been visiting for the summer Independence Day party. Nothing came of that either.

My grandfather's stories had ruined me, made me a romantic like he was. I wanted a great love that spanned oceans and continents—I wanted a love that felt like recognition, like a ship returning home.

And now here was Antonia, out of nowhere. A girl from an Imperialist family, an Alcyrian family, and with no powers at all, but still somehow with that familiarity I had dreamed of. Surely those dreams of her had been given to me for a reason. Was this love? I couldn't be sure, never having experienced it before. But I knew already that it was as different from what I had felt for Rosanna and Dolores as air is from water, dark from light.

36

One night at the beginning of October, as I left for my grandfather's house, my father waylaid me. "By the way, Harlan," he said, "I saw your friend Martin the other day. Asked him about that guitar. He didn't seem to have any idea what I was talking about."

My mother and father exchanged an amused glance. "Oh, that," I said.

"Whoever this girl is," my mother said, laughing, "bring her to meet us before too long."

I didn't say anything. I couldn't find the words. As I walked the two streets to my grandfather's house, I thought sadly of that meeting. How could it ever take place?

I envied them sometimes, my mother and father. In their quiet way, their life had been a great love story too. He had loved her since he was fifteen years old; they had followed each other across oceans. The way I now imagined I would follow Antonia, if she left.

She opened the door fearfully. "What is it?" she said. "Why have you come here so late?"

"I just wanted to see you again."

"I thought something was wrong." She closed the door behind me, and her shoulders sank in relief. "I just made tea."

We sat by the gas fire and drank it. Our relationship, whatever it was, consisted almost entirely of conversation and tea-drinking.

"I'm staying here tonight," I told her at last.

"What do you mean by that?"

"Look, I don't mean anything by it. I'll sleep on the sofa. I just want to talk to you, Antonia. I want to be in the next room to you. You're always alone here. I'll keep you company."

She raised her eyes to heaven, but she didn't refuse to let me stay.

Gunfire from further north reached New Maron that night. The dark was restless and full of wind and stars. The new Alcyrian government was having problems with black-market shipping in the newly opened channel. To pass the time, because neither of us much wanted to sleep, we studied Aldebaran's papers. Antonia had her own ideas about the code and the map. Frowning over them in the light of the gas fire, she was at her most beautiful.

I had a pain in my chest which I could not dispel. I opened the window wide and leaned out to breathe the cold air, and let the wind surround me.

"Close the window," said Antonia. "It makes me miserable sometimes that I can't even put my head out like that. Months now, I've been shut up here."

It was true. With no prospect of getting out of one of the ports, it was looking like Antonia would have to spend the winter shut up inside this apartment.

I looked left and right. All the shutters in the street were closed. It was just past one in the morning. "Come here," I said. "Dim the lamp. There's no one in the street. You can look out just for a minute. There's no harm."

"Are you sure?"

"Come here."

She came over and stood beside me, then leaned far out and breathed in the wind from the street. For several minutes, she watched the lights of ships tossed up and down on the dark waves now that the wind was high. I was not looking at any of that, not properly. I was watching Antonia.

"I can't stay here too long," she said then, moving back inside.

As she turned up the lamp again, the street outside disappeared into darkness, but as it faded from view, I thought I saw something. A shadow moving behind one of the houses.

"Wait," I said. "Dim that again."

"What is it?"

She dimmed the light again, but the place where I had been looking was deserted; no one was standing there.

"Don't worry," I said. "It's nothing. Just something moving in the wind."

I closed the window and the curtains. Antonia, reassured, had returned to the papers and was turning them over carefully.

"There's no point," I said. "Not until we work out the code."

"Maybe people with powers can read it. You should try."

"I *have* tried. Lots of times."

"Try concentrating very hard," she said. "Stare at it. Try not to think of anything else."

Even this I had tried, but I did it again. Somehow it seemed ridiculous. The way I glared at the paper made her snort, and we were both overcome with a fit of laughter.

"It's not done like that," I said at last. "At least, not for me. I've never had the kind of powers that people talk about from the old days. Dreams come to me. I can't reach for them. I have to wait."

Antonia nodded. She put the papers down on the floor and picked up the map. Her face was very serious again as she concentrated. "One of these stars is quite nearby," she said. "Look— this one. Probably only a couple of miles."

"I know," I said. "It's out on the moor—there's nothing there."

"Haven't you ever thought about going there? Just to check?"

"But I don't know what I'm looking for. Surely the writing explains, and if I can't read that . . ."

"I think you should check it anyway. Look, all these others are in occupied territory now. It might be the only one you can visit."

Antonia had a kind of light in her eyes. She put her arms around her knees and looked up at me. "Why don't we go together?" she said.

"How can we go together?"

"Harlan, I haven't left this apartment in twelve weeks. Couldn't we go, in the dark, late at night, when no one could see?"

I thought about it. "Once it gets to be winter, I suppose. When people have their shutters closed. Not before that—I won't risk it. And even then . . ."

"Isn't there a way? Couldn't we go in the middle of the night?"

"At four or five in the morning, maybe. If we walked along the backs of the shops and through the graveyard, we wouldn't be seen. I know the way to get there. I've just never gone because there isn't anything to see, only marsh and swamp and moorland." I traced the spot on the map with my finger. "I don't know what this place could possibly be."

"We'll go together," said Antonia, throwing her hair back from her face. "I'll die if I have to spend the whole winter locked inside. Why not?"

My heart rose at the thought of leaving New Maron with her, even if only for a few hours. "All right," I said. "Once the winter storms come."

37

A burst of sleet attacked the island in mid-November, unusual so early in the year. The sleet halted the fighting between the black-market ships and the Alcyrians for a while, and gave us quiet nights. In the blizzard, the Alcyrian ships were disadvantaged, and the Imperialists who were posted in the small towns regrouped in Valacia, where there was proper heating and mainland generators to run electric light. A letter came from Anselm which, while not exactly cheerful, was hopeful at least, if you read it in a certain light. *The big resistance push is planned for early next year*, he wrote. *This time, perhaps it will be the successful one. Who knows anymore?*

It was strange to think of my brother and sister together on the mainland, right in the middle of the real world. If I hadn't had Antonia, I might have felt very lonely. I might even have decided to join them. This search for the last descendant was weighing on my conscience. Would there ever be any resistance push if they didn't find me first?

I told Antonia about my sister and the way she had protected me so fiercely during our childhood, about my brother and Michael, about the telegraph post they manned through storms and blizzards and blackouts, sometimes alone for months with only each other, thirty miles from the nearest town.

"Just the two of them?" said Antonia. I could tell this interested her a good deal.

"Yes. No one else. Sometimes in just one room, if their firewood runs low. There's no other civilisation in sight. Some people would find that hell on earth, but not Anselm."

"Well, they love each other," she said simply.

Antonia knelt down in front of the fire and warmed her hands. I watched her. Even the gentle curve of her neck was a kind of torture to me.

"Everyone in your family seems to be lucky in that respect. In love."

"Do you think so?"

"Well, from what you've told me about your mother and father. And Anselm. What about your grandfather?"

"He told me he was in love just once, with my grandmother, Amelie."

"They all found love," said Antonia. "One way or another."

"But that's not luck! Look at Anselm. He's at risk of being executed if the Imperialists take the free north as well as everywhere else. There're only a few miles of the whole continent where he and Michael can live safely. Look at my grandfather, spending half his life a widower. Look at me."

She looked so sad then that I wished I hadn't said it. Silence closed in on us.

"Listen," she said then. "Why don't we try and find that place on the map?"

"Tonight?" I listened to the sleet tapping against the glass of the window.

"It's snowing too hard for anyone to see us." She unfolded the map and laid it on the writing desk. "Harlan, I can't stay inside this apartment all winter. My head aches all the time. I'm getting sick, I think, or weak. I don't know what it is. And I can't even play the guitar any longer."

In the cold spell, two of the strings had snapped. I could not find replacements anywhere.

"All right," I said. "We'll go."

"Let's work out exactly where this star is first."

"It's somewhere north and west of here. Up the coast road, and then left near the old mine. It's about four miles—no more than that, I don't think. But that road only leads to bare moorland, as far as I know. I don't see what's going to be there."

"Let's go anyway. I have to get out of this apartment, Harlan."

I listened to the sleet flinging itself against the glass like a spray of shot. It was turning into proper snow, which would obscure our tracks and hide us from passers-by.

"All right," I said again. "No one will catch us in this blizzard."

Antonia didn't have an overcoat, so she put on all the clothes she had and covered her hair against the snow, and we set out. It was the first time she had left the apartment in three months.

The weird snow-world frightened me a little, and she must have felt the same because she shivered and gripped my arm. We went as quickly as we dared down the stairs and out into the whirling snow. Antonia breathed the night air and gave a quiet sigh. The snow clung to her hair and eyelashes. She had never looked as lovely as she did in that moment.

"Come on," I said. "We'll go through the graveyard. I'll show you the way."

We ran along the side of the tobacconist's shop and down the overgrown alleyway that led to the graveyard. Just ahead, two people crossed in front of the streetlamp and made me start. But they were only two neighbours I barely knew, hurrying back home, and they didn't look up.

In the graveyard, the grass was brittle with frost, and every leaf was silvered. We passed my grandfather's grave. I thought of showing her, but I was anxious to get out of the town before we met anyone. We kept going until we reached the edge of the fields.

"There's a shortcut down to the road again," I told Antonia. She followed me under the darkness of the trees, down the hill and out onto the coast road.

We came out opposite the bay by the hospital where I had last seen my grandfather. I had told Antonia about that night. She must have remembered, because she said, "Is this where you saw that vision of him?"

"Yes. There, by the barbed wire—that's where he vanished into the sea. Just in front near the rocks is where he talked to me."

She shook her head in wonder and took my hand.

As we walked on, I told her the things my grandfather had explained to me that night in the summer when he went away from us.

"Before my mother died," said Antonia quietly, "she tried to tell me about singing, in just the same way. She was too sick by then to make very much sense, but it seemed so important to her to tell me. I wish I'd written those things down, or remembered them properly."

We walked for a while in silence. The roads looked different in the blizzard. The wind cut sharply. Through the gusting snow, I could see the lights of army ships surrounding the island. Once, a truck approached and we got down into a ditch beside the road and waited until it passed in a blur of headlights. When I looked up, I found Antonia gripping my arm.

"What is it?" I asked. "Tell me your thoughts."

"I'm thinking that I hope to God they never find us. That this war ends and we can be together, somewhere my father can't get at us."

It was the first time she had ever spoken about the future. Now I found I didn't want to face it straight on. "Come on," I said. "Let's run a little. You're shivering."

But Antonia could not run, not properly. Twelve weeks in my grandfather's narrow apartment had wasted her legs so that she could only hobble.

About a quarter of a mile further along the coast road, Aldebaran's map told us that we were supposed to take a road inland. It took us a while to find the turning in the snow, but once found it was easy enough to follow. The wind on this road was howling, the snow more ferocious. We were climbing onto higher ground. Without the streetlights, the road was utterly dark, except for the snow light, which gave Antonia's face an insubstantial quality. I wondered if it had made her badly sick, staying inside for so long. Certainly, she struggled to get her breath as we climbed the hill.

A great fear came over me when I thought about what would happen if she fell ill. We couldn't call the doctor or bring her to the hospital. "Breathe deeply," I said. "We'll rest a while." I took her hand and gripped it.

We had been walking again for ten minutes when quite suddenly the snow cleared and something very strange happened. I recognised a tree. The particular twist of it, like a woman leaning into the wind. I grabbed Antonia's arm.

"What is it? You frightened me half to death."

"That tree," I said. "I know it."

"What do you mean?"

I stepped closer. "I know this tree. It's been here for years. The bark looks solid, but it's not—it's dry and papery. And on the other side is a love-heart, carved with the initials G.M. and M.B."

I reached out and touched the bark. As dry and papery as ashes, just as I had thought.

This was the place where the former king had hidden in my

dream. Aldebaran's old home. All at once, I understood the meaning of the star.

Antonia was braver than I was. She stepped around to the other side of the tree, scraped off the caked snow and looked. From the way she held herself, very still, I could tell that what I had said was true.

"Where are we on the map?" I asked. "Are we at the star now?" Antonia shook her head. Neither of us knew.

"Either way," I said, "I've dreamed about this place. This track goes across bumpy, rocky grass and it leads to a farmhouse. It's a big grey building with a felled oak tree outside and eight windows on the front. It's where the former king was hiding. I know it is."

"Shall we go up the track and see?"

I shook my head. I didn't know why, but I was terrified. "It's a hell of a strange thing, seeing a place you've seen already in a dream."

"You weren't frightened of me."

"But this is different."

"We have to check what this place is. We can't just turn around and leave. That's what I think about it."

"I don't know." I shivered in the wind.

"Come with me. Take my hand."

"All right. I'll go up to it a little way, but I don't like this, Antonia."

We went very slowly through the blinding snow, over bumpy grass and rocks. The track passed between two stone walls, and the wind swept the snow across our faces. A yard opened up ahead. Antonia let go of my hand and vanished in the snow for a minute. I panicked then and shouted her name.

"I'm only here," she answered. "There's an old tree, like you said. Lying in front of the house. And—oh!"

"What?" I said. "What is it?" I reached for her, but less blindly than before. The snow was clearing again. And I saw what she was looking at.

189

In front of us, where there should have been a square grey house, there was something more insubstantial. As the snow cleared, I saw great charred beams rising at strange angles; blackened brickwork; shattered glass. Not a house, but the skeleton of a house.

"This isn't how I remember it," I said, dread rising in me. "In my dream, the king was living here. Then he left. It was an ordinary old farmhouse. What's happened to it?"

"It's burned," said Antonia.

Still hand in hand, we stepped inside the walls of the house. As we walked from room to room, glass and ash crunched under our feet. The layout was the same as in my dream—at least, the doorways were in the same places—but nothing was left now. In one room, I found a burned stub of candle; in another, cutlery scattered from what had once been a drawer.

"Is it the same place?" Antonia whispered.

"Yes," I said. "I'm certain of it."

Something in the house must have been dislodged by our arrival, because it fell with a shivering crash on one of the upstairs floors. My whole being jarred with shock.

"Come on. Let's go."

Antonia's courage had failed her now. I half hauled her back along the track, stumbling through the overgrown grass, past the tree and down the slope of the moor. Now that the snow had cleared, I could see that this was old farmland, long overgrown. Neither of us said anything until we were back on the edge of New Maron and had left that burnt place far behind.

Antonia was coughing, trembling a little. She could barely go any further.

We had been gone too long. The storm was over. With the snow vanished, I felt strangely exposed entering the town, and Antonia must have thought the same because she let go my hand as we edged along the alleyway and drew her scarf over her face. Somewhere not far off, a truck was revving.

"We'd better get inside quickly," I said. But we were lucky. No one else was out in the night.

I was still shivering when we re-entered the apartment. Nothing had changed. The clock stood at five-twenty. We had been gone three hours.

"You're cold," I whispered, seeing her shiver too.

"I'm fine."

"I don't want you getting sick. That's the last thing I want to happen."

She looked at me strangely. "Harlan, you were frightened, weren't you? Out there?"

"What happened to that old place? Who would want to burn it?"

She shook her head.

That night, huddled on the sofa, I could not sleep. My teeth rattled. I turned over and over, trying to get warm. When I did eventually sleep, close to dawn, I dreamed of the king and my assassinated great-great-uncle, smeared with ashes, weeping, with broken glass in their eyes. I wandered through the house with them, trying to find the way out. Had they burned it before or after the king left for good?

Someone grabbed my shoulder. I shuddered and came to. Antonia was looking down at me. "What is it?" I said.

"You were making this awful noise in your sleep. Like a kind of groan."

"I'm sorry. I was dreaming about that house."

"A vision?"

I shook my head. "Just an ordinary nightmare."

I sat up and rubbed my face. Antonia sat down on the end of the sofa. She had thrown a shawl over her nightdress, but it fell from one shoulder and the streetlamp illuminated the pale curve of her shoulder.

"You're like ice," she said, feeling my feet and ankles. "You're still shivering. You'll get sick yourself, never mind about me."

I shook my head. "It's that dream. I'm not cold."

Antonia did something strange then. She lay down beside me. "What are you doing?" I said. "You aren't supposed to—"

"I'm just going to lie beside you to keep you warm." She arranged the blanket over us both. "Do you want to freeze to death?"

I turned over and, without saying anything, folded her in my arms.

"Harlan," she chided. "It's not safe. I didn't mean like that."

"Who can see us now?"

She resisted for a few minutes longer, but I did not let her go. Finally she gave up and wrapped her own arms round my waist, and we lay like that until I stopped shivering, then a while longer. She began to breathe deeply, and I saw that she was asleep.

When the clock in the town struck seven, it took all my resolve to prise myself out of her grip to dress for work.

I walked through the town that morning, and the damp, grey world seemed like a place where anything might happen.

38

*M*y grandfather once told me: *There are things sometimes in life that just unfold, that seem inevitable. Finding you all on Holy Island was like that. My steps directed me to your door.*

It seemed to me that my love for Antonia was one of those things. What was the point of resisting? I began to be troubled by the feeling that we were wasting these days together, days that would never come again. I knew that war split people apart and sometimes they never found each other. It was what had almost happened with Anselm and Michael. And if I died tomorrow, without possessing Antonia, the great love of my young life, I felt I would die with regret as cold as the ocean in my heart.

A few days later, Antonia caught a fever. I felt such tenderness for her, as I bathed her sweating face and spooned soup into her mouth. I held her clammy hand in mine and kissed her lips. If she'd been awake, she never would have let me. Then I did something I had not yet done: I told her over and over, in her fevered state, that I loved her.

There were soldiers in the town again, and one day towards my eighteenth birthday, late in December, we heard a report on the wireless radio of arrests of Malonian women who had entered into relationships with Alcyrian soldiers. In Valacia, the secret police were raiding houses. The soldiers themselves faced military discipline, but the women were to stand trial and be imprisoned. "Let this be a warning to you," the voice on the radio—General Marlan's voice—thundered. "Immoral love that undermines the cause must be punished." My mother snapped the radio off at that point, but I could see the faint tremor in her fingers. She was thinking of Anselm, I could tell. I was thinking of Antonia and myself.

As soon as I could, I ran back to my grandfather's apartment.

Antonia was almost better, but still pale and wan. After the fever, a tiredness had come over her that no amount of soup and tea could quite dispel. Seeing how grey she looked, I didn't tell her what I had heard on the wireless.

From that night, General Marlan spent more and more time berating our island from the wireless speakers.

"I saw him once, you know," said Antonia. "He came to the theatre to hear my mother sing."

"What was he like?"

She smiled at that. "Short and ordinary. And he had false hair."

"No!" This man was the ruler of a whole empire, and I couldn't believe that he wore something as faintly ridiculous as false hair.

"Yes," said Antonia. "I could tell by the way it sat on his head, like a dead cat."

I laughed at that.

193

"These people," she said, "aren't anything special or important. I've seen hundreds of army men listening to my mother at the theatre, crying their eyes out like children. My God." She struggled for something she could not express. "Zealous," she said eventually. "When I was quite young, I came to my own conclusions about them. If I hadn't been too much of a coward, I'd have declared myself no longer an Imperialist."

"You aren't a coward," I said, very firmly. "You wouldn't love me if you were."

"I am. I'm too weak. I've let my Imperialist relatives pass me about between them, never saying what I feel, never disagreeing, always too scared."

"You've left those relatives. You love me, even though it's a crime. You're helping me work on my powers. You're not a coward, Antonia."

When I said that, her back straightened, and she looked at me very directly.

"What?" I asked.

"Nothing. I'm just more glad than I can say that you came into my father's office that day."

"I think that was what my dreams were for," I said, putting forward a theory that had been forming in my mind over the past weeks. "I think I dreamed about you so that when I met you for real I would recognise you and stop to look again. So that I'd know to help you. I think it was a kind of sign. My grandfather said something once about some force guiding his steps so that he found us again. It was like that. Like powers."

Antonia put her hand on the back of my neck, her touch strangely firm, and ran her hands through the base of my hair. She did it very deliberately. "Isn't it kind of wrong," she said, "the way we submit to their laws? The two of us, who've done nothing but love each other."

I took her hands. She trembled a little, but did not try to resist.

Quite suddenly, I found my mouth dry with anxiety. Antonia was the one who was calm. Something had altered in her. She lit the lamp and illuminated her own face, startling in its beauty. In the half-light, she sat beside me. "You're shaking."

"I don't know why."

"It's all right." She stroked my arms and my hair. "Let's start again, without fear. First of all, I love you."

"I love you too," I told her. "I don't know why I'm shaking like this."

Probably because this was the most important moment of my life.

"Let me shut the curtains properly," I said. "I don't want to be thinking about people looking in."

"Stay there. I'll go."

At the window, she hesitated for a moment.

"What is it?"

She closed the curtains with a snap. "Nothing."

"What, Antonia?"

"I thought I saw someone."

I was on my feet, thinking of the shadow I had seen before.

"No," she said. "Don't open it. They're gone now. They vanished down the street."

"Who was it?"

"I don't know. Someone looking at the house."

My neck shivered. "Watching?"

"Well, maybe not. Just standing on the other side of the road, hanging around. I don't know, Harlan."

"Let me see."

She caught my hand. "Forget it. Forget it. Come with me. This night should just be for us, and forget the world outside."

And perhaps in the circumstances I can be forgiven for doing as she said.

———

I don't know if I should tell the whole of this or not. Perhaps just in parts. Antonia's hands at the back of my head, running tenderly through my hair. Antonia twisting free from her dress and emerging, soft and pale, to take the breath from my lungs. Antonia in my arms beneath the chilly blanket, whispering, "Shh, shh," until I stopped trembling. Antonia's legs and arms entwined with mine so that I hardly knew who was who anymore. Antonia. Antonia. Antonia.

That night, I felt all at once that the world around me was right. My heart had no fighting in it, only stillness. For the very first time, a week ahead of my eighteenth birthday, I had found some kind of peace, and I marvelled at it. I didn't care about that green world, about being anywhere else but here. The room was still lamplit, and the only sound was the ticking of the gas fire as it wound down. I clung to Antonia. Maybe I already knew, with some shadowy premonition I had not yet recognised, that war would try to take her from me.

When she woke, briefly, I tried to talk about running away together. "Governments fall," I told her, stroking the side of her face. "They all have, in the end. Every single one. Just as people die, governments fall and new ones take their place. And maybe the next one will be better. Maybe it will make things better for people like us."

But Antonia just shook her head. "Not this one. It will never fall. Hell itself will freeze over first."

In the dark, I pushed away the truth of what she was saying, and the knowledge that no resistance victory would ever come while they still waited for news from Aldebaran's last descendant.

In the dark, as we slept again, the cold foghorns of the ships seemed to blare our coming separation. When that happened, when they woke me from my dreams, I just clung to her more tightly. I blocked out the future and the past and tried to make time stop.

After that, Antonia and I spent every night together.

I give thanks for that, that in its last weeks our love was nothing but happy, nothing but pure, so that in memories it becomes the one true thing that I believe has been real in my whole life.

I might as well just tell the next part and get it over and done.

39

*N*ight, black and thick with drizzle. February. Two o'clock. Out in the darkness, two drunks groaned insults at each other. This, or something else, must have woken me, and I opened my eyes. The first thing I said, as I always did on waking, was, "Antonia."

She turned her head to me on the pillow and reached out clumsily to stroke the side of my hair. Then she let her arm fall and, with a great sigh, sank away from me again into sleep. While she slept, one hand grasped my forearm, as though to anchor itself. I felt the warmth of her back, the way the breath swelled. Thoughts came to me with a weird clarity during those nights with Antonia, as though someone had spoken them. Now I held the moment before me, carefully, as if I were trying not to spill a glass of water. I breathed in the warmth of Antonia's hair, its rose oil smell. I held my cheek against hers and felt how smooth it was, the firm curve of her flesh across the bone. I wished, as I had wished many times as a young boy, for time to stop.

Is that true happiness, what I possessed in that moment? Is that the ending, the arrival of a life: to be eighteen, waking from sleep with the love of your young life in your arms? Probably; I haven't yet found its equal. The drunks had passed on, but other sounds reached me, dim and unthreatening as noises underwater: a ship's horn, the tobacconist's dog, a passer-by coughing. The gas fire filled the room with a comfortable hiss. The objects around me were just discernible in the dim light through the window: the patchwork blanket I had brought here from home; my grandfather's old desk; the shelf around the wall, occupied by darkness now instead of books and papers. *Never let this change*, I prayed. I remember clearly hearing those words in my head, in my own voice. Maybe I even whispered them aloud. I remember hearing them and holding Antonia, and at that same moment I realised that someone had climbed the stairs and was out on the terrace, and I knew with an awful certainty that something was wrong.

I don't know how I knew. Certainly whoever it was made no noise at first. But there it was again, the sound that had been beyond the edge of my hearing the first time. The squeak of the door handle lifting. That door was chained and barred four times, but someone was trying to open it now. I could hear footsteps on the terrace. One or two hushed words in a man's voice.

Surely it was just a couple of drunks who had climbed the steps to see what was up here. Trapped in the silence, I moved inch by inch until my whole body was shielding Antonia from the door. I lay without moving and prayed that they were just thieves, that they would take the candlesticks from the kitchen cupboards and leave without doing us any harm.

I heard, quite distinctly, a metallic clacking sound that I did not recognise. I learned, a good while later, that it was the bolt on a gun. That, my father said, was the sound that first woke him that night, dragging him through layers of sleep with memories of another long-ago war. Of course, it couldn't have done. My father was two streets away. But all the same, he woke and roused my mother, and the two of them decided to check on me at my grandfather's house.

I heard one of the strangers give a wheezy cough. In my arms, Antonia stirred. She looked up into my face and smiled, her eyelashes heavy with sleep.

"What are you doing awake?" she asked. "Watching over me?"

I put my finger to my lips and whispered, "Go back to sleep, love."

"What's wrong?" She half sat up. "What's worrying you?"

"Shh. Stay quiet, for God's sake."

For weeks afterwards, I would regret that I spoke harshly to her in the fear of that moment.

She tried to drag herself fully awake. "Harlan, what is it? What's happened?"

"Look, just stay quiet, can't you? Please." I think I was still hoping that if we stayed quiet enough they would go away and leave us in peace.

The door of the apartment banged against the wall. A barrage of male voices. Someone shouted, "Get up! Get up!"

Antonia was upright and rigid with terror. "It's all right," I said, taking her in my arms. "It's all right."

Someone flashed a torch into our faces. Antonia screamed. The blaze of torchlight blinded us. Shouting men's voices were everywhere. I was dragged out across the floor, where I bumped against the edge of the fireplace. Antonia screamed, "Harlan! Harlan!"

I was thrown down on the rug. A man stood over me with a gun. I raised my hands over my head automatically. "Don't hurt her!" I said. "Whatever you do, don't hurt her!"

"Stay there on the floor. Keep your hands raised. Tell me your name."

"Who are you? What do you want?"

"Name!"

I got a proper view of the man now. Middle-aged and fat, in a secret police uniform, standing square in front of the mantel-piece. Beside him was Captain Vilnius, our new leader.

"I've seen you before, haven't I?" he said.

"I'm Isak Karol."

"Malonian national?" asked the secret police officer.

I nodded.

"Malonian national? Yes or no?"

"Yes."

"And her name?"

Antonia was thrown to the floor beside me. I reached for her hand and held it, even though that in itself was probably a crime.

"Antonia Fortuna Bercy," she said.

"Alcyrian national?"

"Yes."

There was a sudden commotion behind them on the terrace. My mother and father. It cut at my heart to see them there, suddenly, white-faced and sleepy.

"Stay back," the secret police officer said, knocking my mother away with the side of his rifle. "This doesn't concern you."

"That's my son there," raged my mother. "For God's sake—of course it concerns me!"

I met her eyes, and saw in them a kind of despair I had never seen before. "Mama, leave it," I said, more calmly than I felt. "Stay there. Please—just don't get hurt. I can handle it."

Then there was a strange kind of quiet. They had us all at their mercy, and they must have known it. Captain Vilnius surveyed the two of us, cowering side by side on the living room rug with our hands raised.

"Are you aware that you're committing a criminal offence?" said Captain Vilnius. "You, boy."

I didn't know what to say, so I said nothing. It was Antonia who spoke. "We've done nothing wrong," she said in Alcyrian, sobbing. "We've done nothing wrong."

"This girl is missing from her father's house," said Captain Vilnius, rounding on me. "We've been searching for her for months. We're under orders to return her. And as for you—"

"You can't take her back there!" I said. "They'll kill her! You can't! Please. We've done nothing wrong!"

"And as for you," said Captain Vilnius to me, "you need to come with us now. We're taking you into custody."

At those words, Antonia crumpled. She rested her face on her knees and sobbed. I tried to put my arms around her, but one of the secret policemen kept pushing me away with the butt of his gun. "Come on," he said, more quietly than Captain Vilnius. "Get some warm clothes and belongings."

Behind the door, I heard my mother crying. "I'm sorry, Mama," I said, as I pulled on my trousers, my jacket, my overcoat. "Papa, I'm sorry. I never meant for things to turn out like this. I was going to tell you." Dimly, I realised that this might be the last I spoke to them for a very long time.

I was marched out and down the stairs. Antonia tried to hold onto me. She tried to wrap her arms around my waist and not let me go, but the police were having none of it. They pulled us apart, and two of them pinned her by the arms as she struggled. "We're taking you back home," said one of them. "Your father's here to escort you."

Antonia turned her face away and sobbed. Someone brought my hands behind my back and handcuffed them. I was marched like that out into the street, where a small crowd of neighbours had gathered.

"Antonia!" I called, because I had lost sight of her. "Antonia!"

"Stop that. Stop shouting. Come quietly, or it will be worse for you."

What could they do? I went on calling her name. I just wanted her to hear it as we went out into the dark. I called my mother's name, my father's, and Antonia's most of all; I didn't stop calling as they manhandled me across the street and into the back of a truck.

I pressed my face up against the grimy back window. In the doorway of a building, he stood quite calmly. I recognised that face. Her father. Antonia crumpled to the ground and screamed, "Father, don't take me away!"

Her father, still quite calm, stepped forward. He bent and pulled Antonia's head up by her hair so that she had to look at him. He said something that I could not hear, something that seemed to go on for a long time, then nodded to the men to take her away. No one tried to stop them. Not even the tobacconist, who had been an acquaintance of my grandfather's for seventeen years. No one spoke. Antonia, sobbing, was dragged away from me down the street and pushed into the front of a second truck, her father beside her. Almost tenderly, he tried to wrap her in a blanket. Antonia threw it off and pressed her face against the glass. Then the truck revved up and made a large circling turn, and I couldn't see her anymore. "It will be all right, Antonia!" I shouted after her. "I'll come back and find you! It will be all right!"

After that, it all happened quickly, without ceremony. The front doors of the trucks slammed. The secret police revved their motorcars. As we drove away, I could hear my mother and father calling my name, my real name: "Harlan!"

"I love you!" I called through the grimy glass. "I'll come back!"

Then the truck swung round the corner and everything— the street, the tobacconist's shop, the light in the living room window, my childhood, my lover, my family—everything I had ever cared about—was taken away from me in a roar of diesel.

In that moment, I became a revolutionary in my heart.

V

❧ EXILE ❧

40

𝒲ithout formalities, I was sentenced later that same night to a year at the newly opened Black Heath Labour Camp for Juvenile Lawbreakers in the south of the island.

Black Heath Labour Camp isn't the worst place to end up. I'm older now, and I can see that. As labour camps go, it's almost a paradise. There aren't violent guard dogs, or watchtowers, or floodlights, or midnight strip searches, or unexplained fatalities among the prisoners, or even proper guards. In short, it's nothing like the real prison camps on the mainland. Mostly, there's just a lot of nothing, and that nothing is what you have to contend with, the knowledge that you have been abandoned. On this featureless land—an expanse of black fen that stretches flat and bare to a blurred horizon—huts and buildings have been thrown up haphazardly around the old farmhouse that was once the only landmark. From the soil's heavy depths, the prisoners labour to raise spinach and turnips and beets and potatoes under the eye of the farmer and one or two half-hearted guards. At nights, in the sleeping huts, they shiver under thin blankets and swap stories and cigarettes.

Black Heath Labour Camp isn't a place to send dangerous people. It's a place to send people you want to forget about.

So all in all, things could have been much more serious for me. But that cold morning after I was taken from Antonia, it felt like I was being sent to the edge of the world. I was shoved into the back of a truck with four other boys, and we made our rattling and miserable progress south.

No one talked much, except an anxious and red-faced boy called Sebastian and the thin, stern boy next to him, who had introduced himself as Jakob. Sebastian talked out of nervousness: "Where do you think they're taking us? What's the name of the prison camp? Do you think it will be a decent place?"

Jakob, in contrast, talked to protest his fate. "Damned fool Alcyrians," he growled in the corner. "They'll see what they get for treating us like this."

Eventually even those two lapsed into silence.

Around dusk, the truck swung in a long arc and came to a standstill. The door opened. The guard let us out onto a wind-swept field. Shivering in a line, we beheld the flat land before us. A few lights burned ahead, from the farmhouse and outbuild-ings. "Walk," the guard told us. We were brought through the door of the farmhouse and into an entrance hall. There, the guard made us strip, and our clothes were put into sacks. "For when you're released," said the guard, issuing us with what he called "work clothes," which were grey overalls tidemarked with someone else's sweat. When we were dressed, the farmer, a large and awkward man, surveyed us. Finally he said, "Well, boys. You'd best come in and have something to eat."

We were brought into a brightly lit room where others stood in rows at wooden trestle tables shovelling watery soup into their mouths. We stood in a line. Soup was slopped into bowls and placed in our hands. The other boys were glancing at each other. I could tell what they were thinking: *This is going to be all right after all.* After the stories we'd heard, it didn't seem such a bad place to them. But I couldn't swallow my soup or look at them. How could it be all right—how could anything be all right—when Antonia had been dragged away from me like that?

After dinner, we were taken to a sleeping hut. The wind blew through the walls, but there was a stove, and there were blankets on the beds. No one talked much. Jakob claimed his bed first, then the others. I took the bunk in the furthest corner. By midnight, the others were all asleep.

The pain of regret rested like a stone in my chest. If only Antonia and I had tried to escape the island together, if only we had tried to get to Anselm in Arkavitz. Now where was she? I tried to close my eyes and bring her into my mind, but no picture came to me. I had never had those kinds of powers.

Eventually, because there was nothing else to do, I slept. In my dreams, I seemed to be drifting, and I had no idea where I'd wash up.

When I woke, it was to a haze of birdsong filling the air like static. Sunlight came down through the narrow windows and onto the floorboards of the hut. It illuminated particles of dust and woodsmoke, and gilded someone's tousled hair.

I remembered where I was, and all at once I was overwhelmed with a dread so heavy that it pinned me to the bed and robbed me of air. When the sickness subsided I dragged myself into my clothes and staggered outside, like a swimmer breaking through the surface. The wind whipped my face and brought me to life. A few traces of snow lay on the fields. "Antonia," I said. "Antonia. Mama. Papa."

"You all right?" In the shadow of the hut was the thin boy, Jakob, smoking a cigarette with his eyes closed. Even like that, he had a glare on his face. He was the only one who I believed might have committed a real crime. He must have been wondering the same about me, because he shrugged his jacket up over his shoulders, stubbed out his cigarette, and said, "What are you here for? Revolutionary activities, or some other made-up offence, is it?"

I shook my head. "Nothing like that."

"What, then?"

"I don't know. Being in love with the wrong person, I guess."

"Homosexual offences?"

"No. An Alcyrian girl."

From his face, I could tell it was not what he had been expecting. He watched me through narrowed eyes. "I see," he said at last.

I sat down on the step of the sleeping hut and rested my

elbows on my knees. I felt older than I had ever felt in my life. Jakob continued to watch me. Finally he said, "You a collaborator, then?"

"Of course not." I was out of patience for anyone this morning.

But Jakob did not seem particularly offended. He sat down on the step beside me and said, "You're angry. We're all angry. That's natural. None of us should be here."

"That's plain enough."

He leaned forward. "So what are you going to do about it?"

I did not know.

Jakob picked up a stone from the dusty ground in front of us. He turned it around in his hands. "I was arrested for organising protests in my village," he said. "That's my story. The local police handed me over to the Imperialists. I was taken to a cell and beaten. They were trying to get the names of the other organisers. Every day they beat me. Then eventually they just gave up. Someone else must have supplied the information. They didn't know what to do with me, so I reckon they sent me here to keep me out of trouble for a year."

Jakob turned away and pulled up his grimy shirt. Under it, his back was latticed with scars. He seemed to expect some kind of response, so I said, "That's terrible. What they've done to you."

"You ever read *Violent Disorder*?" said Jakob.

"Is it a book? I've read a lot of books, but not that one, I don't think."

"It's a revolutionary pamphlet. It was written by John Francis, a big man in the resistance on the mainland. I know that pamphlet off by heart. When I couldn't sleep at nights in my cell, I used to recite it to myself, so I wouldn't forget it. I'm going to get my uncle to send it to me here, and then we can make copies and distribute them. Start organising a proper resistance."

"Maybe my brother Anselm's read it," I said, more to be friendly than anything else.

Jakob looked up. "What about you?" he said. "Since you've been listening to our conversation, what's your story?"

Someone was standing in the doorway behind us, so silent I had not noticed him. It was the large and awkward boy, Sebastian. Under our joint scrutiny, he blushed a fierce pink. "What do you mean, my story?"

"How did you end up here? Come on. Sit down. Have a cigarette."

Jakob gestured imperiously to the ground beside him and Sebastian, looking half pleased and half terrified, sat.

"Well . . ." Sebastian's voice came out high and thin. He tried a second time. "Well, you remember when we were meant to hand in an awful lot of books to the Alcyrians? A few months ago?"

"I remember," said Jakob.

"I kept some of them when I wasn't supposed to."

"You were sent here for books?" I said. "What kind of books were they? All mine were burned."

"Mathematics books, mostly," said Sebastian. "And some physics. I want to study mathematics at university. So I kept them." His blush was fading now, and his words came out all in a rush. "They were important mathematics textbooks from my old tutor, on field theory and analytic number theory, which is just exactly what I want to work on. Prime numbers most of all. I mean, later, when all this dies down, if I can get a place at a university, you know."

"Prime numbers?" said Jakob, like he couldn't understand what he was hearing. "What the hell are prime numbers? And what does any of this have to do with revolutionary activities?"

"Prime numbers are the basic building blocks of every integer," said Sebastian. "Every whole number comes from a combination of prime numbers. You can't divide a prime number any smaller and still keep it whole. No one has found a formula yet to calculate whether or not a number is prime. You just have to check it by hand. For a large number, it's impossible. But in the empire, they have new computing calculators that are starting to be able to do it. That's what I want to work on. I want to learn to use these machines, and work on prime numbers. You can use prime numbers for all sorts of things. Secret codes, for one. Mostly I just love them because they're special. They're everywhere in nature too."

"I suppose that might be useful," said Jakob sceptically. "The secret codes part."

"That was what the Imperialists thought too, I suppose." Sebastian's face was full of pale earnestness. "You know, I'd give anything to be back with my grandmother in her front room, or studying at one of their universities. I'm not a resistance fighter. It's all a mistake, their sending me here. I tried to explain."

"Everything you do is resistance," said Jakob. "Wanting to study mathematics is resistance. Isak here asserting his right to love who he chooses is resistance."

"I suppose," he said.

"Look, it's the same for all of us. The same damn stupid story," Jakob said. "Taken away from our lives, brought here, not told when we're going to be released."

"I've been told," I said, and a panicky feeling rose in my chest. "They told me a year."

"That's what they *say*. You think they're going to release you after a year? You think they're telling the truth?"

"I have to leave after a year. I have to go and find Antonia. I'm not staying here any longer. I'll break out if I have to."

"That's right!" said Jakob, punching the palm of his hand. "That's better! We have to stick together. We might be able to help each other. Don't you see—they want to divide us all. You can't act like you've just given up. You won't get back what you've lost without resisting. None of us will."

I didn't care much about resisting, but I did care about getting back what I had lost.

A bell rang somewhere by the farmhouse. "What does that mean?" said Sebastian nervously.

"Time to get up, I suppose," said Jakob. "You two—think about what I've said."

We were shepherded over to the farmhouse, where we lined up to wash under a cold tap and to eat a swill of porridge, then were sent out to the fields to begin picking up stones. Something inside me had altered. I can't explain it, but all my being became absorbed into one wish, one coiled spring of longing: to get back to that night in Antonia's arms. And if it took resistance to get there, then I would do it—do anything.

That night, a dream haunted me. It's a dream that has kept coming back to me ever since. I am walking up the steps of a tall, black house. Antonia's guitar is in my hand. I'm wearing my best blue suit. I am free. I knock, and that aunt with the sour mouth opens the door. "I'm Harlan North," I say. "I'm here to see Antonia." And into my arms, Antonia runs, just as young, just as perfect as before.

41

As time passed, my dreams of Antonia became more shadowy. She cowered in the corner of a room while two dark figures, a man and a woman, beat her. She wept on a bed without sheets, utterly alone. She bent to scrub the floor with a rag, as that old man Mr. Harcourt had done, while her father stood over her in his Imperialist uniform, clicking his boots, snapping his gloves.

I didn't know how I was going to stand a year of this.

To protect myself, I learned to sleep shallowly, with one hand in the cold draught over the edge of the bed, so that I could wake myself if these nightmares of Antonia became unbearable.

By spring, Sebastian, Jakob and I had struck up an alliance. We had almost nothing in common except our situation, but in Black Heath that was enough. Once our day's work was done, no one seemed to care much what we did. The guards went off in their trucks to the nearest village, all except one or two, and we sat on the steps of our sleeping huts or roamed the camp in search of some occupation. On these restless nights, the camp was too small for Jakob. He wandered about, agitating everyone to join his new resistance group, and was forever getting in trouble.

A few weeks after we arrived, he got involved in a fight with one of the other prisoners, a man called Miles Kemp who was also in the labour camp because of involvement with the resistance. After that, Jakob kept to himself for days, nursing his black eye and bruised sense of self-importance. When he finally returned from his dark mood, he had something to show me and Sebastian. He led us across the turnip field and out along one of the irrigation ditches that ran along its edge. Here was a track that must once have been a road, and an old steel shipping container lay half submerged in the water.

"I wonder how this got here," I said. "It must have fallen off a truck."

"Come on," said Jakob, scrambling to the top. I followed him.

From the rusty peak of the container, we could see as far as the village and the grey edge of the sea.

"Look," said Jakob. "The real world. It's still out there." He lit a cigarette and sat down on the edge of the container, drumming on its sides with his feet.

Sebastian was having difficulties climbing, so I lowered a hand to haul him up. "Are you sure this is safe?" he protested as he gained the edge of the platform, red-faced with exertion.

"Of course," said Jakob. "I've been coming out here to think quite a lot lately."

Afterwards, that became the place I went to whenever I wanted to remember that there was a life beyond the camp.

One evening, from the top of the container, we saw a truck arrive in the village. This was not one of the soldiers' trucks but the kind of spluttering, rusty old vehicle that delivered vegetables, or coal. We watched it drive up to the village and stop.

After a while, a figure disconnected itself from the black shape of the village and began to cross the fields towards us. This figure blurred and vanished in the evening haze, then reappeared again. Something about it drew me. Its shape, its walk, the way it held its head. Everything about it was familiar. Wonder brought me to my feet, made my breath shallow.

Without taking my eyes off the figure, I dropped off the steel container and onto the grass.

"Hey, Isak!" Jakob called. "Where are you going?"

I took off across the fields, through the gathering dusk, at a run.

The figure was running now too. She was approaching me.

"Mama!" I called. "Mama!"

My mother and I met in the middle of the bare fields and she threw her arms around me. She was crying and kissing my face and stroking my hair. "My Harlan. They didn't tell us where they'd sent you. They didn't tell us what you'd been charged with or how long you'd be gone. It took them months to let us know. Oh, Harlan."

"Where's Papa?"

"In the shop. He thinks they're watching him. He was worried it would make it worse for you, us coming here when we aren't supposed to visit, but Harlan, I couldn't stay away. I had to see for myself that you were safe."

"I'm all right," I said. "Mama, don't cry."

"I'm so glad to see you. Oh, Harlan, I'm so sorry."

I took my mother's hands. "I'm all right. Really, I am. Please don't cry, Mama."

My mother touched the side of my face. She said, "Who is she? The girl? You never told us anything about her."

"Antonia," I said. It was the first time I had spoken her name to my mother. "I met her by chance, in Valacia. She was trying to escape from her father. He's an Imperialist. I helped her hide. I didn't tell you anything about her. It would have put you in danger too."

"And you love her, this girl?"

"Yes. And I mean to get back to her someday."

My mother stroked my hair.

"Mama, can you try to find out what has happened to her? Her father works for the Censor's Office. He's a bad man, and I can hardly sleep for worrying about her. Can you try and find out where she is? Her name is Antonia Fortuna, and her father is Victor Bercy."

"Fortuna," said my mother. "Like the singer your grand-father loved to listen to." She took a scrap of paper and a stub of pencil from her handbag, and wrote the name down.

"Her father had requisitioned a lawyer's office in Valacia, J. Harcourt and Sons," I said. "I don't know where he is now, but that's where I last saw him. She'll be with him, I know."

"I'll do what I can, I promise. But, Harlan—" She stroked my face again and started to cry a little. "Are they treating you right here? Do they hurt you?"

"They just make me work. It's not so bad as that. Listen, I'm sorry. I never meant to get into bad trouble like this—"

My mother hushed away my apologies.

"And what do you mean, that they're watching Papa? I don't like the way that sounds."

"I don't know exactly. He says he sees people standing out-side the shop, following him home. You know how he gets."

A dog barked somewhere near the farm buildings. She turned towards the noise, and her forehead furrowed.

"Mama, you aren't supposed to be here," I said. "We aren't allowed visits."

Sebastian and Jakob had reached us now and were hovering at the edge of the field.

"I know I can't stay," said my mother. "I just wanted to see you once, Harlan, and check that you were safe."

"What about you and Papa?"

"We're fine. Business in the shop has slowed almost to nothing. Things are still bad in New Maron. It seems like, all of a sudden, everyone's joining the resistance. There's fighting every day in Valacia. We've heard from Anselm and Jasmine. They're safe in Maritz for now. Part of me thinks we should have tried to reach them before the borders all closed, before all this happened. It looks like the resistance push into Capital might happen at last, after all."

"You still could go to him!"

"And leave you here on Holy Island?"

"If Papa thinks people are following him—"

"No, Harlan. Not without you."

It was no good arguing. She rummaged in her handbag. "I brought you this envelope from Grandfather's apartment. We've sold the place now, but I found this in the writing desk and I thought it must be yours. It's Grandfather's writing on the front."

It was the papers from Aldebaran. "Did you read it?" I said.

"Of course not. I just brought it. What is it?"

"Just stories he wrote for me, when I was a little boy."

"It's not something dangerous? Something that will get you into trouble if you keep it with you here?"

I hesitated.

"If it is, we'll hide it," said Jakob, making me start. I had not realised that he was so close behind me in the dusk. "I know where." He extended a hand. "Mrs. K., you must be."

My mother gripped his hand and nodded to Sebastian, who was hovering nervously, stepping from foot to foot. "Are these your friends?"

"Jakob and Sebastian. They've been good to me."

My mother shook their hands. It was absurd and miraculous, this meeting on the edge of the prison camp. But the dog in the farmyard was still barking, and the bell rang to signal that the power supply would soon shut off for the night.

"I can't stay much longer," she said, putting her arms around me. "I'll come again if I can. Listen, promise me one thing."

"Yes, Mama."

"That you won't go getting involved with the resistance. That you'll keep yourself out of harm."

Across her shoulder, I met Jakob's narrowed eyes.

Reluctantly, I let her go.

After my mother had walked away across the fields, Jakob said, "What's inside that envelope?"

I showed them. It didn't mean anything as it was—a book, a map, some encoded pages. Jakob was fascinated by the map. "Look," he said. "This is the country that used to be ours. That's where my family comes from. West Ravina."

Sebastian was more interested in the code. Crouching down in the mud, he leaned over my shoulder, breathing heavily, and studied the numbers. "How did he code this?" he said, taking Jakob's cigarette lighter and illuminating the smudgy pages.

"Careful!" I said. He was holding the lighter clumsily close to the paper. "I don't know how he wrote it—that's the problem. It's some kind of number code I can't break."

"A code. Or a cipher."

"What's the difference?"

"A code requires a codebook. You swap a word, a sentence, for some other set of words or symbols. If this is a code, you're lost without the book. A cipher uses algorithms. It's all mathematics. A cipher can be broken." Sebastian held the pages close to his face and frowned.

"Do you think you could break it?" I said. "Is it mathematics that's needed?"

"I could try."

I hesitated, then handed the pages over to him.

It was agreed that if there was any trouble, we would hide the documents in the hollow roof of our sleeping hut. "It's all right," said Jakob. "I've got cigarettes and spirits and resistance magazines and all sorts up there, and they never search it."

I was reluctant to part with my papers, but Sebastian was the only person I had ever met who might be able to break a code. Mathematical education in the government schools on Holy Island didn't amount to much. And I needed some help right now; I needed a miracle. If Sebastian stood any chance of decoding Aldebaran's words, it was worth trying.

Sebastian sat up late that night on the step of the sleeping hut, studying the pages. "Isak," he said timidly through the doorway at one point. "Are you awake?"

"Yes."

"I need that book as well. The poetry book that was with it."

I didn't know why he needed the poetry book, but I got it out of the envelope and gave it to him. He returned to his solitary post, clutching the papers to him.

When I fell asleep, Sebastian was working something out in the dirt in front of the hut with a stick, its light scratching the only sound in the dark. I thought of my mother, making her long journey home through that night, and prayed that I would see her again, see all of them. My life seemed uncertain and weightless here in this place at the end of the world.

As it turned out, my mother never came to Black Heath again while I was there. Shortly after her visit, work began on a proper fence. Great roaring machines arrived to dig trenches and men in overalls unrolled wire fencing. The workmen were under orders not to speak to us. They worked day and night, and the pounding of their machines made my head ache. There was one advantage, though. By their floodlights, Sebastian was able to work late into the night on my code.

One evening in April, Sebastian handed me back my papers. "I've done it," he said. "I've translated it."

I seized the papers and turned them over. Sure enough, he had written words in neat pencil underneath every coded number. *My very dear nephew . . .* , the letter began.

"How did you do it?" I said, seizing Sebastian by the shoulder. "You must be some kind of prodigy."

He flushed with pleasure. "No, no, it was easy. This doesn't require mathematics, because it isn't a proper code. It's a book cipher, Isak. The only reason I know about them at all is because I've read a little about cryptography. It's a famous old method they used in the last war."

"A book cipher." I had never heard of it. "What's that?"

"Well, you see, each of these numbers really tells you a page number, a line number, and the number of words along that line. You need the right book—the same copy and of course the same edition as the code-maker—to work it out. So for example, here, the first set of numbers is 11143. So you go to page eleven of this poetry book, line fourteen, word three. And you end up with . . ."

I turned the pages and frowned. "*Many,*" I said. "Not *my.*"

"This was the complicated part," said Sebastian. "Because the code also incorporates a simple shifting pattern. The date on the top of the letter, here, gives you the clue. If you go one word along, then one line down, then eight words along, then eight words down, you get the real word, which is—"

"*My,*" I said. "You're right." I repeated the pattern for the next number, and the next, kneeling in the dust before our hut with the papers spread in front of me. *Very* and *dear.*

"I can see why he chose Diamonn," said Sebastian. "He's the poet with the greatest vocabulary in our language."

I knew that fact too; my grandfather had told me so once. "How did you work all this out?" I asked him.

"Trial and error. A lot of error. But there's something unfortunate—he hasn't done this right. He should have told you separately which book to use, not sent it in the envelope with the document. Anyone can decode it if they do the same thinking work that I have."

"The Imperialists have copies of these papers. Will they have managed?"

"I don't know. It might take them a while to work out the part about the date. It took me some time. I only realised because it was so strange, the way he put the date in numbers like that, with no dashes, nothing. Like a code of its own."

"Thank you, Sebastian," I said, running my hands over the pages. "Really, thank you."

As soon as I could, I got away from the others, ran with the papers to the old steel container, and knelt down behind it in the shadow, where I could not be seen from the farm. Only then did I begin to read.

> *My very dear nephew,*
>
> *As I write this, you are still six months from birth. But the sad truth is that you and I will probably never meet—at least not in this world. I pray God reunites us in another. There are people who don't want me to live; the government is falling out of favour with the world. And I am growing immensely old. I can't fight much longer, Harlan.*

A charge went through me. How did he know my name, six months before I had been given it?

*We live in a strange and dark time. I want to tell you
the truth, before it all disappears. This account is to help
you to live, in a world where you will feel like a perpetual
outsider. I have only shadowy pictures of the future. But I
see you in grey rooms, grey stairwells, grey streets filled with
smoke. You will be surrounded by poverty and obscurity,
and you will always wish for another place. And how do I
know this? Because, Harlan, your life and mine—divided
by eighty-five years—are also parallels.*

*I was born on Holy Island, just outside Valacia, the
eldest son of a farmer. My most enduring memory is picking
up potatoes before light, in high fields where the wind was
so cold it seemed to pierce you like broken glass.*

Again, a charge like lightning went through me. Holy Island.
My own life. A boy from the past, picking up potatoes.

*We children had to work in the fields because our
family were tenants on the land and we couldn't earn a
living otherwise. We seemed cursed by misfortunes. One
year the potatoes were diseased, another the corn was
destroyed by a storm. I used to sit watching the clouds and
wish I had the skill to predict these destructions. And
around that time, I began to have strange dreams.*

*I began to dream of another place, a green world far
away where kind hands would reach out to help me.*

*"Do you know, Arthur," my mother used to say, "that I
almost lost you in your birth? Since then you've been special.
Since then you've been out of the ordinary."*

*We struggled to keep hold of our farm. Maybe it would
have been more sensible to leave and search for work elsewhere.
But each acre of that place was written over with our family's
history. In the yard was an oak my great-grandfather had*

dragged from under the earth with a team of horses, an ancient black trunk that had been submerged for hundreds of years in the low field. On a silver birch at our gate were my mother's and my father's initials in a heart, carved in the shaky hand of my seventeen-year-old father shortly after they first met.

Again, my skin turned cold. I had seen that place, with Antonia. It was where the former king had hidden. And Aldebaran was not the only one who had been almost lost at birth.

You have probably grown up in towns, Harlan, and by the time you read this my childhood will be a hundred years in the past. Forgive me if this sounds impossibly romantic. But it wasn't, not then. We never had enough to eat, and my parents lived in permanent dread of a bad harvest. It was no kind of life.

When I was ten, I saw a storm coming. I can't tell you how I knew—a kind of taste on the wind, or a quality of the breeze. I went to my mother and father and told them to harvest the crops. They worked all that night, the three of us children following them with scythes almost too big to lift. Our neighbours said they had gone insane. At dawn, the storm blew in off the sea and flattened everyone else's corn. Ours was the only crop that survived.

From then, our fortunes turned a little, and I had a kind of power of seeing the future.

A few years later I was discovered by the great Lord Sheratan, and I went away from the farm forever. Sheratan taught me nearly everything I know about magic. He believed it was a personal force, a channelling of willpower. But Sheratan was old-fashioned. He believed in training by exertion, by torture, by physical force. It improved my skill, but it made me feel as though I were a soldier readying for some great battle. And that, I believe now, is the opposite of real powers. Real powers are a way of thinking more deeply, not less.

Harlan, I believe that powers come into being for a purpose, and that purpose has everything to do with the violent invasion you are about to suffer, with injustice and war. But those with powers stand arrayed not on the side of war but of peace. That is what I believe.

Around the time of Diamonn, you can find the roots of today's Imperial Order—great landowners who tried to suppress the people, to rule by fear. Around that same moment in our country's history, people first began to believe quite seriously in other worlds. I first read Diamonn's work when I came to the city, at nights in the secret service office when I could not leave my desk. There's a very obscure book, probably completely lost now, called The History of Seeing. *"Imagination," he wrote in that book, "is the art of creating that which is not there in reality, by which I mean opening the pathway to another world. As such, its closest ally is the art of magic. The heart at war makes escape routes for itself, alternative paths to be travelled in times of great need. And since it cannot go forward or backward in time, it goes sideways instead. Magic, like writing, seems to spring up around each act of injustice and oppression because it is a search for another kind of truth, an act of resistance. This magic has always existed. The early people possessed it quite naturally, because they didn't know that they weren't supposed to believe in it. Now it belongs only to the heart at war."*

Again, that strange chill swept over me. *The Heart at War.* My grandfather's last book. It had come from his great predecessor, that title, from Diamonn, and it meant exactly what I had always believed it meant—the heart that was searching for another place and time, some kind green world away from all the fighting. Reading my great-great-uncle's words, I felt the company of others like me, people who dreamed of another place.

I began to be convinced that magic is not manipulation of the world's forces, as my teacher had told me, but that it exists most powerfully in the ability to imagine, to dream. There is no real impossibility in it, just a great power of vision, one that we once perhaps all possessed.

Not everyone likes it, this power of seeing. During the last war, those with powers were kept in special schools which turned out to be more like prison camps. And slowly, something very strange started to happen. Magic began to die. This great gift of seeing, which we still need because the world is just as imperfect as before, is abandoning us. By the time you live, Harlan, it may be gone altogether. But I don't want you to forget. I want you to know the truth.

As I write, a group called the New Imperial Order is threatening us. This group wants only its supporters and its favoured citizens to survive. If they gain power, these people will try to construct a world without freedom to imagine. The first thing they will do is burn the books.

In many of the other worlds that exist, magic has died. You will be the last to believe in these things, if you believe in them at all. But know that, whatever others tell you, powers were once real. I think that sometimes we are given a way out, an escape into another world. Or else we create this way out for ourselves.

The map is for you; it comes from my old secret service days, and charts all places where we once believed there was a connection to another world, a country called England.

Harlan, visit these places. You will find here the answers you are searching for. I want to show you the road back to every last trace of the magic we once believed in. Maybe these escape routes will save you one day. People like you exist to illuminate others by your power of seeing, to bear witness to other realities. Don't forget.

Harlan, this is what I know. Here is the truth about powers:

In the beginning, everyone had powers. These powers allowed them to speak to each other before humans knew how to talk out loud. They allowed the mother to know when her baby was in danger, and the lover to find his destined companion. They allowed us to see all the possible worlds that might exist, long before we had invented stories. They allowed the heart at war to find peace by escaping its reality for kinder shores.

There were a hundred thousand worlds then. Not just ours and England's, but worlds for every possibility. The early people, with their clear eyes, could see them all. They saw places where waterfalls flowed upwards and cities hung suspended in the air, where babies were born speaking and singing, and where old people got younger every day. They saw places where science and technology had already run their course and now lay in ruins, and other places where, to the chip of flint on flint, science was only just awakening. They saw all these things and grew wise, and there was peace.

In those days, it was possible to pass between the worlds. In this way, people travelled the many pages of the universe until they found the place that belonged to them, the life that was theirs. Family and poverty and religion did not dictate your life, and these things were alterable. People lived the life to which their soul drove them, in the world to which *they belonged. Sometimes, people were born in the wrong place. These people lived their whole lives trying to get back to the world they really came from. Usually, they managed, because powers were strong in those days. Then, if they reached that world, the true one, it recognised them and welcomed them home, and their heart, forever at war with itself, felt a kind of peace.*

So all was well.

Then, somehow, powers started to die out. No one knows why this happened in our country. But all at once, people began to be born without the vision for other places they had once possessed.

As soon as they became rarer, these powers became more valuable to those in positions of strength. Soon after the beginning of the death of these powers, which probably happened long before we could write or record anything about it, they began to be seen as precious and were no longer taken for granted. Then they became a commodity, a tool. Those people who had particularly strong vision were sought out and trained. They were given jobs in the government, in the secret service, in the army. They worked for scientists and for engineers. They enjoyed a level of privilege not afforded to the ordinary, powerless people. This, Harlan, was the position that I enjoyed at the end of the last century. They called us "great ones," and gave us fame and riches. This is how I came to be Lord Aldebaran— merely because I saw more than other people could.

But soon, the people who didn't have powers began to be suspicious of the people who did. What were these strange abilities, except a kind of witchcraft, or a kind of illness? Soon, people with powers were no longer favoured. They were hunted and locked away. Experiments were undertaken to find out whether these powers could be bought and sold, could be manufactured. Behind the bars of the asylums and prisons, sometimes the clear eyes of the great ones still saw. But sometimes, their vision of other worlds simply withered and died, and they became just like the people who had locked them up.

Now, powers had become a feeble thing. They manifested themselves not as great visions but as small premonitions and cheap tricks. People who had once seen beyond the stars now told fortunes with playing cards or levitated a coin. These are the powers that I had, Harlan, coupled with a small ability to see the future. Nothing truly remarkable anymore.

This diminishing of powers happened not just in our world but in all the worlds, in various ways. Belief in the power of seeing vanished, and with it the connection between the separate places, whose inhabitants now no longer believed in each other. The worlds, isolated, spun away from each other into darkness. Now, between our own world and the wide universe beyond, only one link remains. We call that place England, and they give our country names of their own, and the sacred connection between the worlds is now a matter for children's stories.

When a species dwindles and dies out, there is a period, impossibly lonely, when only one of its members remains. Biologists say the last sabre-toothed lion roamed thousands of miles in the mountains beyond Arkavitz, looking for others of its kind, until it died and was locked in ice sometime in the first century. They say the last hummingbirds on our continent became separated from each other, and each suffered an isolated death, believing itself to be the last survivor, at the four corners of the known world. In every place where powers died out, the same thing must have happened. There must have been a time when only one person with powers remained. This

person was probably sometimes feared and persecuted,
sometimes hidden, sometimes hailed as a superhuman or a
saviour. This person probably often lived a life of difficulty,
misunderstood and at war with the rest of his kind, with
the world in which he found himself.

Harlan, in our world, I'm sorry to have to tell you,
that person is you.

When I had finished reading, I looked up and saw Sebastian
and Jakob sitting in our usual place on top of the old shipping
container. I had not even noticed them appear, I had been so
intoxicated by my great-great-uncle's words.

"Sebastian told me your great-great-uncle wrote to you."

Sebastian looked away, flustered. "I didn't tell him what was
in the letter," he said. "I didn't say anything about it."

I folded the papers. "It's my great-great-uncle's will," I said.

If this answer startled Sebastian, he did not show it. He kept
his face admirably fixed, allowing only a faint pink blush to
spread over his neck.

"What did he leave you?" said Jakob.

"Nothing," I said.

Jakob let out a hoarse bark of laughter. "Bloody waste of
time then," he said, "putting it all in code."

For four nights solid, I lay on my bunk and looked up at the
ceiling and thought about those words: *Harlan, I'm sorry to have*
to tell you, that person is you.

In my head, two opposing voices were doing battle. The first
said, *I don't want these powers. I don't need them. I'm ordinary, and I*
care about ordinary things: my family, my love, my life. Not some messy
revolution. Not war. Wouldn't it be better to forget all about them?

And the other voice, quieter, told the truth: *You need this.*
You need powers greater than the first feeble hints you possess now, to

bring your family back together, to see your grandfather again. To get Antonia back and find somewhere you both can live. To get to that green world which is your true home. You need them. You have to come forward, and declare yourself as Aldebaran's successor.

I got up and went out into the night. The moon was out. A light breeze troubled the crops. High summer, the last point before the year declines and falls. I knelt in the dust and willed a rock to lift itself. Somehow, after reading Aldebaran's words and believing, I could make it shift on the ground a little. Somehow, within me, the traces of real powers were stirring after all.

42

*I*n December, an envelope arrived for me. The farmer handed it to me as we came in from the fields. "You boys need to tell your families to stop sending things," he said. "I never know whether I'm supposed to pass them on. Quick, before the guard gets here."

I was grateful, not for the first time, that he was a good man. I snatched the envelope and hid it under my overalls.

It had been readdressed from my grandfather's apartment. Crouched behind the shipping container, I ripped the envelope open. A yellow scrap fell out. *42 Plaz Liberte, Valacia*, it said. *Harlan, please come and find me quickly. I don't know how long I can continue like this.*

And at the end, the name I loved more than any other word: *Antonia.*

Something about this scrap of paper, even as I held it to my mouth and kissed it, filled me with dread. The way she had scrawled so quickly on the corner of a shop receipt. The smell of the paper, not a stale cigarette-smoke smell but a charred smell, like the way my books had smelled going up in flames.

Jakob and Sebastian looked down at me.

"What are they doing to her?" I said. "My God. Why does the paper smell burned like this?"

"This must be the address where she's staying," said Jakob. "You can find her now."

"But I've got four more months. And it says, 'Come and find me quickly.' Why does she say that?"

"We'll be free soon," said Sebastian. "We all came here on the same day, remember? We'll be released on the same day too. We each got a year."

"I'm not so sure about that," Jakob said.

"One thing is certain," I told them. "As soon as I get out of this godforsaken place—and I will, one way or another—this is the address I'm going to. Before I even go home to my family, I'll go straight to Valacia and find her."

Sebastian nodded and said, awkwardly, "Good for you, Harlan. Good for you."

On the way back across the field, fuelled by my letter from the outside world, we talked about where we were going when we got out.

"I'm going straight to my rich uncle's house," said Marek, another of the boys who had entered the prison camp the same day as we had on that awful truck journey south, "to take a long bath in a proper tub with hot water."

"I'm going to the city," said Jakob. "Straight to Capital. To join the resistance before this big battle happens."

"Won't it be dangerous?" asked Marek.

Jakob shrugged. "What about you, Sebastian?"

"Me? I'm going to dig up my mathematics textbooks. I'm a year behind with my studies. Not to mention that I've missed any important advances that may have taken place in the time I've been in here."

"I thought you said the secret police found your books?" said Jakob.

"Some of them." Sebastian looked dreamily at the horizon, in whatever direction his home must be. "I've got a whole lot more buried under the pig sty in my grandmother's yard. I'll just dig those up and continue, I suppose. But long-term, I'll have to go to the mainland too. It's the only place with proper universities. I've always known that, though it scares me a little."

"Come with me," Jakob said. "We'll go together. I have contacts there in the resistance and they can get us across the sea."

Sebastian, to my surprise, did not dismiss the idea so quickly as I had expected. "I might, actually, Jakob."

"What about you, Harlan?" Jakob said.

"I'm going to Maritz, in the north," I said. "It's where my brother lives. The free sector. I'll take Antonia and my mother and father and try and get there."

The last months of our sentence dragged out so badly I could hardly stand it. I would soon be nineteen, and I felt like a whole year had passed since I had been a proper person. A mild and rainy winter had brought with it long days of work on the farm. For once, I was glad of the ache in my back because it made me think of something that was not my fear for Antonia. While the wind rattled the windows of the sleeping hut and puffed black smoke out of our old stove back into the room, the exhaustion was the only thing that let me sleep at all.

In sleep, my mind was again full of Antonia, so that I dreamed and dreamed of her.

Again, the same dream.

I am walking up the steps of a tall, black house. Antonia's guitar is in my hand. I'm wearing my best blue suit. I am free. I knock, and that aunt with the sour mouth opens the door. "I'm Harlan North," I say. "I'm here to see Antonia." And into my arms, Antonia runs, just as young, just as perfect as before.

43

*A*gainst all expectations, we were released on the very anniversary of the day that we had been arrested. We were given no warning. The guard just came to our hut, thumped on the walls and shouted, "Up! Up!"

We lined up, shivering. His eyes picked out the three of us from the row: Jakob, Sebastian and me. "Come on," he said. "Time to leave."

The other boys' eyes followed us with a hungry envy they didn't trouble to disguise, across the yard and in at the farmhouse door.

We waited while the guard put stamps on our papers and issued growled warnings about the world outside and what would happen to us if we disobeyed its rules a second time. We already knew, for the world outside the labour camp seemed to have got darker. A few weeks earlier, Sebastian had heard news that his grandmother, the only relative he seemed to have left, had died, and his village was now an Alcyrian army camp. Faced with this, Jakob had persuaded him to go home only to retrieve his buried books, and then follow him to the mainland.

I was given back the clothes I had arrived in. They were too large for me now. But the smell of my grandfather's apartment still lingered on them, and with its scent that whole grim night swept over me like a wave and made me shiver. Still, in my old clothes, I was more myself again. I even had a few crowns in the pockets.

We were ordered to pack our other belongings and report to the gatepost. Jakob, Sebastian and I, walking as if in a dream, followed the fenland road towards the lights of the farm. In the furling snow, my heart felt so tender and light that I struggled to see the world as the same one I had woken up in. A full year had passed since I lay in Antonia's arms and happiness overwhelmed me. I felt at the same time much older and no older. The last year had been the breaking of me, and yet it had also been a dull and circular dream in which nothing had happened at all.

The gates opened. The guard let us out. The gates closed. We were free, just like that. The guard didn't look like he cared one way or another. He shooed us away from the gate and went back to his post.

"Look, Isak, can I be blunt?" Jakob asked as we stood outside, not ready to leave each other just yet.

"Yes," I said. "Go on."

"I think it's a bloody shame you won't consider coming with us to the city."

"My life is here. Everything is here. Here or in the north sector. You won't persuade me."

"What about the resistance?"

"I have to find Antonia."

"Damn you, Isak. You always know your own mind." He laughed. We were all in high spirits, drunk with relief to be outside that gate and free. "Here." He rummaged in his bag and produced the torn envelope that held his release papers. "Got a pen?"

I had a blunt pencil. Resting the paper on his own knee and pausing to wipe thick snowflakes from the page, he scrawled an address. "It's the place we're reporting to in the city," he said. "Keep this safe. Come and find us here if you change your mind."

"Promise you will, Isak?" said Sebastian, unexpectedly. "I mean to say, if you decide to come to the city. It won't be the same without you."

"All right, I promise. But it won't happen, you know. I've got Antonia to think about now. I'll take her to my brother in Maritz, if we can get there. My parents were talking about leaving." Even so, I put the paper in my pocket. Then I gripped the hands of both Jakob and Sebastian.

They turned to go the other way, and quite soon the snow had swallowed them.

"Isak!" shouted Jakob, just a blurry figure now.

"What?"

"I hope you find her!"

Grinning, I waved with all my strength, then turned back into the wind, and all at once I was running, quite weightless in my freedom, towards that life I had been torn away from. *Now, at last, I can find her*, I told myself. *Now, at last, my real existence can begin.* I crossed the fenland and ahead the lights of the real world appeared, and the little fishing towns in their obscurity and poverty had never looked so beautiful.

44

*I*n my elation, I thought that I would walk all night. I was forced to change my mind when I got to the village. At a new checkpoint, soldiers were sitting in trucks with their engines shut off, staring into the snow, while others marched about, checking papers and giving loud orders. On foot, my steps made no more sound than the snow itself, and I was able to get right up to the barrier before they saw me. One of them looked up and said something about papers in fast Alcyrian. I handed them over. He examined them with an impatient flick, scanning them with his electric torch. In its light, his eyes shifted eerily. He met my gaze and launched into a stream of Alcyrian.

"Sorry," I said. "I don't speak—" I did, but my Alcyrian was too rusty.

The man was not willing to speak to me in my own language either. He repeated his command. Eventually I made out the one word he kept coming back to: "*Courefeu! Courefeu!*"

"Curfew?" I said. It was a word that my mother and father had used sometimes, talking about their childhoods in another time of war.

"Yes," said the man curtly. "Curfew."

"What time?"

He showed me on his watch. I had half an hour. I was a hundred miles from my home. No one had told me anything about an eight o'clock curfew on the island.

I just nodded as if it was perfectly normal and I had somewhere to go, and waited for my papers. Once the checkpoint opened, the soldier let me through and I entered the village.

Just a few shabby houses, already shuttered. I walked along the side of the road. Dirty snow was piling up there, making the path difficult to tread. I went as quickly as I dared, but I knew there was no chance of finding somewhere to stay. Trucks roared past me one by one. The clouds hung low as fog.

I began putting out my arm for a lift, but without much hope.

When several trucks had passed me and I was almost through the village and out the other side again, someone pulled over and wound down his window, letting out a cloud of cigarette smoke. He said, in Alcyrian, "Get in the truck."

I had hoped for a Malonian driver. I hadn't expected an Alcyrian would even stop. The man, smiling broadly, leaned over and opened the latch on the passenger side. The door swung open. I didn't have much choice about it. I climbed over the slush in the gutter and into the passenger seat.

The man was about my father's age, quite ordinary, just a man with slicked-down hair in a battered truck. No harm in him, surely. In the back were sacks of cabbages.

"Where you going?" the man said, in accented Malonian.

"Valacia."

"I go to Valacia," said the man. "I take you there, maybe?"

He patted my knee and revved his engine, then offered me a cigarette. Inside the truck, he had made for himself a fog of warmth and smoke, and he drove peering through the windshield into the snow, occasionally taking one hand off the wheel to knock the ash off his cigarette. I looked up at his face; it didn't look unkind, and he wasn't a soldier. But I kept thinking how the last time I had been in a truck was when they had torn me away from Antonia. Couldn't it be some trick?

The truck bumped and slid on the icy road. The cabbages rolled around in the back. We were coming into hilly country now, and towards the edge of a proper town. "About four hours to Valacia," said the truck driver. "You from the labour camp, yes?"

I nodded, though I didn't know how he could tell. Probably by the mud in my fingernails, and the way my ordinary clothes didn't fit anymore.

The sea was drawing closer on our right. I wound down my window and leaned out into the night. Beyond the white noise of the snow, I could hear the sound of the waves. I hadn't realised until now how I had missed it. Longing for my family overwhelmed me: for my mother, my father, my sister, my grandfather, my town—for everything, that whole damn world that had been taken away from me. Antonia most of all. Four hours seemed too long.

Another truck loomed ahead, its headlights filling our cab with light and pricking my eyes. The driver swerved. "It's a bad business, this locking up in labour camps," he said. "What's your name?"

"Isak K."

"Pierre," he said. "I come from a little town in south Alcyria. I'm just here to work, then I go home. I'm not any Imperialist—don't worry."

A few miles further on, the lights of another checkpoint loomed. "You're safe while you're in the truck with me," said Pierre as the truck rolled to a standstill. "All the same, you should get in the back now."

He stopped the truck and ushered me over the seats and into the space between the sacks of cabbages. It was cold back there. We were kept waiting a long time at the checkpoint. The time stretched and stretched itself into hours.

At what must have been around midnight, we moved again. In the dark, I felt the engine come back to life. We drove without speaking to each other. Then, when we were safely out of the town, Pierre let me back into the front of the truck. "It's going to take much longer than four hours," said Pierre. "Sorry."

In the end it was nearly dawn by the time we reached familiar coastline, and I could see the ghostly edges of the white breakers beyond the cliffs. We were not far from New Maron.

I'm going to get Antonia back, I told myself. *I'm going to find her again*. What I was going to do when I found her was unclear to me. Longing must have confused my brain, because I had no fear. I don't remember thinking that there would be any problem with walking up to her aunt's front door and asking for her by name. "Not New Maron," I said, when he slowed. "Take me on to Valacia." I would see my mother and father later. Despite the curfew, I could not wait any longer to see Antonia than I already had.

I must have slept, because when I woke up, Pierre was looking down at me and the engine had cut out. Somewhere, birds were calling with that particular sound they make in high trees at dawn. Pierre opened the doors of the truck and let me out into the world.

"Here," he said. "Valacia."

We were right on the edge of the town; I could tell by the overgrown alleys and shuttered houses.

"When does the curfew end?" I asked.

"Six. Not so long. Keep out of sight. You'll hear a bell."

I unfolded myself from the truck and rubbed my aching legs.

"I've got to deliver these cabbages now," he said. "You can get home from here, yes?"

"Wait," I said, rubbing my eyes. "Do you know where this address is?" I took out Antonia's note and showed it to him.

He frowned. "Dockside quarter, probably. No good place." He held out his hand. "Good luck."

"Thank you!" I called after him, screwing up my eyes against the light. He was already revving his engine, and soon I was left alone in the waking city. It seemed a kind of omen, to get to Valacia so easily.

A single bell tolled, signalling the end of the curfew. I was hungry and thirsty and grimy from the back of the cabbage truck. Now that I was here, I wasn't sure I was ready to see Antonia. It seemed very important to me suddenly that our reunion should be like it was in the dream: that I should wear my blue suit and carry her guitar in one hand, all exactly the same. Otherwise the magic might not work—I might not find her.

But I was here now, and longing for her made me reckless. I walked in what I hoped was the direction of the coast road.

The morning unfolded itself in a haze of sun and a heavy dripping from the roofs and street corners as last night's snow melted. Along the municipal buildings by the docks, new notices proclaimed new laws. The people in the streets seemed hungrier, more grimy. I wondered if my own small town had changed too. And should I have gone there first, to see my mother and father? Should I have made plans to get to the mainland? Sent Anselm some letter?

When I reached the dock quarter, I began asking the way to Plaz Liberte. I started with an old man who was clearly Malonian. He pointed me between two rows of houses, up a narrow alley. There, I found a mother with a fractious toddler who sent me along a chilly avenue towards the dome of what must once have been a religious building.

I asked for directions and walked, asked for directions and walked. Sometimes, fearful that somehow I might be too late, I ran a little way, but people glanced at me strangely when I did that. No one ran in the new Valacia.

And then, quite suddenly, I was there. An Alcyrian sign, plastered with melting snow, decorated the side of a black house: *Plaz Liberte*.

I hadn't expected her to be living somewhere like this. The whole square had a chilly, neglected look, like it was the back face of some proper building. The houses stood very straight and tall, with their walls touching. From behind the door of one came the notes of a piano. Inside another, a baby screamed.

This was the house, the one with the crying baby. Number 42: a narrow building with dusty windows. My hands trembled as I checked the burnt paper. This was the place. Antonia was here.

I am walking up the steps of a tall, black house. Just as I imagined. Antonia's guitar is not in my hand, but instead I grip the note with her name. My hand sweats into the paper. I am wearing the clothes I was arrested in, not my best blue suit. But I am here, and I am free; that is what matters, I assure myself. I ring the doorbell and wait. Inside, footsteps. *I am free*, I keep telling myself. *I am free. I have served my time.*

Eventually someone draws back the chain. It's her: that aunt with the sour mouth. Just like in my dream. I begin to feel that everything may be all right.

"I'm Isak K.," I say, in her language. "I'm here to see Antonia."

She raises her eyes to heaven. She doesn't say anything at first.

"I need to see her," I say. "Please."

The pale aunt sighs and gestures for me to come inside.

All at once, I know that the dream has lied to me—that things aren't going to be the way I imagined.

A great dread comes over me as I follow her into the dark house.

45

"I'm Isak K.," I said as we went along the passageway, in an effort to get something out of her. "Antonia's—Antonia's . . ."

The aunt turned. "I'm quite aware of who you are."

"Is she here? Antonia?"

We entered a dark kitchen with painted plates on the walls. "I'll go and find Mr. Bercy," said the aunt. "I'm sure he'll wish to speak to you about what happened to Antonia."

A sick pain punched me in the chest. "What do you mean, what happened to her?"

"I'll not say anything more. Stay here in this kitchen. If you leave the room, I'll call the secret police." I knew the Alcyrian phrase quite well after a year in the labour camp: *polizier segreda*.

"I'll stay," I said. "Will you fetch Antonia?"

The aunt left, shutting the kitchen door behind her. I walked from one end of the room to the other. The inside of me felt hollowed out, and for the very first time I began to consider that something terrible might actually have happened in this house. "My God," I found myself praying. "Please let her be all right."

That baby began to cry again. It was quite close—in the next room, or the one after. The child went on crying thinly, an enraged and miserable sound, and no one answered. It made my head ache. And all the time, my heart was hurting because Antonia was not here the way she was supposed to be.

The baby wailed as though its heart was broken too.

It must be the aunt's baby, I thought. I had no love for Antonia's aunt, but I felt bad for this child. The way it cried was so miserable, as if it was used to crying and crying and never being answered. That, and nothing else, was what made me disobey the aunt and push open the door.

I found the baby in a small room with a bed and a crib and a pile of cardboard boxes. It must once have been a store-room, and it was still mostly cupboard. The baby was sitting in the dark in its crib, holding out its arms, on a patch of wet blanket. It looked less than a year old. A tuft of black hair stood up on its head, and its cheeks were pink and blotchy from crying so long.

When the baby saw me it quietened down, but not much. It

made a gargling noise and sniffed up the string of snot that was running over its nose and mouth, then resumed its wails. The crib mattress it was sitting on was stained and threadbare. There was nothing of comfort in this room.

"Hush, baby," I said.

I felt sorrier for it even than myself. There was something dark and terrible about the way it was just left there alone. It must be a joyless place to grow up, this house. "Hush, baby," I said again. "Are you scared? What are you frightened of? The dark? Is that it?"

The baby listened. The tears rested in its eyes. Probably no one had ever spoken Malonian to it before.

"Don't be afraid now," I told the baby. "Your mother will be back soon. Hush now. Don't be afraid."

Telling this baby not to be afraid made me a little less afraid too.

The baby stretched its arms out to me.

"No," I said. "I can't pick you up—they wouldn't like it. My people aren't supposed to have any contact with your people. I've learned that to my cost."

I knelt down beside the crib all the same. The baby grabbed my ear with one damp hand and my hair with the other. It swatted at my face. Then it stopped crying and let out a laugh. I could not smile back. I knew already, waiting in that dark and godforsaken house, with this poor squalling baby, that something very bad had happened to Antonia. I rehearsed the possibilities in my mind. Illness. An accident. Death.

I shuddered. "I can't pick you up," I repeated. "But I'll stay with you a little."

I gave the baby my finger to hold. In the half-dark of the room, I waited for the aunt to return, and it made me feel better to have the child's hand in mine.

When she did arrive, it was without warning. The door of the room banged open and she cried, "Up! Up! Leave the child alone!"

I got to my feet. "I'm sorry," I said, and then in her language: "*Escuse*. I'm very sorry. It was crying. No one was looking after it."

"That's the maid's job. If she's too busy upstairs, the baby will just have to wait. Come out of there. You have no right."

When I left the baby, it flung me a disconsolate look, as though I had betrayed it. Its eyes were grey and clear and haunting in the dark.

"Mr. Bercy has left for work," said the aunt. "Come through to the kitchen."

I tried again. "Where is Antonia? She sent me a letter four months ago." I took out the burnt scrap of paper. The aunt reached for it with bony fingers and scrutinised it. "I came as quickly as I could."

"Antonia must have sent this during her illness," she said. "That's the only explanation. Probably she was delirious, or—"

"Her illness?"

"She fell sick a few months ago."

"Sick? No one told me." My Alcyrian broke down, so I continued in my own language: "You knew the address—any letter would have been forwarded to me at the camp—"

"You had absolutely no right to know," cried the aunt viciously, switching to my own language too. "What are you to Antonia?"

"What are *you* to her?" I said. "What the hell are you to her, who never treated her with any kindness?"

The aunt put the paper back into my hand without looking at me. "I'm sorry to have to tell you that she's gone."

"Gone?"

"Dead. She died during her illness. Very sudden. There was nothing we could do."

The words hit me like a blow. I felt my knees losing their strength. It was only the paper in my hands that kept me upright.

"No," I said, the way I'd heard other people say it when they were told bad news. *No, it can't be. No, please, God.*

The aunt was saying more things—"three months ago," and "very unfortunate," and "Nothing we could do, as I said."

I forced the paper into her hand. "Look again."

"I've looked. She's gone. I'm sorry to tell you news you don't like, but that's the truth about it."

In the other room, the baby cried and cried. "I need to see her belongings," I said. "I need to know properly what happened."

"There's nothing to show you. There's nothing to tell you. She got ill. She died."

"How did she get ill? What caused it?"

The aunt shrugged. "A condition inherited from her mother."

Her mother had died young. But older—much older than Antonia, still—forty, or fifty.

"Why didn't you send for me?" I felt tears of rage running down my face. "Why didn't you let me know?"

"You can't imagine we would have wanted that."

"Don't you have a heart at all—you or her father?"

"Mr. Bercy was very upset to lose his daughter," said the aunt. "Very upset indeed." She straightened. "As was I."

Then, all at once, doubt seized me. Something in her tone was all wrong. As sure as she was standing in front of me, I knew that this aunt was not telling the truth about Antonia.

"You're lying," I said. "There's something wrong about this. You're telling me she's dead, but I don't believe it. You've got her hidden somewhere here, or—I don't know what, but you're lying. Say it's not true."

"I will not say anything of the sort," said the aunt. "I'll give you a minute to collect your thoughts, then I would like you gone from my house."

I pushed past the stick-figure aunt and a girl who was eaves-dropping on the stairs—she must be the maid—and ran from room to room, banging open each door and searching behind them, calling Antonia's name. I went all the way through the house, and then I realised I had come to the end of a corridor and there was nowhere left to search. The aunt and the maid were bearing down upon me fiercely.

"She's not here," said the aunt. "She is gone. Now get out of our house. If you come here again, Mr. Bercy will see to it that you are returned to the labour camp."

I had no strength in me. They led me with cold, unfeeling hands along the corridor and down the hall and out onto the doorstep. The door was shut in my face. Then, because the world was spinning around me, I ran. I ran through slushy snow, past the secret police in their grey uniforms, the people with their grey morning faces, the docks, the sea. I ran along the coast road where the wind whipped sharply.

I only came to myself when I was among the familiar streets of New Maron. I collapsed, gasping, against my own front door.

A shadow appeared behind the counter. Bolts were drawn back. "Harlan?" said my father.

"Papa," I said.

"My God, Harlan, my boy. You're back! Are you hurt? What's wrong?"

I fell into my father's arms and wept.

46

$\mathcal{M}$y father sat beside me with his hand resting on my arm, very lightly, in a way that had always made me feel safe when I was a young boy. My mother, on the other side of me, read and reread Antonia's note. I had told them the brief story of our love now. I had told them everything. Between us, we tried to puzzle it out.

At last my mother said, very gently, "And do you honestly think, Harlan, that the aunt was lying? Do you honestly think that Antonia is alive?"

In my mind's eye, I saw only the way her face looked when it was upraised to mine and happy, the soft look of her skin. "Yes," I said. "I believe it."

"Would this aunt have any reason to lie to you?"

I didn't know. I couldn't think of one.

"Look, Harlan, I'm more sorry than I can say." My mother's eyes were wet with sympathetic tears. "But don't let this loss turn you crazy. If she's gone, she's gone."

"She isn't gone," I said. "I know it."

"Then where is she?" My father pored over the charred note again. "There's something sinister about all this."

"I'll have to go back to the house," I said at last. "I'll have to go back and get more answers."

But on this, my mother and father were united. "You can't," said my father, very quietly. "This man, Mr. Bercy, can send you to a prison camp any time he chooses—or worse, turn you over to the secret police. You mustn't be seen to be causing trouble. Things are so much worse than when you left. Much worse. Mr. Cortez is dead, they say."

"Dead? For what?"

"For his part in the resistance, right at the start of the invasion. And the man you used to work for at the shipyards, Mr. Walcott, was arrested on charges of homosexuality, and he's been gone ever since."

"But he has a wife."

"Do you think any of that sort of detail matters to them?"

My mother shivered slightly, probably thinking of Anselm. "Write a polite letter," she suggested. "Ask them to send you a copy of the certificate of death or tell you where the grave is. That's all you can do now, Harlan."

It was a dark day, my homecoming. My mother tried to make an affair of it, opening cans of potatoes and beans and setting the best teacups on the table. The two of them hid their joy quite creditably. But I couldn't eat or drink. I shivered so badly, they became convinced I had caught a fever and put me to bed, but I couldn't sleep. I entered this stupor on the day of my return and lay like that for several days and nights—ill but not with any recognisable illness, sick but with a sickness of the soul.

The thing that sustained me during this time was my letter from Aldebaran.

It sounds strange, but that letter was the only written thing I had left. As a child, unable to sleep on stormy nights, I had read and reread my grandfather's books. Now all I had were the letter and the map. I needed an escape. I needed magic, now more than ever. I studied the map feverishly and imagined that I could travel to these places and pass through into that bright world of green sunlight, and there Antonia would be. I tried so hard to see visions of her, but none came.

After four nights, I surrendered to exhaustion and slept a kind of half-sleep.

And then, I dreamed of Antonia. Not her face or her voice, first of all, but her beating heart. It thudded very lightly in the darkness beyond my vision, but I could tell that it was hers. In the dark, still half aware of my own surroundings, I strained to conjure more of her. Slowly, she came into focus. Her hair, not long and thick as it had been, but unexpectedly short. The curve of one shoulder, thinner and more wasted. Sounds outside the window, not sleet and rain but Alcyrian voices, very real. A small grey room with ornate shutters that threw a fretwork of moonlight over her.

"Antonia?" I said.

My own voice brought me back and I woke, startled. I was sitting up in bed, sweating and shivering like a dying man. My own heart thudded, and made me feel more alive than I had in the last four days. A small miracle had happened. I had seen her, and I knew in my heart that she was alive. I believed that somewhere that small grey room existed, and that if I could find it, there Antonia would be.

Morning, and a cold grey light lay across my pillow. I got up, pulled on my clothes any way I could, and went down to the shop. I hunted around among the tools until I found what I wanted: an old hacksaw blade.

"Harlan?" My father, on the stairs, startled me. He came into the room, put a hand on my shoulder. "Your mother and I have been thinking. It's time we got away from Holy Island. We'll try to rejoin Anselm in the north of the country, now that you're back with us. There's a ship that leaves twice a month for Arkavitz, and they take illegal passengers, for a fee."

"When does it go?"

"Later today."

But this was all wrong. How could I leave for the mainland without Antonia?

"No," I said. "I can't go."

"Harlan, it's not safe for you here. There have been people watching the shop. Announcements on the radio about the search for the North family. They're closing in."

"I can't go without Antonia."

"The ship leaves at six," said my father. "Anselm's sent us the money to bribe the captain and the guard. Don't tell anyone what we're doing, but you have to be ready for the ship."

"I'll be ready," I said. "But I have to sort something out first."

I called goodbye to my mother and father through the door of their bedroom and set out.

47

*A*gainst the wall of Antonia's house—where Antonia was not—I crouched outside the window of the baby's room. I had chosen this window because it was the only one left unshuttered. It stood at just about my head height, with a narrow windowsill. I pressed my face to the glass and looked in. That baby was lying uncovered on its dirty mattress, sleeping, one thumb in its mouth.

I was uncertain how to proceed. I couldn't break the window and risk hurting the baby and waking the house. I had checked every other window, and all were barred with thick shutters. I decided to try the sawblade instead. I had brought it with the thought of breaking in; I knew it worked because we had broken into the store-room that way, one day last year when my father had lost his key. Very slowly, I reached up and began trying to work the sawblade in between the window and the frame, just below where the lock was. I jiggled the blade. The metal let out a rusty squeak.

I got down low behind the front wall of the house and waited until I was certain that no one had heard. Luckily, it was still early enough that no one in the square had opened their shutters. After ten minutes of careful work with the blade, I got the lock free. I leaned on the window and pushed.

The glass in the corner cracked and made me drop behind the wall again, my heart thumping. I must have shoved it too hard. I waited, then pushed the window frame again. This time, it gave way. Inside, I heard the baby murmur. "Shh," I said through the window. "Shh." Giving thanks for the scrawniness I had attained after a year of watery labour camp food, I hauled myself up onto the sill and in through the window.

I could never have been a burglar. My entrance was clumsy and violent and ended in a bruised knee and cut lip. But at least I was inside. The baby cried a little, tentatively. I said, "Shh, shh, shh," and limped over to it. Still crying half-heartedly, it sat and looked at me, its grey eyes very pale and uncanny in the dark. There's something weird about babies, the way they stare. This one troubled me now. But it did not seem particularly frightened. It sucked its fist, and quieted.

"I'm not going to harm you," I said. "I'm here to find out about Antonia. She's the girl who lived here once. She probably used to sleep in this room. In that old bed, maybe. Shoved out of sight like you. I love her, and I'm here to find out if there are any clues about what's happened to her. Is that all right by you?"

"A-ba-ba-ba-ba-ba!" said the baby.

"Good. Just keep quiet while I'm looking, will you?"

I didn't dare turn on the electric light, but the dawn outside was enough to see by. On top of the bed was a pile of moth-eaten coats. I opened a few boxes, but they merely contained ugly china pieces wrapped in newspaper, and brass candlesticks and cutlery—relics of a life in a richer house somewhere. I found a set of war medals that must have belonged to some dead relative, and a crystal decanter. The objects were the kind of things I saw daily in our shop, and none of them had anything to do with Antonia.

In the chest of drawers, I had more luck. I found a few blouses that might have been hers, a wool shawl, an old skirt with a bleach stain on it. I inhaled, and thought that I could still catch the faint scent of her.

All this time, the baby watched me like I was performing a show for its benefit. Poor thing; it must get no attention at all. Its eyes were calm and flat, as though it hoped for nothing, expected nothing.

If it was the aunt's baby, why did she show it no love? Was she simply incapable of loving?

Three of the drawers in the chest were empty. In the bottom one, though, I found some things which must belong to the baby, shoved in any old way in a paper bag so that at first I dismissed them as rubbish. Now I found all the relics of its short life. A little booklet for medical checks and vaccinations, none of them completed. This gave the baby's date of birth as the sixth of October. I looked at the baby again.

"You're five months old?" I said. "Is that right? What are you supposed to be doing right now? Crawling around, or talking? I don't know. You still look very small."

The baby said nothing, just gave me a sudden, dazzling smile, displaying a single tooth.

Something about this baby intrigued me. It was the way its skin looked in the light, very gold for an Alcyrian baby. What were strangest, though, were the baby's eyes. They were definitely Malonian eyes, grey like my father's.

I opened the drawer again and began looking for its birth certificate. I found it at the bottom of the paper bag, stamped and dated by the government authorities. It was written in two languages. My hands were shaking when I unfolded it, and I couldn't yet tell why. The realisation came to me very slowly and by degrees. "Shh, shh," I said, to the baby and myself.

The birth certificate read, *Mother: Antonia Fortuna Bercy. Father unknown.*

The door opened. I staggered back against the chest of drawers. There stood the maid in her nightdress, her mouth hanging open slightly, a lamp in her hand. She turned to shout, but I moved quickly, catching her by the wrist and dragging her into the room. Suddenly, much more was at stake than just my own safe escape from this house, and fear made me think quicker.

"Don't make a sound." I raised the hacksaw blade. "Don't say a word. I'm not going to hurt you, but you have to do as I say."

I don't know what she thought I was going to do to her with the blunt blade, but it worked. The girl wrapped her throat in her hands and nodded.

"This baby," I said. "Whose is it? Is this true—it's Antonia's?"

The maid let out a throaty noise, trying to speak.

"It's all right. I'm not going to harm you."

"I'll call for the secret police."

"You won't."

Another strangled noise, but this time she spoke more clearly. "Yes. It's hers. Antonia's. Mr. Bercy's daughter."

"Who's the father?"

"I don't know that."

In my head, I was calculating. If the baby was born on the sixth of October, it had been conceived sometime in January. There was only one person it could possibly belong to. I turned to the baby and believed that I was looking into my own grey eyes. I was certain.

I knew that if I made a mistake now I would be back in Black Heath Labour Camp by nightfall, and they would take this child from me just like they took Antonia.

"What's the baby's name?" I said.

"She doesn't have a name."

"No one named it? Not even Antonia?"

The maid shook her head. "The mistress says the baby's a cursed little thing and we're not to name her. I tried calling her Trudie, but the mistress beat me. She says the baby's going away to some people on the mainland. There's a reward for handing her in, because there's something wrong with her."

"What about Antonia?" I gripped the maid's wrist too tightly and she half cried out. "I'm sorry, I'm sorry. I won't hurt you— just tell me. What happened to Antonia?"

The maid shook her head, still gripping her own throat as though she was choking.

"What happened to her?" I brandished the saw.

"She ran away! I don't know any more than that, I swear."

"Tell me what you do know."

"She got on a ship to the mainland. That's all I know. I'm only the servant here. They don't tell me these things, I promise you."

"But she's not dead?"

"They think she's dead. They don't know for sure."

"When did she leave?"

"Directly after the birth. Beginning of October."

"But that's not right. If this baby is hers, she wouldn't leave it."

The maid was still having difficulty breathing, but she had begun glancing at the door with greater defiance. I knew that Antonia's father was far more frightening than I was, and I was going to lose my chance if I didn't push her quickly for information, while she was still afraid.

"Tell me," I said. "Why did she leave it?"

"Antonia doesn't know about the baby," said the maid, all in a rush.

"How is that possible? She gave birth to it—of course she knows about it."

"Yes, but she thinks it died after it was born."

"What do you mean?"

"I'm trying to tell you. Stop waving that knife at me. I'm trying to tell you, aren't I?" The maid looked away from me with fearful eyes. "Strange things happened when Antonia was pregnant. She had sort of—I don't know—fits. And things would fall apart in the house when she walked by, if the baby was just kicking. So her aunt kept her at home. For her own safety, she said." She made the old sign of the cross that my mother sometimes made when she was frightened. "Miss Bercy said the baby was an evil little thing."

My mouth felt very dry. "Go on," I said.

"Then when the baby came, it was a bad birth. The doctor gave Antonia drugs and put her to sleep. I don't know why. I wasn't allowed downstairs." She glanced once more at the door and then carried on, in a rush. "Antonia was sleeping when the baby was born. While she was sleeping, the mistress put the baby away in an upstairs room. She showed me how little and frail it was, and she told me it wasn't going to survive. I felt so sorry for it. She said we had to tell Antonia that the baby had died already, for her own good, without letting her see the poor sickly thing fade away. She said she was going to send it to the hospital, and we must pretend to Antonia that it had died and been buried, so that she wouldn't grieve. So I did."

"You told Antonia her baby had died?"

"The mistress said it was for the best." Tears ran down the maid's face.

"What did Antonia do when they told her the baby was dead? This baby, that she probably loved and hoped for."

The maid shook her head. She went on shaking it without saying a word.

"Tell me! Haven't you done enough harm already?"

"It wasn't my fault. None of this was my fault." She became confiding, wheedling. "You know what it's like for us Malonians. I was at risk of losing my position."

"Us Malonians! I don't have anything in common with you. My family fight in the resistance! I've been in a labour camp for a year!"

"*I* was at risk too," the maid told me, with unexpected ferocity. "I'm not saying I thought it was right, what Miss Bercy did, but I didn't dare tell Antonia the truth. They would have known it was me. Who else would have told her?"

"What did Antonia do when you told her the baby was dead?"

"That was when she left. She was still sick, but she got up and left. No one could stop her. She was shivering and feverish, but she left the house anyway. She went down to the docks. Her father let her go. He said she wouldn't get far. I think he was surprised when she didn't come back. Then he went after her all right, but it was too late. They say she was seen at the docks, but she never reached the mainland. They think she died on the crossing. A few ships went down that day, God rest their souls. It was an oversight—she should have been stopped at the border."

I sat down on the ground in front of the chest of drawers. Through the bars of its crib, the baby looked at me. Its eyes seemed to be pleading with me not to leave it again.

All at once, I made my decision.

"I'm this baby's father," I said. "I loved Antonia, and I'll take care of this baby now. I'm going to take it away."

"You're most certainly not." The maid was all fight now, and raising her voice shrilly. "If you so much as try, I'll call for Mr. Bercy and the secret police. They're going to have ten thousand crowns for her!"

"Call them—I'll tell them what you've just told me. And then what chance in hell have you got of keeping your position after that? They'll think you're a revolutionary, the way you've spilled all these family secrets to me just because I threatened you with a rusty saw."

The maid paused, halfway between defiance and shock. In her moment of hesitation, I pressed on. "I'm going to take the baby. When I've gone, go back up to sleep and act as though everything is ordinary. When they find the baby gone, you aren't to tell them anything. Is that clear?"

"They'll know it was you who took the baby. They'll come after you."

"Just do as I say," I told her.

I bundled up the baby in the thin grey blanket. Its weight against me, when I lifted it, was hardly anything at all. I felt its tiny heartbeat, a kind of fluttering. In that moment, love struck me like a blow and I knew—I mean really knew, deep in my heart—that this baby was mine.

The girl made one last attempt to block the door. "She's dead, you know," she told me, with a trace of pity. "She never made it to the mainland. Not the way she was. The master thinks she died of the fever, or threw herself in the sea."

"She isn't dead," I said. "I'll find her again and we'll be together. And then I'll come back here and burn this whole god-forsaken house to the ground. Now stand away from the door."

My anger gave me a kind of violence I had not known I

possessed. The maid stood aside and let me go. Together, my baby and I went down the steps of that dark house and out into the light.

48

*I*n my arms, the baby was squalling, a thin, angry sound. Its cry drew the eyes of passers-by. In my haste, I was holding it like a bag of old potatoes. I heaved it higher into my arms and tried to fold it in my jacket, out of the wind.

I was on the very edge of Valacia when I heard the bells of the police trucks jangling. I knew they could not be ringing for me, not yet, but I also knew that it was not long before Mr. Bercy would find the baby missing from his house and come after me. Even then, I wasn't sure exactly what I had done.

I don't know what idea I had a hold of in my head. I got all the way home without knowing. My one certainty was that this baby was mine, and I was never going to let it go away from me. I had lost Antonia. This child, I would not lose.

I ran upstairs and into the living room and put the baby down on the sofa. It squirmed and cried. While I was still standing there looking at it, trying to get my breath and think, my mother and father appeared from the shop, agitated. The baby lifted up its voice and cried in earnest, surrounded by these strangers.

"Help me," I said, turning to them. "I've done a very bad thing. I don't know how to fix it."

"Whose is this child? What's it doing here, Harlan?"

As well as I could, I told them: that I had stolen this baby from Antonia's house; that it was hers; that however crazy it might sound, I believed it was mine too; that Antonia was not dead, but disappeared, across the ocean, and no one knew where. The baby cried and cried. My mother lifted it and looked down into its face. She said, "What's your name, then? What's your name, eh, pretty baby?"

Her singsong tone calmed us all. With its pale grey eyes, the baby looked up at her.

"No one named her," I said. "She was just living there in a room on her own, with no one paying her any attention. See how dirty her clothes are."

My mother pressed the baby to her chest and kissed its tuft of black hair.

"Did I do right to take it away?"

"You did right," said my mother. "But we have to think now. What are you going to do? You can't stay here. They'll come to New Maron. They'll know it's you who's taken her."

My father touched my shoulder. "Let's look after this poor baby first. We've got at least enough time to make it more comfortable. Poor thing."

My father tore up rags to make a new nappy and filled the kitchen sink with warmish water. He went down to the shop and came up with a set of clothes. We undressed the baby and put her into the water. The stale smell of her old clothes filled our kitchen. My mother shoved them into the bucket under the sink. While the baby went on crying, my father wiped her with a cloth; the grime came away and her pink skin shone.

I reached out and stroked her hair. "Let me take care of her."

My father showed me how to tip the water over the baby's tiny arms and legs, and how to wash her matted hair. Very carefully, I held the baby upright. Her skin folded at the bottom of her round stomach, and creased on the insides of her elbows and knees. When I rubbed soap into her hair, the baby stopped crying and let out a laugh. She clapped her hands in the water.

"She's beautiful," I said. "Isn't she the most beautiful thing?"

"What about Antonia?" said my mother. "Where do you think she's gone?"

"I mean to look for her."

Until I said it, I hadn't known for certain that was my intention. My mother's mouth formed a wordless circle. For a long time, neither of us spoke. Then I said it again: "I mean to look for her. In the occupied territory."

"That's the last place I want you to go, Harlan. We'll leave together, for Anselm's—"

My father shook his head. "We've only got the money for three tickets. That's what Anselm sent."

"The maid said someone was going to pay money for this baby," I told them. "She said the baby was going to be taken away. I can't leave her on Holy Island."

The baby cried again at our raised voices.

"Shh," I said. "It's all right. I won't let them take you away." I lifted her out of the water. My mother found a towel and helped me rub the baby's tiny feet and clenched fists. But she had that silence about her that meant she hadn't said her last words on the subject.

We dressed the baby in the clothes from the shop, rolling up the sleeves. I didn't want to let anyone else hold her, so I sat with her on my lap on the sofa while my mother heated milk. The inside of me felt bruised.

"Maria," said my father, still loudly enough for me to hear, "they'll take the child away from him. You must see that. There's no way to prove it's his, and they'll take it back. There's only one thing to do. Harlan and the baby must go to Anselm in Maritz, and you and I must stay here."

"No," said my mother and I together.

"Harlan," my father called, "the money's in the safe. Go and take it out, just in case. If you do have to leave quickly, you'll need it with you."

That money had been supposed to be for them. I looked at my father with fresh eyes. His face was impossibly sad, but he insisted.

When I came back upstairs, my baby in my arms, the matter must have been decided between them. My mother leaned over the sink, weeping silently.

"I have to go to the mainland, Mama," I said. "But I'll go to Anselm. I'll be safe there, if we can make the sea crossing all right, and get to the north."

"How long until that place is worse than Holy Island to live in? How long until the Imperialists take it too?"

"I have to try. Otherwise they'll take this baby away."

My mother put her hand to the side of my face. She looked at me for a long time; then she seemed to steel herself. "You'll need some milk formula," she said. "It's what you give a baby with no mother. We've time at least for your father to run to the market for some, to take with you on the journey."

My father shook his head. "They won't have it in the market. None of the packet food from the mainland gets here anymore."

"Then I'll make some by hand," said my mother. "The way we used to in the old days. Harlan, get your things together."

Very quickly, I gathered my belongings. A few clothes, my great-great-uncle's papers, the spare clothes my father had found for the baby. My writing notebooks, though I hardly knew why. I put all these things into the old leather backpack in which I had once carried my belongings to school. While I did that, my mother, quite calmly, mixed milk and oats and water and a little honey and heated them for the baby. Then we sat in our living room and I fed the baby spoonfuls of formula. She stopped her crying altogether. My father filled several glass bottles with this watered-down milk and put these too into the leather backpack. He packed rags for nappies, and blankets from the cupboard.

My mother, meanwhile, was attempting to teach me everything she knew about babies all at once. "Keep her warm," she kept saying. "Keep her ears and feet covered if the sea wind is cold. Warm the milk if you can. Test it with your little finger so it doesn't scald her. Hold her against your shoulder like this to burp her after she's fed. Don't put her down to sleep anywhere that someone could roll onto her. If you have to go into the mountains to reach Anselm, don't leave any part of her uncovered or she'll freeze. Not her hands or face."

"Maria," my father said, carrying my backpack into the room and standing in front of us. "Harlan needs to get away before they search the whole town. I know which officials we need to bribe at the docks, but we'll have to go at once."

"What about you?" I said. "We were supposed to go together."

"Maria," said my father. "You go too. I'll stay here."

"No," she said. "I won't leave you."

My father pushed me out and down the stairs. That was the worst part, saying goodbye to my mother. As I looked back at her face, bleak as winter rain, I knew that this was real; I was really leaving my home.

49

I ran through back alleyways with the baby wrapped in my old leather jacket, my father beside me. Once, we almost passed a group of soldiers, but the tramping of boots ahead alerted us and we ducked into the shadows. The baby grizzled and squalled. It squirmed in my arms and clenched its tiny fists.

My father had in his pocket the great sum of money Anselm had sent to ensure our safe passage. Now, it was enough for the baby and me.

"What about you?" I said.

"We'll be all right. We'll join you if we can. I don't know which is safer, staying on Holy Island or making that sea crossing. Harlan, you will be careful?"

"Of course I will."

"I don't know if it's right, taking a baby so small into the hold of a refugee ship, making a two-day climb into the mountains."

"She won't survive here," I said. "They were going to sell her to people on the mainland. People were coming to take her away. It's her only chance."

We did not run as we approached the docks. Instead, we went, very calmly, down to the cargo ship *Star of Valacia*, and my father called into the cabin: "Hello? Anyone there?"

A grubby man in a string vest emerged. "Yes?" he said. "What do you want?"

"I've a letter for you from Anselm A. of the Maritz Cell." My father put a paper into the man's hand. The man nodded. He read and reread the letter. "Eight hundred," he said. "For the three of you."

It was more than the money Anselm had sent. "Not three," said my father. "Just my son and the baby."

The man narrowed his eyes shrewdly and said, "Six hundred and fifty, in that case."

"We've got six hundred," said my father. "We were told two hundred each was the price."

"The crossing has got more dangerous. Price has gone up."

"I'll give you six hundred for the two of them, and no more."

The grimy man sighed. He came up onto the quay and looked at me, hands on hips. The baby wriggled and the jacket fell from her head. "I'm not so happy about taking that one."

"She's only a few months old," I said.

"That's why. You know the kind of crossing we're making."

Other ships were coming in and out of the docks now with a churning and revving of engines, and the confusion in the water around us made the grimy man impatient. A soldier appeared from the shadows of the guard post. I gripped the baby around the middle. All at once, hopelessness came over me. It was too late—they would come after us—and my daughter would be taken away like Antonia had been.

Very carefully, with trembling fingers, my father took out the stack of banknotes and counted out six hundred crowns. He took off his watch, a gift from my mother when they still lived in the city. "There," he said. "For both of them, to the mainland." He pressed the money into the captain's hand.

Somehow it was suddenly all right, because the grimy man let me onto the ship.

Before I boarded, my father hugged me tightly and held on for several seconds. He said, "I love you, son. I've always loved you. Take care."

"When will I see you again? Will you make it to the north sector too? That was all your money, Papa—and your watch—"

"It doesn't matter. Get to Anselm. Keep safe."

With the baby in my arms, I boarded the ship.

The engine started and we left the quay behind quickly, moving between other ships in the churned-up water. My father stood very straight and tall on the quay. I watched him for a long time until he finally receded from sight.

Pretty soon after that, Holy Island became just a grey land mass on the edge of the grey water. I prayed that my mother and father would be all right.

The ship heaved. I sat in the shelter of a draughty cabin, watching my home vanish in the mist. The captain walked about with my father's silver watch on his arm. The baby would not stop crying, so I tried feeding her, warming the bottles as best I could under my own shirt. But she wouldn't drink the milk half cold like that. I held her close to me to keep her warm. Holy Island looked like nothing when you sailed away from it. When we got to a certain distance, you could see both ends of the island. Then it was just a flat, dark stripe on the sea. For the first time since

I was a baby far smaller than this one in my arms, I was crossing the sea, away from all that I had ever known.

The other passengers—a woman and two children who looked wealthy, or at least as though they had been wealthy once—were sullen and quiet. They glanced at me as though they wanted me to silence the baby, but I couldn't do anything. She screamed and screamed. I unfolded her clothes and stroked her pink and screaming face and her tufty hair. I pleaded with her to stop. I walked to and fro and rocked her. I did everything that I imagined a good father would do.

My baby would not let me rest. She refused her food, then took it in great gulps and cried and cried until she was sick. After that, she needed changing, and not long after that she began a different wailing which seemed to have no remedy. Both of us were streaked with milk and vomit, and we were growing infuriated with each other.

After three hours of this, the wealthy woman got up and came towards me.

"I'm sorry," I said. "I can't get her to stop."

"Your baby is frightened," she said, more gently than I had expected. "Mine were like this the first time we crossed the sea. Go out into the wind and let her cry it out, and she'll soon be asleep. That's what my nursemaid did with the little ones, when we made the crossing to the island."

It didn't seem to make much sense, but I did what the woman said. Walking to and fro in the wind, watching my old home vanish, I had never felt lonelier.

When the wind finally died, a thick fog came down. Strangely, that and the cold air seemed to calm my baby, and she sat up in my arms and stared at the mist, entranced by its spiralling. I took a proper breath and sat down in the shelter of the cabin. Then my baby slept, clinging to my shirt the way she had done before. I kissed her forehead in relief.

We were travelling without lights, making for the occupied mainland, towards which Holy Island ships were licensed to travel. At some point in the dark, we would veer north. Towards dusk a ship came alongside, its low throbbing the only sign it was near in the whiteness of the fog. I hid in the cabin, my baby pressed close to my chest. But it was just fishermen, with reassuring Holy Island accents, warning us not to go too close to the sandbars. That was the last I heard of that accent for a very long time.

My baby woke quite contented after her cold sleep. She flapped her arms and let out a chuckle. I held her on my knee in the shelter of the cabin, and let her grab my fingers and face. All at once, like a kind of miracle, it came to me: the name Antonia would have given her.

"Anastasia?" I said.

The baby swivelled her head and stared at me, uncannily, like she understood I was talking to her.

"Anastasia. That's what Antonia would have called you. After her mother."

The baby looked up at me, making bubbles with her spit.

"Anastasia North. It doesn't go well, but it will have to do. Anastasia Fortuna North, maybe."

The aunt had said there was something cursed about her, but to me she was the brightest angel. And what if it wasn't something cursed but something special? What if this baby really was like me?

"Anastasia?" I said, looking into her eyes. "How much do you understand? How much do you know? Did something go wrong at your birth too? Do you have strange dreams?"

The baby gulped milk and, contented at last, returned to sleep. I kept watch, her tiny body enclosed in my arms. My daughter gripped me strongly in sleep, as though she knew I was the one taking care of her now. I thought, *This is my child, a living being with a whole bright childhood and a whole awkward adolescence and a whole tough life ahead of her.*

She settled into her new name quite comfortably. I liked it, because every time I said her name it was a little like I was speaking to Antonia.

VI

❧ RETURN ❧

50

*T*o cross from Holy Island to Arkavitz is to traverse the most dangerous waters on the continent. This the Imperialists knew, and if they were aware of our ship's crossing, they took no trouble to stop us. They must have known that the sea stood a greater chance of doing that.

I first became aware that something was wrong when I was roused by the baby's screaming. The ship was rolling, pitching cold water over us with each toss. It must have come in over the side somewhere. Something thudded as the waves passed under us. The steel of the ship creaked and moaned, as though it were tearing apart. "Anastasia," I said. "It's all right. It's all right."

"We've been thrown off course," said the wealthy woman, clinging to her shrieking children. "They told us to keep down here. They're going to try and get into the shelter of the Strait of Ravina."

The Strait of Ravina, I knew, was occupied territory. "But what about the Alcyrian army?"

"There's nothing to be done. The storm's a greater danger than the Imperialists."

I thought of my father's watch, which he had parted with to ensure our safe passage into the free territory. I thought of Anselm's six hundred crowns. "They promised," I said.

"There's nothing to be done."

The ship gave a half-spin, pitching me onto my knees. Anastasia screamed. "Hush, hush," I whispered in her ear. "Hush, Anastasia. We're safe. I'll protect you."

I thought of my own sea crossing as a baby, the way I had yelled for rescue.

Then, all at once, I considered my powers. If there was any time I had needed them, it was now.

———

I got to my feet. Gripping Anastasia with one arm, hauling myself along the wall by the other, I reached the stairs. "Where are you going?" said the wealthy woman. "It's crazy to take her out there in the middle of the storm. You'll be swept overboard."

"I'll be back soon," I said.

Step by step, I hauled us up. I got the trapdoor open. A sluice of cold water drenched us. Anastasia spluttered, clinging with both hands to my jacket. "Hold tight," I told her, and she gripped more tightly, as though she understood. I got myself out, and knelt on the rain-washed deck, under the force of the thunder and lightning.

"Get back down there!" yelled the captain, wild in the storm. "You'll be swept overboard."

"Are we in danger?"

"It's a localised squall—if we can just make it out the other side . . ."

Through the pitching darkness, I made out the lights of a town. I knelt in the chaos of the storm and pressed Anastasia to my chest. I wished with all my strength for the ship to pass out from under the thunderclouds and attain clear waters. And a strange thing happened. The rain eased for a moment. Light shone through.

The captain hauled on the wheel, and the whole ship shuddered.

Again, I bent my mind to the ship's salvation. Again, the squall held off, hanging a little in the air.

Perhaps I imagined it, but the ship's next pitch was less juddering, less dizzy, as though the storm had lost a little of its force.

Again, I willed us towards the Strait of Ravina.

For several long minutes, the rain assaulted us, the ship rolled. Then, the rain began to ease. The captain, water pouring off him, clapped me on the shoulder. "You can go below deck," he said. "We're going to be all right."

Had I caused it, that deliverance? I did not know. In my arms, Anastasia sat wide-eyed, no longer afraid, watching the last dregs of the storm.

As we passed a few hundred yards off the coast of West Ravina, something plinked off the side of the ship. "Get below deck!" yelled the captain at me. I did not need him to yell twice. I was up and scuttling across the deck, hurling myself down the hatch, Anastasia bundled against my chest. More shots. A sudden rattle of white sparks.

"What is it?" cried the wealthy woman. "I heard explosions."

"Gunfire. It's coming from the port."

Under us, the engine of the ship groaned itself to full throttle. "How close are we to the free sector?" I said.

"I don't know—ten miles."

"Ten miles?" It was still too far.

One of the children gave a cry. In the grimy porthole behind us was framed an Imperialist motorboat, laden with guards.

One of the sailors swung into view. "Stay low—keep away from the windows. We've got to outpace them, and I don't want one of you killed by a stray bullet."

He vanished, leaving his rank sweat smell hanging in the air. I pressed myself against the cold metal, Anastasia under my chest. Beside me, the woman covered her own two children, sobbing drily, without tears. We heard the mosquito whine of their motorboats, the plinking of their bullets. The ship shuddered and groaned; someone yelled above deck.

I willed time again to stop itself, but no powers came to me this time.

Then, after what seemed hours, the motorboat whine seemed to draw off a little. I raised my head. Their boat had turned. It was circling us, heading out into deeper waters.

Another boat had come in view, this one laden with refugees, a boat ten times the size of ours, riding low in the water.

The captain appeared. "They're going after the bigger ship. We'll be safe now; we're almost over the border."

"Thank God," said the woman. "Thank God."

"Is any one of you a doctor? Come quickly."

"Who's hurt?"

"My second mate. Shot badly, in the leg."

We found the man in a puddle of his own blood, propped against the gunwale. The wealthy woman knelt and, with surprising practicality, strapped his knee. "You'll be all right," she said. "See a proper doctor in Arkavitz. I haven't practised since the war."

We passed a guard tower, a curl of barbed wire. "That's the border," said the captain. "We're into the free north now." The wealthy woman threw her arms around me and wept.

The captain eyed me thoughtfully. "One of you refugees is good luck." From his wrist, he unfastened my father's silver watch, and gave it back to me. "Go safely," he said.

As I crossed the docks in Arkavitz, dazed and sick with tiredness, and with the baby clinging feebly to my jacket and squalling again, I thought I saw that red-haired man, Rigel. It came out of nowhere, the feeling of being followed, and I turned and saw him at the edge of the crowd. And then I didn't.

For a moment I stood bewildered while the crowd buffeted me. Then I turned and started to push my way back through the people. The air was much colder here, the accents strange and unfamiliar. "Hey," I called. "Hey, Rigel?"

My own shout brought me to my senses. I must have been half dead with exhaustion. The man wasn't there, and even if he had been, he was a stranger. I hadn't seen that face in ten years.

"Move along, please," said a man holding a rifle.

"Sorry, I just—"

"Move along now. The main road into Arkavitz is that way."

He must be resistance, but I didn't dare ask him the way to get to the telegraph post at Maritz.

I started to walk. We had to walk three miles to reach Arkavitz itself. Though barbed wire was raised high alongside the road, there were no soldiers or Alcyrian voices, only men who must be resistance fighters, on horses or in battered old trucks with guns, guarding the border. Their faces were tired and resigned. This was the last tiny outpost of freedom for a thousand miles in any direction. On the other side of the road were just dark forest and thick snow. Unlike the woods of Holy Island, this one was dense and wild. I wondered if there were wolves here.

The baby wailed with cold and fear. I felt the same way myself. I had left Holy Island behind, and in this strange place that was supposed to be my homeland I didn't recognise the accents or the landscape, and the world felt remade. All I had to go on was a picture in my head of the old square house where Anselm lived, and his address, which I knew by heart from his letters. I had not seen my brother since I was eight days old.

At least Jasmine will be there, I thought. *At least there's that.* I could hear already what she would have to say about my arrival with this baby in tow. Jasmine could be smothering in her wish to protect, like my mother could. Even so, I longed to see my sister, to tell her everything, to have her hug me and make a fuss over me, to tell me in her bossy voice that everything was going to be all right.

But Maritz, I knew, was at least a day's journey further north. I was cold and underdressed, with a miserable, shivering baby and barely two crowns left in my pocket. I had used all the nappies I had and carried them, bundled up and stinking, in my backpack. The baby's clothes were soaked through. As the resistance men ushered us along, I held her inside my jacket, whispering vague words of reassurance. But every few minutes I had to glance around; I felt as though that man was still following me.

I had expected the free north to seem more free, not like the empire with different men holding the guns.

I found a truck station in the centre of Arkavitz. As it turned out, I had to part with my father's watch again, this time for good. The price was fifty crowns to take me to Maritz, and the trip would take eight hours. On the way, the baby cried, then gave up crying. In the back of the truck, we were jostled against the other refugees heading north, all with the same exhausted eyes.

Beyond the windows rose white mountains, bare of all life.

We stopped in Bernitz to refuel and sit half an hour in an inn. I tipped water into my baby's mouth, and attempted to warm her bottles. I took off my own shirt and wrapped it around her. She had gone very quiet, and appeared to be almost asleep, but I didn't like this silence. I wished the wealthy woman was still here to tell me what to do with her.

It was midnight now. The truck set off again, climbing still further, on roads which were now utterly uninhabited.

"Maritz!" called the driver eventually, near dawn. The truck had stopped. I hauled myself out.

"The telegraph post?" I said. "Maritz telegraph post?"

"That house on top of the hill."

The truck growled and left me behind, heading down into the village. With Anastasia in my arms, I began to climb. A square house rose up at last on the hilltop. None of the windows showed lights, though night had fallen a good many hours ago. It was built of wooden clapboard; the boards were slipping out of place and the tiles on the roof made uneven rows as if an earthquake had shaken them loose. It was not how I had pictured my brother's house.

There were footsteps in the snow around the house—at least, I thought there were; I could not be sure because snow had been falling for half an hour and was laying a new cover on the ground. I tramped across it into the front yard, past a woodshed from whose edge great eerie icicles dangled, the moonlight shining right through them. A single fir tree stood in the yard, bearing a burden of snow. The door had no knocker. I banged on it hard with my fist, and waited. Nothing.

The snow was falling harder. I banged on the door again, then shouted Anselm's name. Still no answer. My daughter was groaning, too weak to properly cry. I said, "Shush, can't you?" more roughly than I had intended. "Maybe he's just gone out for a while, eh?" I jogged her up and down. "Maybe he's just visiting someone. If we wait here, he'll come back."

Anastasia screwed up her eyes and gave another disconsolate wail.

Dimly, I wondered if we had even come to the right place. How could I be sure this was the telegraph post where Anselm was stationed? It looked like a ghost house. I sat down on the front step and tried to figure out what to do. Down below, the lights of Maritz spread themselves across the flat of the valley. It was getting to be proper night. A few scattered farms, that was all, for fifty miles in any direction. What if I had come all this way, been almost shipwrecked and shot at and climbed into the high mountains on roads slick with ice, and at the end of it all my brother was gone?

The wind made a constant low whistling above us, and when I looked up I realised that the sound was its voice singing in the wires that ran across the yard from the roof of the house to a small woodshed. At least that was something. Wires were the sign of a telegraph post. But then where was Anselm?

Anastasia was making the soft mouth-breathing sound I had got used to on the sea crossing, her tiny fists clenched against my chest. That sound made things seem better. At least I'd escaped with her, to a place where no secret police could find me. Wherever Antonia was now, her baby was safe with me. I huddled in the doorway and waited for my brother to come home.

In a blaze of light, I woke. I had fallen asleep with Anastasia in my arms. Another truck was coming up the mountain road. Its headlights were what had woken me, and they flooded the yard with light as the truck swung round a bend.

I got to my feet, shielding my eyes with one arm and my baby with the other. The truck came closer. I could hear the driver making mincemeat of the gears as they negotiated the slick ice of the road. With roars and growls the truck advanced. In a final sideways sweep, it gained the top of the hill and drew to a halt at the edge of the yard, the chains on its tires giving a last grim rattle. I remained in the darkness. Two men jumped out of the truck and slammed the doors. The driver swung the truck around, its lights cutting through the falling snow, and began the slow progress back down the mountain road.

The two men had not seen me yet, and in the snow-choked darkness they approached the house. Was one of them my brother? My mouth was suddenly dry as paper. I hesitated, then said, "Hello?" into the night.

One of the men drew a pistol from under his coat. "Who's there?"

"Don't shoot. I don't mean any harm. I'm looking for Anselm."

The men advanced. They were still just shadows. The armed man was not my brother, but what about the other? I strained my eyes to make him out. The whirling snow gave him a strange look—it gathered on his eyelashes and against his mouth so that I could not read him.

"Anselm?" I said.

"I'm Anselm. That's me. What do you want?"

"Careful," said the other man, and touched his arm.

Was it Anselm? I could not tell if he looked like the young man in my dreams. Reddish-brown hair that stood up like the bristles on a brush, strong features, stouter than I remembered. This man looked well into his thirties.

"Anselm?" I said again.

"Yes."

"I'm Harlan. I'm your brother."

Anastasia squirmed against my chest and let out a thin, sleepy wail. The man with the gun relaxed it, then put it down. And as they approached, my brother's face became clearer, solidified, until I knew it was him.

"My God. Harlan? Harlan North?"

"Yes."

In two great bounds, my brother closed the distance between us and pulled me into a rough hug. The baby protested, and for the first time Anselm properly noticed her. He looked at me hard. "I can't believe I'm seeing you. First Jasmine, now you. You've got eyes like Papa's."

"Yes," I said. "I know."

"My God. Harlan." He hugged me again. "Where are Mama and Papa?"

"They couldn't come." Guilt knotted my stomach. "Only us. Me and the baby."

"Whose is it?"

"Mine. And Antonia's. Mama must have written to you about what happened with her."

"The Alcyrian girl." Anselm and Michael caught each other's eyes very briefly.

"Let's go inside," said Michael. "You can explain properly."

"Is Jasmine here?"

"No. She's with the resistance further south now, closer to the border. We haven't seen her for a month."

Homesickness tugged at me. I had been counting on finding my sister here.

Anselm guided us through the door and switched on the light. A room like the one I had dreamed appeared before me, but this version was older and more worn out: a dining table at one end, unwashed plates in a sink, an ancient and sagging sofa, a woodstove, a huge fur rug and mattresses propped up against the wall. Michael put a kettle on the gas ring to boil. My brother steered me onto the sofa. He took the tea Michael brought to us, added sugar and a shot of spirits, and put it into my hand.

"Drink this," he said. "Warm up, then talk, all right? Give me the baby."

"She isn't crying anymore."

"She's cold, that's why."

Anselm unwrapped Anastasia. He rubbed her small hands and feet, held her before the fire. "Have you got any formula?"

I handed him the bottle. He tipped it into her mouth, rubbed her again. "Is she going to be all right?"

"Yes. There's no frostbite. But Harlan—bringing a baby all the way up here, in the depths of winter—"

"They'd have taken her away if I'd stayed. I didn't have any choice."

My brother's eyes were very dark and serious. "Tell me everything," he said.

So I told him.

51

*A*nselm put the two of us to bed on a mattress in an upstairs bedroom, wrapped in furs. There we slept, Anastasia and I, and when I woke it was late and Anastasia was gone.

Hauling myself awake, I heard the tap-tapping of the telegraph machine, far away in another room, and my brother's voice downstairs. I pulled on clothes and descended the worn wooden stairs, which sighed at my footsteps. This old clapboard house must be centuries old. When I paused on the landing, halfway down, I could hear it creaking around me.

I found Anselm at the stove with Anastasia on one hip, warming milk in a pan.

"She needs special formula," I said. "Half milk, half water, then add a little oatmeal and honey. Test the temperature with your finger."

"I know, I know." Anselm extinguished the gas and stirred the milk. "I've done this before. She'll be all right."

And in fact, Anastasia looked quite content in my older brother's arms. From the way he looked down at her, I could tell that he would have liked to be a father.

"Michael's manning the telegraph machine," said Anselm. "And you and I need to talk."

It was afternoon. I could tell by the way the sun was already sinking. My brother made strong tea and set it before me. "Sit," he said.

I sat and attempted to wake up properly. Anselm dropped into the chair at the other side of the table. He lowered his eyes to meet mine. To tell the truth, I was still a little shy of him, with his intelligent eyes and dashing leather jacket. I gave him as much of a smile as I could muster.

The snow outside threw peace like a blanket over the house. It did not seem compatible with Antonia being gone, with the journey Anastasia and I had just endured, with the impending war. "Is it true," I asked Anselm at last, "what I heard in the prison camp—that there's going to be a final resistance attack?"

"I don't know," said Anselm. "That's what I have to talk to you about." He leaned over the table and looked me in the face. "Harlan, you know I transmit messages for the resistance. Intelligence from our spies in the occupied territory; communications between cells in different parts of the country; encrypted mission orders. Anyway, I shouldn't be telling you this, but we picked up some transmissions recently that I can't help worrying about. It's to do with an Imperialist secret police operation—Operation Last Descendant, they call it. Do you know anything about this?"

"A little," I said.

"Harlan, everybody's looking for you. The Imperialists and the resistance both. You know half the old resistance members are still waiting for a sign from Aldebaran. They're hoping this last descendant, whoever he is, will come forward and lead them to victory."

"Should I do it?" Now I asked my brother the question that had haunted me for years. "Should I come forward?"

"I don't know, Harlan. I honestly don't. But I'm worried about you. I worried about you when you were on Holy Island and I worry about you here. I can't work out what Aldebaran meant by naming you—what he wanted you to do—"

"You gave Grandfather some papers for me," I said. "Years ago, when I was a baby. Papers from Aldebaran."

"Do you have them here?"

"Wait." I ran up the stairs for Aldebaran's papers. They were in my leather backpack, a little damp from the long journey, but undamaged. I put them before my brother.

Anselm bent his head over the pages, his tea turning cold as he read and read. At last, he turned to the map. "Do you know what this means?"

"He wants me to go to these places. He says that if I go there, I'll find the answers I'm looking for."

"And what are the answers you're looking for?" With one finger, Anselm traced the stars on the map.

Through the crystal silence of the high mountains, the truth came to me. I was looking for the power to stop time and bring my family back together. I was looking for Antonia.

"I don't know if I should come forward as the last descendant," I told Anselm, a new certainty possessing me. "But I have to go to the places on this map."

"Nearly all of them are in the occupied territory."

"I have to go."

"No one believes in powers anymore," he said.

How could I tell him that I believed I had delivered the refugee ship from a thunderstorm, on the sea crossing? How could I tell him that I believed I was closer every day to stopping time? I couldn't. I drank my tea and jogged Anastasia on my lap, while Anselm continued to trace invisible lines between the pencilled stars.

"This one," he said at last, putting the page before me. "The one between Arkavitz and Bernitz. I know where that is. Old Peter Dewitt's house. He used to be a mountain guide—he was the one who showed me the way through the pass to Bernitz, when I first made the climb."

"Is his house still there?"

Anselm shook his head. "That place was burned down."

"Why?"

"The house was on an old religious site, where there had once been a monastery. I think that was what they wanted to destroy—Imperialists who made a foray across the border. But poor old Peter . . ." He shook his head.

"Could we go there?"

"Yes, but I don't know what answers you'll find in a sad, burned place like that."

"Antonia and I both thought that I should go to these places," I told him. "I think now that maybe my powers will get strong enough to let me travel through like the great ones used to do. There are people there, you know—people who belong to us and have been lost from this world. Maybe Aldebaran himself." I hesitated. "Maybe Antonia."

276

"If it's what you think you have to do, I won't stop you," said Anselm. Even so, my brother looked at me as if he was already preparing for my funeral.

"We'll go to old Peter Dewitt's house," he said. "When the spring comes."

52

*I*n the free north, I was able to listen again to uncensored wireless reports. Now I understood that a change was taking place in our continent. Something was stirring. "The former free sectors of Angel City and Holy Island have been troubled by further unrest," the announcer told us. "The new resistance cells in these sectors continue to take decisive armed action against the Imperialist forces. On Monday, the city of Valacia was under curfew again due to prolonged rioting, in which eighty-seven were killed. Meanwhile, the two resistance factions in the north sector, the Old Partisan Guard and the New Partisan Freedom Movement, have threatened to split after fresh disagreements. The leaders of the old resistance believe that some answer is needed on the issue of Aldebaran's last descendant before decisive action is taken. The leaders of the new resistance favour violent means like those used so effectively by the new cells in Angel and Holy Island, and have threatened to take action alone this spring if the old members do not stand with them. Heavy losses have been sustained in Capital by the new resistance movements this winter, including twenty-three men hanged on Wednesday for the sabotage of a train—"

My brother turned off the wireless. "What does it mean, the new resistance and the old resistance?" I said.

"There's always been a split," said Anselm, "between those leaders who remember the days before the Imperialists and those who came of age under the empire. The old members still believe in the prophecy, the last descendant, the king's return to power.

The new members don't care about any of those things. They want self-government by any means."

"And what if the last descendant came forward?" I said.

Anselm did not answer.

After that night, I avoided the wireless reports.

My daughter, shufflingly, was learning to crawl. She did it sideways, like a crab, and her grey eyes lit with joy as she hauled herself between us on the floorboards, reaching for me with both arms. We fed her mashed banana and honeyed porridge, and Anselm sang her a hundred city lullabies.

Up here in the mountains, still locked in midwinter, it was easy to forget about war.

My brother remembered his promise and drove me down to old Peter Dewitt's house in Arkavitz when he had to go to the city for supplies. It was a journey of eight hours. After loading the truck, we drove out of the city and back into the bare white world. It was almost dusk. Anselm swung the truck around and brought it to rest before a small gully in the forest. Its headlights illuminated the skeleton of a shack. A sick feeling rose inside me. It was just like the house on Holy Island—just the same—the charred remains of a building. Why was someone burning these places?

We got out and walked up to what must once have been the front door. Our feet left dark footprints in the ashy snow. I stood inside the skeleton of the house, shut my eyes and tried to imagine that this place connected me with another, that here the real, solid world around me became less solid, like a haze of heat or a curtain of light. I thought again of that green world, far away.

"Harlan! Harlan!" My brother's voice brought me back. He was beside me, supporting me.

"What is it?" I said.

"I don't know—you looked like you were going to fall. Let's

go home, Harlan. I told you there wasn't anything to see. I don't know what I was expecting."

"I have to go to all these places on the map," I said. "I have to try. Even the ones inside the occupied territory. Both the places had been burned when I got to them. Aldebaran's house and this shack. I feel like—I don't know—I'm racing somebody. It's to do with finding Antonia again. All of this is. That's why I'm doing it."

My brother thought for a moment. "I understand," he said eventually. "But there's something you'll have to face, Harlan, at the end of all this searching."

"Yes?"

"Well, even if you manage to find some miraculous world we've all forgotten about, which is perfectly possible, you must prepare yourself for the possibility that Antonia isn't there."

The way he spoke her name was very gentle. For about the hundredth time, I gave silent thanks that I had found my brother. Still, his kindness stirred something in me, and tears threatened. I turned my face away, but Anselm put his arm around my shoulders and said, "Even if there was magic in the world, it wouldn't bring people back. I remember talking to Uncle about it once."

"But maybe I'm different," I said. "Maybe I can. I think this is why Aldebaran passed these powers to me. It isn't political; it isn't to save the world. It's to save myself, and Antonia. To put right everything that has gone wrong for our family—his assassination; Papa's brother, Stirling, dying that terrible way; Grandfather Harold having to go into exile—and—"

Anselm shook his head. "To put everything right, you'd have to go back into the beginnings of time." He stared up at the blackened rafters above us. "And anyway," he said, "if there'd never been any war in the first place, our mama and papa would never have met. There'd be no existence for you either, no Jasmine. No me."

The truth of what he said cut like a cold blade, but I suppressed it. "I keep thinking," I persisted, "what if there was someone—just one person—with powers beyond what anyone else's had ever been?"

"You think that person is you?"

"I'm not saying that." I didn't really know what I was saying.

"Don't get bound up in these dreams of another life that may not really exist, that's all I'm telling you. You've got your own real life. You've got your baby. What you find in these places won't bring a miracle. I don't want you to go into the occupied territory, taking some crazy risk."

"I dream about Antonia," I said. "I can tell she's somewhere, just not here."

I paced the walls of the old shack. Anselm waited. "If you go into the occupied territory, Harlan, I have one condition," he said at last. "You can't take Anastasia with you."

It was as though my brother had knocked the air out of my lungs. "I'm not going without her!"

"Harlan, it's the middle of winter, and she's not yet six months old. You're lucky she survived the journey over here unharmed. You're going into danger if you go to Capital. It's not the kind of danger you've ever experienced."

"I've been in a prison camp!" My anger made me petulant.

"A *labour* camp, Harlan. And run by our own people, more or less. It isn't the same thing." He sighed. "Look, you must see that if you want to go to the city, it's no good taking a half-Alcyrian baby with you. The Imperialists will want to take her away from you—the resistance will refuse to take you in—"

"Why should the resistance care about my baby? Our love wasn't political. Antonia isn't even an Imperialist."

"Everything's political!" said Anselm. "These resistance fighters have been starving out in the hills for a decade; they've seen torture and death and the worst kind of injustice. It's a question of blood. Many of them would spit on the grave of any Alcyrian, whether the person called themselves an Imperialist or not. They stopped being reasonable long ago."

"Then where can the two of us be safe?" I said. "Where can we live, even after all this is over?"

"Look," said Anselm. "I'll do my best to protect Anastasia. She's safe up here in the mountains. No one passes. Eventually, if we win—*when* we win—she'll be safe enough in that new world. It won't be easy for you, but the resistance are fair. They'll build the kind of world you can live in, Harlan, trust me. It might take them some time to sort out their differences, but they will. For now, though, the world across that border, the world as it stands, is not the kind of place you can take the baby."

It was true, what he said. I had to either stay here and give up the search for Antonia, or leave Anastasia behind.

"I know it's tough," said Anselm. "I'm not doing this for meanness. I'm doing it to protect her. She's my family now too. Stay here, Harlan. Isn't it better to all stay together?"

"All right," I said.

He put a hand on my shoulder, and together we walked to the truck.

"We always thought you were a great hero, Jasmine and I," I told him quietly. "We were always proud of you, fighting for everyone's freedom. I see now that I was right. You're one of the best people I know."

"It's a hell of a lot messier than that," said Anselm.

Back in the kitchen of the telegraph post, at dawn, I mashed apple and banana and fed them to Anastasia. While Anselm went on duty at the telegraph machine, I sat in front of the fire and read my papers again, trying to put myself into this vanished world of powers and magic. But it was no good. I had glimpses of other places, but only briefly—nothing real. "Anyway, Anastasia," I whispered to her as she drifted off, "aren't we all forgetting something? The last descendant isn't me anymore. It's you."

53

*N*ow, I had all but promised my brother that I would stay with him in the north. And yet every night I dreamed of Antonia, her frail arms and hacked-off hair, and woke up sweating, staring into the dark, shouting myself awake.

I couldn't leave Anastasia, but I couldn't stay here either.

One afternoon, when I had been in Maritz for about a month, Michael called me out to help him in the yard. The snow had brought down an old elm tree near the road, taking the telegraph line with it. We worked in silence for a while, cutting up its old limbs and stacking them against the back wall of the house where the firewood was kept. Michael climbed up on a ladder to fix the line. While he did it, he whistled, and the sound was the sharpest thing in the chill air.

"You know," he said, from the ladder, "your brother loves Anastasia. He's glad to have a child in the house."

"I can see that."

I liked Michael: his quiet intensity, his thoughtful expression, the permanently surprised look of his black hair. I watched him work the line out from the tangle of branches.

"If you're going to leave here," Michael continued, "you'd better do it soon. The radio is full of signs of war. You mark my words, this thing's going to erupt, one way or the other."

I looked up at him through the dusk. My stomach felt hollow. "How did you know I was thinking of leaving?"

"It's obvious," said Michael. "Anselm sees it too, though he pretends he doesn't. If you're going to leave, you'd better do it. That's all."

Michael clipped the wire with a pair of wire-cutters, swaying precariously on the ladder. When he had finished, he came down slowly. "This wiring all needs to be replaced," he said. "We can't risk losing our signal if this civil war really begins. Come with me. You can help me do it."

As I held the ladder steady for him in the half-dark of the little shack alongside the house, I asked Michael if the resistance could help me get to the city.

"Maybe," he said, unravelling the new wire and snipping it off. "There's a transport going to the edge of Capital next week."

"So I could go with them?"

"Do you have somewhere to stay? I wouldn't want you going to that city all alone, Harlan. I've been there and seen it—the place is a mess. Not the old noble town it was when Anselm and I were growing up there."

"I have friends there," I said. "Jakob and Sebastian. They were in the labour camp with me."

I hadn't exactly wanted to stay with Jakob. I knew that he was probably at the centre of whatever trouble was going on in the city. But I didn't have anyone else.

"Go with the transport," said Michael. "Go to these friends of yours. But don't underestimate the danger." He leaned closer. "This last descendant story is well known among the resistance. Both sides would like your soul, Harlan. Just remember that."

"I have to go," I said. "It's something I have to see through to the end."

He nodded as though he understood, then said, "There's only one thing. Don't tell Anselm I encouraged you to do this. I don't think he'd ever forgive me. If you are going, it's best to do it soon, without giving him much warning. Too much thinking about it will break his heart."

While we ate dinner, a bedraggled crow came hopping up to the door. I knew this crow quite well now. Its name was

Mick—it had been adopted by Anselm and Michael years ago, and it returned every winter to beg for food. Anastasia loved to watch Mick being fed. She sat up, quite alert, and clapped when he made his clumsy stabs at the crusts of bread Michael threw down in the snow.

I could have lived this life, here in the middle of the snowy wilderness with my brother and Michael and my baby, forever.

But now I knew I was leaving, to see this task of Aldebaran's through to the end. I stayed awake for two nights, just watching Anastasia's sleeping face. She had changed so much already. She sat up quite easily on her own, and kicked her legs. When Anselm knelt before her with a bunch of keys or some other bright object, she would make a grab for it and drag it towards her, laughing. Sometimes she would roll right over, startling herself. She babbled at me and smiled at us, a radiant, single-toothed smile. I did not want to leave her side. I knew that in a matter of hours I would be going a long way from her, into the middle of a war. But I couldn't help it. I had to go. The map was quite clear, and the map was all I had.

One morning, Michael took me aside. "There's a truck going to Capital," he said. "I've spoken to the driver. He's a resistance man—Joe—and he's taking you to Capital as a personal favour to us. You'll go there under the name Isak Karol, your false name from Holy Island. It's vital you don't tell anyone your real name. Don't get involved with them more than you can help. Once you get to the city, move away from them, all right? It's one thing for me and your brother to be in the resistance—and no one was going to stop Jasmine from joining—but you, Harlan . . ."

I didn't tell him that the friend I was planning to stay with was bound to be right at the heart of the resistance. "I'll be careful," I said. "I've got Anastasia to think about now."

"I know. And I hope you'll find whatever it is you're

looking for and come back to us here before any great disaster happens. War is coming, Harlan. You don't have to worry about Anastasia—we'll look after her. But you have to look after yourself. Make sure you come back safe. I don't think your brother would forgive me if you didn't."

"I will," I said. "I'll come back."

I waited until the day of my departure to say goodbye to my daughter.

She was still sleeping, bundled up in her blanket with just a tuft of hair poking out. A second tooth was beginning to come through her gum, making her tearful and fractious during the evenings and sleepy in the mornings. I picked her up and cradled her against my chest and tried to fix this minute in my mind as I had fixed my last night with Antonia, so that I would never have to let it go. "Goodbye, Anastasia," I whispered in her ear. "I love you."

Maybe it was strange, given the unpromising way we had come into each other's lives, but I really did love her, my tiny daughter. "I'll come back for you," I whispered. "I'll bring your mama back too, and we'll find a place to live together."

Anastasia opened her eyes sleepily, then closed them again. I kissed her soft cheek and squeezed her hand.

"No!" said Anselm, when I told him. "No, no, no. You're not to go to Capital."

"The truck's on the way—it's all arranged."

He glanced at Michael, back at me, then sank onto the edge of the sofa, looking sadly at the floorboards between his feet.

"I have to go," I said. "I have to try and find Antonia, and puzzle out this thing Aldebaran's left for me."

"Then for God's sake, take care."

The truck was here, with a growl and a crunch of the handbrake. Michael and Anselm were bundling me out into the snow. Mick flapped around our feet as we crossed the yard. My brother carried Anastasia tightly against his chest.

The man driving the truck was unshaven, and his eyes were saggy with tiredness. "This is Isak," said Michael. "An agent from Holy Island. You'll see he gets to the city safely?"

"Joe," said the man, holding out his hand and gripping mine briefly. "Get in. Sit on the floor in the back of the truck and be ready to get under the blankets if we're stopped."

I stumbled as I tried to climb up into the truck, and Anselm put his hand under my elbow. When I turned to hug him, I had a sudden moment of doubt. Had I come all this way to find my brother, just to leave him again? Anselm must have seen it, because he put his hands on the sides of my face and said, "Harlan, if you don't want to do this, just say so. You don't owe anything to anyone, even Uncle."

I smothered my doubts in fussing over Anastasia. "Does she have everything she needs? And you don't mind taking care of her?"

"I don't mind."

"Let me hold her again, just for a minute. She's confused—I can see she's going to cry."

But Joe was revving up the truck, and I only had time to stroke her tuft of black hair once before I was shut into the dark.

I felt the truck move off along the icy road, away from Maritz and towards that fierce, impoverished country where I had been born, my occupied homeland. Anastasia must have woken up. Over the engine, I could hear her wails as they pursued us down the track. It tore my heart in two, but not enough to make me stop the truck and go back to her. *Stay resolute*, I told myself. *Only in the city, in the place where all this started, will you find a way to bring Antonia back. Have faith in Aldebaran.* It occurred to me once, briefly, that Anastasia had already watched Antonia go away from her across the ocean, but I told myself that she wouldn't remember that.

But when you were six months old, a small voice in my head told me, *you remembered every single thing that happened to you.*

54

I spent most of the journey lying on the floor of the truck, hanging in an odd kind of grey space without time or order. We stopped after what felt like eight or ten hours but was probably less. I got down under the blankets in a rush, my heart running fast. But it was only Joe himself leaning in through the door. He shook my shoulder and pulled me out into the sunlight. "Come on," he said. "We can get something to eat here. The people are safe."

It was just a shuttered farmhouse in the middle of nowhere. "Are we across the border now?" I said. I had expected the occupied territories to look different.

"Yes," said Joe. "But no one lives around here."

We opened the door to the farmhouse and were greeted by a table full of loud-voiced men, eating bread and drinking what looked like watery beer. I moved through them as if I were dreaming. Dimly, I wondered if Anastasia had stopped crying yet.

While the men continued to make their noise in the farmhouse, I went out the rear door into the air. It was milder here than in Maritz; there was no snow on the ground, only the dark stain of recent rainfall. The house was in the middle of empty hill country. Grey clouds hung low, and on the horizon were nothing but a dark stone wall and a tree just coming into leaf.

I climbed the nearest slope and stood at the top, looking out over the emptiness. Then I got out my map from Aldebaran to try and work out where we were. Somewhere in the Eastern Hills, I guessed. If there were mountains in the distance, as there should have been, they wouldn't show up on the horizon because a wave of drizzle was approaching us, blocking them from view.

"Hey!" Joe was gesturing wildly at me from the doorway of the house. I descended the slippery grass while he continued to beckon. "Come on, come on," he said. "It's not safe to roam around out here."

I turned to climb up into the back of the truck, but he caught my arm. "Listen," he said. "There's a checkpoint on the way into the city. The guards at this checkpoint are rotten—we pay them not to give us any trouble. You'll ride up front. If they ask, just say we're collecting hospital supplies to take north."

"All right," I said. I still had the map in my hands. Showing it to Joe, I asked, "Are we anywhere near this star?"

He frowned at the page. "Not really. We're about a hundred miles off. That star looks like it's on Bellame."

"What's Bellame?"

"An old castle. It had an ancient library. The Imperialists torched it years ago. There's nothing to see there anymore."

Why were all these places burned? Did it have something to do with Aldebaran's map, with me?

Joe was looking more closely at the map now. "I don't know where you got this," he said slowly, "but the borders are the old ones. It's an offence to own it. You need to make damn sure it's out of sight when we go through the checkpoint, or both of our journeys will end there."

The roads loomed darkly ahead of us in the truck's headlights. Joe hummed a tune, taking the corners with a wrench of the steering wheel so that the grit crunched under the tires. Eventually we began to pass villages, then small towns. I dozed, and when I woke up, we were driving along the edge of a great reservoir that seemed to stretch to the far horizon. Lights blazed along its edge—proper electric streetlights, such as I had never seen before. A guard patrolled its perimeter. "See that there?" said Joe, gesturing. "That used to be the River Maron. It ran around both sides of the city, Capital. The Imperialists made that their first project. They dammed it and made that reservoir. It supplies Capital with running water and powers those electric lights."

"So there isn't any river in the city anymore?"

"Not beyond this point."

I was disoriented. My only visions of the city came from my family's memories. In those pictures, the city was an island in the middle of a fast-flowing river.

"That's the city up ahead," said Joe. "It's still a long way off, but you can see it, on account of the electric lighting."

It was a mass of lights indeed, so many of them that they made a murky orange glow along the horizon. I could see the shape of large square buildings studded with orange windows. I could see what I thought must be the castle on its rock, high above the rest of the city. Pretty soon after that, the sheds and floodlights of a checkpoint loomed ahead of us. "Keep your mouth shut unless they talk to you directly," said Joe.

Ahead of us, a few vehicles had come to a halt and were standing in a long line with their headlights illuminating the drizzle. Joe rolled the truck in behind a sleek black motorcar with darkened windows. "Bloody bad luck," he said. It took me a second to understand what he meant; then I saw the flags on the back of the car. It belonged to the government.

"Can't we turn round?" I asked.

But as I said it, a tradesman's van rolled in behind us and shut off its engine. We were trapped here in the line of cars now. "Just keep quiet," said Joe. "We'll be fine."

As it was, we were lucky. The guards didn't want to stand out in the rain. They flashed torches over the interior of the truck and briefly checked our papers. "You got permission to be here from Holy Island?" one asked me. Joe gave a quick nod and reached forward. Money changed hands, and they stamped our papers and waved us through.

As we drove across the bridge into the city, over the empty chasm that must once have contained the violent waters of the river, the driver of the van behind us revved suddenly into view. And he had the face of that red-haired man, Rigel.

I stuck my head out the window into the rain, but he had dropped behind again, and it was impossible to see.

"Isak," said Joe. "Keep your head inside. Don't draw attention."

"I'm sorry. I thought I saw—"

Joe leaned across me and rolled up the window very firmly. We were on a city street now, and he pulled over in front of a vast apartment building and shut off the engine.

"This is where I'll leave you," he said. "You're in a Malonian area. You can tell by the bumpy roads and the bad housing, all right? No street lights. Stay in these areas if you can. You'll get into the old city from here, the central part, without trouble. I don't have time to take you any further. If you have any difficulties, you have your papers, and they've been stamped."

"Thank you, Joe."

"You're welcome."

He was waiting for me to get out, so I took my overcoat and my old backpack and went. I turned to wave to him, but he was too intent on pulling out into traffic to notice. Soon I lost sight of the truck. I looked for that blue van that had been following us, but it was gone too. I was alone on the edge of a city that hummed and soared with life, among vast apartment blocks and burnt-out buildings, where crowds of people with strange faces jostled me off the pavement, impatient with my awe. For them, living here was quite ordinary.

My arms ached with the absence of Anastasia's soft weight. *Come on*, I told myself. *You have to find Jakob's house; it's the only place you can go.* I dug the address out of my backpack: 48 Milliner's Lane. Already it was past eight o'clock. I shouldered my pack, buttoned my overcoat and set out.

As I got further into it, the city became stranger and more frightening. Odd smells wafted from cellar apartments. Trucks ploughed the slushy roads. Everywhere in the Malonian quarters were half-demolished buildings, their stones tumbled and doors smashed in. Above them rose apartment buildings. These towers looked like the buildings of the future—great and glossy, stretching towards the heavens with their stairways full of white light. In them the Imperialists must live.

I came to a busy street where ordinary people—women in fur coats, men in business suits, elderly couples—were speaking Alcyrian. It was the first time I had seen them living in our country quite carelessly, as if they owned it. Those who spoke my own language kept to the shadowy side of the road. On this street, which had clearly once been an avenue, spring had already come. Trees put forth twigs, and at the end of each twig was a pale bud, fluorescent in the dusk. Here, the Malonian quarter met the part of the city that belonged to the Alcyrians. I walked along this street that was half ruin, half future, my old leather pack on my shoulder, the absence of Anastasia a burden in my arms.

In a way, all roads in my life had been leading me here, to this city, where none of the ghosts that haunted my family had ever been laid to rest.

55

I wish I could describe the strange hollow feeling you get when you come to a place you think you remember and everything is wrong. The castle on the rock was barely visible behind a mass of guard towers and telegraph aerials. The streets were not lined with bright little shops like the one my family had once run; they were dark and boarded, or flanked with towering buildings whose empty stairwells shone with electric light. People swarmed in great throngs, moving to and fro without looking at each other, without speaking to each other, their fur hoods and woollen caps pulled down over their foreheads.

Soldiers were everywhere. And on the corner of every street, people sat disconsolate, begging in our language. When I glanced up at a tall grey building chequered with windows, I made out a banner with General Marlan's face billowing eerily in the wind so that it seemed to stretch and distort itself, not like a human face at all.

I wanted to ask someone the way to Milliner's Lane, but I was afraid because I didn't know who was Malonian and who Alcyrian. Finally I stopped beside a man selling newspapers. "*Escuse?*" I said, in the best Alcyrian I could muster. "*Come var an sein addressen?* How do I get to this address?"

The man turned his eyes slowly to me. They were sunken in a face made pouchy from years standing in the cold. He shook his head without looking at me directly, then turned away.

Too late, I realised I should have spoken to him in Malonian. I pressed on. My hands were prickling with cold. I wondered if Anastasia was eating her dinner now, clutching hungrily at the tiny morsels of bread which Anselm tore up and fed to her one by one. I thought of her tiny hands, her puff of black hair and her wide grey eyes, and felt such a longing for my daughter that I stopped dead in the middle of the street.

Someone barged into me and knocked my pack to the ground. I began walking again, towards what seemed to be the centre of the city. It was the way everyone else was going. At a busy street crossing, I caught an old woman's eye by chance and she gave me a faint smile. "*Escuse?*" I said. The woman began to shake her head, so I continued in Malonian: "Excuse me, would you tell me the way to Milliner's Lane?"

"You're not from here, are you?" said the woman. "Aye, I can tell that quickly enough."

Her accent was just like my father's. Marvelling at this sudden reminder of home, I almost missed her directions. Left, she was telling me, then right, then straight on. "Then you can't miss it. There's a telegraph shop on the corner of the street. And you'd best make sure you get inside before the curfew."

"Curfew?" So they had one here too.

"You've half an hour."

I took the road I thought she had indicated, and was suddenly away from the crowds. This street was narrow and empty. Up ahead, someone opened a window and made me start. A woman with hard eyes threw a rug over the sill, beat it furiously with a wooden cane and dragged it back in again.

Here there were no banners with the face of General Marlan. Some of the street signs were still in Malonian, and I passed dozens of soldiers, patrolling the perimeter with guarded faces.

By this and other signs, I began to suspect that I was entering the part of the city where the resistance trouble had taken place.

This was surely the part of the city my family had once known too, because there were no apartment buildings here. The houses were tall, their upper windows shuttered and the lower ones blinded by rusty bars. Behind one, I saw a line of candles burning. No electricity here. Or was it a resistance gesture, like the candles my brother had written to me about when I turned five years old? I passed through the debris of a street market, which stank of old fish worse than the docks in New Maron. The paving stones were slippery with scales. Gangs of boys my own age sat around the edges of the square, discernible only by the glow of their cigarettes and their watchful eyes.

I broke into a jog and crossed the dark market, then plunged into an alley, keen to get onto safer ground.

Somewhere far away, a bell rang once—not an old bell, but a buzzer piped through a speaker into the cold air. Instantly, the people near me shifted. They put out their cigarettes and ran for shelter. There seemed to be a kind of panic about it, this curfew. Someone thumped hard against my shoulder in the dark.

Instantly, what lights had shown were put out, the shutters slamming across every window. A cold feeling ran down my neck. In the heart of this city that had been convulsing with life, it was now just me among the Alcyrians.

There was nothing I could do but go on. I walked faster. I must have gone wrong, though, because I finished up in a dead end where only a disconsolate cat limped among the blackened shells of old buildings. I'd have to try again. I was starting to sweat now, in spite of the cold and damp. On the main road, the growl of the trucks was deafening. The petrol fumes left a metal tang in my throat. Hardly anyone else was on the street, but as I turned the corner, a couple of men pushed up against me, and in the confusion I felt my bag being dragged away from me. I yelled out and tugged back and somehow kept hold of it. I ran and found myself in an alley again.

At the end of the alleyway was a high fence. I could hear their footsteps behind me. I threw myself at the fence and began to climb, scrambling clumsily until I was out of their reach. I dropped into a yard. On the other side of the fence I heard yelling, but no one followed.

I bent double to catch my breath. I wanted desperately to return to my old life, to Holy Island and Antonia in my arms, or Maritz, where at least there was warmth and safety and my daughter. What was I doing here? All my dreams of the city— my sister in fur mittens in a whirl of snow, the righteous silhouette of the castle on its rock and nights when the concert halls were full of song—vanished in the dark. I straightened up, and then I saw why they had not followed me into this yard.

Ahead of me, four black shapes were swinging in the breeze. These shapes were like bats hanging from the rafters of a shed. But these shapes were not natural. They were hanged men, swinging in the dark not thirty feet away from me.

Terror overcame me, and in its torments I flung myself back over the fence and ran. At the end of the street, someone caught me. I pulled away, shuddering, but the person said, in my own language, "Hey, hey, hey. Stop there. Where are you going? You're lost, aren't you?"

An old man, bent over a stick, peered up at me. His accent too was like my father's.

"What's that place at the end of the alley?"

"Secret police."

"The headquarters for the city?"

He chuckled drily. "The headquarters for this district. They have headquarters every few yards now, son."

"They hang people there in the yard? For everyone to see?"

"Those young men who sabotaged the train, I believe."

He looked up towards the sky, which was becoming cold and starry. "Where are you going? There's a curfew, you know."

"I know. I've lost my way." I told him the name of the street I was looking for.

He raised his stick and pointed for me. "Go on. Quick as you can now."

As I left him, he called after me suddenly: "Don't worry, son. You'll get used to it here."

At last I found Milliner's Lane. I counted the house numbers, still trying to stop myself from shaking like I had a bad case of fever. The worst thing was, I kept thinking of my daughter. I kept thinking how only that barbed wire fence along the border separated her from this heartless world the Imperialists had made of the rest of our continent.

Number 48 was a laundry. It didn't look like a house at all. Had there been some mistake? I stood in front of it, looking up at the black windows.

But when the wind died away for a moment, I thought I heard voices coming from behind the house. There was a narrow alley, and behind it a yard. Someone's washing was flapping half-heartedly in the wind. I battled my way between the wet sheets to the back door of the building. I listened at the door—nothing. But light was rising from a cellar grate, and the voices were coming from there. The voices led me down concrete steps to a locked door, which I tried without success to open.

I put my ear to the door and listened. Arguing male voices; glasses clinking. The static of a badly tuned radio. I raised my hand to knock, and hesitated. While I was still hesitating, the door gave way, and through the crack poked the barrel of a gun. "Yes?" came a voice. "What do you want?"

"I'm Isak Karol."

The door closed. Chains were withdrawn. When it opened again, it revealed a shabby kitchen, bright with gaslight. Twenty men, a couple of women. The gun remained pointed. But among the faces, I made out one innocent as a moon, upturned anxiously to mine. "Sebastian!" I cried.

"Isak. We didn't think you'd come. What are you doing here?"

The small, dark-faced man with the gun hauled me inside. "And more to the point, what do you mean by spying on our meeting?"

"I'm a friend of Sebastian and Jakob—they know me. They told me to come to this address if I was in the city."

"It's all right." From behind the angry little man, Jakob's voice. He rose from his seat and I recognised him—older and tougher in a sheepskin coat and gun belt, a cigarette behind his ear, cheap wire-framed spectacles, as though he had turned himself into the very picture of a resistance man.

The others were talking all at once now, still angry. "It's all right, Mr. Francis," said Jakob, more loudly. "This is Isak—I know him. I can vouch for him, the damn fool."

The angry little man looked at me hard for a long minute, then put away his gun. "All right. But you gave us all a start. Bloody stupid way to arrive, skulking behind the door like that."

How else was I supposed to arrive, I thought, *except by the door?*

"You could have sent a message," muttered Jakob, as though he had discerned my thoughts. "It's how we do things here."

"I didn't know—I've only just arrived in the city. I've come straight from the north sector."

"Well," said the man who held the gun. "Isak. Welcome. I'm Mr. Francis, the head of our operation here. Are you one of us?"

I did not realise what he meant, but Jakob was mouthing "Resistance" at me behind his head. "Oh!" I said. "No. Not properly. But I—I agree with your cause."

"You agree with our cause?"

"My brother mans a telegraph post up in the north. And my sister belongs to the resistance there. I've been staying with my brother, but I came south to the city to . . . to stay for a while," I finished lamely.

"Are you going to stay *here*?" said Mr. Francis. "In my house?"

I glanced at Jakob and Sebastian.

"He's going to stay here," said Jakob.

"Then you'll have to be sworn in," said Mr. Francis. "Otherwise it's not worth the risk of keeping you."

Jakob took my arm very firmly and hauled me into the meeting room.

"Jakob, wait," I whispered. "I'm not sure I want to be sworn in, just like that."

Jakob's grip on my upper arm tightened. "Even Sebastian has been sworn in; they expect it, if they're to offer you protection."

"Otherwise," said Mr. Francis, "you leave right now. Understand?"

But how could I leave, with the curfew bells still sounding and the streets full of thieves and hanged men?

Jakob brought me to the centre of the meeting room, which was really just a big cellar kitchen with peeling walls. Mr. Francis, who I noticed wore a rough green shirt with epaulets under his jacket, took down a book from the shelf above the stove.

"What is it?" I asked Sebastian.

"*The Complete Works of Diamonn*," Sebastian mumbled back.

"We don't have much interest in Bibles here," said Mr. Francis.

All at once, I felt better about swearing allegiance, if I was allowed to swear it on this book.

The book was opened and my right hand shoved in among its pages. "Repeat after me," said Mr. Francis. "I swear allegiance—"

My voice came out feebly, like a boy's. "I swear allegiance . . ."

"To the Partisan Resistance Army of Occupied Malonia," I repeated, while Jakob, in the shadows, nodded approvingly. "To obey my unit commander, to uphold the resistance's mission, and to work to further its cause, until the occupied homeland is taken back from the Imperialist occupiers, on pain of death."

My voice faltered on the word *death*, but Jakob glared and I repeated it. When I had finished, Mr. Francis gave me the resistance salute, the way I had seen the truck drivers do when they arrived at Anselm and Michael's telegraph post: a clenched fist pressed against the heart. I did the same. Then Mr. Francis gripped my hand, and seated me in a rickety chair near to Jakob. "Welcome to our meeting," he said.

And just like that, I was up to my neck in the resistance the first night I arrived in the city.

56

*T*he meeting was about sabotaging a train, but I hardly listened. "We need to know what the train's actually supplying," a serious young woman kept insisting from the corner. "What's the point of sabotage if all we get out of it is a few mouldy loaves of bread, a pile of coal—"

Jakob growled, "It's about giving a message, a sign—"

"Our cell, the East Capital Partisan Unit, has lost too many fighters already, pointlessly, on your missions, Jakob—"

"And what about the timetables?" Here an elderly man in epaulets accosted Mr. Francis. "They change them every day now—they mean to make fools of us all—"

"We can get the timetables," said a boy, from the corner. "My contact at the supply depot knows about that."

After five minutes of impassioned debate about the timetables of the East Imperial Railroad, the meeting fell apart. "All this talk about how and when and where," cried Jakob, banging his fist on the table leg. "But nothing gets done! Nothing ever gets done!"

"We need to go away and research the timetables," said Mr. Francis, extending a placating hand. "Marta, Pavel, talk to your people at the supply depot. We'll reconvene our cells in two days."

The meeting drew to a close. "Come on," said Sebastian, nudging my shoulder.

Jakob followed us reluctantly, still wound tight, along a corridor into the depths of the house and up a flight of stairs. "We'll show you where we live," said Sebastian. "Harlan, I'm glad to see you. I didn't think you'd actually come to the city. I thought you'd be with Antonia."

"Neither did I," said Jakob. "Maybe I underestimated you."

"I'm not here to join the resistance," I said. "I mean, not *only* that," I added hastily, at the look on his face.

"Then what are you doing here?"

"How long have you been here?" I said, to change the subject, because I wasn't ready to explain about Antonia and the baby just yet.

"A month," said Jakob. "We've already been out on missions. I've been promoted to assistant commander, you know."

"*I* haven't been out on missions," said Sebastian. "Jakob has."

"Well, Sebastian's just a part-time member. Like you will be, for now. It means he goes out to work at an ordinary job, but the time will come when we call on him to support our cell. When we get the signal to begin the final battle."

Sebastian looked slightly sickened at the thought.

Jakob unlocked a door at the top of the stairs and switched on a light. A bare bulb illuminated a large room with a table and packing-case chairs at one side, a sagging sofa under the window and a great black stove in the corner. Two mattresses lay close to the stove, the blankets and pillows in stormy disarray on one and clinically neat on the other. A shelf above a basin in the darkest corner was stocked with small articles: shaving cream and razors and tooth powder. A curtain made out of sacking hung halfway across the window, blocking the orange light of a streetlamp. Against that same wall was a desk buried under a heap of papers.

"Here's where we stay," said Jakob. "That little room through there has two more mattresses—we'll drag one through for you. We don't use that room because it's so cold. It's supposed to be Sebastian's, and this one mine—but I let him come in here with me, and now see what a mess he makes of it."

Sebastian bent his head apologetically, but Jakob was half joking. "The place is all right," he said. "We're lucky to have it. It's because I'm a full-time member that I get the room, and I don't mind Sebastian staying here with me," he added magnanimously. "Or you."

"Jakob's becoming quite important in the resistance," said Sebastian.

"I can see that."

Jakob maintained his stern expression, but a flush of pleasure crossed his face and made its way down his neck.

"What have you done?" I said. "What missions, I mean?"

"We sabotaged a convoy of trucks," said Jakob, counting on his fingers. "Then we broke into a government telegraph office and cut the wires. And—let me see—we went out to the Eastern Mountains to take supplies to the resistance fighters there."

"The Eastern Mountains," I said. "Wait—where? Anywhere near Bellame?"

Jakob looked at me strangely. "Not really," he said. "Why do you ask that?"

"No reason. Go on, tell me about the rest of the missions."

"Then just the usual," said Jakob, getting up and beginning to heave a third mattress through from the little store-room. "We disperse resistance material some nights. Or agitate." Whatever that meant.

"Where's Antonia?" said Sebastian abruptly. "If you don't mind my asking. I thought you were going to find her. I thought you were going with Antonia and your mother and father to the north."

I sat down on one of the packing cases. I had been delaying this moment. As well as I could, I explained. By the time I had finished, they were both looking at me with awkward pity.

"It's all right," I said, though it wasn't. "To tell the truth, I don't believe she's gone. I keep dreaming about her."

"But if her family say she's died . . ." Sebastian began.

Jakob said, "Shit, Harlan. A baby? You've got a baby?"

"Apparently." I was very tired, and my head was aching.

Jakob threw himself on the sofa, which rose to engulf him with loud creaks. "So you're telling me you left this kid with your brother in Maritz, but you're going to go back and collect her and take care of her, her *entire* life—"

"What else am I supposed to do? She's mine."

"But I mean to say, all on your own?"

"I'm going to find Antonia," I said stubbornly.

"But how, if she's dead?" Jakob was impatient with this logic. "Is that why you're in the city, to look for her? Why would she be here?"

I had no answer for this, but perhaps it was a mark of how much he pitied me that he didn't argue anymore. Sebastian twisted his hands in his lap, and he and Jakob exchanged a glance I was evidently supposed not to notice. But to my relief, they began to talk about other things.

That night, on my borrowed mattress, I lay awake a long time, thinking of Antonia and listening to the hum of the city. I could make out all kinds of sounds in the darkness, sirens and gunshots and truck engines and alarms. I had never stayed in a city before. The place made me strangely lonely. For the first time, I began to consider what would happen if I did not succeed in getting Antonia back.

When I slept at last, I was troubled by strange dreams of the resistance, and burned houses, and Anastasia crying and crying. I had no idea what I was going to do once I found all the strange places on the map, if all of them were burned. Waking up in the city, I had a cold feeling in my chest and thought that maybe I shouldn't have come here at all.

Since losing Antonia, I had had a kind of homesickness in me that never went away. Sometimes it manifested itself as a strange exhaustion, sometimes as a pain in my stomach or temples. This morning, it was just an unsettled feeling in my chest, like a bad case of nerves. Sebastian went out early, muffled up in a coat so thick he was almost round, to visit a professor of mathematics. This man lived in a slum on the southern edge of the city, and was teaching Sebastian. From there, Sebastian would go to a restaurant and work in the kitchen for nine hours, returning in the evening. Being Malonian, Sebastian was not allowed to touch any of the food, but he shovelled potato peelings and chicken skin and spoiled sauce down a rubbish chute, carried heavy sacks to and fro, and washed the kitchen floor. The idea of Sebastian doing anything so practical startled me, but even he seemed to have toughened since his arrival in the city. He took two outlawed textbooks, put them inside his coat, and left before it had even got light.

"He's brave, you know," Jakob said. "In his own way. He could be hanged just for carrying those books around."

"Can he not leave them at his professor's house?"

"He doesn't want to risk losing them. Hell, you saw the way he carried them out—cradling them like a child."

I half smiled. Jakob stood at the stove and downed a tin mug of coffee so bitter it made him shudder. He rooted around among the chaos of the shelves and produced a couple of stale biscuits for me. While I ate them and tried to bring myself to life, he sat on the floor folding leaflets with a determination that would have made you think he was engaged in some desperate front-line mission. He gave me one to look at. On it, an Imperialist soldier was dragging a child by the hair. *Nine hundred and fifty thousand unlawful arrests*, read the letters under it. *Four hundred and fifty thousand murders. Two million still interned in prison compounds without charge.*

"There's water on the gas ring," he said. "Pour yourself a cup of tea."

When I crossed the room, I felt achy and irritable. Anastasia occupied my thoughts. Had she stopped crying after I left? She must have done, but in my head she was still tear-stained and wailing.

In a chipped pan, water was boiling. I found a tin mug and filled it with water. Tea leaves I unearthed eventually, at the bottom of an old sugar jar. When I turned around, Jakob said, gruffly, "I'm sorry about Antonia, you know. I've been thinking about it all morning. My God, what bad luck."

I didn't know what to say, so I just nodded.

"It's a damn shame, what happened to her. To both of you. I've no love for any Alcyrian, but I still think so."

"Thanks, Jakob."

He went back to his leaflets. I drank my tea and began to come properly awake.

Around ten o'clock, Jakob went out with Mr. Francis, with the leaflets hidden at the bottom of a handcart full of firewood. I wandered about the room, surrounded by its emptiness but with no inclination to go out into this hostile city yet either. When I looked down from the window, I saw Imperialist soldiers passing, occasionally banging their rifles on the shuttered windows, rousing other neighbours.

I sat down on the sofa and consulted my map. The points that Aldebaran had marked in the city were labelled *Royal Gardens*, *New Square* and *Castle*. Obviously, the castle was out of bounds, since it belonged now to the new government. Instead, I decided on New Square, which was not far from where my family had once lived. I heaved myself up and went in search of an up-to-date map; I was sure Jakob would have one somewhere.

On the desk, Jakob's neat stack of papers had been submerged in an avalanche of Sebastian's disordered ones. I pulled them out. Sure enough, I found a plan of the city among the pile. The place names were in Alcyrian, and the city must have spread since my family lived here because I did not recognise the shape it made on the page. But I looked for a tiny square like the one on my map from Aldebaran, and found it at last: Plaz Capitansk Lucien, and a cross on a building marked *deziert* (disused). That cross was an old religious symbol. It must mean a church. On Aldebaran's map was a square with a church in the same position. That was where the star was.

Out of nowhere, I started to wonder about that priest who had helped us escape the city all those years ago. His church had been beside New Square. Was this the same one?

Partly because I had no other plan, I made up my mind to go to this place, this Plaz Capitansk Lucien, and find the star on Aldebaran's map. Maybe the priest was still there—who knew? I had never believed in the old religions like my mother, but I thought I might feel a little better in my heart if I could find this man who had helped saved my life when I was a child.

I did not take Jakob's map with me—I knew he would not take kindly to that. Instead I sketched a copy of the streets I needed, and put it in my pocket with Aldebaran's. Then I picked up my overcoat and went down the stairs.

The city was sharp with light and cold. I went quickly, without consulting my papers. I did not want to look like a stranger here. There were more people about today, but no one glanced up or smiled, except the very elderly. That suited me well enough. I set out for New Square.

57

*P*laz Capitansk Lucien was a dark patch of earth behind a row of demolished houses. Still, something about the place stirred a memory, as frail as my daughter's tiny heartbeat. I had been here before.

I crossed the packed dirt of the square to reach the remains of a fountain. The pool was empty and crusted with lime, and from it rose the dismembered bottom half of a horse statue. I reached out one hand to touch its side, and on the screen of my mind flashed the image of my six-year-old sister doing the same. I turned, half expecting to see her run across the square in her wool coat and mittens, that child Jasmine had been long ago.

Snow came down without warning out of the grey sky, then stopped as quickly as it had begun. And all at once, at the heart of this grim city, I believed that I truly was in a magical place.

I walked up to the door of the church. It was chained and padlocked and covered with graffiti and a government notice: *Condemned*. Against the grey sky, its dome glittered with the faintest trace of gold. Birds flapped around its roof, the only sign of life. A single ray of sunlight cut down through the window and disappeared inside. On the old board beside the door, I could make out the words *Holy Trinity Church, Mass Daily 6 p.m., Confessions, Extreme Unction, Marriages, Funerals. Priest: Father Dunstan O'Donovan.*

Father Dunstan.

I was right; this had been his church. Was the priest still here? Not hoping for anything, I began to hammer on the door.

After a long time, the hammering drew two people to the square. They appeared at the opposite side and began to advance towards me. As they approached, I saw that they were soldiers. "What are you doing?" called one of them, in Alcyrian. "What do you want?"

I stopped banging on the door and stepped away from it. "Nothing."

They were in front of me now. The nearest one jabbed at me half-heartedly with his rifle. "Who are you looking for?"

"This man." I indicated the old signboard. "Dunstan O'Donovan."

"There are no priests here anymore."

"Can I go inside the old building?"

The soldier looked at me as though I had suggested blowing up the parliament building. "It's been requisitioned by the government. Why do you want to go in?"

"I just want to see it. My family used to live near here."

"Papers." He held out his hand with a sigh.

There was the usual rapid-fire series of questions, but luckily the soldiers' hearts were not really in it today. After examining my papers, they left me. "Leave this old place alone," they called as they left the square. "It's an offence to attempt to enter it."

As they walked away, I saw that someone else had been watching from the shadows. A man just on the edge of old age, with a shock of rough grey hair. He had come out of a doorway at a corner of the square and was standing there watching me. "Why do you want to get into the old church?" he asked me, in my own language. "That place hasn't been open for nineteen years."

"I know."

All in black, walking very straight and tall in spite of his age, he presented a proud and somewhat alarming figure. "I'm Dunstan O'Donovan," he said as he advanced towards me. "I used to be the priest here. I know your face, but I can't recall . . . I'm sorry. Remind me."

I shook my head. "You only saw me when I was a tiny baby. My name is Harlan North. You know my family."

It never occurred to me not to tell this man the truth. "You helped us leave the city," I went on, "when we had to escape. We made it to Holy Island and I grew up there and here I am. I'm nineteen years old."

The old priest was in front of me now, and I was startled to see real tears in his eyes. "Harlan North," he said. "I can't believe I'm seeing you again." He clasped one of my hands between his own. "You're so like Leo. And your family? Are they safe?"

"Yes, I hope so. My mother and father are still on Holy Island. Things are difficult there. My brother is in the north sector, working for the resistance. My sister too. With Michael Barone—I don't know if you ever knew him, but he grew up here too."

The tears in the old priest's eyes threatened to fall. "Yes, I know them. I knew them all. Anselm, and Jasmine, and your mother and father. The Barone family. Yes, yes."

"I didn't think you'd still be here," I said. "Everything in the city seems so different from the place I expected."

"It is," said the former priest. "You can be sure of that."

"Do you still live in this square?"

"Yes. And I will do, as long as anyone remains from my congregation. There are only a few left now. Seven people. I do what I can for them."

"Why is the church still here," I said, "if the government has condemned it?"

The old priest looked up at the dome of the building. "They wouldn't let us use it any longer, and they ordered me to lock it up. They were going to come for the key, but they never bothered. I suppose they just couldn't think of anything else to do with it. They check that it's still locked from time to time, but otherwise they leave it be."

"Do you have the key?"

"Yes."

"I must go inside this church," I said. "It's very important. Would you consider opening it?"

The old priest did consider. "Come inside for a while," he said. "I have to think."

He took me into the shabby kitchen of his little cell and made me tea and questioned me about my family. I told him how we had lived on Holy Island. "And I have a daughter," I told him. "I've been told that my girlfriend, Antonia, is dead. I'm looking for her. That's why I'm here."

The priest gripped my arm in a comforting sort of way, misunderstanding. "I hope you'll find her," he said. "The dead pass on to another, better place, but they don't leave us utterly behind, my son."

I could tell he didn't mean quite what I meant by another place, but it didn't matter, because maybe it would give him the courage to show me the church. The old priest kept shaking his head at the sight of me. A miracle, he kept calling it. "A miracle, Harlan, that you're safe and well."

And at last, he went up the narrow stairs and returned with a bunch of keys. "I don't know why I'm doing this," he said, "when all these years I never had the courage. But I don't care. Too long that place has been in the dark. I might as well open it now."

I followed him across the square. The lock of the church was rusty, and he had to go back to his house for a can of oil. But at last, the rotten door opened in a clamour of dust and splintering wood. The priest coughed and swiped at the cobwebs in front of our faces. Birds screeched and made for the roof. Under the loud snapping of their wings, we stood at the door and looked in.

Light cut down from the broken stained-glass window and illuminated rows of benches standing in thick dust. On a big stone table at the front, a gold cross glimmered, and a ripped and greying cloth flapped morbidly. Rainwater ran down the wall in stripes.

The old priest shook his head. "Look what has become of the place," he said. "I was under orders not to open it, so I didn't. Now it may be too late to save the building. Look at it."

I took a few steps inside. The last birds fled through the empty panes of the window. Now there was nothing but decay and silence. Would I have viewed it differently if I had believed? I didn't know, but I wished the place were less dreary, more as I had imagined it. Why would Aldebaran send me to a place like this?

The priest bent to pick up a great book from the ground, where it lay in two pieces. He put them back together and replaced the book on the little reading desk at the front of the church. I went to the centre of the building and stood right under the dome. I looked into the heights and wished for some sign. *Why did you send me here, Aldebaran?* I thought. *What can I possibly learn about powers, or stopping time, in this dark and dusty place?*

"Father Dunstan," I said, unsure of how to address him.

"Mr. O'Donovan, please. Or just Dunstan. I'm no longer a priest, son."

"Mr. O'Donovan, then." My family had once respected him, and that must have rubbed off on me, because I did not want to use his first name. "I was wondering if this was ever a special place for some reason," I said. "Did anything miraculous happen here long ago?"

"Miraculous? How do you mean? This was a place of faith, certainly."

"I mean, did anyone have a vision or make something—I don't know—impossible happen?"

I wasn't sure what I was asking. Up there in the vaulted dome, there was no trace of magic or of other worlds, only the sadness of our own. When I looked back at the priest, he was watching me thoughtfully.

"It was my great-great-uncle who sent me here," I said at last. "I'm not sure why. Do you know anything about him? Aldebaran."

"Aldebaran? Aye, I know all about him. A good man. Your father loved him. I read the prayers at his funeral."

He was looking at his ruined church so sadly that I thought I should say something about it. I brushed the dust off one of the wooden benches and sat down. "Is this where the people sat?" I asked him. "On these benches, all lined up? I don't know very much about the old religions."

"Yes. These were the pews. Up there was where I led the Mass, by the altar there."

"Altar?"

"That great stone table."

"How many people would come here?"

"Hundreds, at one time."

"Including my mother and father?"

"Your mother and father, yes. From childhood, your father came here. He never believed fully. I was very fond of Leo. I knew he'd grow up to be a good man. Do you know, he once punched me in the face?"

I must have looked shocked, because the priest gave a barking laugh, which dissolved into a cough and filled the old church with echoes. "Yes, he did. It was just after his brother died, so I could forgive him that. Of course I could." The priest finished his coughing and wiped his mouth with a handkerchief. "Does he talk to you about that time?"

"A little."

"That was the saddest thing I ever had to do, telling your father his brother was not going to wake up. Those were the very worst parts of the job, when there was no comfort to give." The old priest walked a few steps towards the front of the church. He knelt at the railing there, and looked up at the shattered window and the rain-filled sky. "Your father believed in miracles," said the priest. "That was the problem. He was looking for the cure to the disease that was slowly killing his brother. There used to be a herb called the Bloodflower. It's the same substance they make synthetically in the government laboratories now, but in those days it was the rarest thing in the world. Anyway, your father was out in the hills every day, skipping school, making himself sick, looking for this flower."

"Did he find it?"

"That was the worst thing," said the former priest. "He found something that he thought was the Bloodflower. He came running home, full of excitement and relief, but his brother was gone."

"And was it the right flower?"

"No. But what was so terrible was the way Leo convinced himself it was. He blamed himself for not running faster. As if it was all his fault that Stirling died. He found his own kind of peace, in the end. I hope you will too."

Sitting there in the dusty, old pew, I felt the cold wind on my cheeks, and reached up to find tears. The crying took possession of me and hunched me over in my seat and made my shoulders lurch. I kept apologising, I remember, telling the priest I would be all right in a minute. He didn't say anything at all. He just sat beside me and put his arm around my shoulder. At last I became calm.

"I'm sorry, Mr. O'Donovan," I said, trying to gain possession of my voice. The priest shook off my apology with a kind little nod.

"She was Alcyrian," I mumbled, wiping my nose on my sleeve. Somehow, I wanted to talk to him about Antonia. "She disappeared in the winter. I was in a labour camp—I didn't know. Her aunt says that she's dead."

"I'm very sorry," said the priest. "I know that's an inadequate thing to tell you, but I am."

I considered telling him my plan, and decided against it. How could I explain to him that I was following the directions on an ancient map, in the hopes of stopping time and making things different, in the hopes of finding her? It sounded absurd, even to me. "When people die," I said instead, "they go to another place? Is that what you believe?"

The priest pressed his knuckles into his forehead. "It's what I hope, but it's not what I believe. Not for certain. I'm afraid to say, my views are not very orthodox. I've never really known where I stand on these matters. I feed my congregation, stay beside my old church. I don't know any more about matters of life and death."

"But if there is such a place," I said, "do you think we could get to it? To be with them?"

The priest frowned. "Now, that's a dangerous thought, Harlan," he said.

I couldn't explain to him that I was talking not about suicide but about the power to live in that world for an hour or a day or a lifetime, the same way my great-great-uncle believed he once lived in England, or as I had once lived ten minutes in that strange green world.

The priest got up to leave. "Mr. O'Donovan?" I said. "Do you mind if I sit here a while longer?"

"No. I'll be in my house across the square if you need me. But don't stay too long."

I nodded.

The priest left, carrying his big bunch of keys in one hand, and I was alone in the silence.

I got out Aldebaran's map. I traced the lines on it and tried to concentrate on a single point, inhabit that point, until I could disappear into it.

I shut my eyes. In my head, I returned to that night when Antonia was taken. I fixed my mind on the way her ribs felt against my side, rising and falling. I tried to make my mind so closed and narrow that her breathing was the only thing I felt. Then I prayed, or wished with all my soul, to be taken back to a world more like that one.

The church didn't vanish. The dim light and dust remained beyond my closed eyelids. But what happened instead was that I heard birdsong. It began in the distance, a kind of seething. Then it became more distinct, high runs as effortless as water-falls from blackbirds and thrushes, the light, insistent chirping of smaller birds, and the throaty caws of rooks and ravens. I listened and the sound became sharper, until it was everywhere around me, thicker and more deafening, like the sound of a tropical forest.

My heart began to beat fast, because I knew I was being afforded a vision, however faint, of another world.

A wing brushed my face and made me leap from my seat. I was still in the ruined church. The sound was gone, and only the cawing remained. The mangy pigeons and crows had re-entered through the broken window, their timidness forgotten, and were flapping and calling in the darkness around me. One of them must have flown too close.

It might have been a sign, what I had heard, but it was not enough. Though I waited a long time in the gathering dark, no other sign came to me. Was this why Aldebaran had brought me here? To listen to some birds?

When I left the church, I could tell that a storm was gathering. I tapped on Mr. O'Donovan's window. He came to the door, dusting flour off his hands. "Did you find what you were looking for?" he said.

"I'm not sure."

"Come back again. It does my heart good to see you. How long are you in the city?"

"I don't know yet. I'm staying in Milliner's Lane."

He frowned. "That's resistance territory. The secret police make raids there nearly every week. Stay out of danger, all right?" He gripped my hand for a last time.

"I'll come again," I said.

He raised his hand, and when I looked back, he was standing there, his hand still raised, a little forlornly, like he was blessing me.

58

*T*hat night, someone tried to burn the old church down.

The stone and wood, damp from years of abandonment, would not accept the flames. The church was only singed a little, but the great book on its stand burned away, and the roof caved onto the altar. I found out the next morning from Jakob's resistance newspaper: a government attack on the old religions, they called it, and Jakob, though he did not believe, was furious.

"Isak?" said Sebastian in private, that night. "Do you think this had something to do with you?"

He had told Jakob nothing about Aldebaran's letter, but now his face creased anxiously. "You need to be careful," he said. "Every other day I hear someone going on about the last descendant. And Jakob's changed. You haven't seen it yet, but you will, sooner or later."

"How has he changed?"

"He's just different."

What I hadn't told him was that every place my great-great-uncle had told me to go had been burned so far. But for the first time, I began to seriously consider the possibility that those fires were related not to Aldebaran's map but to me.

I thought again of the red-haired man, Rigel, and began to be afraid. I had always assumed him to be a good man, because of my dreams, because he had saved me as a child. But why did I seem to see his face around every corner? Was he following me?

I went back to the square that evening, all the same. The church looked no different, except for the black streaks running up its walls. Through the lighted window of the priest's house, I saw Father Dunstan bending over his stove. The old priest was safe; that was what I had been anxious about. I didn't dare to visit him again. That glimpse through the lighted window was the last I ever saw of him.

The resistance, Jakob said, wanted to know why I was living in their house and eating their food but not attending their meetings. So I began attending, and soon enough attending was not enough and I was ordered out on a mission.

We were supposed to be sabotaging a train. The plan was to drive out to the north-east, block the track with our trucks, then hail the driver for help. When he stopped, we would pull him out of the cabin and knock him unconscious (or shoot him, Mr. Francis said—whichever was easier). We would have men stationed along the track to deal with the armed guards. That whole part of the operation should take just five minutes, Mr. Francis said. Then we would transfer the supplies from the train to our trucks, and drive into the hills to deliver them to the eastern resistance. The train was supposed to be supplying the Alcyrian forces on our northern border. Without the supplies, they would be forced to retreat, at least for a short while. Also, the redistribution of the supplies was a symbolic act, Mr. Francis said, to demonstrate the people's wish for equality.

Jakob and Mr. Francis had wanted to use dynamite on the train, but they were outvoted. Sebastian and I had both voted against. "He's not even going!" Jakob raged at me as we put on our overcoats and boots in the gathering darkness. "Why does he get a say?"

"He's a member of the group," I said. "He gets a say. Isn't that how this works?"

"Sebastian doesn't do anything for this group unless I tell him to. Just like you, Isak."

Sebastian, who had come down with influenza the day before, appeared in the doorway and surveyed us anxiously, a scarf muffled round his head to keep out the cold.

"Get some rest," I told him. "Don't worry about the mission."

"Can I have my mathematics book?" he said thickly.

"You can't do mathematics if you're ill," said Jakob. "If you're well enough for mathematics, you're well enough for a mission."

"I'm not going to read it; I just want to have it with me. In case the war comes and we have to escape."

Jakob flung the book at him. I gave Sebastian what I hoped was a sympathetic look.

We were supposed to be holding a pre-mission meeting, but it was raining so heavily that everyone was late. Mr. Francis paced the floor, snapping instructions at us, while the latecomers shuffled in apologetically. "I cannot impress upon you enough the importance of this mission," he said, turning on us all. "If any one of you lets us down, you put the whole unit in danger."

Mr. Francis sent Jakob and me out to put chains on the tires of the trucks. "We won't make it into those hills otherwise," he told us. "The mud's that thick. It's a bastard of a night."

A sly and heartless wind attacked us as we worked. The tarpaulins on the trucks were heavy with rain; it had come down through the roof of the shed and continued to drench us. Jakob frowned, immersed in some silent problem of his own. Anastasia kept invading my thoughts. It was a month since I had last seen her. Did she look older? I wondered. Had she grown bigger? Were her eyes still grey like mine? Away from her, she felt unreal, like she had never existed. I hated that most of all.

"Harlan!" said Jakob. "You're supposed to be passing me that spanner, you bloody fool."

"All right, all right."

"You have to concentrate to go out with the resistance. You can't be lost in your own world. You'll see when you get out there."

We finished fitting the tires in silence and made our way back to the kitchen.

When we got back, Mr. Francis wanted to talk to Jakob about final plans, so I took my great-great-uncle's map and borrowed Jakob's again and sat on the stairs studying them. I had been to New Square, and that had led to the worst kind of trouble. I still had the Royal Gardens to find, but I wasn't sure that I wanted to anymore. There must be some other secret I was missing. Surely Aldebaran had meant me to do more than go to each of these places and attempt to summon my powers? Was there some passageway, some trapdoor?

As I traced the shape of the stars on the map, Jakob came clattering up the stairs. "What are you doing with my map?" he said, ripping it out of my hands.

"Just looking at it. Jakob, do you know what the Royal Gardens are?"

"An old park, I think. Ask Mr. Francis. He's lived here his whole life."

Mr. Francis, preoccupied and glaring like Jakob, did not want to be asked about the Royal Gardens at this moment in time. I asked him anyway. He snatched Jakob's map and pointed with a grimy finger to a vast building marked *Palaz Libertas*.

"What's that?" I asked.

"Secret police headquarters for the entire country. They built it right on top of where the Royal Gardens used to be."

It was deep inside the Alcyrian quarter. "Could I go there? Is there some way I could get inside?"

"You could go there," said Mr. Francis shortly, "if you didn't much mind about whether you came out again."

It was time to leave. We divided into groups and boarded the trucks. I was in Jakob's. We were to leave the city by different bridges, and make pretend deliveries on the way out, in order to avoid suspicion. I was not convinced that Jakob had a licence to drive a truck, but he managed to get us out of the city without incident. Traffic was heavy on the bridge, and Jakob blasted the horn several times and swore out the window. On the other side, we stopped and made a false delivery to a shopkeeper, another resistance member.

I wished I could get out of this mission. I was not in a mood for war. All I could think about was my daughter.

Jakob revved the truck against the mud of the road. The men with me were strangers, a sunken-faced tailor known as Mr. West, and Marco, a boy in his early twenties who worked in the restaurant with Sebastian. They made no conversation. I rubbed the dirt from the tiny back window and watched the road recede behind us. Once we got out into the eastern hills, we drove across grass slick with dew and came to a halt in the darkness. One by one, the other trucks arrived. We were to reconvene here, in the shadow of a disused factory. Mr. Francis got a fire lit by pouring petrol over it, and we sat around it and waited for the dark to set in properly. "We've had new information from Pavel," he said. "The timetables have been changed again. We're too early." The train was not due until half past midnight, and it was only a short way further to the railway line. "We'll have to hope no one knows about this mission," said Mr. Francis.

I thought of the eastern hills my family had known, a land abundant with flowers. Where had that old country gone? I did not recognise it any longer in the places I had seen.

I walked off from the others, out of sight behind the factory building. I knelt down and put my hands on the damp earth. *Aldebaran*, I said, in my head. *Take me back to the days when these hills were just hills, when this sky was black and unlit. Take me back to that time. Show me a vision.*

It was the first time I had ever spoken to him directly in my thoughts. In my head, as had happened in the old church, I felt a faint flickering.

"What the hell are you doing?" It was Jakob, appearing around the corner of the factory.

I sat back on my heels. "Nothing."

He crouched down beside me and jostled my arm. "Why do you want to know about the Royal Gardens, anyway?" he said.

"I just wanted to see them."

"There's something up with you, Isak. Why would you leave the north sector, to come and join the resistance at the beginning of a civil war? You're no revolutionary."

I had no answer. Jakob looked at me with shrewd, appraising eyes. "It's something to do with that letter from your great-great-uncle," he said.

I straightened. "What makes you think so?"

"I'm no fool. His will, you told me it was. As if that's what Sebastian decoded for you! I didn't say anything about it at the time, but I'm watching you, Isak. There's something about you that's never been quite right. Something odd. Unusual."

I maintained my silence.

"Aren't you going to tell me?" he demanded at last. "Your old friend, who stood by you all that year in the prison camp? Sebastian knows."

"There's nothing to tell."

"Fine." He got to his feet, brushed the mud from the knees of his trousers. "Is that all?"

"Yes, Jakob."

Without another glance in my direction, he disappeared behind the factory.

The night dragged on, and we sat in the drizzle, waiting, until at last Mr. Francis stamped out the remains of the fire and said, "Come on. Time to move."

The atmosphere in the group changed. We climbed up into the trucks in a prickling silence, full of expectancy, and in the same silence the trucks, one by one, moved off. The drivers went very slowly this time, leaving their headlights switched off. In the dark I could see nothing behind us or in front. Jakob glanced once or twice in the rear-view mirror, but his face was entirely closed now.

Before I was expecting it, I felt the jolt of the railway lines under the tires, and soon after that the engine cut out. Jakob opened the door. "Come on," he whispered. "We'll leave the truck here."

Mr. Francis was manoeuvring his own truck into place, a short way off beyond a thicket of trees. He shut off the engine and a match suddenly flared. He was checking his watch by its light. "Twenty minutes," he said. "In five I'll turn on the head-lights. The plan is to make out that our truck has broken down on the tracks. Is that clear?"

The rest of us nodded. We waited in silence. Someone tried to whistle a tune, half-heartedly, then stopped, leaving a greater silence.

"Now," said Mr. Francis. He turned the key and the truck coughed into life. Its headlights came on and made us all flinch. We looked strangely guilty, standing about in the sudden light. The drizzle danced in the beams.

"The train is due very soon," said Mr. Francis. "You know your posts."

Mine was easy—I was to remain by the trucks, with Mr. West and the others.

"Those of you who are dealing with the train guard, take your station at the fourth telegraph pole along the track." He gestured towards a blurred grey line in the distance. "Go now."

"Yes sir," Jakob said and jogged into the dark.

"The two of us," said Mr. Francis to Marco, "will deal with the driver."

Marco hauled out large steel lanterns from Mr. Francis's truck. They were covered with red paper to signal danger, and when they were lit they turned the world fiery and strange. The two of them went off at a jog to the turning of the railway track and set up the lights.

Mr. West sniffed and pinched the end of his nose. I stood on the railway line, feeling its cold through the soles of my boots and wishing I were not part of this.

Under my feet, I felt a trembling. "The train must be coming," I said. "Did you feel that?"

I had never seen a train properly before. We had no railways in Holy Island.

"Get out of sight," said Mr. West. I ducked behind the trucks.

It took a long while before we heard its engine; then its lights appeared, moving impossibly slowly across the plain. We heard Mr. Francis shouting, and Jakob, and saw the red lantern beams swinging wildly, a long way off in the middle of a great darkness. The train screeched, and with an awful grinding it passed Mr. Francis and the other two men and advanced towards us. An immense contraption of steel and gears. It was braking, but still it came on, puffing out smoke. "Move the trucks," I said, realising suddenly. "It can't brake properly in this rain. It's going to crash into them."

"And risk being seen?" said Mr. West.

"Move the trucks, damn it, or I will! They're going to derail the whole thing!"

"No, Isak—"

I wriggled free of his grip and ran to the nearest truck. In the end, he followed. I didn't know how to drive, not properly, but Jakob had left the keys in and I revved it off the track, then forced the handbrake, and it stopped. Mr. West was having difficulty with his, but it coughed into life at last. In the deafening scream of the train and the choking clouds of its smoke, the truck leapt forward and cleared the rails. A moment later, the place where it had stood was empty, and the looming engine blocked out the sky.

Mr. Francis and Marco were racing along the track towards us, signalling furiously. I made out the driver's face, scared and white behind his glass.

"Deal with the driver!" Mr. Francis was shouting. "Isak, you're closest! Take him out!"

I had a pistol in my pocket, but I didn't have any idea what to do with it, and the man looked so real up close, slightly overweight and sweating a little as he clambered down the steps.

"What is it?" he said, in Alcyrian. "Has there been some accident?"

In the dark, he couldn't tell we were Malonian resistance. He thought we were friends.

Mr. Francis, cursing me, fell upon the unsuspecting driver. He pulled his pistol out of his pocket and dealt him several hard blows to the side of the head. The driver fell, jerking. Marco stretched him out roughly on the ground and knotted wire around his ankles and wrists. A few frightened passengers pressed their faces against the windows. "Stay where you are!" shouted Marco. "All of you, stay where you are!"

At that moment, we heard a gunshot from the other end of the train, where Jakob was.

"What was that?" I said.

"Quiet," said Marco. "Help me." I took the driver's legs. We manoeuvred him off the track.

I thought I could hear shouting. Then another gunshot, and a third, and a fourth. We stared into the darkness, surrounded by an eerie silence. The train driver lay bleeding slightly from the head. I wanted to apply something to the wound—a shirt, a handkerchief, anything—but I didn't dare to move.

Jakob appeared out of the darkness at a run. "There were four guards," he gasped. "Not train guards but soldiers. The Imperialists must be arming all the trains now. I had to deal with them."

"Are they dead?" asked Mr. Francis.

"Yes."

"All four?"

"Yes."

"Good lad. Well done. Come on."

Mr. Francis turned the train driver over with his foot.

"We can't just leave him like this," I said.

"There's another train along in an hour," said Mr. Francis. "They'll find him then. Now come on, can't you? Form a chain."

We knew our positions, and I went to mine, but I was just a few feet away from the motionless train driver and I did not like to look at him, unconscious on the wet grass in the headlights of his own halted train. Mr. Francis and Jakob were breaking into the wagons one by one with great crowbars. There were only three, and the first held coal, clearly not what they were searching for, since the doors of this wagon were slammed with noises of disgust. But the second must have been worth raiding, because

I saw them climb up and disappear inside it. A moment later, bundles began to move along the line. I didn't know what they held until one of them landed in my hands. A military rifle, still with the factory grease on it, wrapped in a scrap of cloth.

"Wait," I said. "I thought we were carrying food supplies to the border, not guns."

"Someone's breaking the chain down there!" shouted Mr. Francis from the end of the line. "Keep going."

We passed gun after gun and loaded them into our trucks, then boxes of ammunition. Eventually the stream dried up, and we waited while Jakob prised the third wagon open. The way he moved in the dark, I would not have recognised him. He seemed on fire with excitement, clambering about the wagon like a monkey.

"No good!" he shouted hoarsely through the rain. "It's just a lot of new uniforms and Alcyrian flags. Let's go."

"Set fire to them," said Mr. Francis.

A window opened, making us all start. From the passenger wagon, a boy our own age looked down at us, alone in his defiance. "Some of us here have guns," he said, in Alcyrian. "If you set fire to that flag, we'll come out and fight you. It's an offence against the Imperialist government, and you'll all hang if they catch you."

Jakob leapt at the window. With the crowbar, he battered the boy's fingers until he cried out and retreated. Jakob was furious. "Let me get at him!" he shouted. "Filthy Imperialist—"

Mr. Francis hauled Jakob back by the collar. "Leave him," he said. "Do what I've told you and burn the flags and uniforms. We've got to go."

Jakob, in a rage, heaved up a can of paraffin and doused the material. The uniforms and flags went up like tinder. Some of the others, drunk on our success, ran whooping and yelling around the fire. Then we boarded the trucks and drove off into the night.

Looking back, the train made a forlorn picture, halted in the middle of its journey with the driver prone on the ground and fire blazing in its third carriage. And by the light of the flames, I could make out four black figures lying on the ground. I still couldn't quite work out what had just happened, but I wished I hadn't had any part in it.

We reached the eastern mountains, and still no one was after us. Jakob, in the driver's seat, took the mountain track at a pace that made my head spin. "Did you really kill those men?" I asked.

Jakob braked and took a corner at a slide. "Yes," he said shortly.

"Was it difficult?"

"No."

He took another three or four bends in silence, then gave a great sigh. "Harlan, they were coming towards us with guns. Do you think they would have stopped to hear our point of view?"

"No," I said. "I suppose not."

"This is war. Or will be, very soon. I don't think you realise that."

I wondered if this was the kind of thing Anselm did, and Michael. I remembered something my brother had said, when a resistance report from Bernitz made him shake with anger because women and children had been killed. "I think we have to be better than them," I said, repeating his words now. "We're not Imperialists. What kind of country are we going to have at the end of this if we all descend into violence?"

"That's what everyone thinks when they start."

"But killing people, Jakob—"

"Do you think this is the first time?" he said. "Why do you think I was in Black Heath Labour Camp to start with? Why does anyone end up there?"

"All I did was fall in love with an Alcyrian girl. All Sebastian did was hide some mathematics books."

"Well, good for the two of you, but that's not why I was in prison and it's not what I joined the resistance for."

With Jakob driving in such a rage, we almost took flight up the mountain. Soon we were in resistance country: I could tell by the shuttered houses at either side of the road, and the men with guns who loomed suddenly out of the dark and receded again, keeping watch at their own private checkpoints.

At a fork in the road, Mr. Francis, in the truck ahead, flashed his lights to signal to us to stop. Jakob shut off the engine and let out a breath.

"You owe us a hell of a lot more than you've given," he said, into the silence. "Remember that, Isak. We're sheltering you, and don't you forget it."

Mr. Francis drew up beside us and rapped on Jakob's window before I had a chance to reply. "Don't drive so fast, son," he said. "Do you want us to break our necks?"

"All right, all right."

Mr. Francis gripped Jakob's shoulder. "Don't get so wound up. You have to calm down, Jakob."

At three, we reached a compound of barbed wire on the outskirts of a mountain village, guarded by resistance men with rifles. A submachine gun nosed out of a thicket of trees. We delivered the guns at the gate, in silence. Jakob and the leader seemed to know each other. They exchanged a salute, a few brief words.

It was almost dawn now, and we drove home through a grey stillness. No one stopped us as we entered the city, beyond a quick check of our papers. When we got home, Jakob and Mr. Francis shut themselves away in the kitchen with the wireless, but I did not want to listen to it. A great tiredness overcame me, and I went upstairs, pulled the blankets over my head and slept.

Around midday I woke up to someone standing over me. Jakob was waiting very calmly for me to stir, and I couldn't tell how long he had been there. In one hand, he held Aldebaran's letter; in the other was a pistol, pointed directly at me. I reached for my backpack; he had taken the papers while I was sleeping. "Isak," he said, "you've got a lot to explain."

I sat up. My mouth tasted like the bottom of a dried-up riverbed. A strange light had come into Jakob's eyes. "What's all this?" he said. "These papers? What does all this mean?"

"That letter. From my great-great-uncle."

"Your great-great-uncle *Aldebaran*. Nobody told me that."

"Give them back."

Jakob swung out of my reach. "Powers?" he said. "The last descendant? It's you? It's been you all along—all this time? Some kid from a fishing village on Holy Island, in love with an Alcyrian girl?"

I pushed away the covers and made another lunge for my papers. Jakob seized me by the wrist. He forced me into a chair and bent over, his face sweaty and zealous. "If you ask me," he said, "I think it's time this information was brought to light."

"What does that mean, brought to light?"

"Tell the others. Announce yourself as Aldebaran's last descendant."

"Announce myself? Just come forward at a meeting and read them this letter? Or what?"

"Isak, we'd get the old resistance members onside. The ones who are so reluctant—the cells in the north sector, waiting for a sign from Aldebaran, waiting for this damned last descendant to make an appearance. We'd get the *people* onside, Isak. It would start a civil war."

But all at once, I didn't trust him—not even a little. "How do you know that?"

"I'm certain of it."

"And what about my daughter?" I said. "How can you guarantee she'll be safe, if I put myself forward as the last descendant and bring this and my whole family with it into the light?"

"Isak, think about the cause for a minute, can't you, and not your damn girlfriend and your child!"

"I'm only interested in getting Antonia back. And keeping my daughter safe. Nothing else."

Jakob leaned closer. "But think of the means you could have to influence people. Think of what you could do. The last descendant. The Imperialists have wanted you dead for years. Imagine if you appeared, leading the resistance to victory—"

"No," I said. "I don't want to lead the resistance to victory. I want to find out what happened to my girlfriend. That's what I'm going to do with my powers."

"That's crazy! This isn't about you and your girlfriend—this is about the greater cause you belong to!"

"I don't belong to any cause."

"You were supposed to save our country in a time of trouble. I looked it up. Well, save us then!" He looked at me pleadingly. "I'm trying to help you, Isak. I'm trying to bring you into the heart of the resistance, but you won't let me!"

"You're damn right about that. I don't care about being in the heart of the resistance. Haven't you seen that by now?"

Jakob looked at me for a moment, his eyes searching my face. Then he turned away from me, got up and lit a cigarette. "If I were you, I'd be very careful what you admit to, Harlan North." He used my real name with a proprietorial tone I didn't quite like. "Sooner or later," he said, "I'm going to be head of this resistance cell. That's the way it has to be. And until then, I'm your senior in the resistance. You have to do what I say."

"I'm leaving the city soon," I said. "I won't be able to. And give those papers back."

"You're not going anywhere," said Jakob.

"But I can't help you," I said. "I don't see what I can do." And I didn't like it, the way he pointed the gun. "Give me the papers," I said. "I'm leaving. I'm through with this." In desperation I thought of going to Father Dunstan for help again, of hitching a lift back to the north or Holy Island—impossible now.

"You're *nothing* without our help," Jakob hissed, thumping me on the shoulder. "You won't pass any checkpoint unless I let you. If you do anything out of line, we'll know, Isak. You're nothing without us."

"I don't have to do what you say," I told him, very steadily.

"Mr. Francis has got a plan for our next mission. It's a big plan, and it's going to start the civil war this country needs. And you're going to be at the heart of it. So get ready."

"I'm not at the heart of anything. If there is a war coming, I'm leaving Capital to go back north, to protect my daughter."

"You can forget about that. We're all part of something bigger now. Something more important than you and your girl-friend and your baby."

"Nothing is more important than that."

"Not for now. Not until we've finished this war, one way or another."

"Give me my papers."

"No," said Jakob. "I don't think I will." He leapt away from me, brandishing his gun, my papers out of reach now in his triumphant right hand. "Come with me," he said. "You'll do as I say now."

Mr. Francis called us to the kitchen. The resistance cells were coming together in the south, he announced, to intercept General Marlan as he made his annual tour of the occupied territories. This time, there would be an assassination attempt, followed by a bid to take back the south sector. If this was successful, it would precipitate a war. Our cell had been ordered to Anshelle. I told Jakob that night that I was returning to Maritz to my brother's house. But we both knew I was going with them. While Jakob was holding my papers for ransom, holding this secret over me, I couldn't go anywhere else.

One shred of comfort remained. Anshelle, the city that had once been called Angel, might still hold some trace of Antonia.

VII

❧ WAR ❧

59

*T*he city had thawed; we set out on a warm day. General Marlan was in the country, and the Imperialists were in a fever of excitement. He would pass through every major town and address the people. Later, he would cross to Holy Island and make an address in Valacia. The aim was to follow his progress from Anshelle onwards. Jakob was vague about the details of our actual plan, but I didn't care about that. I was going to Anshelle because Antonia might be there, and the first chance I got to cut my ties with the resistance cell, I meant to do it.

I had told Sebastian this, during a whispered conversation the night before we left. But he just shook his head and looked terrified. He too had been ordered on this mission. "You won't get your papers back," he said. "You think you can just take them from Jakob's bag while he's sleeping. He'll kill you."

My daughter was nine months old now, and I had not seen her for three of them. I hadn't seen Antonia for a year and a half. Spring had come, with a profusion of green foliage through which the trucks fought their way on the narrow side roads. I watched the little towns pass by our windscreen without really seeing them. I thought I would do anything to get my great-great-uncle's letter back from Jakob, to get away from them.

We slept by the side of the road. When I lay on my back and looked up, I could see a faint streak of blue along the horizon, beneath the stars. I could tell Sebastian was not sleeping either. For a while, I talked to him about mathematics, just to keep the loneliness at bay.

Jakob slept with his arms curled around the backpack in which he held my papers prisoner, his gun in one hand.

Two days after that, we reached Angel City.

———

Angel was like no other town I had ever seen. Its dusty houses stood arrayed on a wide bowl of hillside, sloping down to a clear sea that was nothing like the storm-troubled waves around Holy Island. Among the buildings, old twisted trees were blossoming, filling the air with their perfume. But Imperialists marched the streets here too. Jakob watched them pass with narrowed eyes. "They're off their guard," he said. "They're distracted by the preparations for General Marlan. That will help us."

Our new headquarters were a short way out of town, up a track so dry that the tires of the trucks sent dust puffing like smoke around us. The local resistance leader came out to greet us and shook our hands. Jakob and Mr. Francis introduced us, barked instructions, ordered us inside for food and water. After we had eaten, a few of the men left to survey the town. "You go too, Isak," said Jakob. "You and Sebastian. Reconnoitre the street they call Strasse Vitor."

This order seemed to amuse him. He knew I would not go far without my papers from Aldebaran.

Besides, we had passed in through a corrupt checkpoint, manned by resistance sympathisers, and they had orders not to let me back out. I knew because I had heard Jakob giving those orders. I no longer understood how Jakob was the same boy who had picked up stones beside me in the prison camp. That boy remained only in fits, submerged beneath someone darker and fiercer I hardly recognised.

Sebastian and I walked down the hill and in among the houses in a bleak silence. The ground was hot under the soles of our boots. Now that we were in the city, the tension in the atmosphere was clearer. Soldiers were hurrying about the streets, putting up barricades and yelling at people who got in the way. Groups of workmen were hauling great banners of General Marlan's face onto all the public buildings. The air had breaths of heat in it now. Sebastian, pink-faced, mopped at his forehead.

We stopped in the shade of an old church, and he lowered himself onto a bench and puffed.

Along the wall of the church were glass-fronted niches where people had put tiny figures of saints and religious leaders, so long ago that now the niches were filmed with dust, the insides cobwebby. Though they had been smashed into pieces, I recognised one or two of them from my mother's stories. I reached into the nearest shrine and reassembled the statue. "Saint Christopher," I said to Sebastian.

"How do you know that?"

"My mother told me about him once, years ago. See? He's carrying the holy baby."

"What are these holes in the wall?"

"Some kind of wayside shrines, I suppose."

A soldier standing under a spreading pine tree on the opposite side of the street blew a whistle furiously and gestured us away from the church.

We went on. "What does Jakob have against you?" said Sebastian. "I've been meaning to ask. I don't understand what happened between you two."

"He read my papers," I said.

Sebastian raised a hand to his face and rubbed it. "All of them?"

"All of them."

"And what did he do?"

"He told me to come forward. He told me to announce myself."

"Don't you want to?"

"I'm worried for my daughter. But Jakob didn't like that. He's got my papers, and he's made clear that I'm to do everything he says."

Sebastian scrunched up his forehead. "Be careful," he said. "Jakob's different here. He's been different since coming to the city."

"What happened to him?"

We stopped in a little square, where a green fountain made a fine mist in the air. Sebastian watched it disperse on the wind. "When we first came to the city, he had a girlfriend. Did he tell you anything about her?"

"No."

"Susanna. A resistance girl, who he knew from his days on Holy Island. They'd been together. He never talked about it. She was killed in one of the early operations in the city. They were sabotaging a telegraph office. The Imperialists surrounded it and made an assault. She was killed by submachine-gun fire, during that first mission."

"He's never said anything about it."

"He doesn't," said Sebastian. "Not ever. Except that first awful night when he came home, and I sat up with him until morning. Then he got up and washed his face and didn't talk about it anymore."

"Is that what changed him?"

"How do I know what changed him?" Sebastian spoke fussily, wearily, like an old man. He took out his folded handkerchief and mopped the sweat from his face. "He's always scared me a little, to tell the truth. Ever since that first day in the prison camp."

It was true—always Jakob had possessed some coldness inside him, some tightly wound thing that I did not like to consider too closely. "Do you think he'll give my papers back?" I said. "Do you think there's any hope?"

"I've heard them talking about the last descendant. He and Mr. Francis, I mean. They think I don't pay attention, but I do. They have a big plan about it. You're going to be part of this assassination attempt."

I rubbed the sweat out of my collar. "I'm not."

"You don't know Jakob the way I do. You need to be careful."

"He has to understand about Antonia," I said. "I have a family now. I'm just trying to get back to them."

"He does understand—at least part of him does—but part of him doesn't. That's what I'm trying to say. You've heard him talking about Alcyrians and Imperialists."

"She's no Imperialist!" I said. "How many times do I have to explain?"

Sebastian spread his hands miserably. "*I* know that; of course I do. But I don't think Jakob does—not properly."

He was trying to tell me something, but I was obtuse and wouldn't understand—any more than I had understood when my grandfather had talked to me about writing. I see that now.

"He knows I love Antonia," I persisted.

And at that moment, as I spoke her name, I saw her face. Antonia's face, staring out at me from the crowd, like a pale ghost of the real Antonia, but there.

60

I ran across the street, dodging trucks and handcarts, and came upon the wall of a bar. It was not her after all, but a poster, buried among a thousand others. I ripped them from the wall. "Antonia, Antonia," I kept saying, trying to reach her picture. It was so torn and faded that it was only just possible to make it out.

Sebastian hovered at my shoulder, saying something about the police. I didn't care. I tore away the posters until I could get the picture free. "It's her," I said. "It's her."

"This says 'Anastasia Fortuna,'" said Sebastian, pointing. "Not Antonia."

He was right. It was ancient, older than I had thought at first. "Anastasia Fortuna, star of the wireless radio, sings," read the poster. "August 1st to 11th, Year 10, Theatre Libertas, Avenue del Strasse." I sat down on the edge of the curb. This faded poster was eight years old.

Sebastian twisted his hands together, uncomfortable in the face of my disappointment. "Did you think it was her?"

It *was* her, almost. The likeness was impossible. All the hairs had risen along my arms. "It's Anastasia Fortuna," I said. "Her mother."

"My grandmother used to listen to her on the wireless radio," said Sebastian.

"I want to go to this place," I said. "Theatre Libertas. Will you come with me?"

"We're supposed to be reconnoitring this street," he said. "We're not supposed to be wandering about."

"Sebastian, please. This is important."

"I don't want to get into any more trouble with Jakob. Isak, haven't you listened to everything I've just been saying?"

"It won't take too much time. Honestly, Sebastian. The town isn't large."

I didn't have the first idea whether it was large or small; all I cared about was finding the theatre. Stupid, really. As if she would be waiting for me there.

I set off at a jog, and Sebastian, puffing, followed me. We passed through a scuffed and dusty park with an ornamental pool: a place I recognised from my dreams. I crouched beside it and looked into its dark water for the fish Antonia had once owned. I thought I caught a flash of orange and gripped Sebastian's arm. "There," I said. "Look there."

"What?"

"It's one of Antonia's fish. The fish that used to be in the fountain in her house, before they had to leave. Well, not the same ones. They must have bred—made a colony." It seemed a sign to me, as though I were drawing nearer to Antonia herself.

Sebastian looked obligingly, but I could tell he wasn't really interested in the fish. He kept glancing around for soldiers and rubbing the sweat off his forehead. "Can we go on, please? The sooner we get back to headquarters, the better. It feels like something is going on here."

Sebastian was right. From the distance came shouting voices and two sharp cracks. Gunshots.

All the same, I couldn't abandon my pursuit of Antonia's face. I hauled Sebastian after me, along the same narrow street. Here the houses were packed tighter, and we walked in black bands of shadow. All at once, we came upon the sea. Further along the shore, I made out a dark semicircle of stone, with little square windows that let the sunlight through. "That must be the theatre," I said.

"It doesn't look much like one," said Sebastian.

"It's an open-air theatre. It's an ancient one, hundreds of years old, I think. An amphitheatre. Come on."

He followed reluctantly, along the edge of the water. We were getting closer to whatever commotion was taking place. I could definitely hear gunshots.

"Let's go," said Sebastian. "It isn't safe."

"I just want to take one look at this place."

The theatre rose up in front of us, its arched walls looming. Through the arches, I could make out rows of seats extending up the hill and the great stone slab of the stage. Posters pasted to every wall proclaimed, "Acclaimed singers from across the empire, every night at 8 p.m." Trucks were lined up outside, and workmen were bustling in and out with what looked like radio equipment. They must be preparing for a concert. Two soldiers surveyed them lazily, but there was another door which was not guarded.

"Come on," I told Sebastian. "We can just blend in."

I dragged him by the arm through the side door before he could protest properly. But here Sebastian, wheezing, resisted.

"No, Isak," he said, with something like real anger. "It's much too dangerous. What do you think Jakob will say when he hears that we've been all the way to this theatre? What will he say if we get caught?"

"Wait here if you're worried, Sebastian, or go back."

"If you go in alone, you'll only get into more trouble." He sighed fussily and straightened his glasses. "Come on. Be quick about it. I'm not staying long."

This way into the theatre was a low, dark passage lit by intermittent floodlights. I ran, and Sebastian followed. At the end, the passage opened out into a kind of vestibule, and beyond that, it led us right out behind the stage. All at once I recognised this place. I was years away in the dark of a summer night when young Antonia crouched behind the floodlight and watched her mother sing. I dropped to my knees in the place she had stood. She was here, within these stones; something of her persisted, remained.

Sebastian tugged my sleeve. "Isak, what are you doing?"

"Remembering," I said, keeping my eyes shut so that Antonia would not disappear.

"Isak?"

"What?"

"There's someone coming."

I opened my eyes. Two workmen were advancing along the passageway. "Hey!" one of them shouted. "What are you doing?"

"Just looking," I said.

"There's a very important concert here tonight. You shouldn't be hanging about. You're lucky it wasn't Imperialist soldiers who found you here."

At a run, we descended into the passageway again and out towards the side door. Halfway down, the floodlights cut out, just switched themselves off with a low *thunk*.

"What is it?" said Sebastian shrilly. "What's happening?"

"Don't worry. We're almost out." I dragged him by the arm to the door, and we escaped into the daylight.

Something was definitely taking place in Angel City. People—crowds of them—were running past the theatre. Soldiers were everywhere, with riot shields and rifles.

"What's all this?" I said.

Sebastian shook his head. "We need to get back to headquarters, right away."

As he said it, something flew past us in a high arc and landed on the ground at the base of one of the palm trees. People backed away, shouting. Whatever it was exploded in a flash of light. I fell to the ground and raised my hands to protect my head, and the backs of them were flayed with flying bark as the tree exploded. A makeshift bomb. Then missiles were raining about us—stones, glass jars, tin cans. People seized everything they could and flung it at the soldiers. Not resistance, but ordinary men and women, spurred on by something I could not guess.

When I got to my feet, I could hear nothing but a ringing inside my head. Sebastian was shouting something in my ear. I began to drag him back the way we had come, between the running people and the riot shields and the swinging batons, towards Strasse Vitor. We were thumped and buffeted on all sides, and more objects were flying now—broken bottles and stones in place of grenades. Somewhere on the left, a puff of smoke appeared from behind the houses, where a building blazed.

Through a world that seemed all at once to be ending, Sebastian and I ran. He couldn't run as fast as me, but I kept beside him, still clinging to his arm. Neither of us stopped until we had left the city behind and were on the dust track to the headquarters. Then we bent double, coughing.

"What the hell was that?" I said. My hearing was coming back.

"I think it's the start of civil war," said Sebastian. "I think it's really starting this time. They've given the signal."

"The signal?" I said.

"There's a signal—I don't know—some signal Jakob's been talking about—some message they're going to transmit over the wireless radio to tell everyone to come out and fight."

61

*J*akob was spitting mad when we returned. He stood in the middle of the dark kitchen, raging.

"Where the hell have you been? You've taken three hours. We're under orders to attack, and I've been left here waiting for you. You were supposed to be reconnoitring Strasse Vitor—that was all."

"We got lost," I said. "We couldn't find the way back."

"Lost? Is that how it is? I'll give you lost, damn you."

"You said we were under orders to attack?" Sebastian broke in. "Attack what?"

"The secret police headquarters in Angel City. It's already started. The other resistance cells are coming down from the hills. We're supposed to take control of the town before General Marlan gets here."

"It's like a civil war down there," I said.

"It *is* a civil war," said Jakob. "That's the point. Come on."

He ordered us into the truck and we set off. At the bottom of the dusty track, he turned right, and we rattled along a pot-holed road between great cypress trees.

"Jakob?" Sebastian ventured. "Where are we going?"

"Mr. Francis told us to meet at the old grain store on the west side of the city. We'll advance from there."

"You haven't seen what it's like in the city," I began. "I don't think we can just—"

"You shut your damn mouth, Isak."

We turned a corner, and the city spread out below us. In the narrow streets, the surge of crowds was clearly visible. Jakob wound down the window and let in the distant sounds of shouting, gunshots and explosions.

"We shouldn't have come here," said Sebastian, rocking in his seat. "We should never have come here in the first place. Why couldn't we have just stayed in Capital?"

We drove on in a charged silence.

The old grain store was visible from a distance by its tall round towers. As we drove down the hill towards it, people began to pass us heading in the other direction. Some were limping, and others came at a run. Outside the old grain store, Jakob swung the truck around and stopped. Still the people came running. Resistance fighters, they must be, from their rifles. But others came too, people in ordinary clothes like the fishermen of Holy Island, gripping sticks and pitchforks, hurling stones.

"It looks like a retreat," I said, but Jakob's glance stopped me from saying more. In front of the old empty warehouse, we waited. Gradually, the flow of people dwindled to nothing. Then it was just the empty square, the sunlight and silence.

"When you got lost," Jakob said, "where did you find yourselves?"

Sebastian cleared his throat. "The old theatre. That one over there." He pointed towards the shore in the direction of the black amphitheatre, which brooded in the spring heat.

"And what did you find there?"

"They were setting up for a concert, they said."

"What kind of concert?"

"They didn't say, did they, Isak?"

I shook my head.

"Jakob," said Sebastian, very gently, "maybe we should go back?"

Jakob didn't reply. But after we had waited another quarter of an hour, he revved the truck into life and turned back the way we had come.

When we got back to headquarters, there was a line of trucks out front, and two people were waiting for us at the door. They came out onto the dust track and waved us down. Marco and Mr. West. "What is it?" shouted Jakob from the window.

Marco had one arm bandaged. "The first attack was unsuccessful. And Mr. Francis . . . Jakob, he fell."

Jakob cut the engine. He rested his forearms on the steering wheel and stared through the mist of dust on the windscreen. "What do you mean, fell?"

Marco put his good hand on Jakob's arm. "He's dead. He was killed in the crossfire when we took the square."

"Is any of the city taken?"

"No. We were forced to retreat."

"Who's in charge of us now?" said Sebastian.

"I am," said Jakob. No one argued with that.

Jakob sat for a moment longer, then drew himself up and jumped down from the truck.

"You'd better come inside, in that case," said Marco. "The leaders of the other resistance cells arrived about half an hour ago. They've got a joint operation planned for tonight. You'd better come in and hear what they have to say about it."

Then a very strange thing happened. I heard, drifting through the warm spring air, my great-great-uncle's words. "Harlan, this is what I know. This is the truth about powers."

I pushed my way through the door and along the corridor. "There were a hundred thousand worlds then," I heard, "worlds for every possibility."

I pushed open the door of the kitchen. In the corner of the room we had all deserted, the wireless radio, unattended, was playing, tuned to the free station. And over the waves, into this room as if Aldebaran himself were speaking them, came my great-great-uncle's words.

"What's this?" I said. "What's happening?"

The others had followed me. Marco's arm was bleeding persistently. Mr. West kept shaking his head, "to get the ringing out of his ears," he said, though I could tell that wasn't the only reason. "What is it?" I said again. "Those words on the radio?"

"It's the signal," said Mr. West. "A small miracle. They discovered the last message from Aldebaran. They say the last descendant is going to come forward now." He tipped his head, pressed one palm against his ear. "Why else do you think all the ordinary people have come out to fight at last?"

While I still stood listening, the remaining members of our cell returned, limping, carrying between them a black and heavy object which turned out to be the body of Mr. Francis. I opened my mouth to confront Jakob, and closed it again. His shoulders were shaking. The loss of Mr. Francis had moved him, for the first time I had ever seen, to tears.

We laid Mr. Francis in the shade beside the track. No one seemed to want to look at him too closely. In the end, it was Sebastian who brought water out to clean the blood off his face. Though I didn't want to, I helped him. Mr. Francis was like my grandfather had been after the spirit left him: the same figure, but altered, no longer himself. I hadn't known Mr. Francis well, but I felt a great pity for him anyway.

Sebastian took two pennies out of his pocket. Without hesitation, he placed them on Mr. Francis's eyes to hold them shut.

"Aren't you afraid?" said Marco.

Sebastian just shrugged. "It's not him. He's gone."

Jakob continued to cry. I had not known he was capable of it. Hot and angry tears coursed down the dust on his cheeks, and he stood with his fists clenched and glared at us all, daring us to look away. We buried Mr. Francis in the green pasture behind the house, and Jakob marked the grave with a resistance banner, which caught the listless breeze and flew, raising its clenched fist to the blue sky. The other resistance leaders, in various states of injury and dustiness, stood and saluted the new grave.

"What next?" said Marco.

"Next," said Jakob, "comes the biggest attack of all." He gathered us around him in the kitchen. "General Marlan's tour is going to pass through Angel City tonight. We thought it would be rerouted after the first attack, but we've learned that he's going ahead as though nothing has happened. He and his entourage are going to arrive at eight. He'll make a speech in the square and watch the captured members of our ranks be hanged. The other resistance cells have come down out of the hills. Tonight, we'll make the attack. Tonight, in the town, timed to coincide with General Marlan's speech."

A few people drew in their breath, but no one said anything. Jakob glared round at us all. "If we fail, we fail," he said. "But we too can fight back. You'll be stationed at various posts in the town centre. We'll set off a series of explosions at exactly half past eight, in the middle of the speech. These are designed to cause confusion. If they leave General Marlan vulnerable to attack in any way, every one of you is under orders to attempt his assassination. If anyone disobeys these orders, they will be shot by firing squad, without recourse to mercy. Is that clear?"

There were nervous nods all around. "What about the last descendant?" said Mr. West. "Is the miracle true? Is he going to show himself tonight?"

Jakob raised his eyes briefly to mine, then looked away. "Time will tell," he said.

"Jakob," I said, as gently as I could, "is this really what they want us to do? Right after we've had to retreat from the town, I mean? Surely we should wait and regroup at least a little . . ."

"No," said Jakob. "It's been decided."

"And what about all the people who will be in the square listening to General Marlan's speech?"

"What right do any of them have to expect mercy? What mercy have they shown us, seizing our homes, marching over our land?" He turned away. "This has all been arranged. Now, are you all clear about the penalty if you disobey these orders?"

None of us wanted to agree, but Jakob left us with very little choice, and eventually we did. One by one, he called us into the next room to give us our orders. The others must have been told not to share them, because they came out in silence.

I was the very last one called in. Jakob did not look at me. He put a pistol down on the table. "Take that, first of all," he said. "You might need it."

"You've got something to explain to me." I rounded on him, with the anger I had not been able to summon while he was weeping over Mr. Francis's makeshift grave. "My great-great-uncle's papers. The wireless radio. You've put me in danger—my whole family—"

"I've nothing to explain to you."

"Are you expecting me to come forward? Are you expecting me to announce myself?"

"You don't need to. The civil war is going to happen whether you like it or not. It's beginning now. The revolution is beginning."

"What am I supposed to do with this gun?"

"You're to go to the old theatre," Jakob said. "Since you seem so drawn to it, you can spend the night there."

"That's all?"

"Yes."

"Just me on my own?"

"Yes. You'll have this portable radio." Jakob thumped it down onto the desk. "It's set to receive orders from here if anything goes wrong. If anything changes, you are under orders to contact us here. Our call sign is Base 232. Is that absolutely clear?"

I put the gun into my pocket and picked up the bulky radio. "How am I supposed to disguise this?"

"Put it in a bag or something."

"A bag?" I weighed the radio in my hands. I couldn't help feeling that the orders I had been given were just a way to keep me out of trouble while they dealt with the important business of their assassination attempt. Or else to get me arrested for carrying an illegal radio, and safely out of Jakob's way. I didn't exactly mind that, but I was startled, especially after my great-great-uncle's words had been broadcast all over the wireless radio, had precipitated what looked like full-scale civil war. "Isn't there something more?" I asked.

"No," said Jakob. "You have your orders. I'm done with you now."

I stumbled out into the light.

62

*I*t was not as easy to get into the theatre the second time around. The doors were guarded by soldiers, and the workmen from before had disappeared. I stayed in the shadows opposite the stage door where I had entered before, and waited, shifting the uncomfortable weight of the portable radio, which I had hidden among all my belongings inside my old leather backpack, as though I were merely travelling. It was far from perfect, but it would have to do. People passed in the streets occasionally, but with heads bowed and keeping to the shadows of the buildings. No one, it seemed, wanted to step outside their houses. Around six o'clock, an ancient man appeared and opened up the ticket office, wincing as he strained to slide up the grille. I approached his little window. "Yes?" he said quaveringly. "What do you want?"

"A ticket for tonight's concert."

"It's sold out," he said.

I was surprised at that. "Even after what happened earlier? Hasn't anyone returned their ticket?"

"It's sold out," repeated the ancient man.

"But the theatre will be half empty."

"Maybe," he said. "But even so, it's sold out."

I must have looked thoroughly confused, because the old man leaned closer and glanced towards the soldiers. "You're Malonian," he said. "This is an Alcyrian-only theatre. Didn't you know that? For you, this concert is sold out."

I turned away.

At around half past six, several motorcars arrived and disgorged a few people at the stage door. Performers, probably. From the chatter that emerged from inside the theatre each time the door was opened, I could tell that others were already inside and preparing. The Imperialists were behaving as if nothing was wrong.

A few other people began to disappear through the door. One of them, a boy about my age, was clearly Malonian. He walked with his back bent, half apologetic, carrying sacks of rubbish and pails of dirty water out of the stage door. When he accidentally got in the way of the arriving performers, he bowed and nodded with a placid smile, spreading his hands, as if begging them not to notice his existence.

I was supposed to be inside that theatre, but I didn't see how I was meant to get there. A few people were queuing at the theatre door now, all well-dressed Alcyrians. The elderly man admitted them in ones and twos. The soldiers who had been standing guard stood protectively around the theatregoers as they waited to be admitted.

A few men, clearly drunk and clearly Malonian, came rolling down the street at about a quarter to seven. I could see the trouble long before it began. One of the men, his torn shirt the mark of fighting earlier in the day, bent to pick up a stone. "Imperialist shits," he said in our own language. "Didn't you hear the message on the radio? Your time is over. The king and Aldebaran and his last descendant are going to come down out of the hills and sweep you all away."

"*Kom er?*" said one of the soldiers. *What's that?*

"Imperialist shits! Taking our town, taking our theatre. This place was standing here when Diamonn was a boy!"

The soldiers faced up to the drunks. Both parties refused to speak the other's language. "Drop your weapon," said one of the soldiers, in Alcyrian.

"My weapon?"

"That stone. Drop it."

The drunk man weighed the stone carefully in his hand. Then he launched it, very deliberately, at the soldier. It made a slow arc and landed with a thump in the dust at the soldier's feet. He and his friends waited for a second before moving in, then they took out their batons and began to beat the drunk men to the ground. They went on even after the drunks had given up all the fight in them. A woman in a fur shawl gave a low cry and turned away. Two of the well-dressed men in the theatre queue stepped back to protect themselves from the flying dust.

The boy, the Malonian cleaner, had somehow been caught up in the commotion. He stood, his pail in his hand, clearly too frightened to open the stage door and go inside, to do anything that might draw the soldiers' attention. Eventually the beating stopped. The three men were dragged away around the corner.

In that frightened boy, I saw my chance. He was allowed free entry to the theatre. Why shouldn't I be? And now—while the soldiers were distracted, trying to calm the panicked Alcyrians in the queue, to assure them that there was no chance of revolution—I had my moment.

I approached and put my hand on the boy's arm. He started and dropped his pail, sluicing both our legs with dirty water.

"Hey, hey," I said, picking it up. "I don't mean any harm. I just want to ask you something—wouldn't you rather go home?"

"I can't go home," he said in a whisper. "Not for another half hour."

"What do you mean?"

"I'll lose my position here. It's treason. We're all to carry on as normal. That's what the governor said on the wireless radio. We're to carry on as if nothing has happened. Everyone in the town. So General Marlan sees us all acting as normal when he arrives."

"Look, I want to watch the performance tonight. I've never been to the theatre." I looked around quickly to make sure no one could overhear. "Let me do the job for you. I won't cause trouble."

The boy shifted his eyes sideways, but he didn't reply.

"Go on," I coaxed. "It won't do any harm. I heard there's going to be trouble at this theatre tonight."

That seemed to settle it. The boy nodded quickly, then put the pail into my hand and slipped something from around his neck. "This is your pass," he said. "We're all casual workers here—you won't be noticed. There's the toilets left to clean, and then you're to stand outside the performers' dressing rooms in case they want anything swept or tidied. Understand?" I nodded. "Don't touch them directly, and don't touch any Alcyrian person's food before they've finished it—they'll beat you. I don't want to hear anything about what's happening here tonight. But I care about my job. It's important you do it right."

"I'll do it right."

I put the pass around my neck. Before I could even thank him, the boy was gone, creeping along the wall of the theatre with the same stooped, apologetic posture, trying to make himself vanish into the wall.

I picked up the pail and went inside.

As I walked along the passageway, the empty pail clanking against my legs, another flash of the past world crossed the screen of my mind. Anastasia Fortuna, in a red dress that crackled with net and satin, leading little Antonia by the hand. I could almost see them walking ahead of me in the gloom, Anastasia pausing to straighten her hair and young Antonia mimicking the gesture, trying to become her glittering mother.

"Antonia," I said, into the dark.

A gaggle of dancers, all long legs and gauze dresses, crossed the corridor ahead of me. "You the cleaning boy?" one of them called.

"Yes," I said. "Yes, madam," I added as an afterthought.

"There's dirty plates that need taking away. Dressing room three."

Carefully, breathing as quietly as I could, I entered the dressing room. Inside, clothes and shoes were heaped on couches, and a powdery litter of make-up covered the dressing table. I found the plates among this chaos and looked for somewhere to put them. Walking back along the corridor, I found a large cupboard with a dripping sink inside. There were cleaning materials here too—mops and buckets and brooms—so I took a bucket and a mop and a brush and went in search of the toilets. I didn't particularly want to clean them, but neither did I want to get that boy, whoever he was, into any kind of trouble.

The toilets were in a dark room at the end of the passageway. Performers bustled in and out as I worked, ignoring me. The radio swung uncomfortably on my shoulder, inside the backpack. I hadn't dared to leave it anywhere. Had Jakob intended for me to set it up? I didn't even know how to use it. This whole mission was ridiculous, a joke at my expense. In the distance, faintly, I could hear instruments tuning—violins and flutes and cellos, like I used to hear on the wireless radio with my grandfather years ago.

That, or something else, carried me back. I paused for a moment, on my knees in the dingy toilet cubicle, and was elsewhere.

When I came back, I could tell that someone else had entered the room and was standing in front of the mirror. I felt her presence, and heard her quietly sigh. I glanced out. A woman with short black hair, hacked quite roughly across the back. I could not see her face from this angle. She arranged a strand of hair, then left.

When I stepped out in front of the mirrors, something hit me with the force of a blow and made me reel. Antonia's memory again, like a ghost. It took me a minute to realise what it was that had brought her presence home to me so forcefully. The woman's perfume, lingering in the air. The hairs on my arms stood on end. It was like her ghost had passed through me there in that dingy theatre bathroom.

It was lucky that I had finished the cleaning work. I couldn't have done any more. I stood outside the closed doors of the dressing rooms instead, and thought of Antonia. *If I get out of this alive*, I told myself, *I'll tell Anastasia how much I loved her mother, how true she was, and how gentle, and strong, and beautiful. I'll bring her to life that way.*

Did I give up hope at that point? I suppose I did. It wasn't a great tragic thing, this loss of hope. It was like the loss of religious faith, the way my father had described it. One moment it's there, then it isn't. Like a force leaving you. Like powers. I had come to Angel City, the last place on my great-great-uncle's map except those that I knew were already burned or destroyed. I hadn't found the green world, and I hadn't found Antonia.

And just at the moment I gave up hope, I heard Anastasia Fortuna's voice. I heard it quite distinctly, as it had sounded on the wireless radio when I was a little boy.

———

I raised my head and walked towards the sound.

In a room somewhere, the performers were rehearsing. Meanwhile, someone was checking the radio equipment; I could tell from the static. Were they just playing a recording of her voice? But it sounded too lifelike, too real. And why would a singer so disgraced, so out of favour with the Imperialists, be transmitted again on a day like this, when they had almost lost control of Angel City to revolutionaries?

I crept closer. But abruptly, the noise stopped, like a radio cut off. Was that really all it had been, just a recording? How strange that Anastasia Fortuna's voice could be at once real and dreamlike.

I was close to the entrance of the passageway now, and I could hear that the theatre was full of people. Just as in my dreams of the place, the front rows were filled with Imperialist soldiers; they were everywhere in the audience, the light blue of their uniforms standing out among the sombre evening clothes of the other theatregoers. Darkness was falling. I stood at the door to the passageway and watched them. What was I doing here?

There it was again: a voice just like Antonia's mother's, and it made my skin prickle uncomfortably.

I turned and again tried to find the sound. Again it escaped me. And all at once I was certain that I was coming close to that other world I had longed all my life to inhabit, that world where time and space could collapse.

Then, in the real world—my world—several things happened all at once, and with a growing unease I became aware of them.

63

*T*he visions came to me unbidden, unfurling in my mind's eye like the pages of a book turning. Lying on the roof of a church with a sniper rifle, Jakob saw General Marlan's entourage move out of range of the shot he had prepared. Heroism escaped him by an inch and filled him instead with rage.

A memory of Anastasia Fortuna's singing surfaced and hovered in the still air of the theatre; it invaded present-day Anshelle, which was about to be torn apart by violence.

And General Marlan, on a sudden whim, remembered that concert, the voice of the singer, and decided to change his route to take in the theatre too.

A sudden commotion in the theatre brought me back. Soldiers with loudspeakers and guns were invading the stage. I could tell from their lack of uniforms that they were secret police. I pressed myself into the dark behind the doorway.

"Clear the theatre," they ordered in Alcyrian. "All but recorded members of the Imperialist Party must now leave. Tonight's concert programme has been altered."

The secret police began moving down the rows, hauling people from their seats. Even some who were quite clearly Alcyrians and Imperialists were unceremoniously marched towards the exits. Some protested. A woman in pearls, a wealthy Alcyrian lady, called loudly for her guards. But the secret police persisted. Quite firmly, they escorted even their own people from the seats. Soon, none but the soldiers and the rich Imperialists accompanying them were left.

Behind me, the dancers were huddling, whispering to each other. "What's going on?" I asked, in my own language, forgetting.

One of them shrugged and shook her head. "It happens sometimes," she said, in Alcyrian. "If an important Imperialist wants to requisition the theatre for a private concert, they just turn everyone out to make sure there's no danger of an assassination attempt. We don't mind. The soldiers come here drunk and try to grab you, but they give good tips."

The secret police were still marching about. I scanned the turbulent ranks of the audience. There was no one here now who could possibly be Malonian. Just lines of Imperialists—rows and rows of pale-skinned, dark-haired people, talking and gesturing easily in their own language, all wearing some sign of their allegiance to the cause—a blue armband, or a jewelled badge with a lion and scythe, or full military uniform.

The secret police were approaching our passageway, four or five of them. The radio on my back bumped conspicuously. I turned and ran down the corridor, looking for a place to hide before they could catch up with me. I ran into the bathroom, but there was nowhere there except the flimsy cubicles. Fear was choking me. The only place left was the little cleaning cupboard. I ran inside, slammed the door behind me and turned the key.

Would they find me here? I had no choice but to remain in the dark and pray they didn't. I could hear the voices of the secret police now, low down and harsh compared to the voices of the performers. There was only one passageway out of here, and it was too late to take it. "A very important guest is now attending the performance tonight," I could hear one of the soldiers saying. "You must make sure that your work is of an acceptable standard. We are now searching your dressing rooms to ensure the safety of our visitor. Please wait here."

And then a girl's voice, broken a little by smoking or poor sleep: "What guest?"

"You'll see soon enough."

I heard them searching—things being overturned; the shatter of a glass or a flower vase. I squashed myself under the sink in the darkness and waited. Suddenly I was back in my grandfather's apartment in New Maron, listening to the door break down while Antonia lay in my arms, and a wave of homesickness came over me, a wave so profound it robbed me of breath.

They paused outside my door. I heard someone scratching at the handle. And I channelled all the power of my mind as I had in the Strait of Ravina, when I willed the storm to pass over, when I summoned a brief trace of powers.

By the time I had recovered, I could tell by the relieved chatter of the performers in the corridor that the secret police had gone.

I got to my feet and turned on the electric bulb. I put the radio down on top of the sink. Should I turn it on and try to communicate with Jakob? I was the only resistance member in the theatre, and I had no idea what was expected of me. Escape beckoned me, but I knew that if I fled I was signing my own death warrant with Jakob. And besides, something else kept me rooted. The trace of the voice of Anastasia Fortuna, still hanging like an enchantment in the air.

I eased the radio out of the bag and set it on top of a can of bleach. I extended the metal aerial. As carefully as I could, I turned the dial so that it was a fraction above silent. I pressed my ear to the speaker. Static, and a confused gabbling.

I pressed the transmit button. "Calling Base 232," I said, the way I was supposed to. "This is Isak K."

I knew that our radios transmitted on different frequencies every day, that the call signs changed, that the resistance leaders used a thousand different codebooks to give a veil of security. Even so, I was terrified that my transmission would be heard not only by Jakob but also by the secret police. I knew already that I was at the heart of something unexpected.

Or perhaps this had been Jakob's intention all along.

"Calling Base 232," I said again.

"Isak K., come in."

Jakob's voice.

"Yes?" I said. "I'm here."

"Isak, listen. Where are you? Still at your post? I've been trying and trying to make contact."

"People got thrown out. Something is going on."

"There's been a change in plans. Our target is going to be exactly where you are in five minutes. There's a device planted under the stage."

"What?"

"But it might not be enough. We're on our way, but we haven't got enough time. Just before the planned disruption takes place, you must act. Twenty-three minutes. Get in there quickly, do what needs to be done, then get out. We'll get there as soon as we can, but everything is up to you now."

"What are you saying? What does that mean?"

"Use what I gave you to take out the target. Is that clear?"

Use what I gave you. The gun. It couldn't be anything else. "Wait," I said. "No, it's not clear. What do you mean, a device? A bomb, an explosive? And I'm not sure I'm happy—"

"Isak, don't bail on us. Don't you fucking dare. I wouldn't have chosen you for this mission, but it's yours now, so don't you fucking dare make a mistake."

"Jakob?" I said. "Jakob!"

But the radio had faded back into static. I was on my own.

Meanwhile, people were stirring outside the cupboard door. I cut the radio and waited in the darkness, listening. Voices, quite close. Had they been close enough to hear?

But no—they were too preoccupied with the change of arrangements. "The General?" one of the dancers was saying, in a high, breathy voice. "I don't believe that."

"It's true. Instead of speaking in the square, he'll attend the concert and speak here. He wants the speech broadcast on the wireless, because of that resistance message earlier. Go and look for yourself. He's just arrived."

I heard quick footsteps go away along the corridor, then return. The first voice again, quietly: "You're right. My God."

"Come along, fix your hair. They aren't giving us much time. Right after the orchestra, we're on stage. The singer comes after us."

"That little Holy Island singer can't believe her luck, I'll guess. She's going to make her career tonight."

"I don't give a damn about her. If we make a mistake with the General watching, we won't go home tonight."

I heard the rustle of their dresses as they passed. In the auditorium, I heard a surge of applause. Then a brassy tune, like the military music I had heard on the wireless in my grandfather's house. The Imperialists in the theatre roared their national anthem in one voice. Trumpets blared. The sound was so loud, it must have risen out of the theatre and filled the whole of Angel City. In a way, it was beautiful, the sound of it. I could see how they were moved.

A bomb, under the stage. I had never considered that the planned disruption might reduce not just the square and the town hall and the military barracks but also this ancient amphitheatre to rubble.

A finer, spindly kind of music rose from the stage. From the way it tinkled and leapt, I knew it must belong to the dancers. I checked my watch. Thirteen minutes to eight. In ten minutes exactly, I was supposed to be attempting to assassinate General Marlan.

Still I remained where I was, hugging my knees to my chest, and again those waves of homesickness came crashing over me. I wished I had never got involved in any of this. Couldn't I have stayed in Maritz, with Anselm? Or couldn't I have remained forever in Antonia's arms?

The first dance was finishing now, and after the applause died away, another began, this one more agitated. If I didn't act, all those dancers on stage would be caught in the explosion. And if I stayed cowering here in the cupboard, Jakob would finish me off just as unpleasantly as the secret police. I was in bad trouble either way.

I got to my feet, put the gun into my pocket and opened the cupboard door.

There was no one in the corridor now. I moved up it in the shadows, one step at a time.

At every step strange pictures of my life came to me, in no particular order. My grandfather peeling an orange with gnarled hands. My mother in her red dress. Antonia's hair falling over the guitar. My sister bending near me, seven years old, and whispering that I was special. My great-great-uncle writing: *I name my last descendant as your hope in times of trouble, a very certain help in the darkness of the road.*

Aldebaran, I thought. *Did you know that in my nineteenth year, everything that had ever made me would bring me here, to this provincial theatre, to shoot the man who took my country from me when I was three hours old? Is that what you meant by "hope in times of trouble"?*

Was that what the star on Holy Island had meant? Had Aldebaran's map been a set of orders, written before my birth, guiding me here?

Seven minutes left.

I prayed for time to stop, so that I could think.

I reached the end of the corridor. For the second time that day, I climbed the steps and entered the wings. Darkness had fallen entirely now, and big spotlights illuminated the stage, dimming the stars. I saw everything very bright and clear, like time really had stopped. In front of me, a great red curtain ruffled like the doorway to a better world. I crept forward and knelt behind the spotlight, where Antonia had knelt as a child.

From here, I could see the first rows of the audience. A man sat in the centre of a phalanx of guards, his hair draped on his head like a floor mat. The man whose face, made flatteringly heroic, had stared down over our country from banners and flags and posters for nineteen years. In real life, General Marlan was small and disappointing.

I took the gun from my pocket. Could I get a clear shot from here? *Aldebaran*, I prayed. *Guide my hand*. Maybe it was just imagination, but I felt him take hold of me and give me strength.

The dance ended. The applause began. General Marlan stood up. He clapped and smiled up at the dancers, and for a minute I felt a stab of pity for him.

I held the gun steady. I waited. If I didn't act early enough, I'd be blown apart too. Still I lingered. Six minutes.

Someone rustled past me onto the stage. I recognised the back of her and the familiar tang of her perfume: the young woman with the chopped hair who I had seen from the bathroom stall. She wore a red silk dress. Her skin was pale and very smooth. She straightened herself in front of the microphone and breathed in, and the radio equipment very clearly caught a sigh and transmitted it.

General Marlan settled himself.

Five minutes.

The woman began to sing. I knew the song: it was from an old Alcyrian opera, in which the lady sees her dead lover as a ghost returned to earth and weeps. The Imperialists in the front row roared their approval. They blew their noses and cried and shouted over the music.

But I no longer cared about them. My hold on the gun weakened. The voice that had haunted me all evening—the voice of Anastasia Fortuna—was hers. And it was the voice I had once heard through a closed door on an autumn afternoon in New Maron, to the notes of a guitar. I was absolutely certain.

Four minutes.

Something strange was happening. But if this was a dream or a memory or something else less certain, I didn't much care, because it was also real.

"Turn around," I said. "Turn around."

A young man, sweating over the ropes of the scenery, frowned at me.

"Turn around," I said again. "Antonia."

The singer faltered. And that falter made the audience shift and mutter, and it brought me back. The bomb. If I didn't get her away from the stage, the floodlights and the orchestra and the singer and the song would all be gone in a heap of rubble.

Three minutes.

In that moment, I didn't care about my great-great-uncle's legacy anymore. I didn't care about saving our country in a time of trouble. I dropped the gun and got to my feet. With all the force I could muster, I shouted, "Turn around!"

My voice must have reached her, because she turned. A face much older than the one I had known, discoloured by smoking or poor sleep, hardened with thick make-up. But still unmistakably hers. Antonia.

Two minutes.

Three times in my life someone came back from the dead. The first was my grandfather, and the second was Antonia. But when a real miracle hits you, it isn't a gentle, joyful thing. It rips through you like the shockwave from a bomb blast. That was how this was.

Antonia stood braced to the spot, looking at me as though I were some spectre. "Antonia!" I shouted. "Get off the stage!"

One or two people laughed, unsure whether this was part of the performance. Others, though, began panicking. The musicians, in a chaos of ruffled evening clothes, started fleeing their positions at the back of the stage, some still cradling their precious instruments.

"Stay where you are," the secret police in the front row ordered. "All of you, stay where you are." Meanwhile, General

Marlan was ushered from his seat, surrounded by guards. Whatever shot I might have had was gone for good.

"Antonia!" I shouted once more. "Get off the stage!"

One minute.

Step by step, she moved towards me, as though she were dreaming. As she came closer, she got more and more real, more and more herself. I could feel tears on my face. When she was almost in reach, the blast hit us. A shockwave of air threw her against me and drove both of us down the steps. As we fell, I closed my arms around her. I clung and clung to her. My ears resounded with silence. Antonia, without sound, was screaming. Wood and scraps of red velvet and shards of thick glass from the floodlights rained down upon us. I clung to her and buried my face in her shoulder. "Antonia," I said. "Antonia." *God, please let us survive this.*

In the new silence, after the debris had settled, I shook her by the shoulder. Antonia, terrified, raised her head. She was shouting something at me, pushing me away. I tried to shout back at her, but neither of us could hear our own voices over the ringing of the explosion. I caught hold of her arms. "I love you," I said, forcing her to look at me. "I love you."

That, she understood.

I pulled her to her feet and away from the chaos, down the stage corridor. The floodlights had cut out again. In the dark, we ran, our hands firmly locked together. We gained the stage door, and I struggled with the lock. I got it open. We were through.

Out in the dark, lights flared and trucks sped, approaching the theatre. Whether they were resistance or soldiers, I no longer cared. I dragged Antonia with me, clutching her hand like it was the only thing sustaining me. And the strange thing was, Aldebaran was still there. I had disobeyed his orders, but he was still with me. I felt him there, in the space all around me, guiding me through the ruins of Angel City.

With a ringing, my hearing began to return. "Antonia," I said, "are you all right? Are you hurt?"

She shook her head. "I'm not hurt." I could hear her, faintly, like a voice underwater.

"Can you run?"

She had lost her shoes and the red rose from her hair. But she was still here, in this world that felt like the end of the world, still with me.

"I can run," she said.

So we ran.

64

I had no time to take in the miracle of her being here. Instead, we ran and ran, through streets black with smoke and past rolling tanks and through alleys where machine-gun fire rattled. At the edge of town, we crossed rough ground, our skin caught on thorn bushes and whipped with branches. The bottom of Antonia's fine dress was cut to shreds. Her bare feet were bleeding.

Dimly, I became aware of her yelling at me to stop. "The restricted zone!" she was saying. "We can't go on!"

"Why not?"

"They've got barbed wire for miles around this area. There's a building inside belonging to the Imperialists. We can't go this way."

I could hear footsteps, not far behind. Was someone chasing us? I could not be sure. Desperately, I dragged her behind me along the fence instead, towards the sea.

"There was supposed to be a bomb blast here—is there no way through?"

"We can't enter," repeated Antonia.

I threw a glance back and thought I made out a shadow across our path. "Come on," I cried. "Come on."

We came at last upon a way through of sorts, a large steel gate, caved in, surrounded by a shallow crater. "No," said Antonia. "We can't go in."

But behind us, the noise was advancing. We had nothing to do but go on. I pushed Antonia in under the twisted bars and forced myself after her. When I looked back, I could no longer tell whether anyone was following. All was smoke and confusion. Across barbed wire and between tall pine trees and down a hillside towards the sea we ran. Great warehouses stood in the dark in front of us. We ran between them, skittering on pine needles. With both hands I clung to Antonia.

Beyond the warehouses, on the edge of the ocean, was a dark silhouette. The ruins of a building—a confusion of pillars and arches and towers—rose above us as we came sliding down the hill. "What is this place?" I said.

"The house of Diamonn, they call it."

The last star on my grandfather's map. Perhaps it had been here all along.

"Let's go in here." I pushed her through the ruined doorway. "Inside here, we'll be safe. There's a reason this is where we've ended up."

Exhausted, bleeding from our struggle through the barbed wire, still clinging together, we collapsed inside the ruined building. We had left the chaos behind now, and the gunfire and explosions were only a low rumble like thunder.

"You're bleeding," said Antonia.

I looked down at my leg. In the middle of the thigh, a bloom of blood stained my trousers.

"It's nothing," I said, but as I put my hand on it I felt something shift inside the flesh, a piece of shrapnel or a bullet, and it made me shiver. Gradually, the pain was advancing on me. "We'll be all right now. But, Antonia, why are you here? What are you doing here?"

"What are *you* doing?" She was trembling. "They told me you were dead. They kept me locked up and wouldn't let me write to you. They burned all the paper. I managed to send a letter at last, but you never replied. Then they told me you'd died in the labour camp."

"I got your letter," I said, gripping her by the shoulders. "Of course I did. I had four months left of my sentence, but then I came to find you. Your aunt told me you had died, but I never believed it. I've been looking for you ever since. Why did you go away?"

"Because I lost you," Antonia said drily, not touching me. "And, Harlan, I have to tell you something. It's awful, but I've got to do it." Again that shudder. "We had a baby." She said it without any feeling at all. "I was very ill during the birth and they had to put me to sleep with drugs. The baby didn't survive. They told me when I woke up. After that, it was like my life ended. I ran away from the house and managed to get onto a ship for the mainland. I don't know what I was thinking. On the crossing, I cut off all my hair. It was stormy and the ship almost went down, but I didn't care; I didn't have any fear anymore. I walked here on foot, in just the ragged old clothes I had. I think I believed somehow I'd find my mother here. I must have been halfway insane, delirious. I was sick—I lost too much blood. I was running a fever. I lost everything on the journey—my papers, my jewellery, my shoes. I thought I'd die on the journey, but I didn't." Again, that dry shudder. "When I got here, it seemed quite natural to start a different life. It seemed like the only thing to do." She touched the back of my hand, then drew away. "The truth is, Harlan, I don't think I can love you anymore. I'm someone different, and I can't go back in time and make things right. They took it from us, that love we had, and I don't have the strength to make another."

Over the sea, shells rose with a cheery whistle. They burst and lit the ruins where we lay. Ash fell kindly, like snowflakes.

"I can't love you," said Antonia. "That's the way it is now."

"We'll find a place," I said, swiping angrily at the tears that took all the strength from my voice. "We'll find a life that we can live, I promise. They've lied to you, Antonia, and they've made you all hard and angry, but if you knew the truth you'd change your mind."

"It doesn't make any difference, the truth."

"It does. It makes all the difference in the world."

But I didn't dare to tell her the truth about the baby while she was like this, so cold and far away from me. Instead, in my misery, I went inside my own mind and tried to make for us, in these ruins that my great-great-uncle had marked with a star without ever telling me why, a small world away from all the fighting, where Antonia and I could make things right.

Pain cut down through my head. Every vein in my body throbbed. I went on willing it into life, this world, and anger at her father and aunt ran in my blood and gave me, for the second time that night, something like real powers. Around me, reality shivered and altered.

The first thing I noticed was the silence. Shells had still been whining, but now they faded away. The machine guns in the town ceased their growling, and when I listened for explosions I could not hear them anymore. What was stranger, my ears were no longer ringing, even faintly. All I could hear was crisp silence.

I opened my eyes. The trees had become statues; the wind did not trouble them, because there was no wind any longer. The flakes of ash had stopped falling and were suspended in the air. They made a kind of white mist that glowed very softly in the dark between us. I plucked one out of the air right beside me, and it disintegrated into powder on my palm. "Look, Antonia," I said. "A miracle. I've done it. I've stopped time. I've wanted to do this my whole life."

Antonia shuddered. "What's happening?" she said. "What are you doing?"

"I told you. Time's stopped, and now I can tell you properly what I have to say. Now we have time to make everything all right."

I didn't find it frightening to see the world so altered. I only wondered if it might be a dream. The old-century light of the shells, which were frozen halfway to bursting in the sky, gave everything an air of unreality. Antonia opened her eyes wide in wonder, and that wonder made her look like the girl I had once adored. I took her hand, and she let me.

"I've got something important to tell you," I said. "Now, while things have stopped. While we have time."

"All right," she said. "I'll listen."

Her voice was more clearly hers in the silence. Hoarser and rustier, but still hers.

I fought for possession of myself, and found it at last. "There's a truth you have to know. Our baby didn't die."

Antonia recoiled as though I'd spat in her face.

"Look at me, Antonia. It's true. She lived. She's safe and well. I found her in your aunt's house and I took her away to the north. She's there right now, with my brother, at the telegraph post in Maritz. She's ours, and I named her Anastasia, and we'll go back now and get her and find somewhere we all can live."

At first Antonia wouldn't believe it. She just sat and shivered. I stroked her hands and hair and told her everything I knew about our baby. I talked for what felt like hours. When time stops, a minute can contain more, can change more. It becomes infinitely powerful. In those minutes, I had all the time in the world to search for the right words and bring them to the surface.

Finally, with a last shudder, Antonia started to believe me. But Antonia believing was more heartbroken than Antonia protected by doubt. Great sobs racked her, and her face contorted in grief. Her hands beat helplessly on the ground, shook with a kind of violence. I had never seen anyone's heart entirely broken until that moment, and it frightened me. "Antonia, stop. It will be all right. I'll take you to her, as soon as I can. You'll see her and hold her in your arms and it will be all right. You're still her mother. We'll find a life."

Then I became aware of someone else moving in that time-stopped world, beyond the walls of the ruined house.

Fear for Antonia made me fierce. "Get down," I hissed. "Wait here."

I got to my feet. Very carefully, I edged to the doorway. Moving along the wall of the house, I heard the stranger breathe. He came into view at last, a tall shadow. A man with red hair, ancient gold spectacles. Cornered, he looked into my face.

"What are you doing here?" I said.

No answer.

"You've been following me," I said. "What for? Is it to take me away? Who are you? What do you want from me?"

"I'm Rigel," he said at last.

"Was it you? At West Ravina, at Arkavitz, in Capital?"

"Yes."

"Why are you here now? To take me away?"

He shook his head. "To watch over you."

"When are you going to stop following me?" I said, desperate, though I hardly knew why.

"When all this is over," he said. "When I'm released from my obligation to Aldebaran, I can go back to England and find my daughter. Those were Aldebaran's orders. To watch over you. Until the very end."

"Until the very end?" I said. "What does that mean?" I didn't like the way it sounded.

Time jerked into being again without warning, like a paused song starting back up. The ash in the air settled, the noises of war resumed, the flares on the horizon finally burst in a flash of light. And a truck's engine roared and came closer. The engine died. A handbrake creaked; doors slammed. Footsteps. Someone was walking towards us down the hill.

Rigel was gone, if he had ever existed, vanished in the darkness. I put my arms around Antonia. I said, "Shh. It will be all right."

"Who is it?"

"I don't know yet."

Several sets of footsteps, not just one. They came from different directions. Twigs snapped. Someone huffed. I heard a sound like liquid sloshing out of a can. "Who's there?" someone called.

Jakob.

"Harlan North!" shouted Jakob. I sat up. My heart was thumping very fast and painfully. "Harlan North!" came the shout again. The ruins echoed. "Come out of there or we'll burn that old building down and force you to show yourself!"

I had no choice. "Stay out of sight," I said to Antonia, then, very carefully, I crawled into the doorway of the ruined house and got to my feet. It was a struggle, because of my leg, which had begun bleeding again as soon as time righted itself. "I'm here," I said. "What do you want?"

Around me, I made out the faces of our resistance cell. Jakob, Sebastian, Mr. West, Marco. Someone lit a torch, and the flame scudded with black smoke and lit the clearing. Jakob stepped forward. In its light, he looked quite insane. He brandished a pistol in one hand. "You bastard, Harlan North," he said. "What have you done?"

I advanced at a hobble. I knew I had to draw them away from Antonia.

"I don't know what I've done," I said. "Why don't you tell me, Jakob?"

"Don't come any closer!" Someone handed him the torch, and he thrust it towards me. "Stay where you are and raise your hands."

I raised them.

"You're a traitor, Harlan. You had orders. I gave you orders!"

In me, something fought back with surprising strength. "I know you gave me orders. I couldn't do it."

"General Marlan's dead anyway. The revolution will come, no thanks to you."

"Then what difference does it make?"

"It's a question of *disloyalty*," said Jakob, as though the word was the worst curse.

"I am loyal."

"When it suits you, maybe."

"You don't understand, Jakob. I'm trying to find Antonia. I never had anything to do with this cause."

"Do you think the men who are dying for the cause right at this moment are loyal only when it suits them?"

The question hung in the darkness.

"What about you, Jakob? Shouldn't you be down there fighting instead of hunting me? What about *your* orders?"

Jakob spat on the ground. In the wavering dark, I met Sebastian's eyes. Sebastian's good, broad face was wobbling with fear and something else. Tears. What had they done to him? In my pain and confusion and concern for Antonia, I didn't understand that he wasn't crying for himself.

"I'm following my orders," said Jakob. "Those orders are to find you and bring you to justice."

"Bring me to justice? For what? I've done nothing wrong."

Jakob's rage erupted. "You know what you've done, you traitor!"

"Anyone could have missed that shot."

"Do you think I'm stupid? I know how many bullets were in that gun. I know none of them were fired."

"Jakob, be reasonable."

"Fuck that," said Jakob, brandishing his pistol. "Move over here where I can see you."

I limped towards the spot he indicated.

"Faster," he said.

"I can't. I've been shot or something. Look, Jakob, where are you taking me? You can't lock me up and try me for missing a shot. That's not a crime, it's just a mistake."

"We're not going to lock you up. We're not going to try you. We don't have time for any of that."

The pain in my leg was making me shudder. I heard Jakob take the safety catch off the gun, and for the first time I was properly frightened.

"Antonia was there," I stammered, "at the theatre. I saw her on the stage. I meant to shoot General Marlan—I had the shot all ready—but . . ."

"You're lying!" shouted Jakob. "You're a damn traitor and a liar. You're lucky I'm just going to shoot you and have done with it. You deserve worse than that."

Jakob's eyes, unblinking, did not leave mine, and all of a sudden I realised I didn't want to die at his hands in this wood in the middle of nowhere without first saying what I knew to be true. "You're the traitor," I said, very quietly. "You've betrayed everything good about this movement and become the worst kind of tyrant. Look at these men. They're terrified. You don't care about the last descendant or about Aldebaran or any of it— nothing but getting your own share of whatever power's going."

"Jakob, let him live," came a voice, very faintly. "Let him live." Sebastian.

This only drove Jakob into a greater rage. "Silence!" he shouted, making a wide swing with his pistol that sent everyone ducking.

Please, God, let me live, I prayed, all in a rush. *Don't let me die now, when I've just found Antonia. That would be the worst cruelty of all.*

They moved suddenly, and both at once: Sebastian and Antonia. They darted towards me, but someone else appeared, much nearer, looming out of the dark behind the warehouse. I knew his face: the red-haired man, Rigel. Jakob let a shot go with a start, then another. From the fright in his eyes, I don't know if he even meant to fire. The red-haired man had come between us, blocking him from shooting again, and Jakob turned and ran into the trees, the rest of them at his heels.

Either way, he had got me. I could tell because I was on my knees in the dust and I seemed to be struggling to breathe properly, and all of me was pain. I heard the crackling of flames; the footsteps of Jakob and the others disappearing; Antonia sobbing.

And yet he must have got Rigel too. There he was, a real man of flesh and blood, not a dream, sprawled a few feet away from me, moving no longer.

Antonia wept onto my face. My blood was soaking her red dress. I wished there was some way to stop it. I saw their faces, Antonia and Sebastian, still somehow beside me. And that man, Rigel, motionless. Then darkness came and I saw nothing at all.

65

I was in a truck and moving. My mouth was so dry I couldn't lift my tongue; my side ached. Something wet was seeping from it at intervals. Under me was something very soft. Antonia, holding me in her arms as she had once, years ago, when we slept side by side in New Maron.

"Antonia?" I said.

"I'm still here."

"What's happening?" My voice came out awful and croaking, like an old man's. "What's happened to me?"

"Hold on, Isak," said someone from the front seat. "We'll be there in an hour."

"Who—who is it?" I said.

"It's Sebastian," Antonia said. "Shh. Lie still. He's taking us to Capital."

"Why?"

"Because there's a proper hospital there."

"Checkpoint!" shouted Sebastian. "Stay down—stay out of the range of fire."

With a smash of splintering wood, he drove clean through the checkpoint. A few bullets plinked off the sides of our truck. "We're through!" said Sebastian. "How is he doing, Antonia?"

Antonia was weeping. I felt her tears on my face, as I had once felt my sister Jasmine's. My whole life, people had been rescuing me, but this time I wasn't certain I was going to make it. "Hold on," she said. "Drink this water, Harlan."

"What happened to Rigel?"

"Drink this water."

I took a sip and coughed, then took another. The truck swung around a corner and skidded. It came to me from a long way off that Sebastian couldn't drive. Still, he was driving now, and my side had stopped hurting, and everything seemed to be all right.

I woke again on a stretcher. People were running with me, and the thumping drew from me strange groans that sounded like they came from someone else. Above me I could see the lights and towers of the city. "Antonia?" I cried. She put her hand in mine. "Is this the hospital?" I clung with relief to her hand, which for a moment I had not been able to find.

"No space," someone was saying. "Take him to the field hospital instead. The old church in Plaz Capitansk Lucien. Yes, yes, they have proper doctors."

I knew that place, but I could not summon the memory to me. "The old church," I tried to say. "Father Dunstan."

I was carried under a stone arch. A great vaulted ceiling opened over me. Voices hummed in the dim light. Someone, somewhere, was crying.

I reached up towards Antonia, and she put her arms around me and kissed my face. A strange shudder went through me. The roof overhead went very dark. I caught hold of her and my last thought was this: *She loves me after all.*

VIII

❦ PEACE ❧

66

I woke a long time later, in a green and pleasant land.

Sunlight, such as I had never seen in my life: green and thick and solid. The sound of the ocean, which became not the ocean at all, but a canopy of leaves hissing overhead. Soft grass under me, and beneath it the cool of the earth itself. Somewhere close by, shallow water glittered.

These fragments came to me from a long way off. I was lying on one side. Nearby a bird was swaying on the branch of an old tree. My head felt like it was clearing after sleep. I sat up. Nothing seemed to alter, but the picture grew more solid around me. I was on a hillside, above a lake, inside the ruins of what might have been a house or a chapel. "Where is this?" I asked, but Antonia was no longer with me. I was alone.

The bird rose from the tree. It flew out of the forest covering and into the full sun, which appeared washed out from where I lay under the trees. I got to my feet and found that my side and my leg were no longer bleeding and I could stand quite straight and tall, as I had before I was shot.

I began to walk down the hill. I passed between branches, and out onto a stretch of grass. I stood in the light of the sun and considered where I was. It seemed to be a valley, because on the other side of the lake, hills rose along the horizon. The green of them hurt my eyes. By the water, rooting around in the shallows with a stick, was a black-haired child, and then she was gone.

When I turned around, I saw for the first time a square white house. I began to walk towards it. Someone was standing inside one of the windows, but all I could see of this person was a black shadow. Their presence did not frighten me. In this green world, nothing did.

I went up to the door of the house and pushed it open. Inside was a corridor with glass cases full of books. I wanted to look at these very much, because I could still faintly remember that where I came from, in the real world, all the books had been burned. But while I was contemplating their spines, I heard light footsteps on the stairs. A child's, accompanied by a very pure singing.

I waited. It seemed suddenly very important, this child's approach. A beam of light cut down through the window and warmed my hair, the way the gas fire at home had done a lifetime ago.

The child swung around the corner of the stairs. He jumped the last three, bent to tie up his bootlace, then gave me a sudden grin. He was seven or eight years old, this child. His hair was very fair, and his teeth were all gappy and uneven. Through them, he grinned and grinned, as though I were just the visitor he had been expecting.

"Who are you?" I asked.

"I'm Stirling," he said.

Of all the people I had expected to meet here, I had not considered this. "Stirling?" I said. "You mean my father's brother? Stirling North? What are you doing here?"

The little boy squinted up at me. "I live here," he said, with a laugh.

I began to know in my heart what kind of place this green world was.

Stirling went out the door I had just opened, and when I looked again, he and the little girl were running together across the grass, chasing something in the air, a butterfly or a wasp, with loud cries of laughter.

The titles of the books in the glass cases now became apparent. *The Darkness Has a Thousand Voices*, *The Golden Reign*, *The Heart at War*. I took out the copy of *The Darkness Has a Thousand Voices* and recognised it, even down to the watermark on the cover. This was my grandfather's book, the one my father and I had burned in the yard outside our shop.

What kind of a place was this, where burned books became unburned again and my father's long-dead brother got up and ran? The book was the first thing I had touched in this strange place, and it felt solid enough. The cover was slightly dusty to my touch. I looked at my fingertips, glittering faintly in the sunlight, and marvelled.

And then someone else unexpected came down the stairs to meet me—my grandmother, who I had not seen since I was a child on Holy Island. Still Grandmother, but with all the kindness in her face and none of the bitterness. "Harlan," she said, as the kind voices had spoken when I hovered between life and death as a half-born child. "Harlan."

I took my grandmother's hand when she offered it. "What's Stirling doing here?" I asked her.

"Stirling is always here."

"He died," I said. "In the year '73. In the silent fever epidemic. Father told me."

My grandmother shook her head. She said, "Stirling got well. He grew up. He always was a good boy, Stirling. Like Leo."

"He died," I persisted. "During the war."

My grandmother was bewildered. "What war? There never was a war."

"Your husband died not long after it, from his injuries. Julian, my grandfather, who was once a very rich man. You told me stories."

"My husband," said my grandmother, drawing herself up with a hint of the indignant self I remembered, "continued work at the bank until he was seventy, in very good health. You remember, Harlan? The house on Cliff Road, with the chandelier and the formal gardens, where you used to come with your mother to visit?"

I shook my head. "In your lifetime alone there have been two wars. In the first one you lost everything—your house and your chandelier and your formal gardens."

My grandmother gave a quick laugh. "What an absurd idea! But I was always so proud of your imagination, Harlan. You used to read me your stories."

That was strange, because she had never been proud of my imagination, or my stories, not in the real world. She was different in all respects. The downward turn of her mouth had faded. Her hair was quite elegant. And yet there was something gone from her, this altered grandmother, some hard-won fierceness which had made her slap and scold in real life but which I had always, somehow, found reassuring. Where was that fierceness now? "What's happened to the real world?" I asked.

My grandmother stood straight and said, "This is the real world. There never was any other." She patted my shoulder and left by the front door.

I continued into the next room. This one too was full of sunlight. And above the fireplace was a picture I recognised. The man had a thin and stern face and my family's shared grey eyes. "Aldebaran," I said.

As if in answer, someone came in from the opposite door. It was the man from the picture, but softened somehow, and younger. He came towards me and held out his hands. "Harlan, my child," he said.

"Where am I? Is this England?"

"Not exactly."

"I never thought I'd get to meet you," I said. "You wrote me that letter. You sent me to all those ruined places."

"I suppose I did," said Aldebaran, as if he couldn't remember. He took my arm and led me through the door, back into the hallway with the glass cases.

"But what about the assassination? You died just before I was born."

"There never was an assassination," said Aldebaran. "I did die the winter you were born, but peacefully, reading *The Complete*

Works of Diamonn in my chair. Just the way I would have liked to go, all things considered."

From the nearest case he took a leather-bound book, its title stamped in gold capitals, its pages unburned. "Climb the stairs," he said. "It will make sense. And, Harlan . . ."

"Yes?"

"You do have a very rare gift. But you don't have to use it. You have my permission to be perfectly ordinary. You'll see what I mean by that in time."

I wanted to ask him now, but before I could, he had gone out the front door and was on the other side of the glass, in the garden with the others, beyond my reach.

I ascended the stairs. The landing was a lofty corridor of dark wood, and at each window, sunlight made a square upon the floor. I looked out and could see a whole lake below me, and cloud shadows drifting over distant hills. Not England, but the England I had always imagined. I continued to the end of the corridor and pushed open a door.

A man sat at an old writing desk with his back to me. He had paused, evidently stuck for a word, when I came in, so that for a few seconds he did not see me but remained lost in his thoughts, looking out the sun-bleached window. His hair was hardly grey, and his face was almost as young as mine. But I knew him by his handsome moustache, his infinitely kind dark eyes.

"Grandfather?" I said.

My grandfather turned and held out his arms, and I crossed the space between us and grasped his hands with their papery skin, cool and strong as they had been when I first knew him. I held those hands for a long time.

"Harlan," he said.

"Where are we? Is this some kind of paradise? Do I get to stay here with you?"

My grandfather shook his head, as though he didn't understand.

A thought came to me from a long way off. "Did you find your wife again?" I asked. "Amelie? Is she here?"

My grandfather seemed taken aback by this question. "Of course," he said. "I never left her."

"She died when you were exiled. Remember? Twenty or thirty years ago."

My grandfather shook his head. "I don't know what you mean. We were all in the city together, in Malonia City, all my life. We were still living there when you were born. It was just after my last book, *The Heart at War*, came out."

That book had never existed, never been written. "People keep telling me these things, but they aren't true." I was beginning to be frustrated. "We weren't all together. You never wrote that book. You told me once that you couldn't find the words."

"Harlan," he said, very seriously, "I've seen you every day since you were born. I've seen you every day for nineteen years, and before that I saw your father every day of his life, and Stirling. Don't talk as if we've been apart."

And when he said it like that, new memories began to multiply and arrange themselves. He had watched me take my first steps, taught me my first word, bought me an atlas to carry proudly on my first day at school. But none of that had taken place on Holy Island after all. Instead, it had happened in Malonia City. He had taught me his craft, as he had taught my father. The years of exile were just a bad dream.

But now things were vanishing too, memories I had carried with me since I was a child and was loath to part with. Jasmine's memories. Anselm's. Even my own. "What about our shop in the city?" I said. "And the fireside and the whirling snow?" I screwed up my eyes, trying to remember.

"There never was a shop," he said simply, and just like that, there wasn't.

And in that perfect world, where everything had been set to rights, a great sadness came over me. "There was," I insisted. "After you left, after Stirling died, my father opened a second-hand shop and made his own way in the world. I'm proud that he did that. I don't want to forget."

"Your father never needed to open any shop. He grew up and went to the university."

"Then what did he do, if he didn't have a shop?"

"He wrote for a newspaper."

I shook my head. No matter how much my father might have longed to be a real writer, the Leo I loved had always been a shopkeeper. And now Holy Island was fading too, every memory I had of it—the grey sea and New Maron's suffocating streets and the way the wind swept over the cliffs, bringing its familiar taste of grey bad weather. And as the memories left me, they became precious, things I was reluctant to part with.

"What about Holy Island?" I said. "Have I ever even been there?"

"We visited it once when you were a boy. Do you remember, or were you too little?"

Into my head came a sea crossing different from the real one—this one in a furnished cabin one evening in late summer. I supposed we had been rich after all, as my grandmother had dreamed. But I didn't want this memory. I wanted to hold on to my own. Even my powers were going. I supposed that in this perfect world there had been no trouble at my birth, and I hadn't needed them.

My grandfather gripped my arm. He said, "What are you thinking of, Harlan?"

"I'm glad to see you." And I was, but the loss of my own real life continued to trouble me. "There's one thing I don't understand. Who is the little girl?"

Then my grandfather grew quite serious. "You'll have to go

out and talk to her," he said. "Ask her yourself. She really isn't supposed to be here, and I don't know why you're seeing her. Something's out of joint."

I turned and hurried down the stairs. In my haste I collided with one of the glass cases, and it let out a soft ringing that followed me across the grass. Everything here was real and not real, dream and not dream. I ran out into the sun. The little girl was standing up to her knees in the shallows. I approached her. The water, pure as ice, soaked the bottoms of my trousers, chilled my bones.

"Anastasia?" I said.

The little girl nodded. "Papa?"

I began to weep. "What are you doing here?" I said. "Didn't I take good care of you? Didn't I watch over you? After the war ended, wasn't I a good father? You're six or seven years old. My God—what mistake did I make that you ended up dying so young?"

Anastasia put her finger on my lips. "I'm not supposed to be here. I don't know why I am. You're supposed to have forgotten everything bad that has ever happened to you, Papa. I shouldn't be here."

"But you aren't something bad that happened to me," I said. "You're the truest thing that ever happened."

"After a few minutes, you'll forget me. The way things are here—set right the way you've always wanted—you don't know me. You never met my mama. Neither of you were ever on Holy Island. She lived all her life in Alcyria and you in Malonia. You never met. As for me, I never had any life to live at all."

"Then where will you go?"

She shrugged. "Where I was before, to wait for birth."

"And will you be my daughter, when you *are* born?"

"No. I'll belong to somebody else."

"Then this has to be changed," I said. "It's not all right; in fact, everything's wrong. Don't go away."

She laughed. "You'll be all right. You have all your family here to live with you."

"Anastasia, I love you more than any of them. I'd rather not see any of them, and be able to see you again, just once. Even Grandfather."

And when I spoke that betrayal, I knew what was wrong with this whole green and sunlit place. I understood, for the first and last time in my life, the trap of time: that it can go only forward, that there exists no power to put it right, because such a reversal would erase everything—all hardship but also all joy—until there was nothing left at all. Nothing comes right the way I had once dreamed. Time goes on relentlessly, in one direction only—a fact to which, sooner or later, I knew that I would have to be reconciled.

And this is the cruelty of time, that at the same moment and all together:

> *a war criminal can sign the form condemning a rich man to destitution;*
>
> *and that rich man's daughter, weeping, can give birth to an unwanted baby;*
>
> *and that baby, crying, can draw the attention of a poor boy in a shabby city apartment;*
>
> *and a gunshot can ring out in the castle walls;*
>
> *and a great man, shot, can provoke the first bullets of a second war;*
>
> *and because of that war, my grandmother's apartment can burn to the ground;*
>
> *and because of that fire, we can cross the sea in the hold of a ship like cattle;*
>
> *and because of that sea crossing, my grandfather can find us;*
>
> *and because he found us, my grandfather can die in obscurity, far from home;*

*and into that obscurity, a great singer's daughter can
arrive, with all her belongings in a suitcase, abandoned;*

*and her father, no kind of father at all, can beat her
and humiliate her;*

*and because of all those things, Antonia and I can find
each other;*

*and because of that meeting, the small spark that will
become Anastasia gets its one desperate chance at life.*

You can't ungrow a baby, or unshoot a bullet, or unfight a war.
How could I have ever thought you could?

And this is also the redemption, if you choose to see it that
way: that out of my mother's disgrace, my father's struggle, the
deaths of half their family, Antonia's loneliness, and everything
that all of us lost when a short man with false hair called General
Marlan dreamed up his great empire—out of all that, my daughter Anastasia rose up and took wing.

To Anastasia, I realised, the world was as green and unre-
membering as this green place was supposed to be. Her life was
just her life, unselfconscious as a bird's, and none of that sadness
was any concern of hers.

The truth came to me with perfect clarity. I didn't want this
green world. I doubted that it even really existed. My lost family
had passed on. But now that Anastasia was living, I had to make
for her a life free from the burden of history that weighed upon
our shoulders. I had to make for her a green world like this one,
but in the real world, not here, because that broken real world
was the only place where she existed at all.

I had to protect her.

Standing in the water, I gripped Anastasia's hands. "We've
got to get away from here," I whispered. "We've got to go back."

All at once, we were running. The green light streamed over
us like falling water. The voices called my name.

In the doorway of a ruined chapel, I saw Antonia, faint like a ghost, and ran faster. "Take me away from here," I said. "Bring me back."

But between us stepped Aldebaran. "Harlan," he said very seriously. "Take my hand."

I could not see my daughter or Antonia any longer. "Let me go to them," I said, weeping. "Let me go back."

"Not yet."

Aldebaran gripped my hand, and the green world began to shatter. It split into shards of glass as if someone had thrown a grenade at its surface. Between the cracks, darkness appeared. Aldebaran led me forward. Ahead of me, a dark expanse of concrete appeared.

The England of my dreams vanished forever, and real England appeared before my eyes.

67

*I*n the distance, an orange glow of smog, lights brighter even than the lights of Capital. Trucks and motorcars swept past, so fast their headlights made streaks against my eyes. Apartment buildings appeared, a line of warehouses, a fence luminous with graffiti.

"Where are we going?" I asked Aldebaran.

"Nineteen and a half years ago, I wrote a prophecy about you. That prophecy said that you would save our country in a time of trouble. You haven't done that yet."

"I had the chance, but I didn't want to take it. I hope you understand. I couldn't shoot General Marlan."

Aldebaran was shaking his head. "Not that, not that. This is your chance, now. Here."

"What is this place?"

"This is somewhere I want you to remember. You'll have to find it again on your own." Aldebaran led me across the weedy and overgrown stretch of concrete, towards the apartment buildings. "In the time when I was not quite living and not quite dead," said Aldebaran, as if this was a quite ordinary thing to say, "the winter before you were born, I appointed a man named Rigel to watch over you. He has been, I think, all your life."

"I know the man you mean. I met him. Is that true, that was what he was doing? Watching over me?"

"He saved you from being kidnapped, didn't he? He tried to bring you here to England. He was persuaded otherwise. So he followed you instead. He was there in the streets of Valacia when gangs of kidnappers were roaming about the school registration office, looking for a mysterious child. He was there when you crossed to Arkavitz with the baby, to keep watch on the road in case of ambush. He was there when you arrived in the city, following you, making sure you reached your friend's house safely before curfew. He was in Angel City, at the start of the revolution, keeping guard. He even took a bullet for you, in the end. You have a good deal to thank Rigel for."

"Where is he now?"

"He died," said Aldebaran. "He's gone."

My head reeled. "Because of me? Because of trying to save me?"

"That was his choice. Don't grieve over it."

I felt the worst I had ever felt in my life, like a dried-up river inside.

"There is one great problem," said Aldebaran. "Rigel did something that I didn't order him to do. He brought the king to safety here after the revolution. He also brought his own daughter, and the king's son, from your country to this one. He would have brought you too, if you had let him. They have been living here ever since, waiting for Rigel to bring word that it's safe to return. But now there's no Rigel to remind them. The king has forgotten the country he came from. He lives here, quite ordinarily, as though he has been here all his life."

"So what can I do about it?"

"Bring him back," said Aldebaran. "In England, there are no miracles. He needs one. I think you can provide it. You need to cross the border between the worlds and find this place, as soon as you recover from your wounds again, as soon as you can. Tell him to return to the country he's forgotten. Tell him he's needed there. You should have died as a baby, but I asked Rigel to watch over you, and you lived. Now here you are, and you have a chance to work a miracle. That's what the stars on the map are for."

"Where is the king? Is he in a palace?"

"He's in this apartment building," said Aldebaran. "Fix it in your mind. We don't have long, and you'll have to find it again without me. I'm not really supposed to be here."

The building was twenty storeys high. All the way up it, along concrete walkways, bright electric lights blazed. At one end was a tall turret that must be a stairwell or a lift shaft. One light burned behind tousled curtains. Damp seeped over the outside of the apartments. Rust leaked from somewhere inside it and ran down the grey walls in streaks. It looked like the future but at the same time very old, as the Imperialist apartment buildings in Capital would look, I supposed, in fifty years' time when their empire was gone. On its side was a sign: *Paradise Court.*

"Why would the king live here?" I asked.

"That's for you to find out," said Aldebaran.

As I looked, the vision shifted. It blurred and rippled, like that great curtain on the theatre stage in Angel City. I knew I was losing it altogether.

"Are you going to let me go back home?" I said.

"Promise me that you will do this thing I've asked. That you won't give up until you've done it."

"I promise," I said.

Aldebaran's face twisted out of shape. I felt dragged

backwards, and both dream England and real England vanished in a blur of light.

68

*T*he light over me came down in solid rays glittering with dust. That light was too bright, and my tongue tasted like raw sewage, and people were talking too loudly around me. I said, "Antonia. Antonia. Antonia."

The voices stopped at once. Her hand was still in mine, and there she was beside me. "Lie still, Harlan," she said. "You'll hurt your ribs."

"Where have I been?"

"You're in hospital. Lie still."

"I've been somewhere else."

"You've been here all along. I've been beside you, holding your hand. Lie still, please."

I tried to move, but every part of me shattered into separate needles of pain. My side was all stitched up with rough thread. My leg was padded with wads of bandage. I coughed, and Antonia was there at once with a cup of water.

"Am I going to live?" I said. "Am I really here?"

"Yes," said Antonia. "Yes, both of those."

"Then there's something I have to do," I said, struggling under her restraining hands.

"Harlan," said Antonia, very seriously. "You're going to be here a very long time. Don't try to get up. Don't move."

"But I'm not going to die? And you'll stay with me?"

"I'll stay with you," said Antonia. "Of course I will."

Three times in my life someone came back from the dead. The first to come back was my grandfather. The second was Antonia. And the third was me.

A long time later, I woke again. I made out something strange on the ceiling above me: stone angels among the cobwebs. "What kind of hospital is this?" I said.

"It's an old church. The one in Plaz Capitansk Lucien. New Square, they call it again now. The old priest gave it for the injured when the resistance fighting started."

"Father Dunstan," I wheezed. "Where is he?"

"No one knows," said Anastasia. "They think he died in the fighting. But either way, he gave the church, so they put the hospital in here."

I started to cry—for Father Dunstan and Rigel, who had saved me and lost themselves. Then I had to stop, because even crying hurt too much. "Where is my family?" I said. "Where's Anastasia?"

"I don't know. We'll just have to wait. You aren't well enough to go anywhere, and telegraph communications are down. But the war is over. The resistance has put a temporary government in place. There isn't going to be any Imperialist army left at all, the way things look. No one realised there were so many who would fight, after the announcement on the wireless."

Memories were coming back to me. A word formed in my dry mouth, and I tried to bring it forth: "Sebastian."

"He isn't here. He had to go. He said he'd try to come back again soon."

"He saved me. Drove me to Capital."

"Yes," said Antonia.

"You'll stay with me?"

She nodded.

My head ached, and I couldn't form any of the other questions that troubled me at that moment. So I said, "Hold onto me," and she did, and after a while I slept.

I woke again and Sebastian was there. He was sitting nervously on the chair beside my bed. One of his arms was in a sling. "Are you hurt?" I asked. "Your arm."

Sebastian shrugged off this question. "Oh, Isak, don't worry about me. What about you?"

I took in air. It entered my lungs more easily this time. "I'm all right," I said. "I'll recover." I said so, and understood it to be true.

"I've got to tell you something," said Sebastian, and I was startled to see his eyes misted with tears. "I've got to tell you about something important. We couldn't tell you, not at first, when you were so sick. Jakob's dead."

I struggled and failed to sit up. "Jakob's dead? How?"

"On the second day of fighting in Angel City. He got shot." Sebastian rubbed at his face with his sleeve. "They've made him into a real hero. They're going to make a statue of him and everything."

I didn't know what to say. Antonia took my hand and tried to pour water into my mouth, but I could not accept it. "Shot? In Angel City?"

"I wish it wasn't this way," said Sebastian. "I really do. But at least you and I won't get into the same trouble that we would have done otherwise. People are going on trial—people who were collaborators or disobeyed their leaders in the resistance. It could have been us. Jakob had it in for us, by the end."

"Who else is left?"

"No one who could testify against you. Just me."

I could not weep for Jakob. But inside, my heart felt constricted, compressed somehow. "We were friends," I said. "The three of us."

Sebastian said, swiping the tears from his good, round face, "We still are."

He turned to the window, and when he turned back again, a long time later, his tears were gone and a kind of resolve had come over him. "I've applied for the university, you know," he said, "to study mathematics."

"Will you go? There doesn't seem much point now in going back to normal things."

He straightened. "Of course there is. Of course I will."

"What's the world like out there?" I said.

He shook his head. "Different. I'll say that much. No one seems to know how to organise things. Some people think we need to search for the king's nearest relative and reinstate the old government. Others think we need to vote for a leader fairly. There's a lot of arguing, mostly. You're well out of it, Isak."

"What about the last descendant?" I said. "Do people still talk about that?"

Sebastian looked at me strangely. "Of course. Everyone's talking about it."

Antonia said, "The doctors here have advised us to keep a low profile. Mixed couples are getting some trouble under the new regime as it is. It might all die away, of course—that's what we hope. But as soon as Harlan's well enough, we'll go to the north."

I struggled to make sense of this. I had always assumed that the resistance leaders, once they got our country back, would know what to do with it. Hadn't Anselm promised me so? That the new world would be a world that Antonia and I could live in.

"You mean to stay together?" said Sebastian.

"We'll go north," said Antonia. "We'll be all right. Until they find the king, no one knows what the rules are anymore."

"I promised Aldebaran something." All at once, it came back to me. "I know where the former king is. Maybe if I can find him, that would help. I need to go now, quickly. Do you understand?"

But the way they looked at me, it was clear they didn't.

"You're a bit tired and confused," Sebastian said, patting my arm clumsily. "You probably need to rest."

Dimly, I realised that I would not see him again for a very long time. But when I said this, Sebastian waved it away. "Of course we'll see each other," he said. "I'll also be working with a research group at the university in the north sector, I hope, a group who work on prime numbers, and it's barely fifty miles to come and visit you in Maritz from there."

He stood, with a straightness he had never possessed before, his mathematics books under his arm.

Then a great wish to sleep came over me again, so I lay down and closed my eyes. When I woke up again, it was dark and the room was moonlit; Sebastian was gone, but Antonia was still there. "Aren't you sleeping?" I said.

"I can't sleep. Not properly. Not until I see my daughter."

In the two months I was in that hospital, she didn't once leave my side.

69

We left Capital on a blustery day in late September. The wind drove wet leaves against the windows of the train as we made our slow progress north. I could sit up now and walk, slowly, leaning on two sticks. As the train rattled north, we passed the remains of former prison camps, their coils of barbed wire rusting on the ground. We passed the reservoir that held the contents of the river. On the edge of the horizon, the mountains rose, with their first covering of snow.

Antonia sat beside me and held my hand. She did not speak, just stared straight ahead at those mountains where our daughter was.

Two months had passed since I had promised Aldebaran I would find that apartment building again and find the king. I had tried to tell Antonia about my encounter with him, but every time I did she frowned and shook her head, as though I was sick in mind as well as body, a person requiring special treatment. "If you had travelled to another world, you wouldn't have been lying beside me unconscious. I was there the whole time. I never let go your hand. It was just a dream, Harlan."

The truth was, dream or not, I had promised him. It occupied half my thoughts. But I didn't want to leave Antonia. Not before she had seen Anastasia. Probably not ever.

Sometime while I had hovered between life and death, I had begun to know for certain that she had started to love me again.

Now she folded and unfolded her hands on her lap, staring north towards where Anastasia was waiting.

"Will I love her?" she said once, her voice brittle and small.

"Of course you will," I said. "I did."

"How does it happen?"

I couldn't explain. "It won't happen all at once. I think the first time I loved her was when I realised there was no one to protect her but me."

Another interminable truck ride. Again, the bare forest of Maritz, already wearing its first dusting of snow. We made slow progress up the road towards the telegraph post. I struggled between my sticks, wheezing, Antonia supporting me at the elbow. If it pained her to go at such a pace, she did not show it. She just walked beside me, her hand on my arm.

As we reached the ridge of the hill, we heard a child's cry. Antonia shuddered at my side. "Is that her? Is that Anastasia?"

"It must be." My daughter now would be nearly a year old. I strained my arms, trying to get up the hill more quickly. As we climbed, someone came out onto the step of the house and shielded his eyes against the sun that was just breaking between the rolls of cloud and the mountains.

"Hello?" he called into the still air.

"Anselm?" I said.

Then he was running, closing the gap between us with a

swiftness I would never again possess myself, though I tried, hobbling on my damaged leg across the yard.

Anselm threw his arms around me. He said, "Harlan! Oh, Harlan!"

"I'm all right," I said. "Look. I'm all right."

"We've been looking for you. We didn't know what to think. Mama and Papa are here too. They got here last week. And Jasmine. We've been sending letters, enquiries—going back and forth to the missing persons office. Oh, Harlan!"

"What about Anastasia? Is she safe? Have you taken good care of her?"

"Yes, she's fine. She's here."

They appeared at the door, my family. Joy and shock came over me in equal measure, made me sway where I stood. "Anastasia?" I called. My mother and father stood aside. From behind the rest of my family, on her own two feet, my daughter came toddling, so different she was like her own big sister, not the Anastasia I remembered. Her hair was no longer a wispy tuft, but a great tangle of black. Her skin had grown golden, no longer translucent. When she opened her mouth, I saw that she had teeth now, a real smile. But her eyes, just about, were the same. We approached each other cautiously, I on my sticks and she on her unsteady legs.

"Papa?" she said.

"She can talk? She called me Papa?"

"Just a few words," said Anselm. "She just started a week or two ago."

"Papa!" my baby cried.

But it was not me she was talking to; it was Anselm. He swung her up into his arms and held her close to me. "*Here's* your papa," he said, very firmly. "Your real papa is back now. Look, Ana. Here's your real papa."

"Anastasia? It's me. Do you remember?"

She was uncertain. She hadn't seen me in six months, after all. She looked at me sideways out of her grey eyes. I reached out and touched her tiny hands, her cheeks, her soft black hair. Then I turned to Antonia. "Hold her," I said. "She's yours."

Antonia shook her head. "I don't love her at all. It's as if she isn't mine. And she won't love me either. It's all ruined now, because I wasn't with her when she was first born."

Something in me much older than my nineteen years reached out and spoke for me. "You have to take her," I said. "She's yours, and if you don't make things right for her—if *we* don't—then they'll never be right. We have to take responsibility for her life now. Do you understand?"

Antonia could not hold in her tears any longer. They spilled, and she reached out her arms for the baby.

"Anastasia," I whispered. "Look at your mama. Look at her properly."

The baby blinked her thick eyelashes, luxuriantly, and reminded me of Antonia waking from sleep beside me in that other life where this story began. She didn't say *Mama* or hug Antonia back, but she looked at her with interest, with half a smile, and I knew this was going to be all right, this family of ours.

In the days that followed, life seemed to be suspended, almost as though time had stopped properly, for good and always. We were all somehow together; we had survived it. Now we listened to the wireless radio, trying to make sense of the new world.

In the city, every day, there were trials and hangings and shootings, as the resistance tried to settle every score left over from the occupation.

I couldn't blame them, not really. I still harboured a strong wish to go to Holy Island and burn down the house where Antonia's father and aunt lived, to get some kind of revenge for the lies they had told us both. But when I said that, Antonia gave a sad smile. "A man like my father won't survive this purge that's taking place. At best, he'll end up in hiding, shifting from town to town, just like your family had to. I can't say I feel much sorrow for either one of them. I would have loved them, but they never let me. Now we'll never see them again. We're free. He's got no allies in the secret police to track me down, no friends in high places to separate us. He can't hurt us any longer."

When she said it, I saw that it was true.

My brother and Michael and Jasmine were not involved in the same grim business the city resistance seemed to be conducting. Instead, the resistance in the north had set up missing persons stations, and they spent each day sending telegraph messages and distributing food parcels and ferrying refugees across the border towards Capital. These refugees travelled in the backs of trucks with their bundled belongings and thin, bleak faces. "For some people," Anselm said one night, coming back after a particularly exhausting day at the camp, "this war will never be over."

Those words robbed me of sleep—those words, and my recurring dream of the apartment building in an English city, which I could explain to no one.

There was a nationwide search for the king, but no news. It seemed the resistance would not set up a proper government until he was found, one way or another. Parties had been dispatched to Holy Island to try and trace him there, but I knew they wouldn't find him anywhere they were searching. As I grew stronger, I knew I would have to honour my promise to Aldebaran. But for the first part of that autumn, I couldn't. When I lay on the mattress in the upstairs room of my brother's house, Antonia beside me and little Anastasia between us with her thumb in her mouth, I knew I couldn't bear to leave them to journey into that other place. We were only just starting to become a family. *Aldebaran*, I prayed. *Couldn't you have given me some other task?*

He didn't answer, but I knew.

$\mathcal{M}$y daughter understood what I was planning. There was something uncanny about Anastasia, just as there had been about me when I was a child. I could tell that she knew I was intending to desert her just as soon as I had found her. Whenever I left her side, she began to wail. Her fits of rage and grief became so intense that I couldn't leave the room without her. She would shriek and beat her small fists on the floor, and the only way to stop her from doing it was to take her in my arms and hold her until the shrieking stopped.

Every day I grew stronger here, surrounded by my family. It pained my heart to think of leaving, but I had promised Aldebaran that I would find that apartment building. I was dreaming about the place. Its electric beacons and stained concrete haunted me each night when I closed my eyes.

I had tried to talk to Antonia about it. But she still believed that place was a dream. Sometimes when I mentioned it, tears ran down her face. "Why do you talk as if you're going to leave us, Harlan?" she said. "It's not real. You have no proof that any of it was."

Then, in October, a great parcel arrived for me. I had been out for a walk along the mountain road with my daughter—the two of us were growing steadier on our feet together. When we got back, there it was, a dirty brown parcel waiting in the middle of the living room, where my family eyed it warily. "Open it, Harlan," my mother said.

The handwriting I did not recognise. I ripped the edge of the paper gingerly. Some kind of wooden box with a letter taped to the top of it. I pulled out the contents. *To be returned to Harlan North on my behalf*, it read. *To be used for his mission. Rigel.*

Seeing his name like that made the back of my neck turn cold. No person who existed only in a dream ever sent letters. Rigel was real. The task was real.

Antonia picked up our daughter. Holding Anastasia to her chest, she watched me prise open the wooden box.

Inside were stacks of paper: banknotes. I pulled one out. I didn't recognise the pink and decorated currency, but I recognised the name of the country, and it made me shudder. There it was, in printed letters: *Bank of England.*

"What's this?" Antonia said. "It's not real money."

"It's foreign money."

"I don't recognise it."

My family didn't seem to want to come any closer. They eyed the money from a distance, as though it were the spoils of war.

"What have you got yourself involved in?" my mother asked. "What does this mean? Who's sent it?"

"I can't tell you," I said. "Not properly. It's just something I promised to do."

Anastasia began to wail. She pounded with her fists against Antonia's shoulders and yelled in outraged grief.

I stuffed the money back in the box and shut the lid, but it was too late. The box was open now.

It remained in the living room. Whenever Anastasia saw it, she cried and turned her face away. Eventually Anselm put a cloth over it, but that didn't fool my daughter. Meanwhile, if I went even six or eight feet away from her, she fretted and reached for my hand.

It was becoming clear to me that if I was going to do this, I would have to take Anastasia with me.

One night in late October, I got up and went downstairs with my daughter in my arms. A rainy wind was troubling the glass in the windows and making the telegraph wires whistle. Michael was up, tapping out some message. Everyone else was asleep; I could tell by the silence.

I drank a glass of water and held one for Anastasia while she slurped noisily, gripping the glass with both hands. "Bird," she said.

It was the old crow, Mick, scratching at the door. I put down a plate of crumbs for him. The night was damp and windswept, without stars. I looked down into the valley at the lights of Arkavitz, stroking Anastasia's hair. All this time I was pretending to myself that I was just standing here because I could not sleep, that in five minutes we would return to the bedroom and lie down beside Antonia.

Instead, I was going to leave them. I had carried my clothes down the stairs, and now I pulled them on hurriedly and put my feet into my boots. I wrapped Anastasia in a blanket. "Shh," I whispered. "Don't make a sound. We'll be back soon. Maybe before they even wake."

I knew that was not true. How long would it take to find a single apartment building in the middle of a country the size of our own? Days, probably—even if I had extraordinary luck. More likely months. And how long, after all, had Rigel been following me?

I dragged Rigel's box from behind the sofa. In the dark, it assumed nightmare proportions, like it had come alive. I took off its cover and lifted the lid. Hastily, any way I could, I began stuffing the banknotes into my old backpack. My hands were sweating so badly that I dropped a handful with a thump, but no one stirred.

Anastasia held onto the sleeve of my jacket while I packed the banknotes away, but she didn't cry. She seemed to realise that she was coming with me, and kept quiet instead and watched with her clear grey eyes.

I packed all the things Anastasia needed: nappies, and water in a bottle, and soft fruit she could eat by herself if you broke it up in pieces, and a spare little dress and shawl and tights that had been drying in front of the fire. All this time, I was telling myself that we would be back in a few hours. That this was all just in case.

I packed my papers from Aldebaran, because I had never gone anywhere without them in the past year, and I didn't mean to now. As an afterthought, I took one of the torches Anselm and Michael kept hanging on the back of the door for night missions.

Outside, it was stormy. Leaves flew from the trees and landed against the walls of the house. I reached for the walking stick I still needed, lifted my daughter onto my hip as best I could, and together we left the house and closed the door.

At the time, I thought I had got away with it. I didn't hear Antonia's quick sigh, or the way she turned over, suddenly awake. I didn't look back even once—I couldn't have done, without losing all my resolve—or I would have seen the window of our small room illuminated as she switched on the light and called my name.

The only place near here that was marked on Aldebaran's map was old Peter Dewitt's house. It was burned, but it would have to do. *Aldebaran*, I said, in my mind. *Are you there? Help me somehow. I'm doing what you asked; give me your help.*

If he was there, I couldn't tell. I tightened my grip on the walking stick and Anastasia, and began my descent. We hailed the first passing truck, and it carried us down.

71

*T*he burned house held memories. Anastasia knew, because she clung to me and hid her face and shivered. "Shh," I said. "It's all right."

Under the wet ash that covered the ground, glass clinked and china crumbled. Great leggy weeds were growing up through the floor tiles. In one room, the enormous bedstead remained. "No," said Anastasia. "No, Papa."

"I know. You don't like it here. It's all right. We're just here for a short time, to find a way through to another place. Then we'll be gone."

But though I searched the rooms, I didn't know how to make the real world disappear. I had never known. The only time I had ever reached England had been inside the ruined church, when I had hovered between life and death. But the Imperialists had burned this place properly. Nothing remained but the faintest of traces. No doorway into another world. The very idea was ridiculous.

What had it been before it was Peter Dewitt's house? An old monastery, Anselm had said. Maybe that place, if any of it remained at all, was where the true memories lay. Maybe that was what I had to concentrate on.

I left the house by the skeleton of the back door and began searching the wet grass for rubble. In one corner of the yard was an old chicken pen, now overgrown and sagging with damp. In another, I found the fixings for a washing line screwed into an old stone wall. I walked about with Anastasia in the windblown dark, searching for some sign. She soon grew tired of this and wriggled to be put down. "Don't go far," I whispered as I set her on the ground. She jigged up and down, then was off at a toddling run, stumbling in the long grass. Keeping half an eye on her, I examined the remains of the stone wall. It was no good, though. This wall was new. It held no magic at all.

"Anastasia!" I called. "Don't go too far, angel."

"Pa!" Anastasia cried. "Pa! Pa! Pa!"

She had turned the corner of the wall, and I could no longer see her. I ran. When I found her, she was jumping up and down on the spot, her face filled with wonder. "What is it, Anastasia?"

And then I understood what had caught her attention. The ground where she was jumping was echoing, because it was hollow.

I knelt beside her and rooted around in the cold, wet earth. Under my fingers was something grainy, like rotten wood. "Anastasia," I said. "Get off there. It might not hold."

She pressed up against my side obediently. I took her hand and began searching about for something to dig with. I found an old slate which must have fallen from the roof and began scraping away the weeds and soil. It was tough work, especially with my side still not quite healed, and I had to keep stopping to rest and gasp in air. "Pa?" Anastasia kept saying. "Pa?"

"It's all right," I told her, as I worked. "I'm trying to find the remains of the old place that once stood here. Maybe there's part of it underground here. I don't know. Aldebaran put a star on all these places for a reason; perhaps there was something underground that the Imperialists didn't know about."

At last the area was clear. In the square I had scraped away was, quite clearly, a trapdoor. I tried to pull it up, but the rusted handle came away in my grip. Instead, I tried stamping on it. Maybe the wood was rotten.

With a splintering, the trapdoor gave way. I was plunged down into darkness and landed hard on my side and elbow. "Pa!" Anastasia screamed from above.

"It's all right," I said, coughing. The fall had half knocked the wind out of me. "Anastasia, be careful. Stay there." I groped around for my walking stick, found it and heaved myself upright.

Anastasia reached out her arms, wailing. I lifted her down and stroked her hair to comfort her. "Let's have a look where we are, Ana." I got out the torch and lit it.

The light brought a whole underground world to life. Under that old burned shack were the remains of another place, much older. The torch brought forth great pillars, worn carvings that must have been statues, a black doorway. "This must have been some kind of underground room," I said. "Maybe they had a chapel here, or a place to hide in times of war. I don't know." I touched the nearest wall. People had carved names and dates on it with knives.

Anastasia's eyes grew so wide, I thought they were going to swallow up all the torchlight. "It's all right," I said. "I've got you." It was strange, but now that I had found this place I didn't feel any fear. I knew that this was what Aldebaran had meant me to find when he marked the map with a star, not the ramshackle building the Imperialists had burned.

Anastasia had to walk beside me; I could not hold both her and the walking stick and still carry the torch. "Let's go this way," I said. "Through this tunnel. Come on. Hold me by the sleeve. Follow me." Together, we ventured into the dark. In the ancient tunnel, water dripped at intervals around us. The torch-light illuminated damp walls, glossy with lichen. Then the tunnel plunged deeper, and the walls became dry and papery, and the silence around us grew so thick that I knew we must be right under the mountain. *How far does this go?* I wondered. It seemed endless.

Quite suddenly, we came to a threshold. Though the tunnel continued beyond it, a stone doorway clearly marked one side from the other. And on the doorway were carved words. I held the torch closer to read them. *The lord Altair passed this way. Here passed the great Nashira. The lady Sarin.*

I knew what those names meant. Those were the people who had been called great ones, those who had once possessed powers. And then, close to the roof and carved in that sloping handwriting, I saw his name: *Aldebaran.*

"He came this way," I told my daughter, clutching her hand. "Anastasia, we're on the right path! He came this way too!"

Anastasia said nothing. She reached out to touch the stone and looked around the tunnel with her wide eyes, taking everything in.

Without thinking much about it, we crossed the threshold.

A cold wind blew. Up ahead, I could see light. I went as fast as I could, hobbling with the stick and keeping close to Anastasia. Another few steps, and brambles trailed and caught us. Fits of drizzle flew in our faces and made Anastasia start, hesitantly, to cry. "Come on," I said, stroking her hair. "Almost there."

A black stone arch, like the entrance to a mine. We came out into the air. A bay spread out before us. Lights shone around its edge, casting streaks of gold across the water. Motorcars growled. A siren blared. Away across the ocean, a sign flashed pink with the words *Bingo Bingo Bingo*.

I didn't know what that meant, but one thing was clear: we were standing on the shore of another world.

I extinguished the torch and lifted Anastasia to her feet.

A large iron structure stretched out across the water on rusted stilts. Under this structure, I could make out a few people, hooded against the drizzle, cradling cans. Along the seafront, girls tottered in heeled shoes, bare legs shivering. I took a few steps out into the world and saw that, very faintly above us, the moon was shining between the rainclouds, and it was the same moon as ours.

"Where this?" said Anastasia.

I didn't know, but I prayed it was England.

72

*I*n the far north-east of England, in a vast and windswept valley surrounded by ridges of moorland, lies a city. To this city I came, with all my belongings in a leather backpack, no proper overcoat, carrying my baby daughter. We must have made a strange sight. Except that everyone on the late-night bus into town was like us, shabby in one way or another. I didn't know if we had found ourselves on the shores of the right city, or somewhere a thousand miles away. I didn't know how far Rigel's money would stretch. I knew nothing about this country.

The city was a place of mist and factory smoke. In the early mornings, pink light edged its smog clouds and made it half inferno, half paradise. That was how it looked when we arrived, stale with exhaustion at the end of a long bus journey. You were only a year old, my Ana, but you sat up and took notice. You knew this was a world that neither of us had seen before. The bus, with a low moan, ascended the hill, and there the city lay, spread out before us with its iron bridges and apartment buildings. And I said to you, very quietly in your ear, "We are here to work a miracle."

You sat up so calm and serious, like you understood.

I held you as the bus descended into the smoke. We passed through patches of orange light from great overhead streetlamps, in and out of the roar of traffic. Neon shop signs made you blink. I held you carefully and felt that the two of us were very alone. Softly, it rained. I still remember it so clearly, that first night in England.

We were dazed when we came out of the bus. It was not yet real morning, so I walked up and down the main street with you until the city came awake. I bought you chips from a late-night van whose lights still blazed on a street corner, and you mashed a few in your mouth and laughed at the hot, fatty taste. All your life, food had been rationed. I drank tea in a polystyrene cup, and then at last I felt properly awake. There was still part of the night left, so we sat on a bench and watched pigeons fight around a grey monument. When it got lighter, we were joined by an old lady. She came waddling up with a trolley on wheels, her whole frame submerged in one of those long coats that very old ladies in England often wear. "Who's a lovely baby?" she kept saying. "Yes, you *are*! Yes, you *are*!" Like she was scolding you. You laughed again. You said, "Ma, ma, ma, ma, ma."

It gave me a pain in my chest when you said that. It was the first time you spoke the word *Ma*, and where was Antonia to hear it?

"Excuse me," I said to the old lady. "I'm looking for a group of buildings named Paradise Court. I don't know if it's in this city, or somewhere else."

The old lady shook her head. "No, love. I don't know any Paradise Court."

"It's a big block of apartments. With walkways along the front of it." I gestured in the air.

The old lady pursed her lips, thinking, and again shook her head. "That's not here."

But we had caught the attention of a man with a little cart, sweeping the road. He ambled over. "Where you looking for, son?" he said.

"A place called Paradise Court. I don't even know which city it's in."

The man took something from his pocket. He tapped and prodded at a small screen. I had no idea what this device was, but it required concentration, I guessed, from the way he frowned.

"I don't understand these new phones, me," the elderly lady confided in a whisper.

Neither did I, but I didn't say so.

The man presented me with the device. On the screen was a colour photograph of some buildings. "This the place you're looking for?"

Even in that grainy picture, I recognised it. "Yes," I said. "Yes, that's the place! That's it! How did you do that?"

He shrugged. "Searched for it. You got a phone or somewhere you can save the address? You got a pen and paper?"

A pencil and paper I had, somewhere in the old backpack. I brought them out, and the man read me an address. I wrote it down. "Is it here in this city?" I said.

He shook his head. "No, mate. It's in London."

———

My daughter and I went south by the late-night coach, towards a greater city. In this one, my daughter and I quickly became utterly lost between great roaring roads and great towering buildings. My heart ached when I thought of my family, of Antonia. But we were almost there now. By street maps and strangers' directions, I navigated our way to Paradise Court.

It was just as I had seen it in the dream. And just as before, one light was illuminated. I held my daughter tightly, and together we entered the building. The concrete stairwells, stinking and daubed with red painted words, were difficult to navigate with my walking stick and the dead weight of Anastasia, who was half asleep by now. Still, I kept going. Once, I passed a hooded man who shrank out of sight along a corridor.

The light was the fifth one along, on the eighth floor. It was easy to find the place. A barred and curtained window, beside a white front door. A crate with empty glass bottles. A little plastic number.

I reached out and tapped on the door.

The tiny spyhole in its centre darkened. Chains shifted. Then a cough, and the door opened.

A man stood in the doorway. He had dark-grey hair and wore an old leather jacket. Behind him, a wireless radio blared, and I could hear over it the soft voices of a family talking, a woman's laugh and plates clinking—all the noises of a home quite ordinary and unexceptional. "Yes?" he said. It was him. I recognised him from the Wanted posters.

"My name is Harlan North," I said. "I'm Aldebaran's great-great-nephew, and I'm the last person from Malonia left with powers. Aldebaran and Rigel sent me here to tell you that the revolution has happened. You can come home. You've forgotten where you come from, and I'm here to remind you."

Because the king looked so discouraged, I added, "Everyone

back home is waiting for you. Everyone is waiting for you to come back and rule."

The man looked at me in silence. Then he passed one hand over his face and gave a great sigh, as though winded. Eventually he said, "You'd better come in."

Anastasia, sensing my disappointment, threatened to cry. The king sat me down at a little plastic table. He poured me tea and turned off the radio. In the next room, the other people had stopped talking. Now they appeared warily at the doorway, hung back a little. "My wife, Anna," the king said, briefly. "My son. His wife, Juliette. Their daughter, Mira."

I had not thought about the king having a family here. I felt awed by them and at the same time disappointed that they were not grander, that they looked just like our family, quite ordinary in the end. My daughter, however, was at home. She wriggled to be let down, all sleepiness forgotten, and ran to the little girl, who knelt down and made much of her.

"Mira," said the king. "Take the baby and let her play with your dolls, yes?"

"Yes, Granddad," said the little girl importantly, and she led my daughter out of sight.

"She'll be safe," said the king. "Mira has a good way with little children."

I waited, watching the steam rise from my tea. An electric clock on the front of some white machine beeped for ten o'clock. The king sat down opposite me. He turned a plastic mat on the table around in his hands, frowning. Finally he said, "I haven't forgotten."

"How do you mean?"

"I haven't forgotten. I know that I have to go home."

"But Aldebaran said—"

"I know what he thought. That if you pass through to England, you start to forget the real world you came from. But that isn't true for me. I remember." The king went to the window. He looked down on the lights of London, and all of that great city seemed to sigh in the dark. "But there's something that Aldebaran would never accept. I told him, but he wouldn't listen. When I go back, I don't intend to rule."

"What do you mean?" I asked.

"I mean just what I say. I intend to resign. I don't intend to rule that country any longer."

His voice as he spoke gained confidence, and it was softer and more foreign than I expected. "For fifty years, I have been the monarch of that country. I spent the first fifteen of those years in exile, the next sixteen as ruler, the last nineteen in exile again. In that time, I've come to realise something I never quite believed until now: I am quite ordinary. There is really nothing about me that is worth the people's superstitious belief that I can make everything all right. That belief, therefore, must stop. It's time for them to see things in their true light."

He paused. "I'll go back," said the king, "but if the people think our country can be fixed by restoring a monarchy that has never been able to protect them from revolution and war, they are wrong. They have to fix it themselves. They have that right."

"There's a lot of hope invested in you," I said. "They're holding off the election until they find you. You can't just go back and tell them you're not going to rule."

"I'll go back, and so will my family, if it's time, though a part of me would rather remain here. We've agreed that's what we would do. My son and Rigel's daughter always wanted to stay there. My wife and I wanted to remain here. Mira is somewhere in between."

The king sighed. "What Aldebaran never understood is that people are beginning to see things differently. Why do you think powers are disappearing? It's just how things are; it's happened everywhere else—in England, and in the other inhabited places that may lie across the universe. People don't want great mythic rulers anymore. You can see, I've become quite ordinary. The old feud between the noble families has torn that country into pieces. My own family took a part in this. But why should our lives overshadow everyone else's? Why is a king any different from General Marlan? Neither is chosen."

"Aldebaran wanted you to go back," I said. "He told me to bring you. So did Rigel."

"And I'll go. But when I go, it will be to tell the temporary government to let the people decide their country's future. They can stop their waiting now."

Tears were running down my face, though I hadn't realised that I cared. "What if they want you to rule?" I said. "What if they choose you?"

"Then I'll ask them to choose again." The king put his hand on my wrist. "I've had nineteen years to think about this," he said. "I'm not going to change my mind."

As I left that group of buildings, my powers deserted me. I felt them go with a great rush like a mighty wind, and my life played itself in reverse: Antonia, the hospital, the ruins, the bomb, the resistance, the sea crossing, Holy Island. Nights when I pored over Aldebaran's writing. Nights with Antonia. My childhood, and realising my difference in the pages of my mother's atlas. My sister whispering in the dark: "Harlan, you're different. Harlan, you're special." The sea crossing. My birth in the city. That time between life and death when I first journeyed to another world.

England righted itself. A light rain fell. Overhead, streetlamps illuminated drizzle and bright concrete. "Come on, Anastasia," I said. "We need to get home."

I realised when I bought another coach ticket that the money Rigel had given me was more than I had first thought. The eyes of the man in the ticket office grew disbelieving when I took out a wad of notes. "You'd better be careful with your money around here," he said. "That's a small fortune you've got there."

I didn't tell him that it was one-fiftieth of what was stowed in my backpack. But I clutched the bag near to me as the coach pulled out of the station. I felt a small stab of regret in my chest that I could not exchange this fairy-tale money, most of it unneeded now, for the real money that would have bought us a safer, better life in Malonia.

As fast as we could, we made our journey north. But something was wrong with Anastasia. She would not sleep. She sat, rocking slightly, with big, wide eyes. When I looked into her face, she did not seem to see me. On the coach, I folded her in my arms. "Nearly home," I told her. "Nearly home."

But when we got back to that city by the sea, there was no way through the tunnel. Instead of a threshold with the names of the great ones carved in it, there was just a concrete wall. I beat my fists against it. I shouted for my family. No reply. Beside me in the dark, Anastasia started to wail.

And then, like a last miracle, I heard Antonia's voice calling me through the weeds and brambles. "Harlan?" she called.

"Antonia!" I yelled. "Antonia!"

Hands reached out for me. Strong arms pulled me from the darkness into the light. There they were, impossibly, under the great steel pier in this gaudy seaside town in the north of England, shivering: my mother, my father, my brother, my sister, Michael, Antonia.

"We followed you," Antonia explained. "I woke up and knew something was wrong. I persuaded them all to come too. I felt like—I don't know—that otherwise we might be separated again. We searched and found the tunnel by the old monastery." She was sobbing. "You promised never to leave me. How could you?"

"I'm sorry," I said. "I promised Aldebaran. I promised Rigel. And now look how this has ended up. I never should have left."

I tried to explain, weeping, that we couldn't get back home now, that we wouldn't return to Holy Island, that we would never see the real world again. But Antonia stroked my face and hair. She held me in her arms. "Harlan, listen," she whispered. "They announced on the wireless that they're looking for the last descendant, just the same as before. It's never going to stop. We would have had to go into hiding to protect Anastasia. We would have had to start some kind of new life. And I'm not going through what we've already been through because of some historic superstition about your family. That's over now. That's gone. I want Anastasia to live a different life. So what I mean is, maybe this has happened for a reason. Maybe we're meant to begin our new life here."

And perhaps I imagined it, but I felt Aldebaran's presence brush over me one last time, and Rigel's presence, at peace, benevolent, before they faded into the night.

"Look," said my father. "The stars here are the same. That's your great-great-uncle's, the one he was named for."

And I saw that low down on the horizon, the red star Aldebaran still shone as it did at home.

"I've got money," I said. "Enough that we won't starve here while we figure out how to get home. Maybe enough to be wealthy."

"It will be all right either way," said my mother. "We'll make some kind of life."

And so, together, hand in hand, we stepped forward across that English shore with its drunks and its bars and its neon lights, and as a cold wind swept over us, I saw all at once that with my family beside me, this was just as much the real world as our own.

73

Because I didn't know where else to go, we remained in that industrial city where the old woman and the street sweeper had shown me kindness, on whose windswept edge the door to my world had closed. I didn't want to go to London. It was too great, too roaring, too endless. This was the only other place I knew.

She was there again by the bench, the old lady, with her trolley and her flapping coat. It seemed like a good omen. "You again, son," she said. "Did you find that address you were looking for?"

"I found it."

"*There* she is," said the old woman, pointing at Anastasia. "Such a dear baby."

"This is my family," I told her, because she was the closest thing to an acquaintance I had in this whole world.

The old woman greeted them with her stiff English manners. She told us where to find the office where they rented out houses. Morning began with a heave of the watery sun over the horizon, and the people emerged onto the streets. Surrounded by their unfamiliar accents, I walked cautiously, holding Anastasia. Antonia supported me by the elbow. Buses passed with a whine, and a motorbike engine made me start. We stopped to change Anastasia at a public bathroom that smelled of stale urine. At last we found the office. It was raining, so I searched around in the backpack which contained all our belongings and found Anastasia's second shawl. The bundled-up clothes gave off a smell of home that made my chest ache. *All that is past now*, I told myself. *A whole world away from us, and we can't go back. Not yet. Maybe not ever.*

A lady brought us to a desk and showed us pictures of houses in a glossy brochure. Anastasia grabbed at it and laughed. I let her turn the pages. In the end, we chose the plainest one to be our home, because the lady said the area was safe. We had to wait for someone else to arrive with a key, so we sat in a café and drank tea which was milkier and less bitter than ours at home, and Anastasia drank orange juice in greedy gulps. I think that was the thing that brought home our situation to me most clearly: the taste of

English tea and Anastasia drinking for the first time the pulpy juice of an orange, disbelieving, wide-eyed with delight.

The English people on their way to work strode as if they were late. Everything about them, from the cut of their hair to their many-coloured shoes, was unfamiliar to me. Where we were from, shoes came in black, grey or brown and were kept until the leather wore through.

While I was still thinking about this, a man arrived in a car. He explained in an accent I barely understood that he would take us to the new house now.

"You got the money?" he said.

Because I was not used to his accent, I had to ask him to repeat once, twice, three times.

"Yes," I said at last. "Money isn't a problem."

"You got leave to remain in this country? All of you?"

"Yes," I said, though I had no idea what he meant by it. It would be a long time before I understood that we were not the only strangers here. England's history is full of wayfarers from across the sea, all making for themselves a different life. That was one thing I came to be grateful for.

"All right," said the man. "I'll take you to the house."

The man had to drive us in two groups because there wasn't space for us all. In Malonia we would have all crammed in, but I was beginning to understand that things here were different. More regulated, more ordered, sterner. Antonia and I and the baby went first, with Anselm and Michael. My brother and Michael were very quiet, but Michael kept his hand on Anselm's arm the whole way and looked out with a kind of hope, a curiosity, at this new country. I asked the man who owned the house when there had last been a war in England, and he looked at me strangely and said he didn't know. "Not in the last few hundred years," he said. "Not *in* England, though we came damn close eighty years ago."

In the back of his car, which purred more smoothly and raced more quickly than any in our own country, I held Anastasia on my knee. The man did not talk to us anymore, just drummed his fingers on the wheel as we edged slowly through the traffic.

The new house turned out to be on the edge of the city. Here the people walked differently, as if they had years to get where they were going. They wore shapeless running clothes, but none of them looked like they were used to running anywhere. A few of them stopped to look at us as we got out of the car. They stood with hands on hips on the other side of the road. The house had no front path; weeds had overtaken it. The landlord had to kick at the door to get it open. We waded through a drift of old letters and papers, and in the half-light the landlord dropped coins into a meter on the wall. With a rush, light entered the house, and it didn't look so desolate. Electric light seems to do that to a place.

"It doesn't look like a bad place," I said. "A nice house. Eh, Ana?"

"Where do you come from?" the landlord said. "Eastern Europe?"

"Yes," said Antonia. "That's where we come from." Neither of us knew where Europe was. It would be another six months before I learned that we were in it.

The man went back for the rest of my family. After he had left, the silence hummed. It was the electricity, I guessed. I sat down in the kitchen and held Anastasia tight while Anselm and Michael went about examining the house. I looked at the pattern in the plastic tabletop. Then I sat with Anastasia, listening to the low hum of traffic on the road and looking out at our overgrown yard in the grey English morning. A great stalky butterfly bush, with purple spires just turning to brown, bowed drunkenly, extravagantly, in the wind.

Antonia put her arms around us both and held us. "It will be all right," she said.

To the ticking of the heating system and the whine of traffic, our first day in England began.

74

*I*n the first weeks in England, I regained a few of my visions, very faintly. Sometimes, in the dim moments before and after sleep, I saw our old home. I saw the king in a small house in Capital, quite ordinary, remembering this place. I saw the search for the last descendant losing ground. I saw people queuing along half-ruined streets to put papers with *X*s in boxes, to elect their leader, and I saw a new world emerging from the rubble, hesitantly, falteringly.

And gradually, England became the real world to me.

There were parts that I didn't want to forget, and those I managed to hold onto. My grandfather's grave in Holy Island, my grandmother's. New Maron, and the surge of the sea. I think my family began to forget; at least, to them those memories began to grow dimmer. All of them found England to be a kind of liberation. All of them had suffered too much in the old world, and wanted to start again. I hadn't realised this until they came to a new place and grew younger and straighter, as my father had done years ago when he gave up cigarettes.

So perhaps it was my burden alone, Anastasia, that I was destined to remember. While you see only the grey skies of England, I remember a place beyond this—not better, nor worse, just different. I remember where we came from, as I once remembered a world before I was born.

Once, I spoke to my father and my brother about it. Then a very strange thing happened. Both of them, from among the few relics they had carried with them when they followed me out of our own world, produced stories. My father's was a battered black book held together with metal staples. It told of his childhood in a world where powers still existed. It told of his father's exile, his brother's death. Anselm's was a stack of yellowing paper. It told of the city as the Imperialists came to power. It told of Aldebaran's assassination. Both of them wrote, quite clearly, of the link between the worlds, and of magic.

Through those stories, our old home remained alive.

"It was because of my father that I first wrote, I think," said Leo. "Because of Harold North."

"I wrote this for you, Harlan," said Anselm. "When you were just a baby. I wanted you to know about the world before you were born. The strange thing is, I'm forgetting it now. I'm forgetting all these things, and I feel like this place, England, is the real one, and maybe these are just stories. I don't mind really if they are."

I thought about my grandfather a good deal as I read the words that they had written. I remembered what he had told me when I was a young boy and troubled by dreams I couldn't reconcile with reality. *Write it down, Harlan. There's no harm in a story.*

Sometimes in those first weeks, I looked up at the English sky and wondered how many of us there were like this, people who came from elsewhere but somehow got stranded here and now, for want of another world, belonged.

In the vast, white-lit shopping centre, I bought a notebook with a plastic cover. I had not written for two years, not since before Anastasia was conceived. But in those first months in England, while she played with her new plastic toys on the carpet of the front room, while she lay entranced by the moving pictures on our second-hand television set, while we learned to be English, I sat and looked at the blank first page of my notebook.

And eventually, this is what I wrote:

My name is Harlan North, and I was born in Capital.

After some thought, I added:

> *My name is Harlan North, and I was born in Capital,*
> *in the year zero, on the night of the invasion.*

I sat and thought some more. Ana rolled on the floor and laughed. Against the window, drizzle fell softly.

I wrote for a third time:

> *My name is Harlan North, and I was born in Capital,*
> *in the year zero, on the night of the invasion. But from my*
> *earliest childhood, I have been able to remember a time*
> *before I was born.*

This, at last, seemed right. In my new living room, in my new country, feeling strangely weightless, I took up the pen and began to record my past. This record spread out like the streak of light behind a comet, recording where it has come from and pointing in the direction it still has to go, so that it doesn't disappear.

My grandfather told me once that all the stories in the world only tell about eight subjects. Once, after a game of chess in his apartment, he laid them out for me in his neat, sharp handwriting on the back of an envelope:

> *Birth/death*
> *Love/loss*
> *War/peace*
> *Exile/return*

"If in doubt," said my grandfather, "start with birth. That's where most things start."

I didn't understand. "But there are other subjects. What about reconciliation?" I said, bringing out the longest word I knew in an effort to impress him.

"That falls under the category of love," said my grandfather promptly. He had a glitter in his eyes. He was teasing me, but I was too earnest to realise it then. I wanted only to appear clever before him, the great hero of my life. He was then. He is now.

"What about families?" my eight-year-old self persisted. "Lots of books are about families, aren't they?"

"That's love. Or loss. Depending how the stories end. Or occasionally, depending on the family, war."

"All right, what about violence?"

"Violence," said my grandfather, very sternly, "is not the subject of a book. It's just something that happens. And anyway, that would come very firmly under the category of war."

"Or what about—"

"Look, Harlan," said my grandfather, ever patient. "I'm only telling you what I know. Of course, I'm simplifying. Every writer does, in order to create a map of his craft. And a time may very well come when you need this map I'm giving you, so listen."

My grandfather was right. A time has come when I need his wisdom. When I was seventeen, all the books were burned. Then I came to a new country where writing, it seemed, was the only way to hold onto those things that I had experienced once and lost. I needed his genius to guide me, as it always had in life.

Look, Grandfather, you'd be proud of me now. Out of our suffering, our journeys, our beginnings and endings, I wove an entire story, as you told me. The fact is, those things endure. Does it matter if they took place in another country? They happened just the same.

There was one thing I decided from the start, as I sat with that new notebook and brought my memories alive on its pages. Whatever happened, this wouldn't be a sad story. It wouldn't be a tragedy. I think that was partly what made our new life in England a reconciliation as well as a loss, in the end.

Seven years after reaching England, I look at my daughter on her eighth birthday and realise there is no weight of loss on her shoulders. Some kind of victory belongs to us for that. I did what I promised when I was nineteen years old and hovering between life and death in that green world. I protected her. With no green world to retreat to, no magic place, we forged one for her in the real world, a home where she could grow up away from war and fighting.

Anastasia stands at the table in our small house which has become a decent home, and looks at her shop-bought birthday cake with wonder. To a child her age, magic exists with an easy grace. Anastasia lives quite naturally here and in the other worlds of her imagination. She can multiply fractions and operate a computer, and she speaks easily with the same accent I first encountered that rainy morning when the old woman and the road sweeper showed me the way. To her, our life here is quite ordinary. But she also believes in a place beyond it, a place to which we all truly belong.

Anastasia, in the light of her birthday candles, has something otherworldly about her. Her hair, long and thick like her mother's, is held back with a plastic clip. On her eyelids there's a faint trace of blue glitter, a gift from a precocious school friend. That's one thing I regret in this new place—how fast their children grasp at adulthood. But not Anastasia, not yet. She's too much a person of her own, quick to pity, quick to love, quick to anger at injustice. She stands very straight and tall, feet together, on the edge of her future, with no idea that she was once the subject of a nationwide search, with no burden of the suffering that has brought us to this point in space and time. Isn't this what everyone dreams of? To be given the chance to escape the shackles of their old life and hand their children a new world?

England has its difficulties, of course. But among its millions of people, after that business of the last descendant, we relish the great gift of being ordinary. And they accepted us here, after a while. The thing about English people is that they distrust you and distrust you and distrust you, and then all at once, when you're ready to give in, they stop distrusting you and become your greatest friend. Then they are a people with warmth and toughness about them, a good people. Or else, I want to believe so.

Anastasia blows out the candles on her cake. In the half-dark, the family we have surrounded her with arrives: Grandmother, Grandfather, Uncle Anselm, Uncle Michael, Aunt Jasmine. My daughter, at the centre of a confusion of crumpled paper and raised glasses and enfolding arms, is radiant and delighted.

And what are these lives we have made for ourselves? My father keeps a bookshop. My brother, who in his quiet way has never been far from the heart of conflict, writes for a newspaper. My mother, here, is a real teacher, my sister a real actress of sorts, mostly unknown outside this northern town. Antonia, in our neat front room with a new and glossy guitar, teaches others to sing. Of course, this guitar is quite ordinary, bought for a few coins as you can buy anything here, but sometimes its notes take me back across time and space to the world we once inhabited.

As for me, I write. I missed my grandfather too much to have considered any other occupation. As my pen moves over the paper, I feel his love propel it, run down it, infuse the words with a trace of his power. I know that even if I never see him again, if that green world does not exist, I meet him again every day in the struggles of our shared craft.

A few months after arriving here, I went to the public library and was issued with a little card which meant I could read any book held within its walls. This seemed, to me and to Anastasia, when I showed her, almost too much to believe. Sitting there under the fluorescent strip lights, surrounded by the elderly and the unemployed, I read and read. And in that reading I discovered something: in an ordinary country where the books aren't burned, it is perfectly acceptable to write stories which may not be true, set in other worlds than this. No one feels threatened, or puts up a Wanted poster with your name on it. It's true here. It's true, I feel certain, in our old country now.

Of course, no one who reads my books believes they are about a real place. Even my father and my brother, I think, are starting to forget Malonia. Even Antonia, the great love of my life, thinks more of England than of home. But Anastasia, my daughter, reads my books and believes every word. "That's us, Pa," she says, breathlessly. "That's our story."

There is something comforting in the way she takes them all so trustingly as the truth about our past.

But now it's time. I always told myself that when she turned eight years old I would tell her, very firmly, that Malonia was make-believe. This world is her future, not that one. And if there was a chance she could find it—if she had inherited the curse and blessing of my powers—would I want her searching? What if she took it into her head to return? What kind of place would she find? She's safe here, and I want her to stay.

Anastasia is at that age, anyway, when children begin to become uncanny and pensive. The other day, for no reason, she said, "Pa, where do people go when they die?" and then retreated into herself to think it through for several hours. Doubt planted in her now will take root, so that it possesses her forever afterwards, if I can tell the story right.

75

*O*n the morning after her birthday, Anastasia comes padding softly down the stairs. I always wake early here, and I am at the kitchen table, writing. Happiness comes over me on such mornings, when the rain runs down the window and the only sound in this safe, ordinary house is the scratch of the pen on the paper, travelling its miles, far further than we have ever come.

Anastasia stands in the doorway. Her hair is tousled from sleep. She hugs her purple dressing gown around her. I turn up the gas heater and fetch her a glass of orange juice, some bread and sweet jam, doting on her as we all do.

"What are you writing, Pa?" she says. "More about us?"

And now I have to do the most difficult thing I have ever done to my daughter. I have to ruin it for her.

And I begin to retell the story.

While I tell her, Anastasia says nothing, but she puts down her toast and stares at me as though I have betrayed her. I forge on blindly. I give her a whole account of our history, of a sea crossing quite ordinary, from somewhere east of Britain when she was a baby, in search of a better life. The fact is, this story makes more sense than the real one. It always has. "There never was another world," I finish. "I wrote these stories. I made them up. There isn't anywhere else, Anastasia, but it doesn't matter. This place is ours."

The rain runs down the window. Never was there a country whose rain was so exquisite, so varied: great hard bullets of glass one minute and clinging mist the next. Now its touch on the glass is like fingertips, a faint insistent tapping.

"These are just stories that entertain people," I explain, "and all stories are true in some way, but not in the real world." I have to plant doubt in her mind. That is the crucial thing, because doubt will gnaw away at her and leave her with a life quite ordinary.

When I have finished retelling our story, Anastasia cries a little. But when I put my arms around her, she stops. "You're still special, Anastasia," I tell her. "That's the important thing. And I can tell that your life is going to be quite remarkable anyway."

She sniffs and rubs her nose on her dressing gown. She wriggles down from my lap. Then, at the door, she says, "If this story is true, you'll see that it isn't finished. We'll always come from somewhere else, and everyone in our family will be born knowing it."

"What do you mean?" I ask, a little in awe of her, my fierce daughter.

"We'll always be born not quite belonging in one place or another. Like you, Pa. Like me. There will always be people like that. This story goes on forever. We'll go back there someday."

But I can tell by the darkness behind her eyes that the doubt cannot be erased now. It troubles her as she dresses for school and combs her hair and packs her books neatly into her bag. Then she lays it to rest.

Anastasia leaves very quietly, in her blue-checked dress and cardigan, hair braided. I watch her walk away from me along the street. On the roofs opposite, a blackbird sings. The air is wet with drizzle, and cool, but the clouds on the horizon are thinning. The rain in this part of England never lasts for long. I like to think that is partly why this place brought forth a hopeful people.

Already, our street is full of families hurrying about their morning business, a place where life is lived. As I watch Anastasia walk away from me through the rain, I feel the last of the magic go from me. Like the smoke from the steelworks in the distance, it lingers in the air and then is gone. And in spite of everything, I start to hope that what she said was right. That even in this new world, where we have made for ourselves a decent life, the power of magic remains somewhere at the borders, to be reclaimed by those with the vision to see it.

That somehow, the story goes on forever.

ACKNOWLEDGEMENTS

The Last Descendants has been a ten-year project, and over that time I've learned, overwhelmingly, that writing is a collaboration; while one person's name goes on the cover, a hundred people make the book. In that spirit, I would like to thank:

Michael Morpurgo, for generous early encouragement. Tessa Girvan, Zoë Pagnamenta, Ariella Feiner, Franca Bernatavicius and Clementine Gaisman, agenting team extraordinaire, thanks to whom *The Last Descendants* found a worldwide audience. Amy Black, Janice Weaver and Suzy Capozzi, for editing the books with insight, wisdom and skill. The international editors and translators who have worked with such care and passion on the books over the years, bringing them to readers in seventeen countries. All of those whose early excitement helped ensure the trilogy's success, in particular Maya Mavjee and Brad Martin at Doubleday Canada, and the team at Random House Children's Books UK, including Georgia Lawe, Lauren Buckland and Philippa Dickinson. Erin Kern, for much-appreciated skills in transatlantic copy editing. And most of all Simon Trewin, quite simply the best agent any author could wish for, from whose initial leap of faith everything else followed.

The Last Descendants is a trilogy about family and I owe the largest debt of gratitude, of course, to mine. I would like to thank my extended family, my international family-in-law, and the many friends who have supported me from start to finish. In particular Jane Wheare, the trilogy's very first reader, without whose unfailing support there would have been no book in the first place; my sister, whose loyalty and sense of humour kept me always on the right track; and Michael Banner, who ten years ago took my writing so seriously he thought it merited a computer, and has encouraged ever since. And finally, my thanks go to Daniele Galloni, the greatest of companions with whom to complete this journey.